The Cleaners
Book 3

THE
DUSTPAN
COMETH

The Cleaners
Book 3

THE DUSTPAN COMETH

JOSH VOGT

WordFire Press
Colorado Springs, Colorado

THE DUSTPAN COMETH
Copyright © 2017 Josh Vogt

ISBN: 978-1-61475-581-4

Cover design by Janet McDonald

Cover artwork images by Jeff Herndon

Edited by Manny Frishberg

Kevin J. Anderson, Art Director

Book Design by RuneWright, LLC
www.RuneWright.com

Published by
WordFire Press, an imprint of
WordFire, Inc.
PO Box 1840
Monument CO 80132

Kevin J. Anderson & Rebecca Moesta, Publishers

WordFire Press Trade Paperback Edition April 2017
Printed in the USA
wordfirepress.com

PRAISE FOR *THE* CLEANERS

"*A fresh voice in urban fantasy and an original new hero. And after reading this novel, you might never again go to the bathroom alone …*"

—Laura Resnick, author of the
Esther Diamond series

"*If you're looking for a fun, fast-paced adventure, give* Enter the Janitor *a read.*"

—A Fantastical Librarian

"*[Enter the Janitor] was funny, exciting, and in some places, a near tear-jerker. In other words, an almost perfect start to a series.*"

—AudiobookBlast.com

"*Enter the Janitor is one of those books that makes you do a double-take when you see it. A book about magical janitors fighting the evil forces of Scum? How could this not be an instant classic?*"

—The Arched Doorway

"*Enter the Janitor is a unique and cleverly written book … bizarre, funny, exciting, and just a bit weird, all of which combine to make it a winner.*"

—Fanboy Comics

"I loved The Maids of Wrath*! This is a worthy successor to* Enter the Janitor. *The Cleaners universe keeps expanding in all the right ways. You'll never look at cleaning professionals the same away again."*

—Jennifer Brozek, author of *Apocalypse Girl Dreaming*

CHAPTER ONE

Dani stared at her palm, waiting for the tornado to arrive. It all depended on this final test. Everything she'd been studying for the last month came to this point.

She hunkered down on an overturned bucket in the middle of the janitor's closet and concentrated. If she could do this, prove she had control of her power over localized natural disasters then maybe, just maybe, she could get Chapter Two in the Cleaners Employee Handbook to unlock.

The manual for her supernatural sanitation employer sat on the floor before her, a white binder big enough to clobber a raging mammoth unconscious. It lay open to the last page of Chapter One, titled: Janitor, Clean Thyself!

The text on the last page merely read: To pass this test and proceed to Chapter Two, summon a miniature tornado that does not bring harm to anyone or anything.

Dani tugged on her power, trying to stir the elements she needed. A rush of air tousled her short red curls as a black thundercloud puffed into being in front of her. Lightning lit it from within as a tiny bolt zapped her hand.

Hissing, Dani released the energies. She rubbed at the stinging spot and glowered at the manual.

"This is all your fault," she said.

The letters flowed together and then back out into a new message.

Incorrect. All is too inclusive a word. Are you giving up?

She slapped her cheeks and rolled her shoulders.

"Right. Focus. I want a tornado. Not a thunderstorm. I got this. I got this."

She jumped up and down to warm up, paced back and forth. The janitor's closet was no bigger than an alley kitchen—one built for a family of gnomes—but it was lined with metal shelving and stocked with bottles of cleaning chemicals, sponges, stacks of paper towels, rags, mops and brooms, garbage bags, and scrub brushes. Her cart sat in the back, laden with similar tools of her trade, both mundane and magical.

She did a few squats and jumping jacks. That warmed her up quick, what with the tan janitorial jumpsuit she wore, complete with black boots and yellow gloves.

Standing before the handbook again, she held her hand out, readying to summon. Then she paused and eyed the manual.

"Hang on. Why a tornado, anyway?"

I like them. They make me think of washing machines. Round and round.

"You've got to be—" Dani sealed her lips before a swear slipped out. "You're joking."

I am a book. I do not have a sense of humor. Another swirl of ink. This is your final chance. Fail and you are finished.

The bold text faded away, replaced by normal text.

A Cleaner must demonstrate Pure focus in any situation. They must not let their attention be sullied by any distraction. Only then can they be effective against Scum and serve Purity in all their actions.

From the table of contents, she knew Chapter Two was titled: On Matters of Bathing. Having been a lifelong devotee to the church of self-sanitation, thanks to her antagonistic relationship with germs and dirt, she craved to discover what that topic entailed. A spell for conjuring hot baths and showers whenever she wanted? She swallowed against a Pavlovian urge to drool at the thought.

For Purity's sake, I'm letting myself get distracted.

Refocusing, she nodded to herself. "I've done this before. I can do it again."

She kept her power mostly contained, activating her Pure energies just enough to draw wisps of air toward her. Directing them ... there.

A breeze swirled over her open hand. Barely breathing, Dani shut her eyes and let her elemental vision take over. She fed her senses into the environment, detecting the earth within the concrete and beneath the building's foundations, and the air wafting through the ventilation ducts. Her power wove out of her like glowing tendrils of energy, latching onto all of this and more.

As a Catalyst—one of the rarest forms of Pure-energy wielders these days—she could churn up an earthquake, crack the water pipes and flood the area, or flare a match into a firestorm.

But she only wanted one tiny tornado, small enough to fit in her pocket. She'd take it home. Call it Swirly. And it would be her Swirly and they would be the best of friends.

If she could just make it work. She needed finesse. To flick the breeze into a miniaturized vortex and stabilize it. Simple. Just break a few laws of physics.

She bit the tip of her tongue and let the barest fragment of her power brush against the still-flowing breeze. A cloudy vortex swirled into being, the tip of it settling on her palm.

Dani giggled. "Tickles."

A thin, airy voice fluttered in her ears. *"Can I help, mistress?"*

Dani growled. "As Ben likes to say: Shaddup."

A whimper, like she'd scolded a child. *"I am only trying to help, mistress."*

"No, you're trying to get a gold star on your report card. I told you I'm not treating any of you any different than the rest. Now leave me alone until I'm actually ready to talk to you."

"Very well, mistress," replied Air-Dani

"And don't call me that. Makes me sound like I should be carrying a whip instead of a mop."

"Yes, mistress."

Dani clenched her other fist. The rush of frustration sent a heat wave across her skin, and her power fluctuated in response. In a blink, the tornado doubled in size. A low roar rose and the room trembled as if in the path of an oncoming train.

3

"Ah, $#@*!"

The Cleaners' foul-filter spell wiped her dirty word out of existence as quickly as she uttered it. No filthy language for paragons of Purity, no sir.

The tornado spun out of control, growing large enough to rattle the shelves. Dani stood rooted, buffeted by the very winds she'd conjured.

She thrust her hands into the swelling funnel as if she could choke it into submission.

"No! Don't you #%$&#@@ dare lose control."

Except the more she focused on grappling the twister, the more her power fed into it. It had no core she could destroy. Her own destructive energies sustained the spell; if it went too far, she'd endanger the whole building and everyone inside.

So Dani whirled about, grabbed the bucket at the end of the cart, and dunked her head into the dirty bleach water. She jerked back out, spluttering and whipping her head around. She felt her energies dissipate, which meant they shouldn't be sustaining the twister any longer.

She turned back to the tornado. It wobbled like a dreidel on overdrive. Then it shrank slightly. Dani's gut unclenched. Breaking her focus had worked! She'd stopped it from—

The tornado exploded, gusts blasting out, with her at the epicenter. She went into a crouch, eyes shielded as everything clattered and boomed around her. At last, she dared to survey the wreck of the room. Shelves had been torn clear, spilling gear everywhere. A bag of de-icing salt had torn wide open, and unidentifiable cleaning fluids splattered the walls and floor. Her cart remained upright and clean, but otherwise the place looked like the Mr. Clean had thrown a temper tantrum.

The handbook, of course, remained pristine.

She scowled. "Showoff."

A flash of light burst from the handbook, blinding her. Her vision cleared just as the binder slapped shut. The thunderclap this produced knocked her back until she caught herself on her janitorial cart.

"Thanks for that," she said through gritted teeth. "Always wondered what it'd be like to get bullied by a book. I can die happy now."

A knock sounded on the door and a young man peeked in. "Are you okay? I was walking by and heard—whoa." His eyes widened. "What happened? Looks like a tornado hit this place."

Dani hopped over and braced the door before he could enter. "I just tripped."

"Tripped?" He glanced around doubtfully.

Dani leveled her best glare. "Tripped."

He coughed. "Okay. Sure. Your mess, not mine."

After he ducked out, she locked the door and leaned her head against it.

"My mess. Sure is."

She turned to survey the scene. The binder caught her eye. The front title, which normally read EMPLOYEE HANDBOOK, now said:

We'll try again tomorrow.

Dani hefted the tome and held it out at arm's length as if it were a baby that had just dropped a nuclear bomb in its diaper.

"You said that was my final test."

For the day. Perhaps tomorrow you will not be so distractible.

"Hey, it wasn't my fault that air elemental wanted to get chatty right then." Dani frowned. "Hang on a sec. Did you somehow get it to pipe up in my ear?"

Distractions of all sorts come at inopportune times.

"You ... little ... cheat! I ought to toss you into the nearest industrial shredder."

I am indestructible.

She narrowed her eyes. "That sounded like a dare."

You are reading me. Not listening.

Grousing, Dani stuffed the handbook into the backpack strapped to the cart. The book's weight made the cart sink an inch and the wheels squealed in protest, but the equipment had been chanted to handle far more physical stress than normal sanitation gear.

Fists on hips, she glared at the wrecked closet and sighed. "Janitor, clean thyself up."

Her radio bleeped. *"Hey, janitor lady, there's been a spill on the second floor, near Room 210. Corpse cleanup."*

Dani didn't answer right away. She could instinctively tell now which channel it came in on. Not a call from the Cleaners. Just mundane work. She plucked the radio from her belt and thumbed it on. "Again? Was it Martin?"

"Sorry. Don't know. Just found it. Nobody seems to be around."

Her skin prickled. Could this be Scum-work? Maybe she could save the day from some corpse-munching Corrupt beast and add another notch to her mop handle.

She grinned. "Be right down."

She tidied up just enough to clear a path to the door. Hoping nobody needed the closet anytime soon, she wheeled the cart out into the halls of the University of Denver's School of Medicine. Good thing it was a weekend if Scum were about. Otherwise more students might be around and in danger. The cart trundled down the tiled halls toward the nearest elevator, passing rooms filled with medical diagrams, dark labs with a few screens glowing within, glass-paneled display cases full of preserved organs, and lecture halls.

Nice of the Cleaners to set her up with a work-study that coincided with her pre-med studies and duties as a Cleaner.

She grimaced. *Of course, I haven't told anyone at the company that I've taken the semester off.*

Dani suspected Chairman Francis knew she'd taken a hiatus from her educational pursuits. Part of her still wanted to work in the medical research field somehow, someday—find a way to protect people from the innumerable diseases and maladies that created so much suffering around the world. Her job as a Cleaner, though, plus her studies with the Employee Handbook took up too much time and energy for her to handle homework and sit through lectures. Not to mention that continued tools training and learning to handle her powers were more immediate priorities.

Besides, I'm still doing the world some good. Maybe even more directly, destroying embodiments of Corruption itself instead of hiding away in a sterile lab.

It gave her a measure of pride, thinking of herself as a guardian of Purity, keeping innocents safe from Corruption in all its mucky machinations. She tried to rein in her anticipation as she wondered what might really be behind the spill she'd been called to handle.

Don't get your hopes up, Dani. Sometimes a puddle of frat boy vomit is just frat boy vomit.

As the elevator hummed up to the second floor, she eyed the radio on her hip. Hang on. Who had called her again? He hadn't identified himself, and his voice hadn't been familiar.

She plucked a squeegee off the cart and held it along one thigh. Best be prepared in case this turned out to be more than just a random muck monster causing trouble.

The doors dinged open and she headed off, senses pinging, power fizzing as she kept it just on the edge of surging free. She turned down the hall ... and into a scene out of a B-rated horror flick.

Ten pig cadavers lay in puddles of glop as if someone had been having a water balloon fight with dissection specimens. Adult pigs, *too. She fought the urge to sneeze against the pickled reek of formaldehyde.* Normally, she enjoyed a good whiff of preservatives—they reminded her of the sanitizer gel she always kept with her—but now she fought against the urge to find something to eat just so she could lose it again.

She blinked. "The #$%^?"

Exactly how could she deal with something like this? She wasn't about to haul all these pigs into a dumpster. They were school property, and she'd need a good excuse for just chucking them.

Dani checked the area for video surveillance, but didn't see any. The Cleaners had scoped out the university's security network for her. Main entrances and rooms containing valuable lab equipment were monitored, but not many of the halls themselves. Of course, whoever was behind this had chosen a section lacking cameras. That meant planning. Maybe a trap.

She tapped the squeegee against her leg. "Okay. Think. What would Ben do?"

She froze. *I did not just think that.* Because knowing Ben, he'd laugh, grab the nearest dead pig, and tell her to go long for a touch-down pass.

Would the Chairman be pissed if she called for a scrub-team in to get rid of this mess? Would that be abusing company resources?

Oh! Company protocol: quarantine any scene to avoid the spread of contamination.

Josh Vogt

She grabbed a pair of Caution: Wet Floor signs off the cart and set them on either side of the hall junction. A touch and spark of energy from her activated the wards they'd been chanted with, which would react negatively to any Scum that got too close.

Satisfied, she turned back to decide what to do with the preserved bacon. Maybe if she used her mop to shove them all into one big pile and then set them on fire? She could handle sweeping up ashes.

"Excuse me, miss?"

Dani spun, squeegee at the ready.

Three men in tuxedos stood in the hallway she'd just come from, a few steps on the other side of the Caution signs. All trim guys with slicked hair and jawbones that could double as sledge-hammers. They looked like they'd come from a fashion photo shoot. Where had they been hiding? Had they ridden the elevator just after her? She hadn't heard the doors ding.

The man in the middle held an arm stiff across his chest like a fancy waiter.

"Are you Danielle Hashelheim?" he asked.

Dani slowly reached for her mop handle. "Who's asking?"

He bowed slightly. "We're the Momma's Boys Quartet, and we have a message for you."

She recounted the trio, making sure they didn't have a shorter member standing behind them. *Quartet?* "Message from who?"

"Sydney."

She aimed her mop like a spear. "If he wants to deliver a message, he can come do it himself."

The man flashed a gorgeous grin. "He thought you might react that way."

"What way?"

"Violently. That's why he sent us as messengers."

"Yeah? Three of you at once, huh? What're you going to do? Hold me down and tickle me to death?"

"No, no," he said. "Nothing like that."

He swayed in place, snapping fingers to a beat.

There, in the middle of a splash zone of pig corpses, the men began to dance and sing.

CHAPTER TWO

Y'know," Ben said, "I's really thinkin' this could work, Carl." Carl bubbled and swayed in the spray bottle strapped to Ben's belt. The water elemental's burbles and splashes, combined with the occasional swirl of geometric shapes, formed a language few, other than the pair, could decipher.

Ben scanned a small book bound in fake mauve leather. He flipped through the pages, using his left thumb and—occasionally—his tongue, to turn the pages as he walked the corridors of Cleaners HQ, barely dodging other janitors, maids, plumbers, and handymen. Would've made for an easier read if he'd had both hands, but the right sleeve of his blue jumpsuit remained rolled up and pinned just below the shoulder.

"Aw, c'mon, buddy. What's the worst that could—"

Carl spouted in alarm.

Ben spluttered and choked. "Right'cha are. Never should say anythin' like that. Just askin' for troublesomeness, ain't it?" He eyed down a page and settled on an entry. "A'ight. Needin' me a test run. Who's lookin' like they need a dose of ol' Benny's sparklin' wit?"

Carl's bubbling translated roughly to: *This will all end in tears.*

"Mebbe if I drank you and got all sortsa sad and weepy. Now shut it and lemme show you what a little educatifyin' can do."

He picked a random man heading in the opposite direction. Striking a dramatic pose, Ben thrust the book out like an accusing finger.

"Would thou wert clean enough to spit upon!"

The plumber, Andy according to the name threaded on the left breast of his suit, stared at Ben as if he'd grown a second head— and a walrus head, at that. "Sorry, janitor? There something you need?"

Ben double-checked the book. "Hmm. A-ha!" He shook the book in the plumber's face. "Lumpish, toad-spotted knave!"

Andy's forehead puckered. "Have there been reports of bilge toads in the Sewers lately?"

The two men exchanged blank stares before Andy shrugged and headed off. Ben frowned down at Carl.

"I's gonna need more practice."

Clipped footsteps made him snap the book shut and shove it into a zippered pocket.

"Janitor Benjamin. What are you doing?"

Ben grinned at the tall black man who strode up beside him. Wearing a white three-piece suit, the Chairman cut a dashing figure compared to Ben's shabby self. The Chairman's features and gaze could've only been sharper if they'd been honed by a metal grinder.

"Tryin' to sneak up on me, eh?" Ben asked.

Chairman Francis doffed his fedora and fiddled with the brim. "I've no need to sneak around the company I run. I was already making my way to you when I heard what sounded like rather archaic insults being slung about. Care to explain yourself?"

After a few seconds of a stare-me-down, Ben relented. He drew out the book and held it up so Francis could see the title.

"*Shakespearean Insults*," the Chairman read. "*Enter the World of Slanderous Wit*." He gave a look so flat it could've cut two dimensions in half. "Benjamin, really. You're still trying to find foul-filter loopholes?"

"Man's gotta have his hobbies." Ben stashed the book before Francis could confiscate it.

"I'd prefer if your hobbies were more private."

"There's a thought. Mebbe I could start collectin' the types of dirt I find under my fingernails after a job."

He tensed as a golden glow shimmered around Francis. Imbued with the Board's authority and a hefty dose of Purity's own power, the Chairman emanated an aura that could largely subdue the wills of corporate employees. He didn't abuse it like the former Chairman had, but he wasn't afraid to use it, friends or no.

"You ain't gonna report me to the Board for this, are you? I'm educatin' myself, see?"

"Is that how you rationalize it?"

"You betcha."

Francis heaved a sigh. "No, I'm not going to report this. I'm busy enough as it is."

Ben chuckled and barely kept himself from bouncing in place.

"Not unless it gets out of hand."

"I'll keep such a good grip on it, it'll be squealin' for mercy." Ben made a fist. "So what'cha lookin' for lil' ol' me for? Got a new assignment for me?"

"No."

"Did'ja need me to go holler nasty names at a new recruit so you look downright cozy in comparison? Play bad Cleaner, good Chairman?"

"Not that, either."

"Then howsabout—"

"Perhaps if you stopped guessing, I could tell you." Francis replaced his fedora on his head. "Your request for rehabilitation trials came across my desk."

Ben opened his mouth. Raised a finger. Hesitated, and then cleared his throat. "Ah. I, um, put that in the Employee Recommendation box."

"Yes. You did."

Ben stared around at the white-tiled halls, feeling like he'd wound up on the decks of an alien ship. "You're meanin' that thing actually works?"

"Despite your belief that it's an incinerator in disguise? Yes, Ben. I take the time to review recommendation submissions, or at least assign an Ascendant to review them on a regular basis. I don't know what my predecessor did, but this is my effort to help the Cleaners constantly improve. Your idea was marked *of interest* and passed up to me."

Ben cringed. "You weren't supposed to really see that. Sort of a joke in the first place. Was thinkin'—"

"I've approved it."

"You what now?"

Francis' smile chilled Ben. "Your theory sounded intriguing enough that I thought it might make for a good experiment, especially considering you volunteered as a test subject."

"Yeah, but ..." Ben grasped for a way to slip out of this unexpected development. The one time the system actually worked, and he ended up on the pointy end. Figures. "But I can't do it on my lonesome. Gotta have folks catchin' me off-guard, otherwise it ain't gonna be effective."

"I've already had people sign up to do so."

Ben blinked. "Serious?"

"Ten, so far."

"Jeepers. Usually need both hands to count that high. Any more and I'm gonna have to take off my socks." Ben eyed the hallway, seeing the other Cleaners in a newly nefarious light. "So ... when's it gonna get goin'?"

"It already has."

Ben sagged. "Aw, c'mon, Francis. Tell me you ain't doin' this to me."

"Technically, you've done it to yourself." He patted Ben's shoulder. "I wish you the best success, and I look forward to your report on the results. Try to take good notes."

As Francis headed off, Carl swished about: *Told you so. Tears. All tears.*

Ben muttered at the Chairman's back, "Bootless, onion-eyed strumpet."

"I heard that," Francis called back.

"Yeah, well, ain't no fun unless you do." Ben scrubbed his forehead. "Dagnabbit. Now I gotta look up what strumpet means."

He refocused on the problem at hand. The trials had already begun? Tarnation. Francis hadn't told him who'd been authorized, either. Could be anyone. Plenty of other employees would have reason to come after Ben. Despite his being officially cleared of any wrongdoing, rumors lingered about his involvement in the death of his wife and the potential causes of the Corrupt disease he'd contracted afterward—the one that eventually cost him both his arm and Pure powers, landing him the ignominious role as a mere "Cleaners consultant."

He studied the nearby foot traffic, wondering if he might already be a target. How could he tell until it was too late? A pair of maids sauntered by, feather dusters strapped to their belts like pistols. A plumber shoved a whole toilet along on a handcart, the lid sealed with clamps while something inside the bowl growled and thumped around.

Ben squinted as a new figure rounded a corner: a chimney sweep striding along in a black jumpsuit, bristle brush resting over a shoulder. It'd been a long time since Ben had seen one of their kind around HQ. This guy looked a swarthy sort, with broad shoulders and dark stubble threatening to spring into a full-blown beard if he didn't savage it with a razor every five minutes.

Not anyone Ben knew, but the appearance of one of the rarer Cleaners right as Francis okay'd Ben's semi-joking suggestions set his nerves on edge. Could this guy have come to HQ simply to take advantage of the open hunting season on the janitor?

He tensed, but the chimney sweep swept past without pause. Ben let out a low breath.

H'okay. I might be a tad too paranoid for my own good. Gotta get someplace safe and shake these jitters.

He considered his hidey-hole options. His van? He could sleep there for a while, like he used to. No. Too many people knew about that. They'd find him there. His room then. Since he'd only recently begun crashing in HQ most nights, not many folks would know to look for him there.

He tapped the spray bottle. "Buddy, keep an eye on my back, yeah? Let me know if anyone starts gettin' all sneaksy on me."

Carl sloshed as Ben jogged for his room. He found the nearest glassway, a floor-to-ceiling mirror where the hall dead-ended, and pressed a palm to it. He mentally triggered the chanted access sigil tucked into his breast pocket. Lacking his old power would've normally kept him from activating the glassways or entering most of the sectors, but the Board had given him the metal sigil to let him navigate HQ without needing a chaperone. It also let them keep an eye on his whereabouts, but he figured it was a small price to pay in order to keep working for the company that had given his life the closest thing to a purpose.

His hand slipped through the glassway's shimmering boundary. Cold rippled over his body as he stepped across and out into another, almost identical hall. He sidestepped a handyman heading the opposite direction. The woman's eyes and hands glowed with an emerald aura, and she looked determined as she vanished past him. Probably heading to heal up a Cleaner or scrub-team coming in injured from fieldwork.

He hurried on, alternating between speed walking and the occasional sprint down a section when no one else was around. No good letting coworkers think he might be panicked. That'd just encourage them.

Navigating HQ required equal parts familiarity, born from working there for years, and a mental focus on the place an employee wanted to reach. Set slightly outside of normal reality, the headquarters occasionally shifted its layout, and glassways didn't always link up to the same sections even if a person passed through the same portal within minutes. HQ's fluidic nature made mapping the corridors, storage areas, conference rooms, and main sectors less helpful in the long-term, and some Cleaners theorized the facility actually held an infinite number of rooms and halls that the Board reshaped and made available as needed to accommodate ongoing operations.

Fortunately, desperation gave Ben a pretty keen focus on his destination, and it just took a few more minutes before he reached the door to his assigned quarters.

Another touch of his hand, another tingle of the sigil in his pocket, and the door whisked open. Ben puffed a relieved sigh as he stepped inside—

And caught a bucketful of water straight in the face. Blubbering, Ben reeled, half-blind. His shoulder rammed the wall and his hip bruised against the dresser, sending him tumbling to the floor. Carl's bottle went rolling away.

Growling, he swiped his vision clear and shook his head, spraying water from his soaked hair.

A husky Hispanic woman stood over him, watching him with a bemused expression. She held a now-empty bucket tucked under one arm.

"#*%#&@#%*, Lu," he said. "Didja have to go for the face? That's the prettiest part of me."

Lucy cocked an eyebrow. "Did it work?"

Ben braced on his arm and took a mental inventory. He reached inside himself, searching for any glimmer of Pure energy the attack might've sparked, but he came up dry.

"Nope." He thumped the floor with his fist, leaving a wet print. "Durn it. Soaked to my britches and not even a dribble of power to show for it."

"Pity. Hang on. I'll be right back." Lucy went into the bathroom, and running water sounded as she refilled the bucket in the tub. She returned half a minute later, full bucket poised to sling. "Hold still."

He scrambled to his feet, still dripping. "Hang on a sec. It ain't gonna help none if I know it's comin'. That's the whole point."

She lowered the bucket. "Spoilsport."

"How'dja even get in my room, anyhoo?" He held up his hand. "Wait. Lemme guess. Francis let you in."

Her plump cheeks bunched up in a grin. "Of course. When he sent out the memo about the series of tests you suggested, I was the first the sign up. I knew you'd run for cover once he told you, so I convinced him to let me duck in here for a little ambush." Setting the bucket down, she reached up and tucked a few loose strands of dark hair back into a bun. "You really think this sort of thing could work? That it could restore your powers?"

He waggled his hand back and forth. "Sorta, kinda, mebbe? Was mostly a joke at first, but the more I got thinkin' about it, the more it made a bit of sense. We janitors got ourselves an affination—"

"Affinity."

"Right. That. An affinatory for manipulatin' water. Most Cleaners get their powers goin' for the first time when they're threatened by Scum or exposed to some nasty situation. So I figured mebbe if I got doused in ways that get my adrenaline goin', it'd wake things up again."

Josh Vogt

"Hydroshock therapy, hm?"

"If you wanna make it sound all fancylike, sure."

Lucy scrunched up one side of her face in thought. "You're assuming there's something still in you to wake up; that Jared didn't suck every last scrap of power out of you."

"Sure enough." Ben wiped droplets off his brow. "But I gotta try somethin', otherwise I'll go crazy sittin' in the penalty box."

"I'm not complaining." She flicked the bucket, making the water quiver. "It's kind of therapeutic for me, too."

"Speakin' of the kiddo, you wanna go give him a howdy with me? Been meanin' to talk to him about what he did to me, and this might be good a time as any to sit down for a little chit-chat."

"Uh-huh." Lucy eyed him dubiously. "You mean since your room isn't safe anymore, you're going to try and camp out in his little quarantine area, where you know most other people can't go?"

"Lu!" He laid his hand over his heart. "That's downright hurtful, thinkin' I'd ever use him that way. What would Dani say if she heard you talkin' like that?"

"She'd say, 'Ben, if you ever dare to use Jared as a shield, I will kick you between the legs so hard your balls will shake hands with your brain.'"

"Huh." Ben scratched his chin. "Probably so. She's gettin' so colorful with her threats." He glanced around the room. "Hey, buddy, where'dja go?"

Burbling led him to the bed, where he crouched and snagged Carl's bottle out from underneath. He hooked the elemental back onto his belt and then waved Lucy to the door. "Whattaya say? Hop along with me and make sure I ain't takin' advantage of our very own weapon of magic destruction?"

She winced. "Only you'd call him that and not realize how scary he can really be."

"Jared? Scary?" Ben blew a raspberry. "Kid's like a little lamby, all sortsa friendly and peaceful."

Lucy snorted. "The last time we visited, he almost set my hair on fire."

He pointed at her. "Almost. But he didn't. That's the important part."

16

"All right." She sighed. "Let's go see what sort of crazy he's creating today."

"You gotta bring the bucket?" He nodded at it. "I'm kinda expectin' you to toss it my way now, which won't help none."

"I'm bringing it in case he starts burping flames again."

Ben opened the door, motioning for Lucy to follow. "I'm tellin' you, the kiddo's gotten a lot better at keepin' things under control. Soon enough, he's gonna show the Board he don't need no quarantine. Why, I reckon you'll think him a little angel, all sortsa prim and proper."

He stepped out into the hall—

And took a soap-soaked sponge to the face.

"#$#%^@@&$!"

CHAPTER THREE

ani gawked as the performers moved in choreography, stepping carefully across the slick floor. The leader winked at her. In surprisingly honeyed tones, he launched into song while the other two hummed an *a cappella* soundtrack.

You promised me a chance to change.
I've fought hard to make you proud.
Let's unite as we arranged.
I promise to be true.
Meet me for just one evening.
I'll show my world to you.

As he crooned the last word, they bowed in unison, each with an outstretched hand.

Dani lowered her mop. Sydney had sent a singing telegram to ask her out? Well, okay. Kind of sweet of him, though with plenty of self-preservation undertones. Definitely Sydney's style. And she had promised him a date a while back, in order to secure his help in saving the life of a newborn demigod. She owed him. But she'd ignored several of his ongoing attempts to contact her, including notes left in her van and even a perfumed letter somehow delivered to her quarters in HQ. This new approach certainly caught her attention, but she remained leery of spending any time alone with the Cleaner-turned-Scum.

"That's nice," she said, "but I'm really busy these days. He'll understand. You guys will still get paid, right? I mean, it was a nice performance and—"

The lead singer struck a saucy pose and clapped once.

"All right, guys," he said. "Same song, second verse. A little bit hotter, a little more perverse."

In a swift motion, he tore his shirt off, revealing a sculpted, tanned torso. The other men started bumping and grinding the air, making their hips and shoulders move in impossibly fluid ways. Their self-generated music took on a thumping tempo, making Dani think of techno music.

She backed up as they advanced. "What ... what're you ..."

The leader started singing again, but in a huskier voice. He threw in heated glances along with his swiveling hips.

> *I knew you'd say no. I knew you'd resist.*
> *I wanted to be honorable. I truly tried my best.*
> *But I realized there's only one way to succeed.*
> *Dani, will you go out with me? They won't stop until*
> *you accede.*

The men danced toward her, a more horrifying sight than the dead pigs littering the floor around them. They spread out, still gyrating in disturbing ways as they moved in.

Dani opened her mouth, but only a squeak of dismay escaped.

Not a singing telegram.

Sydney had sent a strip-o-gram.

As they neared, Dani retreated, gorge rising at the thought of them actually rubbing up against her. She choked down a swell of nausea, trying to think up a way to keep the strippers back without hurting them. No good triggering an earthquake or windstorm, or conjuring lightning from the nearby electrical sockets.

She had a brief thought of squirting sani-gel all over them to ward them off. *Oh $&%, no! That'd just make things worse.*

She settled for thrusting the mop out again, making the nearest stripper jump back to avoid being hit in his chiseled chest.

"Stay back."

Their leader tried to shuffle closer, but she jabbed the mop at him, flicking water at his face. "Please, lady. We have to do this."

"Or what?" she asked.

"Or we get punished." His lusty façade cracked, exposing hints of panic. "Please. Just accept the invitation and we'll leave you alone."

"Punished?" She lowered the mop slightly. "Sydney threatened you? With what?" When the men hesitated, she planted the mop by her side. "Look, I know what he can do, but it's okay. I'll protect you. You don't need to do this."

"You ..." The singer hung his head. "You don't know what that monster is capable of. What he'll do if we don't follow his orders."

She squeezed the mop handle, imagining her fingers around Sydney's neck. "Let me guess. He turned things to dust and said he'd do the same to you if you didn't come here and try to grind all up on me."

"Not all of us," he said. "Just certain parts of us."

"Parts?" she echoed.

He grinned sheepishly and did a little bump-and-thrust with his hips. "Ones that'd make it difficult to keep doing this sort of work."

Her eyes widened. "Oh. Oh!" She shuddered, but gathered her composure a moment later. "Listen, I can handle Sydney just fine. You don't have to be afraid of him anymore. All your ... parts ... will stay put, I promise."

The singer's voice wavered. "Oh, thank god." Looking ready to cry, he rushed her, arms raised for a hug.

She snapped the mop out, handle in both hands to push him back just in time. "Whoa! Back off, Perky!"

He blinked, tears welling in his eyes. "But you said ..."

"Oh, &$%, you're not actually going to cry, are you?" Dani contained another shudder, thankful she'd invested in the extra-thick cleaning gloves. "What kind of protection means you've got to rub your epidermis all over mine? Don't you know how many diseases are exchanged by physical contact?"

"Um ..."

Dani sighed. "Sydney and I have an ... an arrangement. As of now, you all are officially under my protection, so if he tries to anything, he's going to have to deal with me first."

A low chuckle caught her ear.

"My, my, Dani. Don't tell me you're still in the habit of adopting any strays you come across."

She turned to see Sydney watching from down a side hall. He leaned against a wall, smirking, arms crossed. He looked both thinner and paler than usual, with his light blond hair now streaked with platinum. His shabby T-shirt read: *If You Can Read This, Your Life is Still Meaningless.*

He straightened and clapped black-gloved hands. "Oh, do give them a round of applause, m'dear. I think they performed rather admirably, don't you?"

She glowered at the ex-handyman. "How long have you been there?"

He walked toward her and stopped just on the other side of the chanted cleaning signs she'd set up. "Long enough to enjoy the spectacle. I wondered how you might react to their little routine."

Dani snarled softly. "How did you think I'd react? Take them all on in a hallway orgy?"

The strippers stepped back as one, looking more afraid of this suggestion than they had of her threatening to impale them with her mop.

Sydney shrugged. "Who knows what dark desires lurk in the hearts of others? Could be that you would've found the comb-ination of formaldehyde and male musk to be quite the aphrodisiac. But it's lovely to see you're saving yourself for me." As she tried to splutter an outraged response, he waved at the men. "Gentlemen, if you could give the lady and me a bit of privacy, I will consider our bargain concluded. Your companion is waiting for you."

After the strippers raced each other out the nearest doors, Dani shot Sydney a look. "Companion?" she asked.

He nodded. "You did notice they numbered three, yet called themselves a quartet?"

"I wondered."

"Well, some people need persuading to do a job well. I simply kept one of them indisposed so the others would be motivated to do their best to woo you my way."

"Woo me? Yeah, I'm feeling totally wooed. It's every woman's dream to be asked out with the help of hostages, dead pigs, and strippers." She glared. "What did you do to their fourth member? You better not have aged him or anything."

He fluttered his hands. "Nonsense. After they retrieved the porcine specimens, I simply left one of them in the laboratory freezers and dissolved the lock. It'll take them a bit of time to reopen the door, but he should be perfectly fine, if a little frosty."

She pressed fingertips to the bridge of her nose. "Sydney, this is all a bit vile, even for you. How could you scare those poor men like that?"

"Quite easily," he said. "You simply have to know what a person values most and threaten to take it away." He nodded at the warded signs she'd set up in the hall. "Would you mind removing those?"

"I would, actually." She went to stand just across from him. "Why? They make you uncomfortable?"

"I'll admit they do raise my hackles a bit."

"You have hackles now?"

"Droll as ever. But I'd rather not forcibly remove them. The clash of energies might gain us unwanted attention, and I'm not in the mood to flex my metaphorical muscles at the moment when I could, instead, be spending time with a gorgeous and scintillating specimen of the female sex."

"She sounds like such a lucky lady."

"The rarest of sorts." He flourished theatrically. "One worthy of my time and attention."

Dani snorted. "Golly, gee. Now you've got me all a-flutter. How can I refuse?"

"I'd rather you not do anything of the sort." He inched closer to the warded boundary. The air crackled, and Dani's ears popped. "Truly, Dani, I am here simply in the hopes that you'll honor our agreement. A single date. A chance to get to know each other better. Presenting myself like this, putting myself at risk to appear here is ... well ..." He looked aside. "A bit grating on the ego, I must admit. I'll not grovel, but merely appeal to your sense of decency, courtesy, and unspoken desire for myself."

Dani studied him for a minute, filtering through his little speech. Shifting aside his penchant for the dramatic and the overestimation of just how much she wanted to bake him pies and have his babies, she sensed a subtext to his act. He'd stopped just shy of admitting being nervous; that he, in fact, feared being rejected by her. More, he was also worried that poking his head out of whatever hole he'd crawled into put him in danger of being targeted by the Cleaners once more.

Sydney admitting to being antsy? The only other time he'd done so was when they'd taken an emergency shortcut into a realm known as the Gutters to avoid being mashed into a homogenous paste. With the Gutters existing outside of normal reality, certain laws of physics—like the second law of thermodynamics—didn't apply, robbing him of his entropic powers and leaving him practically helpless.

The last time she'd seen him, he'd been duking it out with his older brother, Destin, the former Chairman of the Cleaners—before the revelation of Destin's nasty affair with a member of the Corrupt Pantheon, resulting in the birth of a godling with both Pure and Corrupt powers. Once the Cleaners had trapped the kid, Sydney had wanted to put him down like a rabid dog, citing the boy's unnatural manifestation and the likelihood of him putting the whole world at risk.

Only Dani's offer of a date had convinced him to spare the boy. Sydney had then fled in the ensuing chaos when Destin tried to slaughter his own offspring. She'd made a devilish deal and always knew she'd have to see it through sooner or later. But she'd always hoped it'd end up being much, much later. Sometime around the heat death of the universe, preferably.

"Why now?" she asked.

His smile returned, a shade relieved, perhaps, that she hadn't given an outright *no*. "Why not? You've been unresponsive to all my other overtures and it's been too long since we've enjoyed each other's sparkling company. I thought it'd be lovely for the both of us to enjoy a bit of downtime."

Dani glanced over to her cart and the backpack hanging heavily off the side. An evening out would mean time lost that she could spend getting through the next Employee Handbook test. She'd also have to explain to her coworkers what she was up to. Francis and Ben knew of the arrangement, and the Chairman would have to approve her taking the evening shift off.

"I've been busy," she said. "The job takes up a lot of my time."

His expression clouded over. "You remember I warned you of that, yes? The Cleaners will take advantage of your every spare moment, every last ounce of energy until you are drained and left as ashes to be swept under the rug. What's the worth of work if you don't take the chance to enjoy life outside the corporate environs from time to time? All work and no play would make Dani very dull indeed."

"Since when do you enjoy life?" she asked. "What happened to the Sydney who lectured me about how pointless everything is?"

"Perhaps his perspective has shifted." He held a palm up. "Perhaps he's still capable of learning and caring for certain aspects of life more than you might have expected of him."

Or perhaps he's being a sly little shyster like before. Once an evil mucker, always an evil mucker? Or can murderous Scum really have a change of heart?

Dani wondered at this. While she'd heard plenty of stories about Cleaners falling to Corruption and going Scum-wise, she realized she'd never asked if the reverse ever occurred. Could a servant of decay and destruction turn Pure? Could a handyman-turned-entropy mage regain his healing and constructive talents? If so, would her denying Sydney send him spiraling down even deeper into the murk his mind and soul wallowed in? If she did give him the pleasure of her company and they had a decent evening, could it convince him to come back to the side of the ... well ... not angels, but the clean and shiny?

"Rules," she said.

His eyebrows rose. "Rules?"

"Rules. We need some."

"Ah. Such as leaving room for Jesus between us at all times?"

"Sure, if he wants to chaperone."

"I suppose boundaries would be wise," he said. "Wouldn't do to spoil every surprise on our very first date."

Nice try implying there'll be more than one. Dani raised a finger. "Rule number one: No trying to convert me. If I get even a hint of you trying to get me to switch teams, we're done, then and there."

He nodded. "Understood, and I'll submit a rule of my own: Neither of us will wield any of our powers. We'll remain entirely mundane and simply enjoy a night without supernatural interference."

"I can live with that. You also don't get to bring any Scum friends along."

"Nor do any of your coworkers get to turn this party into a crowd."

"Fine. Wouldn't want any of them to see me with you anyway."

He flashed a grin. "Excellent. Privacy with the lovely lady, at last."

"And there's a time limit."

"Such as Cinderella dashing off before midnight lest she reveal her origins as a bumpkin?" He tapped his nose in thought. "Actually, that's not the most horrendous idea. What if we set a definitive end at, say, breakfast?"

She glared. "You get three hours of my time. After that, you don't stop me from leaving."

He glanced up, thinking. "Very well. I'd hate for you to get bored. Tomorrow night then. Eight o'clock. We'll meet downtown by the clock tower."

Dani's stomach tightened, as did her grip on the mop. She shifted her boots, planting them more firmly to keep from dashing off as the first nervous quivers waved hello. Was she really going through with this? It'd been years since her last real date. Not that she viewed his advances as anything nearing real romance, but the last time she got involved with a guy, it ended in so many showers she'd nearly drowned. Admittedly, this all occurred before she'd discovered her ability to wreck everything around her—but Sydney's own abilities kind of canceled that out.

"One last condition," she said.

"Yes?"

She gestured with her mop. "Get rid of the pigs."

Sydney grimaced. "Surely you jest."

"Surely I am not getting paid enough to deal with your &%^$. And do you want me wasting hours cleaning this up or do you want me getting ready for our date?" She leaned her mop against the cart and picked up the cleaning signs, dispelling the ward energies she'd invested in them. Stepping aside, she nodded at the pigs. "Well? Are you going to put on your big boy panties or what?"

Sighing, Sydney tugged his gloves off and walked around to each of the carcasses. When he bent over to touch one, a purple aura flared around his hands. Yet when he touched the pig, it merely rippled and sagged like a deflated football. Sydney frowned and his face creased in concentration. The auras darkened and, at last, the pig popped like a fleshy bubble, reduced to dust in moments. He repeated this with all the others until the hall stood empty but for the two of them and several smelly puddles.

"Much better," Dani said.

Sydney wiped his hands on his jeans, even though his powers could leave his skin entirely sterile, should he wish it. "So glad you approve. I shall now take my leave in anticipation of a heavenly evening, devoid of distractions other than our own simmering desire." He headed down the hall he'd appeared from, but paused after a few steps to look back. "Oh. I'd remind you that you did promise to wear a dress. I'd prefer a gown rather than, say, a frilly French maid skirt, but I'll leave that up to you."

He blew her a kiss and strode off.

Once he'd gone around a corner, Dani clutched the front of her jumpsuit in horrified realization.

Oh, &~$#@. That means I have to take off my uniform ...

CHAPTER FOUR

Dani careened through HQ, boots thumping, backpack whacking her spine with every step. Apologies streamed from her lips as she dodged coworkers in her haste.

"Sorry, sorry, whoops, sorry, oh %*$@, that'll bruise, you should get to Maintenance, excuse me, pardon me, sorry, sorry …"

She whipped past an Ascendant, whose golden aura flared in surprise. Dani spun and jogged backward for a second, waving at the woman who glared out from under her white fedora.

"Nothing wrong! Honest. Everything's totally fine. Keep on being awesome." She turned forward again and sidestepped just in time to avoid colliding with a maid, who held up a toilet scrubber like a shield. Regaining her momentum, Dani raced for the nearest glassway.

She tugged her radio off her belt and clicked it onto a private channel. "Chairman … Francis … any chance … you know where Ben is?"

The speaker crackled. *"Janitor Dani? Is something wrong? You sound distressed, and I believe your shift was supposed to continue for another hour."*

"Had a little … run-in. Had to clock out … early."

"May I inquire as to the problem?"

"It's … it's Sydney. He's back. I've got to … got to let Ben know what's up."

Static burst so loud from the other end, she stumbled and stared at the radio, worried it might be acting up. "Chairman?"

"All's well," he said. *"Simply alarmed at the news. Do you need me to accompany you?"*

"No, it's okay. I got this. Just need a little pep talk."

"Very well. I believe he and Janitor Lucy were visiting Jared to check up on the boy. But I should warn you—"

"Thanks a heap."

She rushed ahead, weaving through a crowd of Cleaners who were plodding along, ragged tears and dark stains marring their jumpsuits. Even as she hurried by, though, their uniforms sealed up and the blotches started to fade.

After a jump through a glassway, she reached the foyer where a pair of Ascendants guarded a set of plain double-doors. The doors stood open, and the Ascendants stood off to the side, chatting with each other, suggesting Ben and Lucy remained inside the quarantine area. Ignoring the Ascendants' startled looks, she shot past them and down the hall beyond.

When she reached Jared's quarters, she staggered to a halt and swung the backpack off and to the floor. Unburdened, she planted hands on knees and wheezed.

"Ben! I said yes! Oh, ##%, I said yes. What ... what am I su-supposed to do?"

She sucked deep breaths until a gurgle made her lift her head. A huge orb of water filled the middle of the room. Ben floated within it, thrashing as air bubbles streamed from his mouth.

Lucy stood off to the side, arms crossed, scowling. "For the last time, let him go, kid, or I will spank you so hard, you'll be a wave pool for life."

"Ben!" Dani ran to the edge of the water and tried to grab the janitor. Her hands bounced off a rubbery surface.

Ben swiveled within the water to face her, cheeks bulging as he tried to hold his breath.

A voice interjected with Dani's thoughts.

"Hello, Dani. We are playing a game. Want to join us?"

Dani projected a mental reply. *"Jared, did you ask permission to play with Ben first?"*

"No. He asked for surprises. I gave him one. Isn't it fun?"

"You're drowning him, Jared. That's not good for his health. Let him go, please."

"Oh." A sensation of guilt formed like a knot of lead in Dani's chest, and then vanished. *"Okay. Sorry."*

The orb collapsed, letting Ben *splat* on the floor. Lucy rushed to him as the liquid drained into a self-contained river that wove off to a corner of the room. Dani helped Lucy get Ben upright as he gagged and coughed. She pulled back and shielded her face as he shook himself like a wet dog, spraying them.

"You okay?" Dani asked.

"Sure, just …" He hacked and spat. "Just gimme a sec."

In the corner, the water congealed into a humanoid form; the image of a teenage boy, bare-chested, wearing jeans and sneakers—but made entirely of clear water. Jared ducked his head sheepishly as Dani studied him. His liquid body reminded Dani of the time when Ben's partner, Carl, had communicated with her through her elemental tethers.

As Lucy tended to Ben, Dani went over and checked over the boy. "Jared? Why are you made of water?"

"Don't know," the hybrid said. *"Woke up this way."*

Dani frowned. Ever since they'd brought him to HQ, the kid had manifested an ever-evolving and seemingly random slate of powers. Would these chaotic displays ever end? At least his speech had gotten better. Instead of piecing together phonetic jumbles, he could manage clear phrasings, though he still refused to speak out loud for some reason.

She put a hand on his shoulder. Water slicked her palm and miniature currents swirled under her touch. "Hang here for a minute, all right?"

"All right. I'll be good."

When she withdrew her hand, her skin dried immediately. She returned to Ben's side as he stood, looking less like what the cat dragged in and more like what the cat ate and then hacked back up. He coughed again and swiped his long hair out of his eyes.

"Heya, princess. Thanks for talkin' a bit of sense into the kiddo. Got a little carried away there, mebbe."

She squinted at him. "Ben, what's going on? Why did Jared just try to drown you?"

"Er …" Ben gathered his hair into a ponytail and squeezed, dribbling water down his back. "That mebbe coulda been my fault. Weren't thinkin' too well when I told him about what we was up to."

Dani looked between Ben and Lucy. "And what exactly is that?"

"Tryin' to get my powers gunnin' again."

She shot Lucy a look. "Is he …?"

"He's being serious," Lucy said. "Ben thought a little water shock therapy might somehow jolt his Pure energies back into action. So he suggested a series of tests where he'd get hit with unexpected watery attacks, thinking the adrenaline rush and survival instincts might help him tap into the elements. He mostly meant it as a joke, but the Chairman approved it."

Dani sighed. "Seriously? But why'd Jared get in on it? And why's he made of water?"

"Found him that way when we dropped in," Ben said. "Guessin' it's his new way of showin' off his powers, though I ain't sure he's meanin' to."

"Great," Dani said, glancing at the boy. "Well, at least he looks normal, otherwise. So long as he's stable like this, maybe we can get a better idea of what's going on with him."

With a whoosh, Jared burst into flames.

The three of them stared as his previously watery body transformed into a column of writhing fire. The room's temperature rose a few degrees, and waves of heat slapped Dani's face. He blinked back at them with eyes made of blue flames.

Dani winced against the glare. "Uh … Jared? Does that hurt?"

The teen studied his flaming hands. *"No. Kind of cozy, actually."* He grinned, teeth backlit by an orange glow. *"Why didn't anyone tell me being fire could be so much fun?"*

This version of him made Dani think of her fiery doppelganger—a particularly rude and crude elemental summoned during a cultish ceremony intended to turn Dani into a goddess of apocalyptic proportions.

As if my powers aren't hard enough to deal with, as they are. One day, it's as easy as breathing. The next, I might as well be trying to suck wind through cement blocks while running a marathon.

She briefly shut her eyes and snaked out tendrils of power, looking like glowing lines to her inner vision. When they brushed against Jared's fiery self, she sensed nothing but flames, a super-condensed reservoir of elemental potential. She opened her eyes to see Jared watching her in return, an odd expression on his face—or perhaps that just came from the heat waves rippling out from it.

"Should we put him out or somethin'?" Ben unhooked Carl's spray bottle from his belt.

"Don't bother," Dani said. "He seems fine except for, you know, being fire. And with how hot he's blazing, Carl would evaporate before he even touched him."

The water elemental spouted in alarm. Ben flicked the bottle. "No worries, buddy. I ain't gonna make you sizzle for nothin'."

"Should I play a game with Ben again?" Jared stepped closer, his body brightening to hot white. *"Maybe this time—"*

"No!" Dani and Ben shouted in unison.

The teen hopped back against the wall, hunched. His voice ricocheted through her mind. *"Sorry sorrysorrysorry ..."*

Dani came as close as she dared, hands raised. She wanted to give the kid a hug, but his touch left char marks across the wall and floor. "You didn't do anything wrong, Jared. It's just, the way you are right now, it could hurt us if you got too close. I'm sure it'll change soon."

"I don't want to hurt anyone."

"That's good! That's exactly the right thing to not want. Remember our lessons? Hurting people is bad. Helping people is good."

"But I wanted to help Ben before and almost hurt him, didn't I? Doesn't that make me dangerous?"

Dani met Ben's eyes. "Can you put a little positive spin on this, please?"

"Sure 'nuff." He leaned in to Jared, close enough for steam to start rising from his damp suit. "Lookee here, kiddo. Are you dangerous? You betcha."

"Ben!" Dani cried.

He held his hand up to her. "But so's each of us here."

Jared tilted his head quizzically. *"You are?"*

"As dangerous as rabid rhinos in a fluffy bunny shop. I mean, look at Dani. She's a Catalyst. She can toss all sortsa natural disasters right in your face, from earthquakes to blizzards to locust plagues."

"I can't do locusts," Dani said. "Or rivers of blood, or frog rains, or the whole killing-firstborn-children thing."

He shrugged. "Eh. Probly better that way. Anyhoo, all she's gotta do is get nice and riled, and soon she's whippin' up a nasty mess that takes us forever to fix."

"Gee, thanks," Dani muttered.

Ben winked at her. "And then there's Lu, who—"

Lucy cleared her throat. He hesitated.

"Well, Lu, she's the only one I've ever seen send a pack of blot-hounds scamperin' for their nest just 'cause she didn't get her mornin' coffee. All she had to do was give 'em one good glare, and they practically piddled themselves scramblin' for cover."

"Thank you," Lucy said.

Jared's forehead wrinkled in thought. *"But why are you dangerous, Ben? You don't have powers anymore."*

Ben grinned and tapped his head. "Too smart for my own good, don'tcha know?" At Lucy and Dani's low groans, he puffed his chest up. "It ain't all about how big a stick you got to swing around. It's havin' the experience to know when to swing, how hard, and what soft spots you gotta hit to make 'em puke blood. And that's where I got all of y'all beat. I got enough field work and Scum-savvy, I could be usin' one of them silly swirly straws and still poke out someone's eye if I aim right."

"What's a silly straw?" Jared asked.

"Bendy, twisty little plastic tube you use to drink things." Ben wove a forefinger in the air, tracing loops and swirls.

"Those sound fun. Can I have one?"

"Mebbe once you aren't fire, otherwise you'd melt it before you even got a sip in."

"Oh."

Dani stepped in. "I need to talk to Ben and Lucy for a couple minutes."

"Can I read a book while you do?"

She noted the stack of books by Jared's bed. She and Ben had brought the kid a wide range of titles to keep him entertained, from comics to sci-fi paperbacks to Aesop's Fables and plenty more. But she figured it wouldn't do his mood any good if he accidentally reduced his reading pile to ashes.

"Probably best if you don't," she said. "Just hang out there for a little. See if you can figure out a way to stop being fire."

"I'll try." Jared shut his eyes, face tightening in intense concentration.

Dani turned to the others. "Back to your self-imposed water-boarding. What possessed you to even think of this? It sounds a little crazy, and this is coming from someone who knows crazy."

Ben waggled his eyebrows. "Sometimes the best ideas are the craziest, princess."

"Ben, your powers are gone." She nodded at his missing arm. "You told me yourself, and everything since then's confirmed it. Jared took all you had."

A thought floated over from Jared. *"Didn't mean to."*

"S'okay, kiddo," Ben said. "No one's blamin' you."

Just what we need, Dani thought to herself. *A godling with a guilt complex.*

Ben reached over with his other arm and touched the nub wrapped in the rolled sleeve. "He drained me, sure-for-shootin'. But just 'cause the gas tank's dry don't mean it ain't gonna get refilled sooner or later. Gotta have some hope, princess."

"Fine," Dani said. "You have hope while I have a nervous breakdown."

"Eh?"

"Something wrong?" Lucy asked.

Dani pointed back to the room's entrance. "Didn't you notice how frantic I was when I rushed in here?"

They exchanged looks, and Ben shrugged.

"Sorry. Was a might bit busy gettin' drowndified."

She rubbed her head. "I said yes."

"Yes to what, princess?"

Dani steeled herself before blurting it all out. "Sydney. He's back. And he's taking me on a date. The one I promised him. And

I don't know if I can go through with this. But I have to. I mean, I promised. He was going to hurt Jared if I didn't, and I don't know what to do, and it's all just a little too much right now."

"Oh." Ben puckered his lips. "Jeepers."

Lucy frowned at him. "You want to explain what she means by all that?"

A thud made them look to Jared ... who now stood in earthen form, his body a stony composite covered in lichen and crumbling dirt. The floor had cracked underneath his sudden weight. He patted himself down, hands clacking across his rocky texture.

"Not fire anymore!"

Dani ran over and gave the kid a quick hug. "Good job. I knew you could do it."

He hugged her back, and she grunted against the bruising force of his literally rock-hard arms as they wrapped around her. She disengaged and patted his shoulder, making pebbles drop away. "Go ahead and read for a bit. Just try not to tear the pages."

"Okay." He pounded over to the bed, crunching floor tiles with each step. Like the rest of HQ, the structure would heal itself over time, but Dani cringed when he sat on the edge of the bed and cracked the frame in half. Jared thumped to the floor. He stared down at the ruined bed.

"Oops."

"Don't worry about it," Dani said. "We'll get it fixed. Just ... don't move much right now."

He picked up a book with thick fingers, fumbling to open it. Once he became engrossed in the latest sword-waving, laser-flashing adventure, Dani returned to Ben and Lucy.

Lucy glowered at her. "So, you've got a date. With a Scum murderer."

Dani winced.

"Ain't as bad as it sounds, Lu." Ben held his hand up. "Is Sydney nasty news? You betcha. But he also helped keep our skins intact and got Destin chucked outta the Chairman's seat."

Lucy turned her glare his way. "I read the reports, Ben. He's responsible for dozens of Cleaners disappearing for good, and has sabotaged more operations than the Board is willing to admit. Most of his file is locked up tight, so who knows what terrible things he's done that we don't even know about?"

"A'ight. Mebbe it is as bad as it sounds."

"Hang on," Dani said. "You don't know the whole story."

She started with her and Ben's initial run-in with the entropy mage, his fixation with turning her Scum-side, and how he'd tricked her into meeting with an extremist group known as the Cleansers, who wanted to end all life in a fiery apocalypse. Then she explained how she'd bargained with Sydney for Jared's life when the boy had been rendered temporarily helpless.

Lucy crossed her arms, face even stonier than Jared's earthen features.

"He's Scum," she said. "You never have to keep a promise with Scum. You should never, ever make deals with them, because they'll always find a way to twist the terms in their favor. They do work for Corruption, remember?"

"We set up rules," Dani said.

Lucy flung an arm out. "Oh, well, rules. Girlie's got rules. That just makes everything right with the world, doesn't it? Sounds like you two are going full on with the whole Romeo and Juliet shtick. Need me to point you toward the nearest priest with some poison?"

Dani scowled. "Hey, I'm not looking for a soul mate with this date. I'm just looking to survive following through on my promise."

"Survive?" Ben asked. "Y'think he's up to something nefertirious?" He frowned at their looks. "What'd I say wrong this time?"

"Nefertiti's an ancient Egyptian queen," Dani said. "I think you meant nefarious."

"Mebbe I did, mebbe I didn't."

"And no, I don't think he's out to hurt me. Not directly. But something still feels off." Dani splayed her hands. "Look, this is Sydney we're talking about, right?"

"Unless someone went and changed the topic when I weren't lookin'," Ben said.

"Well, if I didn't know any better, I'd say he's gotten desperate."

"Desperate?" Lucy asked.

"Yeah." Dani sighed. "He's been escalating his attempts to get my attention. Little notes. Then flowers. Then cards. Then long letters. Then perfumed letters with flowers and chocolate. Even all-expense-paid salon trips. Now this whole setup with the strippers." Her face blazed as the two janitors stared at her. "Aw, &$%#. I didn't mention the strippers, did I?"

"Why not start at the beginnin'," Ben said, "and go over that part in lotsa juicy detail."

She sighed. "Male strippers, Ben."

He grimaced. "What's the fun in that?"

Lucy punched his arm hard enough. "Don't be a Neanderthal."

"Why not?" Ben rubbed where she hit. "Those were simpler times. Plenty of meat. Cozy caves. A guy could spit and grunt and scratch himself without gettin' a lecture on not scarin' any nearby kiddos, and women was waitin' to cook up whatever dinosaur you brought back from huntin'." This time, Dani knuckle-shot him in the same spot. He groaned and shifted to shield himself from further abuse. "Gangin' up on me's just provin' my point."

"If we could get back to me having a date with a potential psychopath who has the hots for me?" Dani asked, voice rising an octave. "Sydney would never admit it, but behind all his theatrics and bluster, I got the sense he's … well, almost like he's running out of time, somehow. That he wants to have this date with me before something bad happens."

The other woman narrowed her eyes. "Something bad happens to you or him?"

"No clue," Dani said, "but either way, I just don't have a good feeling about any of it."

"Nobody here would cry if he bit the dust," Lucy said. "In fact, we'd probably throw a party knowing one less entropy mage was around."

"I get it. Everyone here hates him. He's a dangerous traitor. But he does have a twisted sense of honor."

"Emphasis on *twisted*," Lucy said.

Dani sighed. "I trust him enough to keep to his word when he states it as straightforward as he did. We agreed on certain limits. No powers. Just a few hours, and we're done. He won't bring any Scum. I won't bring any Cleaners. Just the two of us."

"And Dani was never seen from again," Lucy mumbled. "Cause of death? Being groped by an entropy mage."

Dani glared. "Not. Helping."

Lucy grinned lopsidedly. "But I am. Listen to reason, girlie. You let him get his hooks in you like this, and there may be no coming back. At best, people around here are going to wonder if you can be trusted after getting chummy with Scum like him."

"I'm not stupid," Dani said. "I'm not putting this up on the bulletin board or anything, and I trust you guys to keep this quiet. That's why I came here." She nodded to Ben. "I need a chaperone."

He made a face. "Me? But you just said no third wheels allowed."

"I don't want you breathing over my shoulder or butting in for a dance. Just stay at a distance, keep an eye on things."

"Why me? Why not Lucy or someone who could actually do something in case things go topsy-turvy?"

She gripped his arm. "Your powers."

He eyed her askance. "I ain't followin'."

"You still don't have them."

"Don't gotta rub it in."

"No Pure energies," she said. "That means Sydney won't sense you. You can follow us and keep watch, make sure everything's okay, and he won't know the difference. Besides, technically you're an independent consultant, not a full Cleaners employee."

"Aw, I hate when we start arguin' technicutleries. That's just beggin' for trouble."

Dani held her hands out. "I can't do this alone. I need to know I'm not going in by myself."

Ben tugged and pushed on his cheeks as he mulled this over. "Could work. I'd need to gussy up a bit so's he don't spot me right off. You sure you want my help with this, though? You even sure you wanna go through with it?"

"I have to," Dani said. "If I break my promise, it could make things worse. Give him a reason to lash out, not just against me, but everyone he knows I care about." At his dubious look, she huffed. "Come on, Ben. You got a second chance. Why can't he have one?"

Ben and Lucy eyed each other, a mix of displeasure and resignation on their faces.

"You're really wanting to do this?" Lucy asked.

Dani firmed up. "Yes."

The other woman sighed. "Hang here for a minute. I'm going to find some rope so I can tie you up and stick you in a closet until you come to your senses."

A slap made them look over to Jared, who had let his book tumble to the floor.

The teen's boulder-head turned their way. *"I hear screaming."*

"Screaming?" Lucy asked. "How many voices? Are they saying anything?"

He whacked the side of his head. *"A man. Maybe a woman, too? No words. Just lots of yelling. Like arguing."*

Pebbles fell off from him in greater numbers, creating growing piles on the floor. Jared started to rise, but an arm and leg cracked at the joints, sending stone shards flying. He slumped to one side.

"Jared!" Dani ran over and grabbed the kid's head between her hands. "What's happening?"

He blinked up at her with gold-flecked eyes. *"I don't feel so good."*

His entire body collapsed into a pile of sand, and his head drizzled down through her fingers.

CHAPTER FIVE

S omeone get a dustpan," Ben hollered.

Lucy rushed out of the room, while Ben ran for the kid—or, at least, what remained of him. Dani had gone to her knees, grabbing up the clumps of sand that had been Jared moments before. She scooped handfuls aside as if she might uncover a tinier version of the boy buried beneath the piles.

Ben grabbed her wrist before she could scatter the piles more. "Hey now, princess, let's hold off on playin' in the sandbox."

She tried to pull free, one hand still digging around. "But he's sand!"

"Yuppers. And if that stuff is his body, you really want to be tossing it around willy-nilly? What if he comes back together with an arm sticking out of his noggin' 'cause you mussed things up too much?"

She jerked her hands back and stared at the piles of grit. "$&%#, didn't think of that."

"Probly shouldn't sneeze none, I reckon."

A swirl of dust spun up from the piles, accompanied by Jared's voice. *"I'm still here."*

Dani reached out again, but stopped herself. "Jared. Oh, thank Purity. What happened?"

"Don't know," he said. *"I was fire and water, earlier. Then earth. Now ... dust?"*

Ben frowned. "Woulda figured you puffin' into air, if we was goin' with an elemental rundown. Don't suppose you can pull yourself together?"

The sand shifted, hollows forming the appearance of eyes and a mouth. *"I don't think so. Just talking is hard."*

Lucy returned with a hand broom, dustpan, and bucket. Dani took these and began sweeping Jared into the pan and dumping the sand into the bucket, down to the last grain. The three of them gathered around as Jared's face formed on the surface of the contained pile.

"Am I in trouble?"

Ben patted the bucket. "Naw, kiddo. You ain't done nothin' wrong."

A chime sounded, and Francis' voice emanated from everywhere at once.

"Company-wide alert: We have reports coming in of a sudden desert appearing in a downtown park."

"Sudden desert?" asked Dani, eyes wide. "Like, what? It dropped out of the sky or something?"

Ben chuckled. "If it did, that's sure gonna make some weather reporters start lookin' for new jobs."

Lucy hushed them both as Francis continued.

"Please notify your superiors if you observe any oddities regarding dust, sand, or other uncharacteristic elemental manifestations."

The three of them stared at each other, and then down into the bucket.

"I'm in trouble, aren't I?" asked Jared.

"Did you make a desert in the middle of Denver?" asked Dani.

"No." The sand rippled. *"At least, I don't think so."*

Ben picked up the bucket and handed it off to Lucy, who held it out as far from herself as possible. He unclipped his radio and pressed the speaker button. "Francis, we got ourselves a funny little co-inky-dink here with Jared. Howsabout a conference call?"

With a flash of light, one wall turned into a viewscreen, revealing Francis at his desk in the Chairman's office. Another man stood off to the side, almost out of sight. Ben recognized the chimney sweep he'd passed by earlier. The guy nodded to Francis and edged out of sight a moment later.

Francis fixed on the bucket Lucy held. *"Is that ..."*

Ben nodded. "The kiddo's been poppin' all random-like into elemental bodies. Right before you made that announcement, he turned into his own personal sand dune."

"I see. I assume these transformations haven't been voluntary?"

"Don't look it. Was thinkin' it was more of his jumpin' and jivin' powers, but this last little trick seemed a might bit too on the nose. What's it lookin' like from up in your ivory tower?"

The Chairman clasped his hands atop his desk. *"I've just received a rather disturbing report from a maids team. Apparently a sizable portion of Cheesman Park—including most of the Denver Botanic Gardens— transformed into a desert mere minutes ago. The maids were heading to clean some houses in the area and witnessed the desert consuming almost a quarter of the park right before their eyes."*

"Desert?" Dani asked. "Like sand and cactus and cow skulls?"

"No cacti or skulls. Merely several square blocks of rolling sand dunes where there used to be trees, sidewalks, and grass. The initial elemental probing suggests the change goes all the way down to the bedrock. Any structures in the area, such as waste bins, benches, or the like appear to have vanished as well."

"Anyone hurt when it happened?" Lucy asked.

"Too early to tell," Francis said. *"We'll keep scanning for missing persons notices or bodies turning up—animal, human, or otherwise. In the meantime, I'd like Janitor Dani to visit the site and see what she can sense. Janitor Lucy, please accompany her. While we had a glassway connected to the Botanic Gardens visitor's center, it appears to be inactive or destroyed. Driving will be most expedient."*

"Me?" Dani looked taken aback.

Francis nodded. *"Your connection with the elements might let you probe deeper into the environment there. You could give us better insight into the cause of transformation. I'll alert the Cleaners on-site to expect you."*

Ben considered a request to go along, eager to get on a job of any sort—plus use it as an excuse to slip out of HQ and avoid further dousings for a bit. But what could he offer here?

Mebbe I could bring a big ol' broom along and start sweepin' up the place? Naw. Let the princess have her fun before she's gotta play spin-the-bottle with Scum.

Dani saluted. "Can do, sir. I also have a request to make for time off tomorrow afternoon. Remember the deal I made with Sydney back before you became Chairman?"

A voice murmured off to the side of the magically projected scene. Francis frowned that way before refocusing on her.

"Ah. The date. I assume this relates to your mention of him earlier?"

"Yeah. That."

"Excellent." Francis picked up a golden pen and began jotting notes on a blank form. *"I will form a scrub-team and gather several Ascendants who should be able to neutralize him once you lure him into the open."*

"Um ... actually ..." Dani cringed. "I promised him no Cleaners would get involved."

The Chairman blinked and paused his writing. *"You actually intend to go through this as a romantic evening?"*

"I don't want any romance," Dani said, "but I can't go in like an undercover agent. This has to be on the up-and-up, otherwise all bets are off."

"I've hardly known any Scum to be on the, as you say, up-and-up. Most likely he's trying to take advantage of your prior desperate offer to bring you in harm's way."

She rolled her eyes. "Sir, I'm not desperate. It's not like I'm going around throwing myself at just anyone."

Ben chuckled. "I's thinkin' he means whatcha did to save Jared. Offerin' yourself like a lil' lambie in exchange for his life." He scratched his stubbly chin. "Huh. Got a ring to it. Little Lambie Dani. Mebbe I oughta start composin' sonnets."

Dani's gaze snapped his way, eyes flared, and he almost imagined a tiny flame flickering in the depths of them. Her low voice simmered. "Look, gramps, you should count yourself lucky I let you call me *princess*, still. You try adding other cutesy bits to that list, and so help me, I will tear off your arm and beat you with it." She blinked and looked abashed. "Sorry. A little on edge with the whole situation."

Ben held his hand up. "S'ok. Everyone gets them first-date jitterbugs. I know I did when Karen finally said yes to a night out on the town."

"It was hardly a night on the town," said Lucy. "You took her to an all-you-can-eat seafood buffet."

"Yuppers." Ben grinned. "Who'da guessed she had an appetite for Rocky Mountain oysters? That's when I knew it was love."

Lucy just sighed and shook her head, but Dani cracked a smile.

Still, Ben studied her closely for a few seconds. Ever since a servant of Corruption had infected the Cleaners with an emotional virus—a magical construct capable of bypassing their protection against diseases and other foul infections—he'd been keeping an eye out for any odd behavior that might suggest its return. The original virus had triggered spiraling bouts of rage and despair, leading Cleaners into murderous frenzies or near-catatonic hopelessness. While the Board assured them measures had been set in place to prevent the repeat of such an event, occasional emotional aftershocks still flared up among the employees. Was this one of them? Could Dani be feeling a little too loosey-goosey where Sydney was concerned? Being emotionally vulnerable without even realizing it?

Mebbe I's overthinkin' the situation. We all took a beatin' with that not-so-warm-and-fuzzy muckery. Hard to trust our thinkin' when we can't even trust how we feel. Bein' human sure is a lousy deal, sometimes.

"Chairman," continued Dani, "I don't think I'm in any danger here. Sydney has never really tried to hurt me before."

"'Cept when he threatened to turn you to dust the first time you met," Ben said.

"He was bluffing to keep you from killing him," Dani said.

"Or when he had those Urmoch ambush us in the Sewers?"

"They just knocked us out."

"Or howsabout the time he tossed you to that fire cult so's you could become their goddess?"

"I'm not sure he realized how far they'd go," she said. "Don't you see? He's never done anything to me directly. He's always had others handling the physical interaction. It's like he didn't want to risk actually having to use his powers on me."

Lucy huffed. "Purity help me, you're disturbingly good at rationalizing."

"All those events remain points of concern for both myself and the Board," said Francis. *"Sydney is well aware of your powers and what a terrible weapon you could be if turned to Corruption."*

Dani lifted her chin. "But, sir, what if I could convince him to return to Purity?"

"It is far easier to Corrupt than to Purify. The instances of Scum joining our side are extremely rare."

"But it's possible?" Dani looked to Ben. "What about you? You got majorly Corrupted with the Ravishing and were cured."

He grimaced, never enjoying reminders of the horrible infection that had weakened his powers, rapidly aged him, and isolated him from his fellow Cleaners for years. "That weren't my choice, first off. We still ain't got no clue what rightly caused it. Sydney chose to become Entropy's errand boy. And second, remember what it took to save me." He nodded at his rolled-up sleeve and then to Jared. "Not resentin' the kiddo suckin' away my powers and whatnot, but whatcha think it's gonna take to get Sydney to repent of his sinful ways? Some sweet talkin'? A few cuddles? You gonna smooch the badness right outta him?"

She made a face. "$%#^, no. It's not like I want to seduce him. That's just gross." She pulled out a tiny bottle of sani-gel and poured some into a hand. "But if he sees I can be trusted, maybe that'd let me discover more of what drives him. Understand him and figure out ways to bring him back to us."

Ben frowned. "Why're you so dead-set on bettin' he's still got a good side to save?"

"Because I've actually talked to him," said Dani. "I've seen him scared; seen him helpless. Underneath all the power he's got, he's still a person. And on top of all that, he's Destin's brother."

Ben twitched at her naming the former Chairman, who'd betrayed the Cleaners by having an affair with a member of the Corrupt Pantheon itself—a disgusting dalliance resulting in Jared's hybrid nature. Ben had known the man for years and never suspected him of being rotten, which was partly what kept him second-guessing everyone and everything. One reason he wanted his powers back so badly was because it'd let him detect both Pure and Corrupt energies in others, let him sniff out the baddies instead of having to wait for them to be revealed. Give him a little more certainty that all was well.

'Course, that didn't help none with Destin. If I couldn't spot that kind of Corruption when it was so up-close and personal, would I do any better once I got back in action?

"What about Destin?" Ben asked, trying to keep his doubts and worries concealed.

Dani held her hands up parallel to each other. "What if he was the reason Sydney went bad in the first place? Destin ran nationwide Cleaners operations and worked alongside the Board, all while hiding his Corrupt dealings for who-knows-how-long. What if he engineered Sydney's fall to use him as a distraction while he kept on with his own dirty business?"

"Girlie," said Lucy, "you're reaching so far right now, you're going to tear something important."

"Actually," the Chairman frowned, *"it is an intriguing theory, and one I've previously considered—though from a different angle. The Board and I have discussed whether Destin and Sydney might have been coordinating their efforts to some degree."*

"Any proof either way?" asked Lucy.

"Unfortunately, no. Destin's files on his own brother proved surprisingly sparse. There's nothing that would immediately link the two. It might bear further investigation, though."

"Lookit, I'm all for figurin' out just what's been swept under the rug," said Ben, "but if we start tossin' around too many Cleaner conspiracy theories, eventually I'm gonna start wonderin' if even Carl here is plottin' against me."

Carl bubbled in his bottle: *We are forever partners.*

Dani shot the water elemental an odd look. "I'm not saying he's innocent," she said. "I'm just saying maybe he's not as bad as everyone thinks. That he might even be a victim to a degree. And, Ben, you and I should know more than anyone else what it's like to be hunted down for all the wrong reasons. Destin was involved then, too."

Ben glowered down at her, trying to not be swayed by her arguments. Sydney had killed Cleaners, yes. That couldn't be denied. But what if she was right, and Destin had a hand in his brother's fate, as much as he'd twisted company resources to try and eliminate Ben and Dani during her employee orientation? What if Sydney could be salvaged if the Cleaners did something other than attack him on sight? After all, Ben hadn't shied from fighting alongside the entropy mage when their goals aligned—though, admittedly, with plenty of assurances in place that he wouldn't betray them.

Francis remained as hard-faced as ever. *"While I admire your attempt to defend his soul, if you intend to meet up with Sydney, it will be with Cleaners waiting to scrub him out—or not at all."*

Dani's shoulders sagged. "But, sir—"

Trying to shake off his uncertainty, Ben forced himself to a quick decision and came up beside her. "Tell you what, princess. You go do your Catalyst voodoo-whatsit at the park and I'll talk at the Chairman and get him to give you a chance."

"Will you really?" Francis asked.

Dani looked to Ben. "You're sure?"

"Sure-for-shootin'." He winked at her. "Go make sure we don't get no more sand sneak attacks."

She hugged him, but then backed off quick and gave Francis an embarrassed look. Lucy came over and handed Ben the bucket handle.

"Looks like you get to babysit Bucket Boy," she said.

He raised Jared's container. "Here's to the adventures of Bucket Boy and Mop Man."

The women snorted in unison before leaving for the job. Once they'd gone, Ben peeked down at the sand, which continued to shift and swirl.

"You lemme know if you feel like your body's comin' back together," he said. "That way, we can pour you out before you wind up with your head stuck in a bucket."

Jared's dusty face appeared briefly. *"Okay, Ben."*

Francis flipped through a folder he'd drawn from a desk drawer. *"If memory serves, didn't the boy once take control of and communicate via a dust devil, back when we first recruited Janitor Dani?"*

"The kiddo ain't to blame, here," said Ben. "If anythin', my gut's tellin' me he's nothing more than a victim of circumcision."

"Circumstance." Francis pointed with his golden pen. *"And your gut also once told you to eat a whole gallon of the cafeteria's chili."*

"It can be right about more than one thing at once. That chili was delish. Just 'cause you had to take me to Maintenance after don't mean I didn't enjoy every bite." Ben set Jared's bucket down to cross his arms, then realized he had only half-accomplished his desired goal. "Now lookee here, Francis, I'm one of them consultants now, right? Only one the Cleaners got, too. So you gots to be respectin' my input on this here situationalism."

"Actually, most consultants are overpaid to deliver opinions and programs the company never actually implements," the Chairman said.

"Good thing you's knowin' better, 'cause I got a couple'a reasons you oughta stow the shotgun and let Dani stay out past curfew."

"Let's hear them, then. This should be … intriguing."

Ben squinted, figuring Francis had swapped in that last word at the last second, instead of, say, "amusing," "ridiculous," or "stupidly crazy."

"Dani ain't goin' at it alone," he said. "I'm taggin' along as a chaperone, see? Since I ain't got my powers, Sydney won't have no clue I'm there, and I can step in if he starts goin' all octopus-hands."

"That's hardly the worst-case scenario I envision. And, unfortunately, sending you in fails to comfort me. Part of my job is to help protect company assets whenever possible. Putting both of you in the path of a known killer without taking the chance to eliminate him would be foolhardy."

"It's not a mission. It's personal between them two."

"Anything involving Scum or any manner of Corruption involves the Cleaners. Which makes this a corporate matter."

Ben squared up and prepared to pull out his final trump cards. *Princess, you're never gonna know how much I bent over backward to get you a date. Better be worth it. You better be right.*

"'Cause you trust me." As Francis opened his mouth to reply, Ben added, "And you owe me."

The Chairman sat back, looking warily amused. *"I've already showed you considerable leniency by bringing you on as a consultant rather than delivering a severance package after you lost your powers. And I uncovered everything we know about the situation surrounding your wife's death. What more could I possibly—"*

"New York City," said Ben. "Halloween Parade. The gal in the sexy plumber costume. I gotta keep goin'? You let this happen, and I forget that ever did."

Francis went quite still. After a minute, he flipped the folder closed and tucked it away.

"Very well. I won't interfere with Janitor Dani's evening. However, I would recommend keeping your radio with you in case you need to call in reinforcements. I doubt you would've been able to face down the entropy mage on your own even with your powers."

"Gotta love a boss who gives great motivational speeches." Ben tapped the wall. "You might needs to try a more positive thinkin' management approach, mebbe?"

Francis cocked an eyebrow. *"The Federal Correction Institute in Englewood. Your second shift there. Must I continue?"*

Ben went still, before slowly lowering his hand. "You ever thinkin' we knows a might bit too much about each other?"

"Every single day."

The wall went blank.

Ben dug into his pocket and pulled out his book. He flipped it open one-handed and scanned a section. Nodding to himself, he scowled at the wall and mumbled, "Malmsey-nosed haggard." He paused, then shrugged. "Eh. Not bad. Gotta look up what 'malmsey' means, though. Sheesh. Who knew swearin' proper made a fella do so much learnin'?"

The bucket by his feet trembled as Jared spoke. *"Ben? I know what plumbers are, but what is sexy?"*

"Hoo boy." Ben tucked the book away and ran his hand through his shaggy hair. "Kiddo, there are some things you're just gonna have to wait to learn until you're older."

"How old?"

"You'll know when you get there."

"Oh." The sand shifted, hissing against itself. *"Ben?"*

He sighed. "Yeah?"

"Were you and Francis telling each other funny stories? They sounded funny, but I couldn't understand."

"Sorta. But they ain't quite the sort I can tell you. Kinda secret stories."

"Do you know any funny stories you can tell me?"

"Oh, I dunno. Can't rightly think of anythin' here and—"

Carl swirled loudly: *Your bachelor party.*

Ben scowled down at the spray bottle. "Now don't you go gettin' started!"

CHAPTER SIX

Dani slathered sanitizer gel on the steering wheel and seat of her Cleaners van before hopping into the driver's seat.

"Why do you do that?" asked Lucy, eyeing her from the passenger's seat. "You realize our Pure energies keep us safe from common germs and dirt. Or did Ben skip that part of your training, too?"

Dani sniffed as she started the van and headed out. "Just because we're protected from that stuff doesn't mean I have to like it touching me still."

"You're an odd one, girlie." Lucy slurped from a thermos the size of a ballistic missile. The smell of burnt coffee already filled the van.

"Oddness is merely a social construct," said Dani, easing into downtown Denver traffic from HQ's underground parking lot. "It's a spectrum along which we are all points."

Lucy slurped again and nodded. "Just proving my point."

Dani sped up as she drove for Cheesman Park. They quickly transitioned from the smaller urban center, swapping out skyscrapers and steely architecture for tree-lined walks. Would've been faster to pop through a glassway, but that required a clean, glassy surface linked to the network, and few of those ever got set up around city parks. Besides, a couple janitors showing up out of nowhere and without a vehicle could've garnered them a little more unwanted attention. Driving offered more camouflage, plus backup supplies and weapons if anything went down on location.

Whenever she drove her van, she usually enjoyed feeling like a SWAT team in a postal truck, heading to take out the bad guys incognito. No one ever took notice of the generic, white vehicles most Cleaners used—even if hers did have pink stripes painted along the sides.

This time, though, the debate she'd just had tumbled around in her brain, distracting her from the anticipation of actual field work. Had she really been trying to argue for Sydney being a poorly misunderstood man? She'd seen his powers at work and listened to his nihilistic diatribes. The reason behind his romantic obsession with her remained a mystery, no matter how much she pondered it. It couldn't be as simple as mere loneliness, could it?

Despite the van rattling along, she became aware of the silence ballooning between her and Lucy. She tried to ignore it, but it kept pressing on her mind.

"Are you mad at me?" Dani asked, once she couldn't stand it any longer.

The other janitor eyed her sidelong. "Mad?"

"For defending Sydney. I know everyone sees him as a crazy murderer, so me speaking up for him must seem insane."

Lucy sat up straighter, making the seat creak. "It's not just about people getting killed. I've killed. So has Ben. So've most Cleaners. You'll have to as well, at some point."

"I don't want to kill anyone! I want to save people. That's why—"

"I know, I know." Lucy waved her off. "That's why you're trying to finish your medical studies. To do some good."

"Actually ..." Dani sighed and ducked her head. "I put that on hold for the foreseeable future."

Lucy turned to look at her directly. "Really. Why?"

"It was getting overwhelming, trying to juggle college and potential grad schools while dealing with everything at HQ or the field assignments. Besides," she grinned wryly, "even though it's hard, I kind of enjoy being a Cleaner more than a student."

"Does Ben know?"

"Does he need to? It's my decision. I don't need his permission."

Lucy sat back. "Guess so. You know there are Cleaners who live in both worlds, right? There are some of us who aren't in uniform all day, every day. They have other jobs. Families. Hobbies, even. Being a Cleaner can be more of a moonlighting position."

"I'm not sure I could split myself like that. It's hard enough for me to focus on the work here."

The other woman shrugged. "Well, whatever you decide, the reality is it's never about doing good."

"What's it about then?"

"Doing your job. Whether you're a Cleaner, a doctor, a cook, or a barista—it's about doing what you do well. That's what lets me sleep at the end of a day, whatever happened during it."

Dani alternated between watching the road and glancing at the woman in incredulity. At last, she shook herself and chuckled. "Wow," she said. "Let me know which Asian buffet you got that fortune cookie from so I can never, ever go there."

"Careful." Half of Lucy's face crinkled in a scowl. "Tweak me enough, and I might let Francis know you're unfit for field duty again."

"That's an empty threat, and we both know it."

That darkened Lucy's scowl. "How do you figure?"

"Because you're too honest."

Dani struggled to maintain a stare-down with the other janitor while keeping them on the road. Running over a stray child wouldn't help her employee record.

Then Lucy snorted. "Honest, huh? All right. You want the truth?"

"Oh, yes, please, ma'am."

Lucy turned to look out her window. After half a minute of quiet, she muttered. "I'm worried."

"About what? Being proven wrong?"

"About you."

Dani bit the tip of her tongue until a few sharper responses she'd prepared retreated down her throat.

"I've seen what you can do," Lucy continued. "Yes, you're a good and a hard worker. Maybe too good."

"Is there such a thing as too good?"

"If it's all skill and no smarts, absolutely. You've got raw power and are learning to handle it well, but you still lack tons of real experience. You're such fresh meat, you could be used to bait wolves. I mean, have you even finished studying the Employee Handbook?"

Dani's cheeks heated. "The Handbook hasn't been as easy to get through as I expected." *And I was going to ask you for help on how to pass the test for Chapter One, but maybe I'll just go to Ben for a cheat sheet.* "So you're saying I should put my head down and just do the work? Don't ask questions? Don't try to look at things from a different angle?"

"Could put it that way, if you want to sound sulky. What I'm saying is you've still got a lot to learn, and it doesn't all have to be the hard way. One quick lesson I can give you is that it's a lot easier and more effective to eliminate the bad and let the good grow back in its place. Or at least get rid of the threats so the good has a better chance of surviving."

"That's a pretty take-no-prisoners perspective."

"Scum don't take prisoners unless they want to Corrupt them. Why should we return the favor?"

Dani scrunched her brow. "We do take prisoners, though. That's what the Recycling Center is for, isn't it?"

Where we nearly died, too, when the whole place imploded. Worst security failsafe ever. I wonder if it's grown back yet …

Lucy coughed a laugh. "If we stashed anything or anyone there, it was either to study them so we could learn how to fight Corruption better, or because something proved a little too troublesome to destroy." She raised her thermos to glug more coffee.

"So you think Ben and I should've died there?"

Lucy choked and spluttered, spraying the windshield. She fought for breath, wiping at the dribbles down the front of her suit. Once recovered, she looked at Dani with shock.

"For Purity's sake, what makes you think that?"

"You were right there," said Dani. "One of the people Destin sent down to stop us from escaping."

Lucy looked taken aback. "I was just—"

"Doing your job. And if you'd done it well enough, he and I would both be dead." She nudged her coworker. "Want to know who saved us after your crew high-tailed it for safety?"

Lucy stuck her thermos on the floor and crossed her arms.

"Sydney," said Dani. "He used his powers to break us out into the Gutters, right before we would've become smaller than pin-dancing angels."

"Self-preservation," Lucy muttered. "What other choice did he have?"

"Come on," said Dani. "You accused me of rationalizing things earlier. You're clinging to what you want to believe, too."

"Sure, except my belief is backed up with evidence."

"Just like you believed Ben was really Corrupted? Did you really believe that, or was it easier to just follow orders?" When Lucy continued to glower, she pushed a little more. "And my opinion of Sydney is based on experience. I think there's a good person somewhere behind that act."

Lucy spoke in a tight voice. "Some people are just bad, through and through, no matter how much you hope otherwise. With Scum, you can't ever let your guard down. It's the safest way." She jutted her chin ahead. "Let's focus on the job. Bigger issues right now."

Dani grumped as she drove on, wanting to continue probing. But Lucy didn't seem in a talkative mood anymore.

They cut through suburban neighborhoods, with cozy, brick homes alternating with art deco quadruplexes in areas defined by well-tended lawns and gardens, root-cracked sidewalks, apartment high-rises, and the occasional corner boutique shop. On this Friday evening, plenty of runners should've been sweating and slumping their way through sadistic fitness routines, wearing unhealthy amounts of spandex while fighting off entropy in their own way. However, the area looked quiet, with minimal foot or road traffic.

Then she turned a corner and nearly slammed the brakes as the view shifted.

"Holy #$%@."

She may as well have driven onto a movie set. Up ahead, between one block and the next, the entire geography changed. Concrete sidewalks, asphalt, and stretches of grass and trees abutted an enormous swath of desert. Pale yellow sand stretched out in gently rolling dunes, flat enough to see across several blocks to where yards and homes resumed on the other side.

She'd brought them in from the north, angling toward where the Botanic Gardens adjoined Cheesman Park on the east side. However, the whole of the garden center looked to have been swallowed up by the dusty anomaly. Even the center's structures—from the large, glass-domed indoor exhibit to the visitor's center to the many sculptures and facility buildings—were nowhere to be seen.

Dani's throat clenched. There had to have been visitors or staff in there. What happened to them? Or anyone in the affected part of the park?

Another cleaning van idled ahead, half a block from where the desert began. Dani pulled up alongside, and Lucy rolled down her window to speak to the Cleaner in the other driver's seat—a black lady who had to be in her late sixties.

"What's the situation?" Lucy asked.

"Same as we reported," the woman said—Phyllis, by the name stitched on her jumpsuit. "One second, everything's normal. Next, we get a desert dropped in our laps."

Dani leaned into view. "Did it just appear? All at once?"

Phyllis blinked as she thought back. "Actually, I suppose it kinda ... grew? Like it started somewhere and then spread out to where it is now in a second or two. Quick, but I guess not quite all flash-bang."

"How're locals reacting?" Lucy asked.

She nodded over to a few groups clustered along the sidewalk. "Most folks are steering clear, but a couple of kids were playing around like a blizzard dropped a few inches of snow. Saw some cops who've started blocking off a few streets to redirect traffic, but they haven't made it up this way yet. Not sure how much time we have before needing some good excuses for being here."

Lucy thanked the woman and nodded Dani ahead. "Best get to it, then."

Dani drove a little further and then parked the van along the sidewalk on the opposite side of the street from the desert. They hopped out. A handful of people stood nearby, but they ignored the newcomers to continue gawking at the environmental phenomena. A few brave souls squatted by the edge to scoop up handfuls of sand and let it drizzle through their fingers. One young man edged out onto the nearest dune, acting like someone standing on a frozen lake who expected to plunge through at any second. A petite Asian woman peered out from beneath a floppy gardening hat, while several young couples chatted among themselves. An elderly man had emerged from a house to stand on his deck, dressed in nothing but oversized boxers, dress socks, and sandals. Typical suburban riffraff.

On the edge of it all, though, a sense of foulness pinged off Dani's senses. Not just her elemental tuning, but her Pure energies as well. The feeling turned into the subtle sensory hallucinations she'd come to recognize as Corruption. A subtle whiff of decay. A hiss of laughter. A slopping sound, like someone trying to pull a huge clog of slimy hair out of a drain.

Lucy came around beside her.

"Getting that?" Dani whispered.

Lucy nodded. "Scum. Or some sort of Scum spell." She scanned the area slowly. "Can't pinpoint it though."

Dani frowned, studying the area. The homes and their surrounding vegetation provided plenty of hiding places. What might it be, this time? Alongside the Employee Handbook, she'd tried studying up on various types of Scum and their ilk. These included ones she'd already faced, like fleshmongers, mudmen, blot-hounds, and gnash, to muck-monsters she hoped she never would, like sloughs, gags, and rotskins. Yet her research had proven overwhelming, and after reading about a creature that literally fed on people's dirty thoughts she'd retreated to a scalding shower, followed by all-night cuddling with her bearded dragon, Tetris, for comfort. So many possible threats. Too many manifestations of filth and decay in the world. It'd drive her insane if she tried to take it all in at once.

So ... time to focus.

Dani rubbed her palms as her power simmered inside her, eager to be unleashed, almost as if it'd grown hungry in the presence of Corruption.

Lucy retrieved a mop and leaned against the van, thermos in her other hand. "I'll keep watch."

"Going in," Dani said.

As she headed for the sandy border, Lucy grumbled behind her, "Be careful."

Dani smiled softly. Once out of earshot, she focused internally and whispered, "Hey, crew. Might need your help on this."

No response, but she knew her elemental helpmates—or slaves, as some of them preferred to label themselves—were awake and aware of the situation. They never slept, for one, and they remained connected to the world through her, so they couldn't really avoid it, for another. The question would be just how grudgingly they might lend their assistance.

Reaching the edge of the desert, she crouched and hovered a hand a few inches from the surface. Faint heat radiated up, but nothing unnatural. She tried to focus on the hint of Corruption in the area. This close, she should've been able tell if it emanated from the desert itself, but it felt as faint as ever.

She glanced back at Lucy and shrugged. "I don't sense anything."

"How deep can you dig?" asked Lucy.

Frowning, Dani turned back and dared to stick her hands into the sand. She winced, but ... nothing. She wiggled her fingers, feeling the grains grinding against her gloves. She drew random patterns through the grit and poured a few handfuls out.

Closing her eyes, she shifted her vision to the elemental plane. Her Catalyst energies snaked out from her in glowing lines of power, eager to latch onto elements in the area and stir up localized natural disasters. With the right prompting, she could likely summon a dust storm that'd engulf a couple blocks, or perhaps whip up some sand twisters to wrench nearby trees out of the ground. An earthquake wasn't out of the question either.

Dani hesitated. *Reality check. Exactly when did I start thinking of creating dust storms, tornadoes, and earthquakes as a normal thing? That can't be healthy.*

She refocused, and discovered that before her laid a vast expanse of ...

Emptiness.

Impossible emptiness. She hadn't felt such a lack of anything, even when tromping along on a dead world in the Gutters.

She tested her senses by probing everything around her except the desert. Plenty of earth, with concrete forming home foundations, rocky lawn substrate, and even the asphalt congealed as a hot—if immobile—sludge. Air swirled as breezes wrestled one another. Electricity crackled through the power lines and into the homes, mere sparks away from starting fires. Water sloshed through pipes as people ran faucets and flushed toilets.

She thrust her powers back into the desert, searching for something, anything, she could latch onto. Yet the emptiness seemed to go on forever, a bottomless pit that would swallow up whatever fell into it. A void in the world, as if this part of existence had simply been erased.

All at once, her elementals started screaming. Dani screamed in response and clutched her head as pain lanced through it. Several arms wrapped around her from behind and yanked her back to the pavement.

CHAPTER SEVEN

Dani thrashed against the people pinning her down. Her vision went dark, despite her eyes being wide open. She bucked and tried to claw out, tried to lash out with her power. But her arms remained pinned and her power, while present, seemed frozen.

As she gathered her strength to try to shake free again, three voices spoke in unison.

"*Relax,*" said a gravelly voice.

"*Relax.*"

"*Chill, fleshbag,*" said Fire-Dani.

She stilled, recognizing the speakers—especially the sniping tone of the last. A groan escaped her.

"Really?" she asked. "Now?"

The hands released her and there came a disgusted noise. "*Fleshy humans are so squirmy. It's disgusting.*"

Dani blinked as her vision cleared. She sat up in the same spot she'd just been in, but in a world locked within a moment. Nobody else, including Lucy, was anywhere to be seen. Not a leaf or blade of grass twitched. Not a grain of sand stirred, and the clouds looked pinned in place.

Turning, she sighed and studied herself in triplicate. Three other Dani's clustered there, except they appeared in elemental forms, much as Jared had earlier. Stone-Dani, Moss-Dani, and Fire-Dani looked back at her. While the fiery version of her radiated constant flames, the heat didn't so much as singe Dani's eyebrows.

"What's up?" Dani nodded back at the desert. "I'm kind of busy."

Fire-Dani flipped a hand. *"You're welcome."*

"For what?" Dani asked. "I don't recall asking for a spontaneous ticklefest."

The flames of her doppelgänger's eyes went white-hot. *"We were saving your stupid, fleshy life!"*

Dani frowned, looking to the other two elementals. Stone-Dani and Moss-Dani remained silent, with Stone-Dani not even manifesting a mouth below the emeralds she used for eyes.

These three appeared to be the main spokespeo … er … spokeselementals for the lot of them, and Stone and Moss often deferred to Fire-Dani. According to them, when Dani's abilities manifested, she'd bonded to a whole host of major and minor elementals, which was what gave Catalysts so much raw power.

She hadn't seen much of her water elementals, not since Carl had used them to communicate privately. She still seethed at his making her stay mum on the fact that Carl and his elemental cohorts had been keeping tabs on Ben. She so wanted to give him a few swift kicks and see how much she could make his rumpus ripple.

"Saving my life?" she asked. "From big piles of sand?"

Fire-Dani rolled her eyes. *"Yes. Big piles of sand that magically appeared and wiped out a huge part of a city park and everything in it."*

Dani gestured to the desert. "Do you know what this all is then?"

"It's Nothing."

"If it's nothing, then why the big fuss?"

Heat waves shimmered out from Fire-Dani's flaming hair. *"I meant nothing as in* Nothing. *Capital-N Nothing, you fleshwit. Get that into your fleshy head already."*

"Pardon me for not being all-knowing. Give me a $&%#%&$ brea …" Dani trailed off and stared at her alternate self. "Wait. Are you using *flesh* and *fleshy* as swear words?"

Fire-Dani pouted. *"Might as well be. Flesh is vulgar enough."*

Dani clapped. "Hah! Copycat. Now that the foul-filter affects you, too, you're totally imitating my circumvention strategies."

"Am not. I just picked the most horrible words I could find."

"Oh, yeah? Why don't we see who can come up with the worst?" Grinning, Dani clapped her hands. "This should be pretty flaming fun, don't you think?"

"You wouldn't dare ..."

"Flame you, you flaming flamesack."

Fire-Dani crossed her arms, glaring. *"I hate you so fleshing much."*

"You're going to need more variety, otherwise that'll get old quick. Ben said he was working up a new swearing angle, but I'm not sure what it is yet. Maybe you can collaborate."

If I ever tell anyone else about my elemental entourage, that is. So far, Dani felt it safer to keep her companions a secret from the other Cleaners. None of her coworkers seemed to know exactly how Catalyst powers worked, and she worried that claiming to see and talk to elemental minions might make the others worry about her mental stability—something Catalysts were already renowned for lacking.

Dani swept a finger through her curls. "Vulgarity contest aside, get back to this desert-that's-really-Nothing. Wouldn't that mean it's harmless? How could Nothing hurt me?"

Fire-Dani pressed fingers to her temples and massaged. *"Meat-for-brains. If you were standing on the edge of a bottomless abyss, would you: A. Back away carefully? B. Put up warning signs and a guardrail? C. See how far you could reach over the edge before you fell in?"*

Dani frowned. "Is this a trick question?"

"You were feeding your power—yourself and us both—into what's basically a big hole in reality. Nothingness. And if you reached too far, you could've toppled in and wiped us all out. We could've become Nothing, too."

"Ah." Dani pointed at the elemental. "That's why you saved me. Nice to know you finally believe my death could destroy you, too."

Fire-Dani scowled. *"You think I helped because I love our little chats? And I don't totally accept your theory of mutual destruction. It's just a chance I'm not willing to take yet."* She marched past Dani to look out over the desert. *"There were other elementals here. All sorts. And now they're gone. Erased from existence. They're Nothing."*

A chill tensed Dani's shoulders. "People must've died here as well. Anyone in the affected area just turned to dust."

Fire-Dani shrugged. *"Sure. People, too."*

Dani grabbed her alternate's arm and forced Fire-Dani to face her. "Hey! They were innocents. What makes their deaths any less important than an elemental's?"

Fire-Dani jerked free. *"People come and go. Elementals are, for all intents, immortal unless actively destroyed. So long as there's life in this world, we're here, helping maintain it. Without us, you fleshbags wouldn't even have a biosphere. So show a little respect."*

"Kind of hard to do when you act like a whiny brat every time you show up."

"I don't care how you treat me," Fire-Dani said. *"I doubt you and I will ever get along, and I'm not telling you to bow down to me. I'm saying you should respect life in general. Existence."*

Dani crinkled her nose. "People like to exist, too, you know."

"Life is life, whether it's humans, insects, plants, whatever. It's hard enough to exist as it is without your kind threatening it at every turn."

"Says the creature that urged me to bathe the world in endless flame."

Fire-Dani bared teeth like candle flames. *"We've been over that. I'd just been woken by the Cleansers ceremony. I barely had any sense of self then. And I didn't want to end the world, if you'd remember right. We could've broken free from their control if you had let me be in charge."*

"Never going to happen."

"Fine. I can wait."

"Wait?"

"To elementals, your species might as well be mayflies." Fire-Dani gazed around at the neighborhood in obvious disgust. *"You're all so proud of your civilization, never thinking about how small and short-lived it is in the bigger scheme of things."*

Dani snapped fingers in front of her other's face. "Focus. I know you like to wax all rhapsodic about how superior you are to me. Sure. I'll die someday and you can finger paint with my ashes. But we're here now. We're linked. You to me. Elementals to humans. I don't think any of us want the world to die."

Fire-Dani grimaced. *"We can agree on that, at least."*

Dani indicated the Desert of Nothing. "This, though, looks like the work of someone or something who doesn't care about life. So we've got a common enemy. Anyone in your bunch have a clue who or what could've done something like this?"

"Entropy," responded Stone-Dani.

They turned to Stone-Dani, who's lower face now had a crack in its rocky mask.

"Say again?" Dani asked.

Stone-Dani tilted her head, causing pebbles to dribble out of the scraggly lichen forming her hair. *"Entropy. Concentrated in one spot by a powerful being. Might accomplish such as this."* She gazed at the desert, posture mournful. *"The earth knows Entropy. We feel its power with every wave on the shore. With every breeze that brushes over the mountains. In the melting glaciers and shifting sea. It is everywhere, and it is inevitable."*

Dani frowned. "Sydney's power is based on entropy, both the big and little E version. Could he be behind this?"

Fire-Dani hissed through her teeth. *"Possible, but he's hardly the only Scum capable of it. And from what we've seen, he usually ages things out of existence instead of leaving random deserts behind."*

Dani pondered this. Could Sydney's reappearance and pursuit of their date be a ploy to let him experiment around the city without being immediately linked to the disasters? Or might another Scum be responsible? Why would he bother approaching her, though, when he could've made the desert without alerting the Cleaners to his presence? That didn't make sense, but it did make her hopeful he might not be resorting to old, destructive habits after all.

But doubt still rustled in the dark outskirts of her thoughts. He'd targeted her from the moment they'd met, and hadn't let up. Could he be playing a long con, using her as an "in" to cause the Cleaners long-term damage? And why, despite knowing what he could do and what the others said he'd done, couldn't she shake her interest in him? Was it intuition that there might be more to him? Something that everyone else refused to see? Or could it be—dare she admit it—a ridiculous sort of infatuation?

Sighing, she scanned the area, wishing other humans didn't disappear whenever she went into this mental space with her elementals. "When we got here, Lucy and I both sensed Scum in the area, but we couldn't pinpoint the source. Any chance you could help with that?"

"We'll try," Fire-Dani said. *"Send your power out through the elements and we'll see if we can triangulate the source of Corruption. Oh, and don't forget to avoid the Nothing."*

Dani eyed her. "You really think I'm that stupid?" Fire-Dani opened her mouth, but Dani raised a finger. "Don't."

Smirking, Fire-Dani turned to face the rest of the street. Stone-Dani and Moss-Dani did the same.

Dani sensed her helpers stretching their awareness out through their respective elements. She wondered if they might even be interacting with minor elementals in the area, having little exchanges in a language that humans could never comprehend. Would they be discussing deep philosophy relating to the spread of the nearest algae bloom? Or would it equate to, "Oh, hey there, little dirt elemental. Seen any Scum around lately?"

Breathing in, she coiled her power up within herself. As always, even in its most subdued state, the energies pushed back against her control. It wanted to be unleashed in a torrent of Pure power, latching onto the elements and whipping the world into a frenzy. There could be earthquakes, floods, and fires. There could be windstorms and hurricanes.

Dani kept a tight grip on it all, refusing to let it loose beyond what she allowed—especially knowing people stood nearby. She breathed out and unspooled tendrils of power, letting them snake out into the environment. Her awareness expanded with it, even more sensitive than usual thanks to the elementals lending their heightened focus.

Closing her eyes, she could still form an internal map of the street and sidewalk, the grass-and-rock patches of lawn, the wiring and piping and wooden frames making up the homes. She felt the pressure of car tires pressing against the asphalt. The ripple of wind through leaves. All of it formed a raw sketch of the world around her. She tried to ignore the yawning emptiness at her heels, and the sense that she might topple backward into it and never stop falling.

Corruption tinged the whole area, almost like static hissing in her ears. Could this be a side effect of the desert's creation, or a spell intended to camouflage the Scum's location? Either way, it clouded her attempts to single out its origin.

Dozens of cords of power wove about, probing spots briefly before moving on. Normally she could only stretch her awareness so far before losing control of the energies or having her power dissipate altogether. Yet with the elementals bolstering her, she found her focus remained strong.

Then she realized several threads of energy had warped around a particular spot, not far off. A slight shift off the course she set them on, forming a small gap in what she could sense. She concentrated and found the place lay along the sidewalk, over near where a number of people had gathered. Her power hadn't touched on the spot because there was nothing to touch. It felt empty, devoid of elemental substance and any spark of life. A hole in existence—just like the desert. It had to be the Scum, acting as an innocent spectator.

She fixed the location in her mind. "Got it."

The trio of elemental Danis turned back to her.

"*Good,*" Fire-Dani said. "*We'll let you get back to your job so long as you promise to stop almost getting yourself killed.*"

"Perish the thought." Dani gave a little wave. "See you all soon."

"*Why do you have say such depressing things?*" Fire-Dani asked.

Before Dani could reply, the elementals vanished and the world lurched back into motion. She stumbled and caught herself on a hand and knee.

Lucy hurried over, mop poised. "You all right?"

Dani rose and dusted herself off. "Yeah, I'm good. Just lost my balance."

"You sure?" Lucy eyed her with more than a little worry. "Last time I saw you like that was at the hospital, when we were trying to save Ben. Like you were having a fit or something."

"Not a fit. My power just backlashes at times."

"Backlash? Like when you formed a giant sinkhole and swallowed that house?"

Dani winced at the memory. "Sort of, but not quite." She looked to where she'd picked up on the aberrant elemental feedback and immediately spotted her target. "Woman in the big, floppy hat and purple sundress. She's Scum."

Lucy squinted that way. "How do you know?"

"Picking up a weird vibe from her," Dani said, jogging to the van.

"Vibe, huh?" Lucy followed, still staring over at the lady. "You must have better Scum-sense than me. I'm still just getting a vague nasty feeling from the whole area."

"Maybe it's a Catalyst thing. Why don't we go say hello?" Dani grabbed a rag and spray bottle of all-purpose cleaning solvent. She also stuffed a black garbage bag and a few zip-ties in a pocket. "We'll confirm either way."

A few people gave them odd looks as they approached. Hopefully they'd assume the two Cleaners had been working in a nearby house and were drawn out by the spectacle like everyone else.

Lucy stayed a step behind Dani, who marched toward the Asian woman with grim determination. The other janitor whispered as they closed in, "Careful, girlie. Don't know what we're dealing with here."

The woman stood further back from the rest of the onlookers, not talking to anyone. She simply stared out over the desert as if enraptured, which made Dani all the more certain she had something to do with its appearance.

The gardening hat shadowed her pale features, but Dani glimpsed large, wide eyes and a pert mouth beneath a sharp nose. Short black hair clung to her neck and ears.

Dani slowed as she neared, ready for any threatening movement. A few steps away, the women suddenly turned to face her. She smiled prettily. "So that's what you look like. You're very pretty." She swept a hand at the sand dunes. "Do you like it?"

Dani hesitated, unsure what the woman meant by the first comment. Did she know Dani? Dani had certainly never seen her before. Then she fixed on what the woman's question implied.

"Like it? You're admitting you caused this?"

"Created," the woman said, "not caused. There's a difference. Now, be honest. How can I improve?" At Dani's disturbed look, the woman made a welcoming motion. "Don't be shy. I can take criticism, so long as it's constructive."

"Why did you do this?" Dani asked.

"Practice." The woman shrugged. "How else to perfect my art?"

"Art? You killed people here." This close, the Corruption rippled out from the woman, making Dani feel like she stood in a wave pool filled with sewage. She braced against the sensation and tried not to gag. She aimed the spray bottle at the woman. "Who are you?"

The woman's gaze flicked down to the bottle and back to Dani. "Aw. You're so cute. So dedicated to your work."

"Listen, $%&#@#, I've got really good aim and this stuff will hurt you worse than holy water on vampires."

"Vampires aren't real," Lucy whispered.

"Not now," Dani said through gritted teeth. She narrowed her eyes at the woman. "You've got three seconds to tell us who you are, otherwise I'll melt your face and then cut you a new mouth so you can tell us then."

"You really want to do this here?" The woman gestured at the nearby suburbanites.

"I'll do it here," Dani said. "I'll do it there. I'll do it in the rain. I'll do it on a train. Doesn't matter where you run. I'll take you down, you filthy Scum."

Lucy made a choking noise, while the woman merely raised an eyebrow.

"Very well." The Scum held her hands out, wrists pressed together. "I suppose you'll be wanting to take me in for quarantine and questioning?"

Dani stared, wondering what the trick was. When the woman didn't move, Dani handed the spray bottle to Lucy. "If she twitches funny, aim for the eyes."

"Up the nostrils is funnier," Lucy said.

Pulling out the zip-ties, Dani eased closer, trying to figure out how she could explain her actions if anyone watching asked. Maybe she could claim she was a rogue maid thieving from homes, and maid services took care of their own?

The Scum remained still as Dani looped a tie around her wrists. As Dani cinched it, the woman's tiny grin widened.

"Oh, that's nice and tight. I do love when someone isn't afraid of getting a little rough." She winked at Dani as she tugged at her bonds. "Thank you for the help."

"Help?" Dani echoed, tensing again.

"I have places to go, more to practice. Getting around through mundane means would've worked, but I'm not allowed to pull this little trick, though, unless I'm trapped. He considers it such a waste of power, otherwise."

She yanked against the plastic cord and the zip-tie sliced through her wrists. Her hands fell to the ground at Dani's feet, exploding into clouds of dust when they hit.

Dani jumped back. The Scum appeared unfazed by the loss of her hands, especially as more dust flowed out of the stumps of her arms like grit waterfalls.

The woman's voice gained a rasping undertone. "My masterpiece will be finished soon. I do hope you'll attend the unveiling."

She smiled wide. Her perfect teeth crumbled and sand spouted from her mouth. Her eyes shriveled and more dust poured from the sockets. Her body sagged, collapsing in on itself as more holes opened and let sand stream out. In seconds, her entire body collapsed into a heap of grit, an almost identical replay of Jared's collapse earlier.

A moment later, the pile of sand spun up into a vortex. It grew twice as tall as Dani, a roar sounding as it increased in speed.

People screamed and ran in all directions. Dani reached out with her power to try and cut off whatever spell the woman had enacted—but as with the desert, her energies couldn't latch onto anything.

The dust twister quickened and widened. A shrieking wind snatched at Dani's hair, and blasts of grit stung her face as she shoved more power at the whirlwind. There had to be a way to stop or take control of it.

Someone grabbed her shoulder from behind.

"Not now," she shouted, thinking her elementals were interfering again. "I won't fall in."

"Fall into what?" Lucy yelled in her ear, tugging her back. "Time to run, girlie!"

With a last frustrated glance at the twister, Dani turned to join Lucy as they raced for cover. Just a few steps in, the twister exploded with a thunderous crackle. Dust blew out in billowing yellow clouds. A sheet of sand slapped at them and knocked them both to the ground.

Dani's gloves protected her palms from getting gouged on the pavement, but she still hit with bruising force. She lay gasping for breath for a second; Lucy sprawled beside her. As silence descended on the neighborhood, they roused and looked to each other.

"All right." Lucy turned her head and spat. "What just happened?"

Dani straightened and stared around at the desert, plus the fine layer of grit now coating everything within a hundred feet.

"I think we're going to need a bigger bucket," she said.

CHAPTER EIGHT

Sitting in a corner of the cafeteria, Ben hunched over his tray, using Jared's bucket as a shield as he glowered at the rest of the room. His shaggy hair lay matted and soaked from the last glass he'd had splashed in his face by a passing coworker. Water dribbled down under the collar of his jumpsuit. A small puddle formed around his feet, and he figured he looked like a soggy scarecrow.

Guess I sorta deserved this. Francis done learned me a lesson, that ... that ... He reviewed a few memorized phrases. *That villainous crook-pated puttock.*

For the moment, Cleaners came and went without giving him a second glance, but he eyed them all with suspicion, nerves jittery. Who among them was already plotting the next ambush? Would it be a bucket to his handsome mug? A spritz into an ear? Maybe a sponge chanted to contain a whole pool's worth of water?

Sure, he could've snagged a bit of grub and eaten in his room, but he didn't enjoy feeling like a coward. He'd brought this trial-by-water on himself.

Jared shifted in his bucket. *"Ben?"*

Ben spoke around a mouthful of garlic mashed potatoes. "Yuff?"

"Will I ever be normal?"

Ben swallowed and belched softly. "Aw, don'tcha worry, kid. You ain't gonna be stuck as sand forever. We'll get'cha fixed up right and good, sure-for-shootin'." Even as he said this, Ben hoped they'd find a way to follow through with that promise.

"No. I mean normal. Like you and everyone else here."

Ben snorted. "If we're your definition of normal, you gotta get a better dictionary. We ain't exactly your everyday joes and janes."

Jared churned around, grains scraping against the side of the bucket. *"I know people are scared of me. I don't like it."*

"Ain't so much as scared as worried."

"Is it because I can do things they can't?"

Ben scratched his chin. "Sorta, kinda, mebbe? I mean, everyone can do things nobody else can, if you figure it right. You're different, sure. So what? You're yourself. I'm me. Dani's Dani. We all gotta be okay with that, otherwise we'll all go crazy sooner or later."

"Like my dad did?"

Ben frowned. They hadn't told Jared much about Destin, the former Chairman, but the kid seemed to have inherited a certain amount of knowledge from his father and knew more than he should've—about the Cleaners, HQ, and Destin himself. Despite Jared's good behavior so far, Ben worried about what else might've been handed down from father to son. Fortunately, Jared hadn't been affected by the emotional virus Dr. Malawer had unleashed. If the kid had succumbed to a supernatural rage, who knew what he might've done before they got him back under control. If that would've even been possible …

Shucks, we even gotta tone down playtime, sometimes. Keep him rememberin' to act all proper, even when he's havin' fun. Share your toys, Jared. Clean up the mess, Jared. Don't become an insane, unstoppable force of Corruption, Jared.

"Might be," he said. "Destin sure did forget who he was and got dragged down into the muck 'cause he didn't have no firm footin'."

"Maybe that's why people are scared. They think I'll be like him someday. That's why the Board wanted to get rid of me, isn't it?"

Ben frowned. "Ain't gonna lie. Some folks might be thinkin' that way. Fact is, though, any of us could go sour if we aren't careful. Nobody's pure mud and no one's pure spit-shiny. But you're a good kid, Jared. I know it. Dani knows it. Francis knows it. You ain't gonna wind up like your daddy."

Jared remained silent, and Ben took the opportunity to shovel a few more forkfuls down his throat. At the same time, Jared's questions poked at a few sensitive worries of his own—mainly, what might be causing the kid's current predicament. Ben never much liked the Board, even in his heyday, and never fully understood the extent of their inhuman powers.

Could the Board itself be messing with Jared's physical presence, experimenting with ways to neutralize him? He drew on powers from both the Pure and Corrupt Pantheons, but none of his behaviors so far suggested any nasty inclinations. He enjoyed adventure stories and comic books, kept his room clean for the most part, and followed instructions—though sometimes it took a bit of explaining the rationale behind certain requests for him to acquiesce.

Aside from his fluctuating powers, he came across like any other kid plucked off the streets, even if his mental and emotional maturity lagged a few years behind what his normal body suggested.

He tapped the bucket with his fork. "Tell you what. Once I'm done stuffin' my gullet, we'll get'cha down to Maintenance and see what a handyman or two might make of you. Mebbe one of 'em can figure out how to get'cha back to your old self."

Jared mumbled a response, seemingly lost in his own thoughts. As Ben tried to think of another way to encourage the boy, a figure entered the cafeteria. His black jumpsuit contrasting sharply with HQ's white walls, tiled floors, and the colorful array of other Cleaners' uniforms. Ben recognized the chimney sweep he'd passed in the hall, and had also seen meeting with Francis earlier. He kept an eye on the guy while chomping through a pile of taters and a dense cube covered in red sauce the cafeteria menu claimed was meatloaf.

After a glance around, the chimney sweep went down the food line, ending with a heaping tray of nothing but cheesecake slices. His brush was strapped to his back in a modified leather holster with a strap that ran from his belt to his shoulder.

Ben tried to think of the last time he'd seen a chimney sweep around HQ. Certain types of Cleaners were more common these days than others, and chimney sweeps definitely didn't have the presence they used to.

Eh. Ain't none of my business, whatever he's doin' here. Don't gotta be nosy with everyone here. Ben refocused on his meal, turning his thoughts toward Dani's date.

"This seat taken?"

Ben looked up to find the chimney sweep standing across the table from him, tray in hand. A stocky bull of a man, the sweep could've stood in for many of the brick fireplaces he most likely worked on. The white threading on the left breast of his black jumpsuit read *Rafi.*

Ben gestured for him to sit. "Naw, it ain't. But I's warnin' you, that there's the splash zone."

"Oh, I know." The sweep slid onto the bench, setting his tray down. "It's an interesting test you're running. Never heard of anyone trying to recharge their powers. Though," he frowned, "I guess I never heard of anyone losing them."

"First time for everythin'." Ben checked around to make sure nobody was sneaking up on him with a glass of water—or a bucket. "How'dja hear about that, anyhoo? Francis nudge you to give me a dousin'?"

"No." Rafi picked up a slice of cheesecake and ate it in two bites. "Spotted the announcement on one of the bulletin boards."

Ben spluttered. "It's on the bulletin board?"

The sweeper nodded. "And the latest company memo."

Groaning, Ben swiped droplets from his brow. "I really oughta start payin' attention to the memos."

The chimney sweep extended a hand. "Rafi."

"Ben. But everyone 'round here usually just calls me 'hey, you' or 'get 'em!'" They shook. "Where you comin' from, Rafi? Ain't seen you 'round here that I can remember."

"I was transferred to the European HQ for a couple years," he said. "Solo operation that required some top security clearance."

Ben nodded. The Cleaners had a presence in practically every government and major business across the world—after all, office buildings and military compounds still needed trash cans emptied and windows wiped down—and a chimney sweep's abilities made for excellent infiltration work. They often got assigned to what the Board liked to call "white ops," slipping in and out of highly secure facilities to deal with Scum and Corruption even more covertly than usual. He'd even read a report that suggested Scum had been kept from getting their hands on a few dirty nukes thanks to a chimney sweep's intervention.

"European HQ, huh?" Ben waved his fork around. "Fancy. Why come back here?"

"Aside from completing my assignment?" Rafi said. "I'm actually back on the Chairman's orders. Special gig that needs a little extra muscle."

"Yeah? What's Francis got you doin'?"

The sweep's expression turned rueful. "Sorry. I'm not allowed to say. It's—"

Ben took another bite. "Above my pay grade. I get it. I ain't gotta know everythin' he's up to, and honestly, I don't wanna know. So, whatcha trottin' my way for? Ain't figurin' it's 'cause you're wantin' to recruit me for the company talent show."

Rafi blinked. "There's a talent show?"

"Oh, sure. You oughta see Francis ride a unicycle while jugglin' flamin' sponges. Carl and I," Ben patted the spray bottle at his hip, "were workin' up a few magic tricks, like pullin' dust bunnies out of a hat and tellin' fortunes with a squeegee board. Dani was thinkin' of tryin' a bit of ventriloquism with her lizard."

"Lizard?" The sweep's eyebrows rose.

"Yuppers. Cute little fella named Tetris. I was gonna put a suggestion in that he be made the company mascot, but now I'm worried they'd take me seriously."

Rafi had that look—the one people got when they couldn't tell if Ben was being serious or not. Sometimes it just didn't feel like the day was complete until he'd gotten that look at least once.

"Well, as interesting as that all is, it's not why I wanted to talk to you."

"Figured as much. So what's the catch?"

"No catch. It's just that, with being on the other side of the pond for so long, I lost touch with a lot of current events over here. I was hoping to get caught up to speed. Fill in the gaps so I can feel more on top of things when I start working on my current assignment." Rafi picked up another cheesecake slice and pointed it Ben's way. "From everything I've heard, it seems like you and some of your friends have been at the center of some of the bigger happenings here. You and that apprentice of yours—"

"Whoops." Ben wagged his fork in warning. "Dani ain't my apprentice no more, and unless you wanna get her in a right ol' huff, you gotta avoid callin' her that at all costs."

Rafi raised his hands. "Thanks for the warning. I've asked around a little, and you've got a ..." He coughed into a fist. "A reputation."

"I does, huh? For what?"

"For being honest. For not hiding behind the bureaucratic bunk a lot of Ascendants pad their reports with."

Ben grinned. "Upper management sure does love their paperwork, don't they?"

Rafi returned the grin. "Muck and mutter, yes. That's why I've never applied for a raise. I like where I'm at."

"You and me, both. I've worn that suit once, and ain't never goin' back."

The sweep's disbelieving look returned. "You were an Ascendant?"

Ben waved that off. "Dusty old history. Don't give it much thinkin' these days."

"I see." Rafi studied him with renewed interest. "And now you work as a consultant?"

"Yuppers. I've been around, up and down more than most, if you can believe it. Seen some muck that'd drive a man mad. Even went a bit loopy myself for a bit. Francis don't want none of that experience to go to waste." He glanced around. "And I got some unfinished business of my own I aim to see done and dealt with, sooner or later."

Ben's radio crackled on his belt, and Dani's voice came through. *"Ben? We're coming back and could use an extra brain or two to figure out exactly what happened out here."*

He grinned at Rafi, patted the radio, and then thumped his own head. "See? So long as my noggin' is intact, they'll keep payin' me to use it." Rising, he put his hand on Jared's bucket. "Tell you what. I gotta go help a few folks, but howsabout we meet tomorrow and I can getcha all caught up?"

Rafi saluted with yet another cheesecake slice. "Sounds perfect. I'll find you sometime in the afternoon."

"Ben!" Jared cut in. *"Look out."*

Rafi snapped his head from side to side. "Where's that voice—"

A splash of water blinded Ben for a moment. He blinked his vision clear and looked behind himself to see a janitor standing with an empty cup, smiling sheepishly.

"Did it work?" he asked. "Should I try again?"

"Aw, c'mon! We was havin' a conversation here." Ben swiped at his face and flicked water back at his latest tormenter.

Every last drop flowed off his face, onto his hand, and flew in a liquid ball to strike the other Cleaner straight in the chest. The janitor jerked and dropped the cup. He gaped at Ben, as did Rafi and several other nearby Cleaners.

Ben shot to his feet. He patted his face, finding it entirely dry. He stared at his hand, and then at the janitor, who looked back in shock as water ran down his suit.

A grin spread across Ben's face. He focused inward, searching for what he knew must be there. Deep within, the tiniest flame of Pure energy burned. A moment later, it guttered and extinguished. He reached for the puddle on the floor, straining to stir up the slightest ripple. He couldn't sense the element anymore, but it had been there. His old power. Just for a few seconds.

"Well, bust my britches wide open." He glanced around the cafeteria. "Anyone got a fire hose handy?"

CHAPTER NINE

Dani sat on her bed quarters in Cleaner HQ and glowered. Specifically, she gave the Employee Handbook a good scowling where it lay on the floor a few feet away. After another minute of this, she grunted and flopped back on the mattress.

This is ridiculous. I'm having a staring contest with a book. Worse, it just won. Stupid no-eyes, unblinking manual.

She ground the heels of her palms into her eyes, stifling a yawn. She'd spent much of the previous evening hashing out the encounter with the desert-summoning Scum with Ben and Lucy, with little to show for their effort.

Ben had been a bit bouncy at first, annoyingly cheerful with his claim of some spark of his old power coming back—which he couldn't prove in the slightest, when asked. Yet he sobered up and focused when the women described what had gone down at the park-turned-desert.

He and Lucy agreed—grudgingly so on Lucy's part—that it didn't fit Sydney's MO, though they also noted the woman's powers must be linked to the Corrupt Pantheon member, Entropy, who embodied its namesake. Her identity remained unknown. Dani had provided the best description she could, mentioning her sense that the unnatural desert represented a whole lot of Nothing, avoiding mentioning how her elementals helped her realize this.

The other two had headed off to the Records section of HQ to research possible leads on the mystery. She, on the other hand, retreated to her room, planning to study more of the Employee Handbook. Except she'd fallen asleep ten minutes in and woken up bleary-eyed, shedding dreams of dust devils chasing her across an endless desert.

There was no word from either Ben or Lucy today, even though it was now well into the afternoon. That must mean they hadn't turned up anything substantial yet, if they even still worked on it.

She propped herself up on an elbow and looked to the dresser, where a sunlamp lit up a large terrarium. Inside, Tetris gobbled down the mealworms she'd tossed in earlier. The orange-and-red speckled bearded dragon twitched his tail as he scurried from one corner to the other.

Dani quirked a smile, enjoying his antics, but then her focus strayed to the sandy bed of his home, and her mirth faded. It reminded her too much of the desert and the people who'd been caught in the senseless destruction.

A tiny part of her felt like a failure for not bringing back more substantive information, as well as letting the Scum escape so easily. And if there was one thing she hated almost as much as germs and dirt in general, it was failing.

She replayed the final scene in her head, seeing the woman turn to dust over and over like a sand-filled scarecrow with its guts sliced open. What could Dani have done differently? How could she have subdued the woman without even knowing everything she might be capable of?

Huffing, she rubbed her temples.

I'm trying to distract myself, aren't I? Been doing it all day, I guess.

She'd even willingly gone to a training session for most of the morning, letting herself get bruised all over at the hands of several combat and gear instructors. Then she'd dawdled in the cafeteria for a long lunch, and then spent an hour cleaning and organizing her van—which in no way needed it.

Dani checked the clock on the wall. Three o'clock. Just a couple hours, and she'd have to head out if she wanted to meet Sydney on time.

Just that thought sent icy worms squirming over her skin. She hugged herself until the sensation dissipated. She wondered if the reaction came from the idea of exposing herself to a date in general or whether it came from Sydney's involvement. Even with her defending the entropy mage to her coworkers, the man remained a muddle in her mind. At times, he'd seemed so sincere, and yet underneath he kept that teasing, almost taunting tone, as if he could never resist showing off his superiority. Maybe the date would settle the matter for her once-and-for-all.

She checked the clock again. Three-oh-one.

Oh, for Purity's sake. Am I going to sit here and stew the whole time or am I going to put on my big girl diaper and deal with this?

Still, she had time enough for one more attempt to pass the Chapter One test. Maybe if she managed that, she could head out for the evening in a better mood.

Sitting up, she eyed the Employee Handbook.

"Tiny tornado?" she asked.

The letters on the cover swirled. No. I now desire for you to bring me a shrubbery.

Dani stared. "Excuse me?"

That was an attempt at a joke.

She scrunched her eyes up in suspicion. "Since when do you joke? Is this another test?"

I have discovered different people learn via different means. You appear to enjoy a certain level of witticism, so I wanted to determine if incorporating it in our interactions would be effective.

Dani shot to her feet. "Wait, you're observing me during the day? All the time I'm lugging you around, you're scoping me out?"

Of course.

"That's ... that's voyeurism! Are you saying I'm stuck with a pervy Employee Handbook?"

I do not take pleasure in watching you. It is merely to gather data for your own good.

Dani glared. "That's it. Anytime I take a shower, you're going in the closet."

Is this your attempt to avoid the test again?Growling, Dani woke her power and latched onto the air in the room, drawing it in and churning it up over her upraised palm.

"I don't avoid challenges," she said.

She formed a mental image of what she wanted—a small tornado spinning over her palm, not disturbing anything else—and tried to assert her will over the formation of the spell. The energies were slippery, wanting to spread through the whole room and beyond to inflict as much damage as possible, which made it all the harder to stabilize a natural disaster in miniature.

A fist-sized, light-gray cloud formed and began to swirl. Dani focused on it, her vision tunneling in until she could only see her creation. Power pulsed through her, trying to shoot down into the growing tornado and whip it up, larger, faster, deadlier.

She throttled her power back even as it shoved harder against her, urgent, a painful pressure that gripped the back of her neck and made every muscle tense.

The twister wobbled, and she jerked her arm around to try and regain the balance. But this just threw her off more, and the twister swelled and burst. She slammed onto the bed, while the Employee Handbook didn't get so much as a page ruffled.

Dani raked fingers through her hair and winced as she caught a few snarls. "$%#@$&@#%^@#! I thought I had it that time."

Are you giving up? the book asked.

Refusing to be baited, Dani stood and paced, trying to think of a different approach. Brute forcing it didn't seem to be working, and her abilities rarely helped with anything requiring finesse. She could visualize what she wanted just fine, but turning that into a reality was where it all broke down.

She should've taken the Borrelia sisters up on their offer for air-manipulation training sooner. The twin maids could fling tightly spun vortexes with their feather dusters or brooms; they could even briefly fly with their powers, shooting their bodies about on sudden gusts and alighting with perfect poise on their leather cowgirl boots. Dani could fling bodies about, for sure, but the results would involve broken bones and an unhealthy amount of splattering.

Her thoughts turned back to her friends' use of feather dusters and brooms. Most Cleaners employed magically enhanced sanitation tools as focuses for their powers. Dani had learned to wield some as well, though her power hardly required it. But what if she employed a focus for this test? Maybe that was even part of the test—identifying a flawed approach and fixing it.

She didn't keep any tools in her quarters, however, and didn't have enough time to trot down to Supplies to retrieve any. She cast about the room, seeking something that might suffice.

Then she fixed on Tetris' terrarium again, and an idea sparkled in her brain. She went over and removed the lid enough to scoop out a small handful of sand. Cupping the grit in her gloved hand, she summoned another mental projection of what she wanted to create, but not of just a twister this time.

Instead, she thought back to confronting the sand-Scum on the edge of the desert. She pictured the woman turning to a pile of lifeless dust ... and then she envisioned herself summoning a sudden wind to spin the woman about in the process of transformation and keep her trapped in midair. Anger rose in Dani at having let the woman get away. She channeled this anger into her spell, using it to bolster her control while honing her focus to a squeegee's razor edge.

Wind tousled her hair as the sand in her hand spun up into a diminutive dust tornado. Dani took ferocious pleasure in the imagined cries of despair the Scum might've made as her escape was neutralized. She saw herself proudly bearing the woman's trapped form, whether dust or flesh, back to HQ where it could be contained so she'd never hurt anyone again—followed by the admiration of her fellow Cleaners at a job well done.

Caught up in this fantasy, it took Dani another moment to realize she'd been maintaining the spell for a full minute. She glanced at the clock and waited until another minute passed. The twister stayed spinning in a tight coil, fed by her raw power, yet not wavering in the slightest.

She turned and presented the dust tornado to the Employee Handbook.

"Satisfied?"

The book flipped open to the title page of Chapter Two. The letters shifted once more.

Test complete. Access to chapter two granted. Congratulations, cleaner.

Josh Vogt

"Yeah, yeah. I'm still tempted to discover if you're really indestructible or not."

She looked to the sandy twister still spinning, and made a fist. The dust exploded as the spell collapsed, spewing sand everywhere. Dani grimaced and shut her eyes as grit blasted her face, bed, and left yellow streaks on the floor.

Okay. Maybe that wasn't the smartest thing. But that's what I'm going to do to that Scummy witch the next time we cross paths.

She licked her lips without thinking, and gagged at the grains suddenly scouring her tongue. Spitting like a machine gun, she ran to her backpack and found her biggest bottle of sani-gel. She swigged a mouthful and swished desperately.

That burns so good. Even in her most zealous anti-germ days, however, she never would've done anything so stupid as ingesting her sani-gel, but one perk of being a Cleaner meant being immune to most of the hazardous components of the cleaning compounds they worked with.

Still, she lurched into the bathroom and spat out the gel until only fumes wafted from between her lips. Then she swished with water until the taste faded to bearable levels. Overkill for a few particles of dust, maybe, but Tetris had been crawling over the stuff, and she didn't want to be haunted by nightmares of lizard germs crawling through her innards.

Botulism … Trichinellosis … Campylobacteriosis!

Dani clamped down hard on her thoughts as her brain tried to pick up its old habit of citing potential health hazards. It did nothing except spiral her down into hysteria where every possible contact with people or surfaces involved microscopic bogeymen, leaving her hyperventilating.

Keeping her breathing even, she went and picked up the Employee Handbook. She wished she could spend the evening poring over Chapter Two, but that'd have to be her reward for surviving the date. She stuck the book in a desk drawer. She was out of excuses to delay getting ready for her date.

Turning, she eyed herself in the full-length mirror that doubled as one of her closet's sliding doors. Her tan jumpsuit, gloves, and black boots had become such an integral part of her ever since she'd

88

joined the Cleaners. Damage-resistant, the outfit gave the wearer an extra layer of defense from mundane infections, disease, and other impure exposures—not to mention the ability to clean itself, given enough time. She only ever took it off for her regular showers, and donned it again immediately after. She'd even worn it to class when she'd been enrolled, which got her more than the occasional odd look.

Crackles of fear shot down from her skull to her toes, little shocks as if she'd licked a battery. Dani hated admitting to being afraid, but ... exposing herself to the world again? Without this level of protection she'd come to love?

She took deep breaths and met her reflected gaze.

"I can do this. I know I can."

Dani reached for the zipper of her jumpsuit with a shaking hand.

Start with a shower. Everything is better after a shower.

Just as she started to tug, a knock on her door made her jump and squeak. For Purity's sake, how could she be so nervous before even stepping out the door? She was in one of the safest places she knew when it came to keeping her uncontaminated; how would she deal once she got out into the world without the safeguards she'd grown used to?

She opened to the door, heart still thumping double-time.

Ben grinned at her so broadly his cheeks had triple dimples.

"Heya, princess."

"Ben." She slowed her breathing. "What're you doing here? I'm just starting to get ready."

"Brought'cha somethin'."

She eyed him warily as he rummaged about in a pocket. "I swear, Ben, if you're about to hand me a condom ..."

"Now that'd be just downright rude of me, wouldn't it?"

"Something you absolutely never are."

"Besides," he winked, "I figure a smart girl like you keeps plenty of safety measures handy."

"Of course. It's called ginormous amounts of personal space." Dani sighed heavily. "Ben, please don't make this harder than it already is. I need your support here."

"That's what I'm here for." He opened his hand to reveal a mini-bottle of whiskey. "I ain't one to drink while workin', but sometimes a hard job needs a hard shot afterward. But I figured you could use it more than me tonight. Besides, ever tried to open one of these things one-handed?"

Smiling softly, she pocketed the teeny bottle and gave him a quick hug. "Thanks. I appreciate it. Really. Now scram. I'll radio you when I'm heading out so you can get in position."

He saluted and headed off, whistling to himself. Dani watched him go, bemused. She hadn't seen him this cheerful in a long while. Hopefully his claimed flicker of reawakening power wouldn't turn out to be a fluke. It'd be fantastic to work with him in the field again, but she didn't want to see his hopes crushed.

Closing the door, she steadied herself, leaning back against the wall as she refocused on removing her suit. Her hand shook slightly less this time as she started to tug the zipper, one slow inch at a time.

Another knock made her cringe. Scowling, she stomped to the door and yanked it open.

"I told you I'm—"

Lucy stepped back, brow raised. "Bad time?"

"Sorry," Dani said. "Thought you were someone else."

"Ah." Lucy half-smiled. "Getting ready for the big evening?"

"Trying to, but I keep getting interrupted."

"Right. Well, I brought you something." She held up a small black bag. "For your ... date."

Dani took the bag and drew out two objects. The first was a round aluminum cartridge with a trigger on top, which one would thumb down to activate. The other was a thin, rectangular device that'd fit in her hand, with a switch on one side and small metal prongs on top.

Both were hot pink.

"A Taser and pepper spray?" Dani asked in disbelief.

Lucy shrugged. "You did say you couldn't use your powers, right? Assuming Sydney's even going to respect that rule, there's no promising he won't try to get gropey on you. I figured you could use something for a little self-defense backup."

Dani blinked at the items for several seconds before grabbing Lucy in a hug. "Oh $%&. You're the best. I almost want him to give me an excuse to use these now."

Lucy squirmed in the embrace. "Yeah, yeah. Let me go, girlie, before you leave me spasming on the floor." The janitor clomped off, mumbling to herself. Dani thought she caught, "Not enough coffee in the universe …"

Smiling despite her still-amped nerves, Dani once more sealed herself inside. After she stuck Ben and Lucy's gifts on her desk, she found her hand had stopped shaking as she reached for the zipper this time.

The moment her gloves, boots, and suit came off, though, she bolted for the shower and turned it on as hot as she could stand. She showered and scrubbed off thoroughly, and once dried, applied a generous helping of sani-gel as an added precaution. Creeping on tiptoes back into the bedroom, she opened the closet and studied her options.

When the Cleaners first recruited her—or absconded with her, more like—they'd also gathered all her personal belongings, which had been returned once she officially joined their ranks. Since then, though, she'd never worn anything aside from her company uniform. Why bother? Could a floral blouse shield her from bile spewed from the orifice of a Sewers-tunneling bilgeworm? No. No, it could not.

But she'd promised Sydney a dress, and regretted that part almost as much as the date itself. Too much potential for exposure. Still, her parents had gifted her several for birthdays, and she had never gotten around to tossing them out.

Finally picking out a blue-and-white striped outfit, she struggled into it as quick as she could, working with unfamiliar straps and pinching spots. A comfortable pair of black flats went on last, because there was no way she'd be caught running from Scum in heels. Once done, she studied Dani-in-a-dress in the mirror.

Well, it wasn't so terrible. At least, she didn't think so. Though, most of her previous fashion choices were based on how easy the outfits were to clean—or how quickly they burned, should someone sneeze on her.

Make up? No way. She hadn't used the stuff in years; if she tried now, she'd likely end up looking like a clown. Besides, cosmetic contamination was a real thing, right? She might as well be putting on a bacterial facemask.

Realization blazed through her, her cheeks turning a shade of red that almost matched her hair. She ran to the dresser and grabbed up her radio, dialing to a private channel.

"Chairman? Sorry to bother, I know you're busy."

Francis answered moments later. *"Yes, Janitor Dani?"*

"Um … any chance the mirror in my quarters could be used as a glassway downtown?"

Static popped, and she winced.

"It's possible. It might take a little longer to connect to an outlet, depending on exactly where you need to exit. May I ask why?"

"It's just off the 16th Street Mall, downtown. Plenty of windows that'd probably work. I figured since this is a personal outing, I shouldn't be using the company van."

"You do realize one of our main physical exits is downtown? It wouldn't be a far walk."

Dani sighed and bumped the radio against her forehead, trying to dislodge the words. At last, she admitted, "I really don't want to be seen walking through HQ in a dress, sir."

"I see." The static barely disguised his cough. *"I'll make the arrangements and notify you when all's ready."*

"Thank you, sir. I owe you."

"You work for me."

Once he signed off, Dani checked for final details. She didn't want to lug her backpack around all evening in this getup, so she snagged a large, black purse. She tucked the TaserTaser, pepper spray, and mini-whiskey in there, as well as her Cleaner radio. Those, along with her ID, credit cards, and a bit of cash still left plenty of space. She looked around for anything else she could bring along. Something that might help her feel a bit more comfortable and secure while spending quality time with a guy who could wipe things out of existence with a touch.

The closet mirror shimmered for a second, throwing dappled light across the walls. In the same instant, as if the mirror had been a light bulb popping into being over her head, an idea came to her.

A grin crept across her face as she double-checked the space left in her purse.

"Perfect."

CHAPTER TEN

Ben's radio went off right before he shot himself in the eye. He lowered Carl's spray bottle as Dani's voice crackled over, echoing through the garage.

"Ben? You ready? I'm about to head out."

Sighing, Ben hooked the spray bottle on his belt and took up the radio. He leaned a shoulder against his van. "Gimme five minutes? Was just about to see if a little spritz in the eye might kick this stubborn ol' power back into gear."

"I can't be late for this, Ben, and the glassway they're opening for me is temporary. If your powers are waking back up, they'll still be there later."

"Guess that's true." He eyed the radio speaker. "You ready for this, princess?"

A moment stretched until a sigh came through. *"No, but what choice do I have?"*

He kicked one of the van's tires. "Plenty of 'em. Just 'cause Sydney's bein' a stickler about this don't mean you gotta go through with it."

"I'm not the kind of person to back out of a promise."

"Even if it means mebbe puttin' yourself in danger?"

"That's why you're tagging along. I trust you to have my back."

"Speakin' of backs ..." Ben coughed. "You remember the part about my powers not really bein' *back* yet?"

"I know you. You'll figure something out. Probably already have a few ideas of how to tackle him if he gets out of hand. Which he won't."

Ben frowned, both honored and yet uncomfortable at her placing so much trust in him. *Guess I could always try and run the sucker over.* Of course, if things got that desperate, Sydney would likely be using his powers again and could just turn the van to dust once it got close enough. Ben pondered the possibility of a van sneak attack, but had a hard time imagining pulling off an ambush with the rattling, rumbling vehicle. Fortunately, aside from his work belt, he'd dressed incognito for the part, with jeans, a plaid button down, and a Rockies baseball cap.

"You get Jared taken care of?" Dani asked.

"Lu's got him," Ben said. "She figured it ain't the best idea for me to be cartin' around a pile of sand when folks're flinging water my way. He asked for you to pop in after you get back, if it ain't too late. Had some questions for you."

"Questions? Like what?"

Ben couldn't help grinning. "Like what it means to be sexy."

She remained silent so long, he wondered if she'd gone off-channel. Then her voice popped back on. *"Exactly what did you tell him I was going to be up to tonight?"*

"Better get goin'," he said. "You don't wanna be late, right?"

Her huff came through loud and clear. *"Fine. But stop sticking me with all the grown-up talks with him, okay?"*

Clipping the radio back to his belt, Ben started to open the driver's door when a voice called out, "Janitor Ben!" Rafi jogged up the parking lot toward him, long chimney brush in hand. "Is this a good time to talk?"

Ben patted his van. "Gotta say it ain't. I was just headin' out for a lil' evenin' excavation."

The sweep's brow wrinkled. "Do you mean excursion?"

"Sure. That thingamabob. Point is I'm clockin' out for the night."

Rafi's shoulders drooped. "Sorry. I was tied up today and just got free."

"Don't gotta make no excuses," Ben said. "We all lose track of time."

"No. Literally tied up. I offered to help a crew clean a pack of bogwebs out of the Sewers and there ended up being a few more of them than anticipated. They trussed a couple of us up before the rest of the scrub-team arrived. Just got back to HQ and was looking for you."

"Ah." Ben tapped his radio. "Well, I'm helpin' Dani on a teensy secret mission of her own, so gotta post the pony on our chat."

Rafi grimaced. "Oh, her date."

"You know about that? I ain't thinkin' that got stuck on the bulletin board, too."

"I was in the Chairman's office when you all discussed it. I didn't mean to eavesdrop." The sweep glanced around and lowered his voice. "Is she really fraternizing with Scum? And an entropy mage, of all things?"

"There's a big ol' story behind all that and I'd be pleased as cherry pie to lay it all out for you." Ben patted his van. "After I get back."

Rafi nodded. "I guess we'll coordinate something then. I'll be in touch."

Once the sweep headed off, Ben slid into the van and drove it out into the evening traffic. Despite the crowded roads, it only took him a few minutes to find a parking spot a couple blocks north of the downtown clock tower. He didn't want to get too close in case Sydney staked the place out. The former Cleaner would recognize one of the company vans easily enough.

He set the van to idle and got the radio out again. "Dani, you there?"

"Just about to step through. What's up?"

"I'm in position, but was thinkin' of somethin'."

"No, Ben. I'm not backing down on this. And no, I'm not bringing any condoms, so knock it off."

"Weren't nothin' like that. I was just thinkin' mebbe Carl could plop off a drop or two and send them your way. Could stick one in your eye and one in your ear. Then I could do the same and keep a closer watch on things. Just like when we was runnin' like hares with our bushy tails on fire back in the Recycling Center."

"I appreciate the thought, but no. I don't want there to be any chance of Sydney picking up on Carl's presence. Plus, you'd chatter in my ear the whole time, or try and go Cyrano de Bergerac on me, and I'd get distracted or flustered and he'd realize something was up."

"I would not!" Ben glared out the windshield. "Okay. Mebbe I would." He checked out his reflection in the rearview mirror. "You think I got the nose to pull that off? Now I'm kinda self-conscious."

Her sigh came through loud and clear. *"Look, I'll radio you if I need anything. Otherwise we go silent until this is all over. Less complications that way."*

"With Sydney, I'm thinkin' everythin's a bit more complicated than we'd like." He studied the passersby. "Good luck. And, heya, princess?"

"Yeah?"

"Mebbe have a little fun."

"I've got a Taser and whiskey. How could I not?"

▲ ▲ ▲

Dani shivered as she stepped out of the windowpane and into the warm downtown Denver evening. Francis had connected the glassway from her quarter's mirror to a row of windows outside an upscale barbershop—fortunately already closed.

A homeless man stared from across the street, where he lay in his sleeping bag in a doorway. He rose slightly, having noted her sudden appearance. Cupping his hands, he yelled over, "Hey, lady! You a witch or something?"

"No," she called back as she oriented to the clock tower. "That's the maids' department. I'm just a janitor."

He blinked before ducking back under his coverings.

She finally spotted the clock tower's peak just a few blocks away. Tonight it was lit up a radiant purple and pink. She didn't know if it was for a special occasion, but she took a little silly comfort in having her favorite color on display. Pink definitely had become her spirit animal. Not that she'd ever admit that to anyone.

Her gaze turned to the sidewalks. *Got my destination, now just have to get there without any serious exposure.*

Evening strollers and revelers packed Denver's main downtown pedestrian thoroughfare. Restaurants and bars thumped music out into the balmy night, while someone played a saxophone off in the distance. Nights like this, Denver almost felt alive, buzzing with a mirthful energy that suggested the city didn't take itself too seriously once the sun set. People wearing everything from yoga pants to faux-cowboy getups moved along with the air of those who worked hard to play hard—who spent their mornings in the office, their afternoons in the mountains a short drive away, and their evenings with everything from sports bars to wine flights to jazz concerts in the nearest park.

Dani took a minute to steady her breathing, soaking it all in and trying to feel like she belonged. Her private war against all things dirty hadn't given her a penchant for much of a social life. In fact, most of the people she'd ever had sustained interaction with while growing up had been others in the support groups she'd been made to attend, or patients in the clinical research trials her parents enrolled her in.

Maybe I don't belong in the real world. Maybe that's why I feel more at home with a supernatural sanitation company than I ever did with my own family. And maybe ... maybe I'm just stalling.

Fortifying herself for the inevitable, she looked for gaps in the foot traffic. She soon realized she'd just have to be quick about it. *Safety in speed. Minimize possible contact and deal with any exposure on the other end. Go!*

She speedwalked for the tower, analyzing on-comers for any spaces she could slip through easiest. As she rounded the corner, a man's voice boomed out from across the street.

"Shoe shine! Everybody needs a shoe shine!"

She glanced over to where an elderly black man stood on a corner. He wore a dusty cowboy hat, faded leather jacket, and the shiniest boots she'd ever seen. The guy picked a random person out of everyone passing by.

"You, sir! You need a good shoe shine. No woman can love a man with dirty shoes."

Folks laughed, and Dani's lips quirked as she headed on. She'd have to ask Ben if the Cleaners had a shoe shine division. Who knew? Maybe that guy was a coworker.

She picked her way along, side-stepping larger groups and jumping into the more open middle path between rows of trees and light poles, using the transit buses as walls-on-wheels until they sped away.

Up ahead, one of the horse and cart rides stood blocking her path as the driver fiddled with the harness. Dani dodged back onto the sidewalk, shoulders pinched in to make herself as skinny as possible.

A sudden surge in the crowd filled the space so, for a moment, she couldn't see anything but other people—potential germ carriers. People who might not have bathed or washed their hands in the last week.

Just like that, all her old survival instincts rammed into the small of her back and propelled her forward in desperation. Teeth clenched, purse clutched safely in front of her, she bolted along, not caring what anyone thought of the crazy redhead sprinting in a skirt.

Thank Purity I didn't wear heels.

She hurried to pass a trio of men leaning on the railing of an outdoor bar patio. One of them caught her eye and grinned.

"Hey, babe." He chucked his chin at her. "Where you going so fast?"

Motion caught her eye and she realized he was reaching for her. She whirled and thrust a finger out. "You touch me and I will make you eat a plunger!"

He jerked back as she kept on with nary a misstep. Finally, she raced across the last intersection, ignoring the taxi that blared its horn as it missed her by a few feet. She stumbled up to the clock base and caught herself with a gloved hand against its stone siding.

Panting, she took stock. Had she brushed against anyone? Torn anything? Had anyone spilled anything on her? As she stepped, her right foot stuck slightly to the walk.

A klaxon sounded inside her mind, and she choked back a squeak.

Gum. On the bottom of her shoe.

She needed a razor. A blowtorch, maybe? Could she ditch the shoe and spend the rest of the night hopping on one foot?

After getting the jitters under control, she forced herself to settle for dragging the foot along as hard as she could, scraping the offending wad of flavored wax to crumbled bits. It wasn't like she intended to lick the bottom of her shoe anytime soon, but she couldn't take chances.

"Would the fair lady care for a ride?"

She froze. Sydney's voice. He'd been close enough he had to have seen her mad dash and subsequent gum-related shoe mangling. Cheeks burning, she turned. Stared.

Stared some more as she worked the words out.

"You've ... got to be ... $&%##@^& me."

Sydney wore a dingy white tuxedo with a black rose stuck in the lapel—and he sat in the driver's seat of a horse-drawn carriage, holding the reins. The draft horse stood quietly with its mane done up in red pompoms. It flicked its tail; Dani stepped back reflexively.

"Where did you get this?" She waved at the whole setup.

"You should know by now, my dear, how persuasive I can be." He raised a hand gloved in black leather. "And before you accuse, as you've already opened your mouth to do, no one was harmed in the process. Though I did wipe down the seats and interior, decontaminating them thoroughly. And that is the last time I'll use my abilities until our time is ended."

He scooted over and patted the seat beside him.

Dani gulped. She looked to the horse. Weren't they awfully dirty animals? They rolled in dirt, had to have their stalls mucked out, and always had flies buzzing about them. Yet this one looked amazingly clean, even to her scrutiny. How long had Sydney spent prepping all this to try and make her comfortable?

She looked back to Sydney, who smiled. A warm smile, for once, rather than his usual smirk.

"Have I mentioned you look incredibly lovely this evening?" he said. "When you promised a dress, I feared you might show up in your uniform and a tutu."

She glared. "Hey. I look good in that uniform."

"Certainly. You'd be ravishing in a burlap sack, but I hear those are dreadfully itchy." He held a hand out.

Swallowing. Dani minced over and took his hand. He pulled her up, his grip strong but careful not to jerk her off-balance.

She perched as primly as she could and cleared her throat. "Before we go, you should know that I have a chaperone."

He cocked an eyebrow. "Do you now? I've been keeping an eye on the street sweeps, but none of them contain Purity's power."

She unzipped her purse and drew out a wriggling Tetris. She patted the lizard's head and whispered, "Sorry for the bumpy ride."

One of Sydney's cheeks twitched. Dani assumed he was attempting to conceal an *Are you crazy, woman?* look. His words came in a measured tone. "You brought your lizard?"

Dani lifted Tetris Sydney's way. "His name is Tetris. Remember? You kidnapped him when we first met. Besides, you brought a whole horse."

"Yet I've no intent of being chaperoned by a horse." Sydney pulled back slightly as Dani raised Tetris higher. "What are you doing?"

She looked at her pet meaningfully. "Say hello and promise you'll be on your best behavior."

Sydney eyed the bearded dragon. "Does he have a tiny shotgun he intends to threaten me with if I don't have you home before curfew?" At her narrowed eyes, Sydney sighed and reached up to give a scaly claw a shake. "Charmed. I can assure you, sir, I will be the very model of a gentleman. Do you give me your blessing with this woman?"

Dani placed Tetris back in her purse and then sat with her hands on her knees, making sure to keep as much space between her and her … her date as possible.

"Where to?" she asked.

He took up the reins again. "I thought we might begin by enjoying a picnic in City Park."

Dani's back stiffened as she thought back to what had recently happened to Cheesman Park. Why would Sydney have chosen this location for their outing?

He beamed at her. A flick of the reins set the carriage in motion.

"Tally ho," he said.

CHAPTER ELEVEN

Ben did not enjoy the feeling of being watched. Especially when he needed to focus on keeping track of Dani at as much distance as possible.

He had to admit, Sydney showed a bit of style in his approach. Though he hoped the man had a plan for his likely stolen horse and carriage other than turning them to dust after he dropped Dani off for the evening.

He kept the van a block north of the carriage as it trundled along, checking down alleyways and connecting streets to ensure Sydney didn't veer off. They headed east along 16th Street until they reached the end of the walking mall, at which point Sydney turned north, toward 17th Avenue. Ben cut the van in behind a large delivery truck until the carriage headed east again. Ben let them get several blocks ahead before easing back out into traffic. The carriage remained off to the side of the street, but a few larger cars still had to shift lanes to get around it.

Where in tarnation are they going?

As he wondered, he continued to feel that itching sense of being watched. He tried to glance around, to see if he could spot anything off about nearby drivers or the surrounding area, but didn't dare take his eyes off the distant couple for more than a few seconds. He wanted to scratch the back of his neck, but had to maintain his hand on the wheel.

Glad I don't gotta drive stick, at least. Would have to hold the wheel with my teeth, and that don't sound at all tasty.

He shifted in his seat, making Carl slosh a bit.

"You feelin' that, buddy?" he asked. "Like we're bein' scoped out by someone who ain't exactly got our best in mind? Feels like I'm gettin' the hairy eyeball from somewhere."

Carl gurgled: *Eyeballs can be hairy?*

"Figure of speechification," Ben said. "I mean we's bein' givin' the ol' stinkeye."

A fizz and swirl: *I am unable to smell like you do.*

"Huh. Actually, I ain't never thought about that. You elementals can see and hear and whatnot, but what other senses y'got?"

Taste.

Ben blinked. "Really?

Yes. Everything I touch, I can sense at least the outer chemical components and detect what you might consider taste.

"So … when you've been rollin' all over my skin, you's tastin' me? Or when I've sprayed you over Scum to take them down?"

Correct. Automatic function. I can't turn it off.

Ben cleared his throat. "I got any particular flavor?"

A miniature spout whirled up: *Citrus, rubber, and a hint of taco seasoning.*

"Huh. Ain't what I woulda guessed." Ben glanced down at his partner. "You, uh, don't mind it, hm?"

It's an acquired taste.

"Fair 'nuff." Ben refocused on his target as the carriage reached an intersection. On the other side lay an expanse of greenery, with running paths and service roads cutting through broad lawns and tall trees. "Looks like they's headin' for City Park. He gonna try and take her to the zoo? Ain't exactly the smartest move, knowin' her. That many animals in one place might get her a little topsy-turvy."

Bubbling translated to: *She should not go upside down in a dress.*

Ben frowned as he eyed the park. The carriage would have plenty of maneuverability, but his van would be far more exposed beyond the normal traffic routes.

"Looks like we're gonna have to take this one on foot here soon, buddy."

He started searching for a parking spot. Fortunately, Sydney kept the horse at a plod, which meant a light jog would catch him up if need be.

Up ahead, Dani turned to look at Sydney, obviously saying something, though he couldn't tell her mood at this distance.

Sure wish I could know what they're talkin' about.

⋏   ⋏   ⋏

Sydney breathed deep, as if enjoying the night air—though it mostly smelled of exhaust, to Dani.

"Tell me," he said, "as a child, what did you want to be when you grew up?"

She eyed him sidewise. "Are you also going to ask about my favorite color and ice cream flavor?"

"I'd love to know," he said, far too cheerily. "While we've shared some harrowing experiences and deeper thoughts on the meaning of life and death, sometimes it's just as delightful to learn a person's snacking habits or fond childhood memories."

She made herself the teensiest bit more comfortable on the seat. "You really want to know this kind of stuff about me?"

"I want to know everything there is to know."

"That's a lot."

"Good thing, then, that we have several hours ahead of us."

"Are you going to return the favor? Tell me about growing up with an older brother? Your first pet? The favorite role you played in your middle school drama team?"

Sydney cocked his head. "However did you know I belonged to a drama team?"

She grinned. "Lucky guess."

He grinned back. "I propose a trade. A question for a question."

Dani thought this over and nodded. "I can handle that. Ballerina astronaut."

"I beg pardon?"

She nodded up at the sky, where stars glimmered.

"One of my first dreams was to become an astronaut and spend all my time living on a space station. The rest of my life, even. I would've settled for being a colonist on a moon habitat, too."

"Why that particular career?"

She sighed in fond memory. "Because to me, space was a lovely sterile place where I could be far from all the muckiness of the world. I could spend all my time in an environmental suit, eat and drink heavily filtered substances, and enjoy knowing nothing could touch me."

He made a chuffing noise. "So you were averse to contamination and whatnot from a rather young age."

"Oh, yeah." She tugged her gloves so they fit more snugly. "One of my earliest episodes was when my parents caught me trying to set our backyard sandbox on fire."

"But why the ballerina part?"

"Zero-g lets you spin really well. I've never exactly been light on my feet."

"I see."

"And that was several questions wrapped in one. No cheating."

He held a hand up. "Ask away."

She hummed in thought. "What was your favorite thing to do as a kid?"

"Catch little animals."

She leaned back slightly. "You didn't, like ..."

"Torture them? Sacrifice them on an altar to my dark master?" A puffed laugh. "No, Dani. I was a chubby little boy. I could barely chase down a turtle."

An unbidden image rose in her mind: Sydney as a miniature version of himself, still wearing the same ridiculous tux, but now with a protruding tummy and pudgy cheeks, waddling after baby deer.

She snorted. Then she giggled at her snort, which made her snort again, until she bust out with a full-on cackle. Turning her face away, she choked through the laughter.

"I'm sorry. Sorry. I shouldn't but ... oh $#%...."

He chuckled. "Never fear. I look back on those times and can't help but remember them fondly. See, it turns out the only creatures

I could get my hands on were wounded ones. Birds with broken wings. Cats that had been maimed in an alley fight. Baby raccoons that had apparently been abandoned, or their mothers made into road kill. That sort of thing." He gazed down at one of his palms. "I'd bring them home and try to nurse them back to health. If they lived, I let them go free and felt I'd done something to make the world a better place. If not, I gave them a proper burial, knowing I'd at least done my best."

His smile turned sadder. "Then there was the time I found a squirrel beside the road on the way home from school. A car had run over its hind legs, but it was still alive. Barely. I brought it into our garage and put it in a box with a towel, some food, and water." He looked into the distance. "My parents tried to brace me for the inevitable. I'd had animals die on me before, but for some reason I so wanted this one to beat the odds. In the middle of the night, I snuck down to it and found it just lying there, twitching, barely breathing. I picked it up and held it to my chest and wished with all my might that it would be healed."

Dani held her breath until she couldn't stand his silence.

"What happened?"

He made a fist. "My hands glowed green. Energy rushed through me, and the squirrel was healed. Fixed just like new. My cries of joy brought my parents running to see the squirrel bounding about the closed garage, desperate to get free, while I stood there with the essence of Purity beaming out of me. That's when I discovered I was meant to be a handyman."

She stared. "What did your parents do?"

He shook off his maudlin air and leaned on the seat back, affecting a jaunty pose.

"Oh, my parents were both Cleaners," he said. "By that point, Destin was already employed and clambering his way up through the ranks. But my parents were overjoyed, as genetics is no guarantee of manifesting powers. It may be a contributing factor, but then there are cases such as yours, seemingly utterly random."

She grimaced. "So how did you become—"

"Please." He turned his head aside. "The story of my fall is not one I would like to sully this evening with."

She crossed her arms, glaring. They wheeled through the park in silence and the growing dark as light posts flickered on, casting deep shadows everywhere. Still, people wandered and ran about, throwing Frisbees, barbequing in lit picnic areas, and playing under the bright lights of several tennis courts. A few cars roamed the streets, headlights spearing through the trees.

"If you could be any color," she asked, "what would it be?"

Sydney glanced over, a smile once more giving him the handsome look she knew she shouldn't admire. "Octarine."

She frowned. "I don't think that's real."

"Precisely. I prefer the impossible, since I know plenty of it exists. Favorite toothpaste brand?"

"Oh, I'm still running comparison studies. Was thinking of making it my thesis, if I ever make it to that point."

They chatted like this for a while longer as Sydney navigated along the park roads. To her surprise, Dani found herself actually enjoying the exchange. It felt unthreatening. Fun, even.

At last, he stopped the carriage near a long building that reminded Dani of a small monastery, with its yellow brick and stone construction and red-tiled roof. It overlooked a lake with an island in the middle. A few spotlights lit the area, though darker corners remained in abundance. The area smelled of wet grass, though a mustier smell wafted by on the occasional breeze. Crickets provided a background chorus alongside the occasional honks of geese that waddled about.

Dani eyed the ground with trepidation, as goose droppings smeared a healthy portion of the walkways and grass. It'd be like walking through a minefield.

"Excellent," he said, hopping down and sweeping an arm to display the spot. "A measure of privacy, though I hope it's not too isolated for your tastes."

A few couples wandered nearby, some hand-in-hand, others lounging along one side of the building, with the occasional orange spot flaring near their faces to suggest some sort of smoking habit being indulged.

"It's nice," she said. "I think it'll work."

His smile flashed, and he helped her step gingerly to the ground. She briefly opened her purse to give Tetris a tickle under the chin. He scrabbled at her hand, but she kept him contained.

"Lots of mealworms and crickets after this, I promise," she said. "You are such a good purse lizard."

Sydney reached into the carriage's main seating area and removed a blanket that had been covering a lump. She'd figured it to be horse-tending equipment or feed, but it turned out to be a picnic basket. Hefting this, he tilted his head toward the tables.

"Shall we? I don't know about you, but I'm famished." However, after a step, he paused and looked from side to side. "Do you feel that?" he asked.

"What? The wind?"

He squinted around. "The sense of being watched."

Dani realized it'd been a bit since she thought about Ben being her backup. Had he lost them? She studied the area and didn't see any sign of his van. *Am I alone with this guy? Am I going to be on my own after all, if things turn nasty?*

She shrugged, forcing herself to sound casual. "There are still a lot of people around. Somebody's probably just checking out the guy in the tux."

"Hm. Perhaps."

After a second, he shrugged and led the way toward a set of metal tables. Dani picked her way along, worried that stepping into something too squishy might send her scrambling back for the safety of the carriage. By the time she reached the table he'd selected—one situated well in a lighted area—he'd set the basket down and swept off his tailcoat. He wore a black T-shirt underneath, printed with a faux bow tie and button down shirt.

He proceeded to use the jacket to wipe down the whole table and surrounding seats. At her look, he grinned. "I'd use my powers to sterilize the area, but we did have an agreement."

"Thanks," she said. "I appreciate it."

He resumed his cleaning efforts. "It's fascinating, if you think about it."

"What is?"

"Sterility. It's something of a paradox in itself."

Dani frowned. "How so?"

He hummed to himself as he worked. "It just seems connected to elements of both Purity and Corruption at the same time." He straightened and flapped his coat, taking care to do so facing away from her. Then he swirled the jacket about and slipped his arms through the sleeves. "Applied in one manner, sterilizing something can be a method of cleaning. Applied in another, it can lead to destruction and the absence of life. Sterile men, for instance—"

"Okay. We go down that path and I'm going to lose my appetite." She crossed her arms as another breeze raised goose-bumps on her arms. "I thought we were going to avoid any heavy discussions tonight."

His lips pursed in amusement, but he bowed. "My apologies. It's just I do find your perspective on things quite refreshing."

She eyed the basket. "You know what I'd find refreshing after all this talking? A drink. I don't suppose you brought along bottled water or something? Because I'm not sipping from that lake."

Sydney gestured for her to take a seat. Once she complied, he stood on the other side of the table and spread his arms, framing the basket like a magician about to pull an elephant out of a hat.

"It so happens I did bring a few libations. A meal without beverages isn't truly a meal at all." Poising hands over the basket, he met her eyes and bobbed his eyebrows. "Now, m'lady, prepare to feast your eyes, and then your palate upon …"

He flipped open the basket lid.

They both stared at the contents. She looked up to find him looking as befuddled as she felt.

"Sand?" she asked.

Yellow sand filled the whole of the basket, gleaming in the harsh lights like gold dust.

He plunged a hand into the stuff, digging around as if the meal might be buried within. "I don't understand. This was a delicious spread meant to tantalize even the most demanding taste buds. Fine cheeses. Wine. Cured meats." Pulling his hand out, he let a handful of sand pour back inside. "What happened? Where did it go?"

The sand stirred, though Dani felt no wind at the moment. She eyed it, a crazy idea coming to mind. She leaned in and touched the side of the basket.

"Jared? Is that you?"

The surface bulged, and she jumped up from her seat as a sandy globe formed atop the basket, looking vaguely skull-like. Two horns protruded from what might've been a forehead.

Sydney squawked. "Dani, get away!"

He grabbed her shoulders, and she stumbled away with him. She looked back just as the basket blew apart. With a roar of grit-filled wind, two demonic figures made of sand soared into the air on dusty plumes.

CHAPTER TWELVE

Dani didn't care how many goose droppings she stepped in as she ran from the table.

People in the area also ran, screamed, and pointed, while a distinctive, "Whoa!" rose from the smokers off to the side.

She reached the carriage, Sydney at her side. They stared up at the two creatures now hovering at roof-height. Their lower bodies looked like sandy tornadoes, while their upper torsos, arms, and heads were humanoid.

She grabbed Sydney's lapel, breaking off the black rose as she did. "Dust devils! Why'd you bring a basket of dust devils?"

He looked from her, to the creatures, and back. "Dani, I didn't do this, I swear."

"For some reason, I find that hard to believe."

His face pinched in hurt, but she shoved aside her guilt at the accusation. She should've known this was all a big setup. She should've known she was being manipulated. Ever since her powers had manifested, people just saw her as a pawn to be played with.

"What were you going to do?" She spit the words out. "Is this a loophole so you could kidnap or attack me without actually using your powers?"

He gripped her shoulders, seething through his teeth. "I would never do such a thing. On my honor."

She snarled. "Let. Me. Go."

He pulled back with a shocked look, as if surprised by his own actions. They turned to study the monsters, who remained hovering above the table. The dust devils shifted about, but didn't seem to be focused on the couple.

"What are they doing? Why aren't they attacking?" She glanced at him. *Unless he's ordering them not to. Can entropy mages create dust devils? I hate feeling so ignorant.*

One of the dust devils plummeted into the nearest rooftop. The building trembled as brick and tile shards flew everywhere. The creature went into a frenzy, grinding into the structure and raising a cloud of dust. This prompted most of those lingering in the area to scream and flee, though a couple remained, cheering and recording the action on their phones.

A few seconds later, the creature rose back into the air, leaving a gaping hole where it had attacked. The dust devil appeared slightly larger than before, and more solid.

"They're gathering substance," Sydney said. "Building their strength."

The second dust devil performed the same maneuver, while the first lowered enough for its lower half to start grinding away at the concrete.

"I didn't know dust devils could fly," Dani said.

"They usually can't. It would take an intensely powerful creator to invest their cores with enough energy to achieve this."

She gritted her teeth. "We have to stop this before they hurt someone."

She and Ben had faced one of these Scum constructs before, back during her very first outing with the janitor. This, at least, gave her some idea of how to handle the creatures. All constructs had one thing in common: their cores.

Most times, any spells cast were sustained by the caster's focus and channeled energy, whether they were creating a gust of wind, a watery barrier, or fiery flare-up. Once that focus ended, so did the spell. However, if someone wanted a conjuration to exist longer and act independently, it needed a core of power—a knot of energy contained within the center of its being. Destroy the core, end the threat.

"You're right," Sydney said. "Please forgive me for what I'm about to do."

Dani glanced at him. "What do you—"

His gloves vanished as purple auras flared around his fists. She jumped away, desperate to be out of reach of his insidious touch.

"Sydney, no!"

He stalked forward, coat flapping in the breeze the Scum churned up. Once halfway between her and the dust devils, he took up a boxing stance.

"Excuse me," he cried, "but you have interrupted our lovely evening and upset this beautiful woman. That shall not stand. Face me and suffer the consequences of your rudeness."

The dust devils oriented on him, horned heads tilting in unison as if trying to determine who dared to call them out.

"That's it," he said. "Come on, then!"

One dust devil shot down at him. Sydney raised his fists, which blazed with entropic energy. Yet as the creature neared, the auras suddenly winked out.

He hesitated for half a heartbeat, then leaped back just as the dust devil slammed into where he'd been standing. His cry struck Dani's ears as she shielded her face from a wave of grit. The horse whinnied in fear, and the carriage rocked behind her.

When the dust settled, Sydney lay before her, gasping. He pushed up to his feet, looking first at his hands, then her, then the dust devil, which had once more risen to stare down at them.

He gave her an utterly perplexed look.

"My power," he said. "It isn't working."

She shoved her purse at him. "Here."

He clutched it, looking bewildered. "What—"

"Get in the carriage. Stay down, and ..." She thrust a finger into his chest. "Keep. Tetris. Safe. At all costs."

She pushed him toward the carriage, side-stepped, and then spun to face the dust devils. With each second, their swirling lower bodies churned up more debris, adding to their forms.

Focusing inward, Dani envisioned her elementals standing just behind her, adding their strength to hers. *Hey girls, you ready to sweep the floor with these guys?*

A silent chorus answered. She grinned as energy pulsed through her, prickling her hairs.

Dani raced forward and flared her own power as the dust devils soared down at her.

▲   ▲   ▲

Ben muttered as he untangled his empty sleeve from a snarl of thorns. The sleeve had torn loose from its pin as he tried to hunch through a set of brambles, and his incoherent cursing had drawn more than a few curious looks from trail runners—negating any of the stealth he'd been trying to achieve.

As he got the last burr loose, he flung it to the ground and stomped it good. Then he picked up the squeegee he'd had to set down to work himself free, shaking it at the bush he'd just wrestled into submission.

"You better be thankful I'm a patient guy, otherwise I'd be takin' a flamethrower to you right about now."

Temper, temper, Carl said with a slosh.

Ben thumbed at the thorn bush. "He started it."

Yes. I saw how it ambushed you from a stationary position. Very unfair.

"Hush it." Ben scowled at his partner and clipped the squeegee back on his belt. "So mebbe tryin' to sneak up through the pricklies weren't the biggest brain bubble I've ever blown. I ain't never figured myself for a ninja, so keep your mouth shut."

Carl's gurgle had an amused undercurrent: *Would need one, first.*

"With your sense of taste, you're one big mouth, ain'tcha?"

Human logic is fascinating.

Ben got the sleeve rolled back up and pinned in place at the shoulder. His janitorial uniform would've let him push through the thorns, no problem, but he kept having to reorient himself to the situation: no powers, no suit … he'd even hesitated bringing Carl along, since Sydney would make short work of the elemental if things came to blows.

Tugging his baseball cap down to cover his face better, Ben shuffled back onto the path, steering clear of any tempting shortcuts involving questionable vegetation. He followed the gravel and dirt-packed route past the tennis courts, where a couple of women vented their suppressed rage on an innocent ball. The road paralleling the path curved around toward an oversized duck pond, with a red-roofed events center squatting on the shore. People milled around the area, as did a small flock of geese that hissed as Ben's stride scattered them across the lawns.

"Yeah, yeah," he muttered. "Everyone's a critic."

Four porta-potties stood along the walkway approaching the events center, and Ben used these to shield his advance, just in case Sydney had one suspicious eye out. Out of habit, Ben checked the porta-potties as he scooted by. All stood vacant and padlocked, already secured for the evening.

Reaching the far end, he peered around and spotted the carriage a couple hundred feet away. Dani and Sydney had gone twice that far and were talking to each other near a cluster of tables.

Ben craned his neck, squinting to pick out details. "Is he … naw … can't be pullin' this kinda stunt."

Carl fizzed: *What's happening?*

Ben blew a soft raspberry. "Boyo really knows how to put on a show, don't he? Fancy suit? Horsey and cart? Picnic basket? Next he's gonna bust out some wine and start quotin' poetry and gettin' all smarmy."

The water sprite rippled waves around: *Isn't he smarmy already?*

"Guess so. What's that make it then? Smarmier? Smarmiestest?" He checked on the couple, again, but saw nothing amiss. "Dagnabbit. And here I was hopin' for a chance to steal his horse and ride in like the cavalry."

Short ride, Carl said.

Ben nodded. "Yuppers. Better be, 'cause I sure-for-shootin' don't know how to ride worth nothin', anyhoo. Guess there ain't nothin' to do but get cozy and hope they don't start smoochin' too loud."

Leaning back against the porta-potty, he dug into his back pocket, where he'd crammed the book of *Shakespearean Insults*. He thumbed it open to a random page and started scanning.

"Varlet? What in tarnation's a varlet?"

His partner bubbled and spouted.

Ben frowned. "That's it? Not nearly as dirty as I was thinkin'. Or hopin'." His gaze settled on one line. "We leak in your chimney and your chamber lye breeds fleas like a loach?" He chuckled. "Ain't gotta clue what that second part means, but I oughta let Rafi know 'bout the first bit. Bet he could use it like blackmail with a few folks."

Sighing, he skimmed more pages. "Y'know, I woulda started readin' more than comics earlier if folks had told me words could be just as fun without the pictures."

A gush made the spray bottle rock.

"You never did." He bopped the book against the bottle. 'Sides, am I gonna take readin' advice from a blob who can't even smell?"

A trickling noise: *Smell and reading are connected?*

"Sure, there's a connection. I just ain't got the time to 'splain it proper right now."

Carl burbled his equivalent of: *Uh-huh.*

A sudden whooshing noise sounded as the porta-potty furthest from him rocked slightly. Ben chuckled as a few thumps came from inside.

"Whoops. Looks like someone went and took a nap right before they was lockin' the johns up. What say we see if we can't lend 'em a hand?"

You only have one, Carl said.

"And that's all I need." Ben clapped the book shut and tucked it away again. Sauntering down to the noisome porta-potty, he knocked on the door.

"Hey in there," he said. "You need a little help? Didn't fall in and get stuck now, did'ja?"

"One moment," came a woman's voice. "I'll be right out. Just pulling myself together."

Ben frowned at the padlock. "Not so sure about that. Unless you're gonna pop the top and crawl out thataway, they got'cha pretty stuck." He tapped the spray bottle. "Whatcha think, buddy? Can you bust the lock?"

Before Carl could answer, a soft hiss made Ben step back. Splotches of rust appeared over the padlock, consuming it in moments. The lock drizzled into dust and puffed away from one blink to the next.

Ben had the spray bottle in hand, spinning to aim it at Sydney, who must've snuck up on him. Yet the entropy mage was nowhere in sight. Besides, didn't he usually have to touch objects to make them decay?

He turned back to the porta-potty as the door swung open. A woman stepped out, wearing a floral dress and a floppy gardening hat. Ben backed up, finger on the trigger, trying to figure out just what was going on.

The woman lifted her head just enough for him to glimpse shadowed eyes under her hat's brim.

"Oh, hello," she said, smiling so brightly her teeth gleamed, even in the darkness. "Did you come to enjoy my show?"

Bleach my britches, Ben thought. *You gotta be kiddin' me. Another entropy mage? She sure does match Dani's description of the woman who turned to dust earlier.*

"Show?" He glanced around, trying to stall long enough to figure out how to handle the newcomer. Spraying Carl her way would likely get the elemental obliterated just like the padlock—if the woman was responsible for that. "You pullin' some sorta ... whatchacallem ... flashy mob prank or somethin'?"

"Or something," she said, still beaming prettily. "I've been preparing for this for a long while, and I'm always delighted to have an audience."

"Oh yeah? You gonna sing? Mebbe dance a bit?"

"It's a magic show," she said, winking.

"Gotta love me some magic," Ben said. "So what's your shtick? Pulling elephants out of your bonnet? Cutting rabbits in half and putting them back together?"

She waved at the surrounding park. "I make life disappear."

He sighed. "Y'know, I was hopin' you wouldn't say somethin' like that."

Her pout made her look almost childlike. "But life always ends. I just make it happen in much more entertaining ways."

"Like makin' deserts out of thin air?"

She clapped. "Yes! Isn't it novel? I came up with the spell all on my own. Although," she lifted her hat brim to give him a sly look, "I did have a very good teacher."

"So you ain't gonna deny whippin' up that desert back over at Cheesman Park?"

"Why would I? If I could, I would've signed it properly, like any proud artist."

"Hey now. People died. Ain't you got no shame?"

"Shame? Of course. I just learned to ignore it."

"Lady, I's gettin' the feelin' you's a … a …" He scrunched his brow up, trying to recall a particular term from his book of ye ol' insults. "A villainous reeling-ripe popinjay."

Her smile disappeared. "That, sir, is no way to speak to a lady."

She thrust her hands out, fingers curled. Ben's neck hairs prickled, and it took him a moment to realize this reaction came from more than her creepy behavior. He was sensing Corrupt energies—something only a person with Pure energies should be able to do.

Threads of purple mist appeared above her palms, knotting around themselves as they thickened. The threads quickly condensed into balls of foul energy, which sprouted thorny tendrils.

Cores, Ben realized. This woman was Scum, and she'd just manifested a pair of cores in a matter of seconds. Dust swirled in and around the cores, thickening and swelling into twin forms. A couple of breaths later, two dust devils stood on either side of her like goon bodyguards.

She waved Ben's way. "Kill."

"Uh …" He backed up a step. "Mebbe I was a bit hasty with the popinjay part."

Her smile would've made a rabid badger reconsider its life choices. "Too late." She turned and headed for the nearest patch of shadows.

Ben triggered Carl, who shot out into a long, watery blade. Water glommed over Ben's hand, securing the weapon to his hand. He slashed this about as the dust devils came at him, claws reaching. The water sliced off chunks of dust with each hit, but couldn't penetrate nearly as well without being reinforced by his old powers.

He dodged a haymaker from the one on his left and twisted to chop as hard as he could along its wrist. Its hand fell away, puffing into a tiny cloud when it hit the ground.

"Hah!" Ben jabbed at it.

But as the dust devil rounded on him, a brand new hand reformed and reached for him.

Ben grumbled as he retreated. "Forgot you guys are downright, rotten, dirty cheaters." He eyed the construct's body of grinding grit. "Though I'm guessin' the dirty part is kind of a given."

The creature lumbered a bit faster. Ben let it come in and then jumped aside again. It swung a fist back that clipped his arm in a glancing blow that still spun Ben around and sent him staggering.

Ben recovered just in time to jerk back from another claw swipe that would've given him a few extra holes in his skull. He ducked a grab, and then threw himself past the dust devil, cutting Carl's blade along its side. It gouged deep, but not nearly enough to reach its core.

As Ben braced for another blow, the second dust devil rammed into him from the side. Ben went sprawling across the pavement. He tried to catch himself on instinct, but his hand hit the asphalt so hard Carl's bottle tore loose, taking the elemental with it.

Stunned, Ben barely had the wherewithal to turn over. The dust devil that had knocked him flat stomped over and raised a foot. Ben spread his legs and that foot cracked into the pavement right between them. The dust devil raised its other foot as he tried to drag himself away with one elbow.

A figure in a black uniform dashed in from the darkness. Rafi charged on eerily silent footsteps, his chimney brush held in both hands like a battle hammer.

He swung as he reached the dust devil standing over Ben. His brush connected with the creature's chest and tore through it, ripping its core out through its back, stabbed through by the bristles. Rafi spun without losing momentum. He swayed to let the other dust devil's claw whiff inches from his ribs, and then brought his brush up and over his head.

It came down and shredded the construct from top to bottom. The brush struck asphalt and shattered the core that had been stuck on it. The two halves of the other dust devil tumbled apart. Rafi reached out and snatched the second core from midair before it had time to fall—and crushed it in his fist.

He stood there in the aftermath, barely breathing hard, while Ben had to remind himself to breath. That had been some mighty fine handiwork. Even with his powers, it would've taken Ben a bit of a tussle to down those constructs on his lonesome.

"Thankya there." Ben held his hand out. "I reckon I owe you one, huh?"

Rafi's gaze snapped his way, eyes wild, teeth bared.

Ben drew back. "Hang on, bucko. You can hold your jets ... or cool your horses, or whatever the sayin' is. They ain't comin' back from the beatin'—or brushin' you just gave 'em."

The chimney sweep didn't seem to hear him. Rafi raised the brush over his head as if in salute.

"For the Chairman," he said.

He sprinted off again, this time in Dani and Sydney's direction.

"Hoo boy. This ain't good." Ben got to his feet and retrieved Carl, who sloshed about in relief. With his partner back in hand, Ben raced after the chimney sweep.

CHAPTER THIRTEEN

Dani whipped cords of her power into the surrounding elements. Briefly shutting her eyes, she drew on this connection to create an internal view of the world. The earth quivered beneath her feet. Air swirled about, distorted by the dust devils' method of flight. An expanse of cold, murky water lay off to the side, waves lapping the shore, ripples left in the wakes of fish and fowl alike. And within the building the constructs had damaged, exposed wiring crackled with electricity, waiting to be discharged.

She summoned a gale that tore through the tree branches and blasted over her head, striking the dust devils as they flew her way. It sent the creatures tumbling and crashing back against the building, raising great plumes of sand. A wall sagged and tiles exploded, any people in the area had long fled.

Stirring up the electricity in the building's wiring, Dani unleashed a miniature lightning storm, sending white-hot strikes streaking around the dust devils at random. Several bolts struck, turning portions of their bodies into glass chunks that dropped and shattered.

Yet no lightning hit their cores, as she'd hoped. Continuing to pull on the electrical output, harrying the creatures with ongoing blasts, she fed more of her power into the duck pond and sent the wind roaring that way.

Algae-covered water swirled into a waterspout that reached for the sky. Dark clouds condensed as she fed more moisture into the atmosphere. Thunder joined the lightning.

Dani fought to keep her volatile energies under control. Every time she unleashed them, creating localized natural disasters, the raw power fought to be loosed, to rampage. It would fix the problem faster, obliterating the dust devils—but likely taking out plenty of property and any lingering bystanders in the process.

Sweat made her dress cling to her skin as she wrestled her power into submission, using her training and sheer will to keep it all reined in. She might be fantastic at destroying things, but she would only destroy what deserved it.

Sheets of rain swept across the area, punctuated by flashes of lightning. The brief glares illuminated the dust devils while the waterspout grew. Wicked-looking clouds jostled for space overhead, and a frigid downpour doused the area.

Moving the waterspout felt like trying to puppeteer a sock full of marbles and mashed potatoes. Dani nudged it this way and that, shifting it straight toward the dust devils, which still struggled to regain their flight.

The watery twister dredged up mud and grass as it reached land and crawled toward the building. Its top touched the thunder-clouds. A chilly mist rose all about, punctuated by the few lights left flickering in the storm.

At last, the spout's tail reached the building. Electrical arcs shimmered up its sides. With a cry of triumph, Dani released the energies sustaining the spout. Countless gallons of water collapsed over the constructs, swamping them. Eyes still shut, Dani flared the electrical outpouring from the building as it sizzled through the water.

To her elemental sight, the dust devils appeared as blotches on reality, with dark knots of energy at their center. Yet the water thinned out their substance just as lightning discharged through them. She clearly saw as the cores disintegrated, and the constructs became so much silt that flowed away into the miniature flood.

Opening her eyes, Dani surveyed the aftermath. One wall of the event center lay in complete rubble, with heaps of weed-packed mud slopped about. Water streamed everywhere, coursing through the pit of silt the dust devils had turned the concrete walkways into. Branches lay strewn about like mangled arms and legs, while clumps of mud plopped down from those nearby trees still standing.

She straightened and rolled out her neck and shoulders.

I wish field work would count for extra credit when it came to passing the Employee Handbook's tests.

"That's how you do it." She looked back, surprised to find the horse and carriage had remained put. *Good thing the horse is wearing blinders and is used to lots of noise.* She started to wipe her hands off on each other, and then froze as she realized she stood drenched by pond water. In her haste to eliminate the dust devils, she'd briefly forgotten her dress offered no supernatural protection from disease like her Cleaners uniform would've.

This water could contain … *Giardia. Cryptosporidium. Schistosomiasis!* Not to mention any of the diseases carried by the birds that flocked around the place. She might as well have taken a slip-n-slide down a sewer grate and dunked herself in pure excrement.

She hugged herself, shivering and shuddering at the same time. Her breath came in pre-panic hiccups, and she blinked away an encroaching dizziness. Fainting here would just create more exposure. Her gel. She needed her sani-gel. That should keep her collected enough to get back to HQ without breaking down.

She turned to the carriage just as Sydney's head poked up from within. His blond hair was plastered to his forehead, and his tux hung drenched, making it look like he wore a giant, soggy sock.

"That was …" He stood, regarding her with a measuring look. "Effective. You've been training." She ran over and snatched the purse from him. "I kept your lizard quite safe," he said. "He's likely drier than either of us at this point."

Hands trembling, Dani undid the clasp. Tetris clawed at her as she reached in, and she shot him a mental apology as she snagged her gel and sealed the purse back up. After hooking the strap over a shoulder, she poured half the bottle into a hand and began working the gel over her arms, neck, and face. The alcohol odor cut through the pond stink, letting her breathe slightly easier.

"Sydney, I ..." She almost licked her lips in nervous habit before realizing that'd potentially draw goose germs right into her mouth. "I need to get back."

"Back?"

"To HQ. I'm sorry." She squirted more gel and slathered it down her bare legs. "I need to ... um ... take care of some things."

Sydney's gaze swept over her, and she realized how much the soaked dress clung to her. However, she didn't detect any of the lechery he indulged in when they first met. Instead, his eyes held resignation. "Oh," he said. "I see."

She winced. "Sorry. I just ... you know how I am."

A sigh. "Indeed. And it would be extremely childish of me to insist you remain out in this state. If you desire, I will provide an expedient ride back to the nearest glassway so you can tend to yourself properly."

Dani blinked. "Wait. Really?"

"Of course." He stuck hands in his jacket pockets and shrugged. "What would demanding you see the evening through prove other than my petulant selfishness?" He looked over to the remains of the fight. "I do hope you at least believe I didn't actually plan or cause the appearance of those creatures."

Dani studied him for a long moment, her thoughts and feelings a snarl she couldn't even begin to untangle. Whenever she thought she'd figured him out, Sydney showed another unexpected side of himself. She could've handled one of his rants or sulking fits, but him acting mature about the whole ordeal? Respecting her wishes? Was this another ploy?

She swallowed a sigh. If she kept looking for the next deception, the next hidden agenda, she'd exhaust herself. Where would it stop? Eventually she'd start interrogating Tetris, demanding the lizard tell her all his secrets.

She needed to stop wavering at some point, for her own sanity's sake. If she made the wrong choice, she'd deal with it, survive, and be smarter the next time around. Hope for the best, prepare for the worst.

Dani nodded. "I'll believe you. For now."

Sydney's face brightened, and a ghost of his former smile returned. "I suppose that's all I could hope for. Perhaps you'd allow me a second chance at an evening out? I dare say we were rather enjoying ourselves."

She shifted in place. "I don't know. I need to think about it." His expression fell, and she hastened to clarify. "It's just I had to argue pretty hard to even be allowed to go through with tonight. I know it didn't go how you wanted, but I'd probably get plenty of pushback if I asked for a do-over."

He chuckled dryly. "Ah. Yes, I would hate to cause any sort of office drama, sparking rumors of your fraternization with a known enemy. Wouldn't do well for your reputation."

"I don't see you as the enemy," she said.

"No? Then what?"

"A person."

"I believe the word you're looking for is: Scum."

"Hey, nobody's perfect. We're all a little messy."

"Careful," he said. "You're almost making me sound human. And you might get written up for employee insubordination if you go around speaking that sort of heresy where an Ascendant might hear."

"Then I'll just drop an anonymous note in the Employee Suggestion box."

They shared a smile for a few moments, until a breeze made her shiver again, her soaked frame cooling rapidly in the evening chill. The sani-gel bottle was almost empty, and her anti-germ jitters started to gnaw on her brainstem again, like rodents with a caffeine addiction.

He swept his coat off and started to offer it to her, but then paused as fresh rivulets of water dribbled off the tails. "I don't suppose this would actually do any good."

"Probably not. Thanks for the thought, though."

Sydney stepped aside and waved at the coach. "Shall we? Wouldn't want you to be ignominiously struck down by *Streptococcus pneumoniae*."

She smirked and headed for the driver's seat. "Now you're just showing off."

"Only now?"

"I do wonder," she said, as she prepared to clamber up. "If you didn't create the dust devils, where did they come from?"

"I'm at a loss. A state of being I truly despise." Sydney frowned. "Speaking of our erstwhile picnic pouncers ..." He gazed over her shoulder. "Are you sure those ones were truly vanquished?"

She nodded. "I saw their cores be destroyed. Why?"

He pointed to where the dust devils had last been. "Because I'd then be curious as to what is causing that."

Dani turned to see a yellow splotch several yards across, centered on where the dust devils had been destroyed. It visibly grew, spreading in all directions, sending out tendrils of ...

Sand, she realized. *That's a big patch of sand. Purity, please don't let this be what I think it is.*

The sand raced outward from its epicenter, looking somehow eager to consume. Everything it touched collapsed into dust, adding to the mounds of filth already coating the area. Another of the building walls collapsed, and the furthest surviving picnic table crumbled into rust which wafted off on the wind. All the water pooling about from the storm she'd created evaporated the instant the patch reached it.

Terror filled Dani's throat, but she choked out the words, "Oh, $#%&. It's happening again."

"What is?" Sydney asked.

She started to grab his arm, wanting to drag him to the carriage, but couldn't force herself to make contact with another person in her already-vulnerable state. Instead, she waved frantically as she hauled herself up into the front seat. "We've got to get out of here. This whole area's about to become a lifeless desert. If we get caught in it, it could kill us both."

"Desert? Dani, you aren't making any sense."

She looked beyond him to the dust eating away at the landscape. It moved as if alive, ravenous as it devoured every inch, converting it all to barren wasteland. The words babbled out of her.

"Part of Cheesman Park got turned into lifeless desert, taking out the buildings and anything or anyone alive that got caught in it when it appeared. It's Nothing. Absolutely Nothing. And if we don't move now we're going to die, too."

Sydney donned his jacket again. "First, our meal is ruined by those devilish minions, and now the earth itself wishes to chase us off?" He marched toward the growing Nothing, which swept in relentlessly.

Dani grabbed the reins. "Sydney! Come on!"

He struck a pose, hands flared at his sides and shouted. "You are my power. I control you and ... You. Will. Work!"

Right before the sandy edge reached him, he dropped to his knees and pressed his hands to the ground. Purple-black auras appeared around his hands. An instant later, a length of earth simply vanished in front of him. The gap grew on either end, curling around to form a seemingly bottomless trench. The void continued to expand, concrete, metal, and raw earth puffing away into emptiness. Yet it couldn't contain the entire desert. A portion accelerated into the park in the opposite direction and beyond sight.

Dani watched in horror as the entire event center slumped and dispersed into a massive sand dune. Trees fell into sawdust, and the whole lake drained into a bone-dry bed. The sand rolled into the distance until she couldn't track its growth any longer.

The only mercy was she didn't hear any screams—and she prayed that wasn't because they were too far away.

At last, a final ripple went through the newly formed desert, and she sensed whatever awful energy fueled the transformation dissipating. Everything went still and quiet, except for the thumping of her pulse in her ears.

She caught her breath and climbed back down to join Sydney by the miniature ravine he'd created. He stood, arms crossed in satisfaction.

They stood in silence, looking over the obliterated landscape. Finally, Dani tapped the ground with a toe, indicating the trench Sydney had created.

"How did you know to do that? How did you know it would stop it?"

He flourished a hand as if showing off an artistic masterpiece. "Instinct, I suppose. If this Nothingness, as you called it, didn't have anything to transform, then how could it advance?"

She peered over the edge, but couldn't see a bottom in the darkness. "How deep does this go?"

"Deep enough."

Movement caught Dani's eye off near one end of Sydney's trench. In the distance, almost concealed by shadows, a diminutive figure in a dress and floppy hat waved cheerily at them.

"No," she breathed. "You're not getting away again."

Holding her purse tight, Dani charged for the Scum, ignoring Sydney's shout. Yet she only made it halfway there before the woman once more collapsed into a pile of sand. Growling, Dani ran in and aimed a savage kick at the dust left behind—realizing her mistake when a cloud of it puffed up into her face and blinded her for a second.

She spluttered to get grains out of her mouth, wiping her lips clean. Then she spat more as she tasted a lovely bouquet of pond water.

"What in all the worlds was that about?" Sydney asked as he reached her side.

Dani shook a fist at the dust. How could a faceless pile of sand look up at her so mockingly? "It was her!"

"Her? Her who?"

"The woman. The one who made the desert yesterday."

"Desert?" Sydney looked over across the sandy expanse. "Like this one?"

"Yeah. It's as if she's some sort of entropy mage like you. Turned herself to this"—she pointed at the sand on the wrong side of the trench—"to escape when we confronted her."

He grabbed her shoulders, and she jerked to try and free herself. "Let go!"

"Dani!"

His barking her name combined with his extremely worried expression made her pause—though she bunched a fist to give him a bloody nose if he kept hold much longer.

"What?"

His fingers flexed. "This woman. What did she look like? Did she tell you her name?"

Dani shook loose. As she gave him a brief description of the few details she had, she reapplied gel to where he'd touched her. After she checked on Tetris again, she realized Sydney had gone quiet. He brooded at the dust pile and desert in turn.

"Do you know her or something?" she asked.

Sydney faced her and opened his mouth to answer. Just then, a man in a black jumpsuit raced into view. He wielded what looked like a giant brush, bristles stiff as he aimed a blow at Sydney's back.

She pointed. "Look out!"

The entropy mage turned, hands rising, but too late.

The brush connected with Sydney's head—which blew apart in a cloud of dust.

▲　▲　▲

Ben tried to follow Rafi, bracing against a sudden gale that slung stinging rain into his eyes. He ducked a tree branch that whirled over his head and decided it might be wiser to hunker down until the storm blew out.

Betcha this is Dani's work, sure-for-shootin'. Go get 'em, princess.

He raised his arm to shield his face. The chimney sweep had disappeared ahead of him, black uniform helping him blend into the night once more.

He hollered, "Rafi! Get back here!" but the wind swallowed his voice.

At last, a final wet gust sputtered out and the world returned to a semblance of sanity. Ben rose and started to pick his way through a snarl of mud, fallen limbs, and churned-up stone. He tried to reach out with his hoped-for power to sweep some of the water aside and clear a better path; while his skin prickled and he felt that brief flicker inside him, the elements remained unresponsive to his efforts.

However, in the distance, he sensed a sudden crackle of foul energy that burst and expanded exponentially. He plodded ahead as fast as he could, and broke through a last line of brush to see …

A desert. An impossible expanse of featureless sand where trees and paths and ponds should've been. He halted at the sight, blinking to make sure he wasn't seeing a reverse mirage, swapping out a desert in a park where one might see an oasis while crawling across burning sand dunes.

The desert remained stubbornly present.

Carl burbled in his bottle, sounding distressed. *All elementals there are gone. Destroyed.*

Ben set his hand on the bottle in a weak attempt to comfort his partner.

"All of 'em?" he muttered. "Even the earthy types?"

All. Erased. Gone.

Carl fell still, as if in shock.

Ben scanned the area and finally spotted Dani and Sydney. The pair stood at the edge of some sort of ditch. They had their backs to him and looked to be studying the desert as well. A tight band of worry loosened in Ben's chest on realizing they hadn't been caught up in the devastation.

However, his breath hitched again as a dark figure appeared, running in from the side, brush raised to strike. Rafi moved so quickly, Ben didn't even have time to blurt out a warning before the chimney sweep reached Sydney and struck his head off his shoulders.

"No!"

Ben's cry echoed Dani's, and the two of them stared as Sydney's body slumped to the ground. Rafi stood as if frozen, with his brush held in the follow-through position. Then he snapped his brush straight by his side like a spear and stepped back, soldier-like.

Dani looked at the other Cleaner in disbelief. Then her gaze shifted to Ben. She appeared utterly stunned, visibly trembling.

Ben ran in and grabbed the chimney sweep's shoulder. The bone beneath Rafi's flesh buckled oddly and slipped out of his hold. He turned to face Ben.

"Yes?" he asked.

"Yes?" Ben repeated. "That all you got to say? For Purity's sake, man. This was supposed to be a neutral thing. Nobody stickin' their noses in. Whattya think you're doin' bargin' in here and swattin' down Dani's date?"

Rafi cocked his head, eyes and tone flat. "I'm acting under the Chairman's orders."

"The Chairman?" Dani shook herself out of her shock. Now both her body and voice shivered with growing fury. "Francis sent you? After he swore he wouldn't get involved?"

The chimney sweep swayed in place, using his brush like a staff to steady himself. He looked around, confusion replacing his previous look. "Wait." He pressed a hand to his forehead. "This isn't right. Where am I? What's happened here?"

Rafi backed up, and Ben reached for him. "Hang on, bucko. You got a lot to answer for."

Ben grabbed for the Cleaner, but Rafi's arm bent like rubber, evading his touch. The chimney sweep stumbled back and raised his brush to ward him off. "No," Rafi said. "This isn't right. I completed my job. It's over."

"Your job?" Dani's voice rose and Ben sensed power ripple through her in response. "This was murder!"

Rafi shook his head. "No. Orders. This had to be done."

He raced off and vanished in moments, leaving Dani and Ben standing over Sydney's body.

Dani stared back down at it in horror. She crouched and held a hand just shy of touching.

"#$%&, Sydney, I ... I didn't mean for this to happen." She looked up at Ben. "What do we do?"

He grimaced. "Sorry, princess. Unless your med schoolin' has taught you how to go all Frankenstein and switch heads back on, ain't much we can do." He glanced around. "What happened to his noggin', anyhoo? Looked like Rafi blew it to smithereens."

"Um ... Ben?" Dani pointed to the jagged stump that remained of Sydney's neck. "It looks like he's made of sand."

Ben crouched beside her and squinted. Sure enough, no bone or blood was visible. The neck ended in a jut of grit, as if Sydney had been packed full of sawdust.

"What in tarnation ..." He checked to the side and noticed yellowish streaks on the ground in a spray pattern. "Lookee here. I ain't ever heard of no Cleaner spell that coulda done this. Not even with chimney sweeps."

"A chimney sweep?" Dani looked to where Rafi had run off. "Is that what that guy was?" She huffed. "#$%&, what does that matter? This is Francis' fault. I am so going to make him pay for this." Refocusing on Sydney, she frowned in confusion. "It's almost like that woman, when her body turned to dust. Is that something that happens with entropy mages?"

Ben scratched his chin. "Don't rightly know. I ain't exactly been pokin' 'round too many of their bodies lately."

With a shushing sound, the streaks of dust animated. They flowed together into a sphere, which rolled over to Sydney's body and stuck itself back on his neck. The grains shifted to form a familiar face, and color swirled across the surface to make him look human once more.

Sydney's eyes opened and he blinked up at them.

Dani and Ben pulled back as the entropy mage sat up and shook his head. He probed at his neckline, grimacing.

"Did someone just try to kill me? That was a distinctly uncomfortable sensation." He glanced over at Ben. "Oh. Salutations, Ben. I don't suppose you'd possess any clue as to what is going on?"

CHAPTER FOURTEEN

Dani stared at the resurrected Sydney. With a trembling hand, she dug into her purse, found the tiny whiskey bottle, and slugged its contents. It burned her throat, unfortunately reassuring her that she wasn't stuck in a nightmare.

Sydney stood and popped his neck from side to side. "Seeing how the evening was already devolving, perhaps an assassination attempt shouldn't have caught me so unawares." He sized Ben up. "Odd. I didn't sense you before, but now that you're here, there's something a little off about you. New haircut? Are you actually showering and using deodorant these days?"

Ben grinned. "Y'might say I'm on somethin' of a new health regime."

"Regimen," Sydney and Dani said at the same time.

"Yeah, yeah. You all with your proper spellin' and vocabularifics." Ben snorted. "We's standin' on the edge of a desert with a buncha dust devils that just tried to wallop our tushes, and you gotta make a guy feel downright uneducatified."

Sydney eyed him. "Your sudden arrival here suggests you were shadowing us." He looked at Dani. "Were you aware of this?"

She cleared her throat, trying to think of a response, but he sighed and held a hand up.

"Don't bother with excuses. I'd like to say I'm surprised but I suppose it's only logical that you'd harbor a certain level of suspicion toward me still. But I'd hoped ..." He shook his head. "I think I rather preferred the lizard as a chaperone."

"Sydney, I'm sorry." Dani gestured to the mess of a landscape they stood beside. "You know what a worrier I am. I needed some boundaries and safeguards in case, well, something like this happened."

"You mean in case I caused something like this to happen," Sydney said. "Yet you said you believed I wasn't the source of the dust devils."

"I still believe that." She frowned. "I mean, I believe it now."

He sniffed. "So glad to finally see what it takes to earn your trust. I'll be sure to have unknown enemies ambush us in order to force me to protect you whenever we cross paths."

Dani jabbed a finger at him. "I'm giving you an enormous benefit of the doubt, right now. The last time I trusted you without thinking things through, you turned me over to a cult that tried to use me to create a fiery apocalypse, remember?"

He lifted his chin. "An error I've sought to rectify ever since. I'd hoped that my actions afterward might have made some difference in your estimation of me. After all, you did agree to go on this date, knowing my reputation."

She stepped in. "We had this date because we made a deal so you wouldn't murder Jared." The words came out sharper than she intended, and she cringed internally.

Sydney's expression darkened. "I see. So that's all it ever was, hm? From the beginning, you only wanted to relieve yourself of feeling beholden to me. You could've simply said you no longer desired my company and I would've dissolved the arrangement."

"Right," she said. "Like you would've taken that well."

"Whatever you think, I am more than the sum of my pride. Yet you seem to be little more than the sum of your fears."

A tiny growl escaped her as hot flashes of anger tensed her muscles. She started to reach into her purse, unsure if the pepper spray or Taser would be more satisfying. Ben stepped in the way before she could choose, however.

"Hang on a sec," he said. "Before you go spoutin' off all sortsa things you's gonna regret, you oughta know Dani here went and argued all fine and fierce about how you was worth givin' a chance. She coulda stayed in HQ and sent a whole squad of dustbusters after your hide, but didn't."

Dani tilted her head. *Dustbusters? Is that some sort of scrub-team or something? How many divisions and subdivisions of Cleaners are there?*

"Thank you for rising to the defense of your friend and ally," Sydney said. "I'd expect nothing less from you. Yet this is not your quarrel, and you are not welcome here. Besides, in light of the attempt on my life, how am I now to trust that this wasn't all a setup on your part from the start?"

"I made Francis promise he wouldn't get involved," Dani said.

Sydney tugged at his lapels, tightening the jacket around his slim shoulders. "And we all know exactly how trustworthy those acting as Chairman have been in the past."

"He's not like Destin." Dani glanced at Ben. "At least, I didn't think he was."

Ben frowned. "He's got somethin' to answer for, you betcha. But mebbe we ain't exactly seein' this right."

Sydney chuckled. "What else is there to see? Enough evidence has been laid bare for conclusions to be reached and actions to be taken. I shall bid you adieu." With an arm across his chest, he bowed, and then headed for the carriage.

Dani slipped past Ben. "Sydney, wait. There are still things we have to talk about."

He turned, impatience crinkling the skin around his eyes and mouth. "I don't really see how there's much more to say. If you're worried I'm going take some form of retribution on your coworkers for tonight's underhanded dealings, fear not. And while I would offer you a ride back, I think you'd likely be more comfortable in Ben's van which, I assume, is parked nearby."

"Just wait. I need to know. How are you still alive?"

He frowned. "What do you mean? I've suffered worse injuries than a mere blow to the head."

Dani reached out, but drew her hand back. "But you totally lost your head."

"I certainly did not." His back stiffened. "I feel I remained quite calm and capable in the face of such unexpected adversity."

"I mean literally." She pointed off into the distance. "The guy who took you out whacked your head right off."

Sydney's hand went to his throat again. "Are you jesting with me?"

"Saw it m'self," Ben said. "Your head went kablooey into a big dust cloud." He mimed a small explosion. "*Poof.* Then, after he ran off, you put yourself back together. That's more of a handyman maneuver than entropy mage—but I ain't thinkin' a handyman could stitch herself back up after what he did."

Sydney's expression turned perplexed. "I don't understand. Are you saying I actually died?"

"Was that some sort of entropy mage trick?" Dani asked. "Becoming dust to avoid being killed?"

"I am afraid I must admit I've no idea what you're talking about." Sydney fluttered a hand. "If you're trying to divert my attention from the underhanded dealing you've pulled at my expense—"

"I swear we're not." She stepped closer. "Please. Something's not right here. With you."

Ben strode over to Sydney and, before he could pull away, poked the entropy mage in the side. Sydney grunted and jerked back. "Must you?"

Ben frowned. "You feel real enough to me."

"I am real," Sydney said, now clearly frustrated. "What am I supposed to make of what you're saying?"

"That maybe you should stop throwing a tantrum and realize there's something bigger going on here than just a ruined date?"

He scoffed. "This from the woman who threatens to crack open the earth beneath someone's feet if she doesn't get her way?"

A rush of heat prickled down Dani's scalp and along her neck. *I never do that!*

A quiet chorus in the back of her mind whispered back: *You sure? You do have a tendency to make violent threats pretty often.*

She couldn't tell if it was her bonded elementals or just her conscience making a nuisance of itself. Sometimes she thought it'd be nice if that conscience would physically manifest so she could give it a good smooshing under a boot.

I only threaten Scum like that, she shot back. *Or people who really deserve it.*

Dani sighed and clamped down on the internal rationalizing. She realized she and Sydney were having a glare-off. While his eyes had narrowed in restrained anger, they still had a glint of mirth in them. What was he finding so enjoyable about this whole situation?

"If you think I'm being bratty," she said, "then maybe you can help by showing a better example."

"What would be the fun in that?' he asked.

"This is not about having fun anymore." She flipped a hand at the desert. "We're standing right beside a catastrophe. People might've died."

"Perhaps you forget that everyone dies. Worlds die. The universe and reality itself will all die, one day. Have you also forgotten that I serve Entropy itself?" He nodded at the sand dunes. "This is practically a monument to that member of the Pantheon— one which I once might've sought to create myself if I didn't have other considerations distracting me."

"You would never do this," Dani said.

"That's one of the things I like about you. Always sounding so certain even when you have no idea what you're talking about."

Dani bit her tongue to keep quiet, knowing the foul-filter would just negate everything she wanted to vent. Her hands shook with the desire to slap him so hard his cheeks would switch places, but she still couldn't make herself touch him in her exposed state. Maybe if she had a bucket of water … soapy water … straight to the face. Get a little in his eyes, even …

Ben came up and once more interposed himself between them. He took the bottle off his belt. "Lemme try somethin'. Just a quick little test to see if any funny business is really goin' on with you."

Sydney considered the bottle warily. "Exactly what do you intend?"

"Just a little scratch." Ben triggered Carl, who sprayed out a few inches and congealed into a small blade. "Mebbe we can see if there's somethin' a little different with you under the surface."

The entropy mage's face scrunched in disbelief. "Are you serious?"

"C'mon." Ben waggled the bottle. "You afraid of eensy, weensy cut? Mebbe you's just too afraid we're tellin' the truth."

"Nothing frightens me." Baring teeth, Sydney held a hand out, palm up. "Very well. I will humor you this once. But when I shed a single drop of blood, we part ways. For good."

"Can't say I ain't likin' the sound of that."

Ben flicked the water blade across Sydney's palm. The entropy mage didn't flinch.

That is, until he looked down to the cut itself. All his bluster and pretense dropped away, and he joined the two Cleaners in staring as grains of sand trickled out from under his flesh. The cut sealed over a few moments later, leaving a yellow scar that shifted to match the rest of his pale skin.

Sydney touched his hand, pushing and scratching it slightly. Then he pulled his coat off and yanked a sleeve up to bare a forearm. He made a claw of one hand and raked it down the exposed skin of his other arm, gouging deep furrows into himself that revealed nothing but grit and dust beneath.

These too filled with more sand in seconds and reverted to an appearance of normal, unbroken skin. Sydney raised his hands, gaping as he turned them this way and that, flexing the fingers and popping the knuckles.

"This is unprecedented."

"What are you?" Dani asked. "Who are you?"

Sydney patted his cheeks and down his chest. "I am myself. As I have ever been and will be. At least ... I think I am."

"First your powers weren't working like they should," Dani said, "and now you're made out of sand? Sydney, something's really wrong with you. We need to figure out what's happening."

"Your powers ain't workin'?" Ben asked.

Sydney gave Dani a long-suffering look. "Thank you for revealing that. Do you not have any respect for privacy?"

Ben jumped in before Dani could retort. "What if we getcha back to HQ and have a handyman took a looksee at'cha? Figure out what's goin' on with yourself."

Sydney eyed him dubiously. "Truly? You want me to simply surrender myself to your employers, who just attempted to kill me? At the very least, they seal me away again, and I highly doubt you'd find it as easy to free me again as you did the first time." He looked at Dani sidewise, making her flush again. "Your deception, despite the intentions, leaves me dubious that you'll be entirely forthcoming with me moving forward."

Sirens blared in the distance, and the three of them turned as lights flashed through the night, indicating police cars, fire trucks, and other emergency responders heading toward them through the park. Helicopter rotors chopped overhead, and a spotlight sliced down to sweep along the far edge of the desert.

"I'm thinkin' we oughta skedaddle before folks find us and start askin' all sortsa uncomfortable questions." Ben pointed Carl to the west side of the park. "Got my van parked thataway. What say we scoot and sort out the details once we're safe and sound?"

Sydney glanced around, looking cornered, despite having plenty of directions he could sprint off in. "That still does not solve the matter of my fate should I let myself be at the mercy of those who would see me permanently done away with."

"A'ight. I hear you. Howsabout Dani and I go talk to Francis first. If we can figure out what's goin' on, mebbe we can sort things out for you. Cut a deal. We'll get you sittin' pretty somewhere quiet until we signal the all clear."

"Yeah." Dani scowled. "I want answers. I want to know why he lied. Because if I can't trust my own boss, I'm not sure I can even be a Cleaner anymore."

Ben raised his hand. "Hold on, princess. Francis can be a bit of a stiff suit, but he ain't never been a liar. Fact is, he's way too honest for his own good, most times."

She glowered at him, but he just shrugged as if Francis' actions spoke for themselves. Dani satisfied herself with fantasies of making Francis eat his own fedora. Thinking of fedoras turned her thoughts to hats in general and then to one floppy gardening hat in particular.

"Before we go, there's one other thing," she said. "I almost forgot. The woman. The desert. She was here."

Ben looked at her in concern. "You saw her again? And you's sure it was her?"

She nodded, making fist. "She made sure I saw her. She wanted me to know she was responsible for another desert."

He scratched his nose. "Guess that makes two of us. I had a lil' run-in with her, too, just before I got to you all."

"You did?" Dani leaned closer, eager to get any information she could about this other Scum. "Where? What happened?"

"Let's save it for when we're in the clear, yeah?"

She turned to Sydney. "When I told you about her, you acted surprised. Almost shocked. Like you knew. But then that guy …" She looked at Ben in question.

"Rafi," he said.

Dani scowled. "Then Rafi interrupted and killed you. Or tried to. But you were going to tell me something. Do you know her?"

"I may," he said, slowly. "If so, I can't promise her presence would explain everything here, but it might be a start."

"Who is she?"

He gave her a coy smirk and waggled his eyebrows. Dani groaned, realizing he'd slipped his old flamboyant affectations back on like a mask—a defense mechanism. She had her gel. He had his off-putting personality.

"That, dearest, will remain my secret for now. Seems I know something the Cleaners might value highly. Something they may even agree to spare my life to learn, should I agree to temporarily return to HQ."

Dani crossed her arms, trying to ignore the slickness still clinging to them. She'd be showering for hours at this rate.

"Fine," she said. "Have it your way."

His grin turned devilish. "Oh, I intend to." That grin vanished as quick as it came. "As soon as I figure out why I'm sand, of course."

"Good to see you got'cher pretty birdies worked out," Ben said.

Sydney and Dani exchanged a confused look, until Dani sighed.

"Priorities, Ben," she said.

"Ain't that what I said?"

CHAPTER FIFTEEN

Ben stepped out of the glassway into HQ just a second after Dani, but she was already halfway down the hall. She shot ahead like a missile—if a missile wore a water-stained dress, had a mop of red hair, and shoes that still squished with every step.

"Come on, gramps," she called back, adjusting her purse strap. "Let's get this over with."

He jogged to catch up. "We still ain't sorted out any plan of approach. Gotta be strategified with bein' insubordinate. Otherwise, you just come across all whiny and complainin'."

She growled. "Oh, I know exactly what I'm going to do and say. I'm going to go get that Employee Handbook. Then I'm hauling all two-thousand pounds of it up to Francis' office and using it to club the truth out of him."

"You are rememberin' he's the Chairman, yeah? You're thinkin' a big ol' book is gonna get him cowerin' behind his desk?"

Dani chopped a hand down. "I'm already sick of dealing with that book's smart-$#@ attitude. It can at least do something useful and act as a blunt object. And if Francis owns up to being a lying &^%@#$&, I can light the thing on fire and use it as a resignation letter."

Ben frowned at her, unsure how to respond. The book's attitude? It'd been years since he'd flipped through his copy—he couldn't exactly recall where he'd left it last, anyways—but he remembered it being nothing but bone-dry procedural outlines, company policies, Scum overviews, and rundowns of various departmental duties. Exactly what was she picking up on that he hadn't?

"You really thinkin' of quittin' over this, if it turns out to be true?" he asked.

Her steps echoed as she wove through the halls, while other Cleaners shifted out of the way of her warpath marching.

"Wouldn't you?" she asked.

"Nope."

She glared up at him, not breaking her stride. "Why not? How could you work for someone you can't trust? Especially someone who holds so much power?"

He patted Carl's spray bottle. "'Cause the work's gotta get done, princess. And you ain't never gonna find anyone you can trust one hundred percent, all day, every day."

"I trust you."

"Aww." He sniffled and mimed wiping a tear away. "But you didn't always. When we first started workin' together, I had my secrets. Things I wasn't all upfront about, like the Ravishing disease eatin' away at me—and that it coulda infected you too, if I weren't careful."

She frowned. "You had your reasons."

"Sure 'nuff. And if Francis called out a hit on Sydney even after he said he wouldn't, cross his heart and hope to dry clean, he's got his reasons."

"I'd love to hear them," she muttered.

"I ain't saying you're gonna want to hear those reasons, or even agree with 'em, but let's be honest. He ain't gotta answer to you or none of us."

"Then who does he answer to?"

"The Board, of course. And the Pantheon."

"Not good enough."

Ben chuckled. "Don't let 'em hear you say that, princess. Might just get their feelin's all sortsa hurt."

He followed her around a corner, where they had to quickly stick themselves against the wall to let a dozen Cleaners run past. Several scrub-teams heading out, Ben guessed, by the look of it. Plumbers, maids, janitors, even a couple window-washers and handymen. All geared up and looking for trouble.

Dani peeled off the wall and watched their backs until the last turned the corner. She looked nervously to Ben.

"You don't think they sensed ..." She swallowed the rest of what she'd meant to say.

He shook his head. "Naw. I'm bettin' there's a big ol' heap of sand out in City Park that's got their attention."

"Oh." Dani frowned in the direction the others had gone. "I figured they would've responded to that by now. What with that Rafi guy being on the scene, wouldn't you think he'd have reported in to Francis by now? He saw the desert, too."

"You'd think." Ben rubbed the back of his neck. "Ain't quite sure all's too steady with him. He weren't lookin' too peachy back there." He was worried about the chimney sweep, despite the man's murderous actions. *Whatcha got yourself into, bucko? You just get back into town and all a sudden you're hot for hittin' on folks when they're already down? Ain't like you was makin' it sound yesterday.*

He'd considered trying to call Rafi up over the radio, but Dani had insisted they not broadcast what happened or their return to HQ, to try and catch Francis off-guard.

Dani resumed plowing down the hall, and he trailed along in her wake.

"Who is that guy, anyway?" she asked.

"Just met him," Ben said. "A chimney sweep just back from workin' overseas. We was chattin' a bit, what with him bein' a little outta the loop 'round here. Seemed like a nice enough fella."

"We have chimney sweeps? And operations overseas?"

"We got a lotta subdivisions and specialists, you betcha. And what'dja think other countries did to deal with Scum, huh? How'd you imagine I'd handle it if I got sent to France or China?" Dani winced, and he nodded. "Yup. Now, want in on another little tidbit?"

"Please."

"Every regional HQ gots its own Chairman. And all of those guys and gals? No matter how shiny their suits are, they've gone and screwed the pool more than they'll ever admit."

"Pooch," Dani said. "Not pool."

He frowned. "Now why would you ..." He shook off that line of questioning before it took him down a few dark and deep rabbit holes, where nobody would ever hear him scream. "Don't matter. My point is, even the best of us—" He paused and raised a finger to clarify. "Not that I'm ever gonna claim to be any sorta best or brightest, hear? But even the best of us make mistakes. We're all human 'round here. Mostly. Sorta. And those who act like they're above all the mess of life are just lyin' to themselves."

She stayed quiet for a few more twists and turns. When she spoke again, a little of the heat had left her voice, though plenty enough remained to spark a wildfire if she passed through dry brush. "Fine. I'll keep an open mind. But if the truth is that he lied to us ..." She paused. Blew out hard. "... then I'm going to want to bash his open instead."

"Fair enough. Just figure you ain't gonna have much success at that."

"I don't care. I just have to try and do what's right."

Ben chuckled. "I'm pretty sure that's what he's tryin' to do, too."

After another corner, he realized that instead of heading toward one of the glassways that would direct them to the Chairman's office, Dani was weaving through the corridors leading to personnel quarters. She stopped in front of one door, which Ben recognized as hers because of the smiley sticker on it.

She tapped the door with a finger to open it. "Hang out here for just a minute, okay? I need to deal with this." A gesture indicated the general mess of herself.

"You got it. Go get all spiffified and then we'll see what Francis has to say."

Dani dashed inside. The door slid shut behind her—but not fast enough to cut off her words as she caught sight of herself in the closet mirror.

"Holy $&#@, I look like a #$%&^@!&$ walrus puked on me!"

Ben grinned as he leaned against the wall to wait. Knowing her, it'd be more than just a minute; but after what she'd gone through, she deserved to recover a little balance before whatever came next. Who knew? Maybe going through her decontamination rituals would calm her down.

As he waited, he turned the issue over in his own mind. Losing Karen, plus his infection and the way the company had treated him in the aftermath, had jarred more than a few of his old convictions about the Cleaners loose—if not knocked them out altogether, leaving his sense of trust with more than a couple of toothy gaps in its grin.

Destin's betrayal of the whole company and the Pantheon he'd sworn to serve had rattled Ben further. He'd worked alongside the man for years, and while they'd never been pals, there'd been a sense of mutual respect.

Ben scratched at his stubble. *Did I ever sense his going Corrupt before it happened? Was I foolin' myself the whole time, lookin' the other way whenever I got any heeby-jeebies from him? If I'd paid more attention, could I mebbe have kept things from gettin' as bad as they got?*

He let those thoughts and doubts swirl around, distracting him as he waited. After twenty minutes, though, he'd begun to worry slightly. Hopefully Dani hadn't taken a shower and then passed out from exhaustion.

He frowned at the door, wondering at the wisdom of interrupting her self-care. For the next several minutes, he kept raising and lowering his hand, pulling back just on the edge of knocking. Just when he worked up the courage to intrude, a voice called out.

"Ben?"

He looked up as Lucy strode toward him, a mop over one shoulder. He smiled to himself. *Well, there's at least one other person I'd trust to keep me in line, no matter what. If I ever gets too uppity for my own britches, she's always gonna punch me back down.*

"Heya, Lu." Ben faced her and gave a little wave. "Whatcha doin' here?"

The other janitor planted her mop and looked up at him with her usual not-quite-a-scowl that rumpled her cheeks just so.

"Here?" she asked. "You mean in the section of HQ where I live? I don't know, Ben. That does seem kind of weird."

He harrumphed. "Just thought you mighta been out to deal with the new desert we've got in town."

"You know about that?"

He sucked in a breath through his teeth. "Let's just say I got a bit up close and personal, this go-round. It's why we're back a little earlier than expected.

Her surly expression turned to alarm. "You guys were out at the park when it hit? Ben, what happened?" She nodded at Dani's door. "I take it the date didn't go so hot?"

"Actually, seemed to be goin' just fine, for the most part. Sydney was all gussied up with a whole horse and carriage ride and picnic and whatnot. From what I saw, kinda looked like they was havin' a decent time of it."

"And for the least part?"

"That'd be when the dust devils showed up, and Dani wrecked half a buildin' takin' 'em out."

"She what?"

"It was all good self-defense on her part. 'Sides, that was just before that Scum lady popped outta the porta-potties and scuttled up another couple of dust devils to sic on me."

"Porta-potties? Wait, which lady? *That* lady?"

Ben leaned back against the wall again. "'Course, that was also just before we got ourselves another big ol' desert appearin' outta nowhere and eatin' up the park like a sand dune with the munchies."

Lucy's thick eyebrows bumped together. "Have you reported any of this to Francis?"

He grimaced. "About that ..."

Dani's door opened, and she stalked out, dressed in her Cleaners outfit and looking mostly recovered with a face so freshly scrubbed a few spots matched the shade of her hair. She had the Employee Handbook tucked under one arm like a slab of marble.

Lucy gave her a concerned look. "Hey, girlie. Just what's going on—"

Dani snarled and waved a fist under Lucy's chin. "How dare you lie to my face and then try to murder my date! I can't believe you could be such a total $#%*!@&."

Ben eased a step back.

For once, Lucy looked bewildered instead of peeved. "I ... what?"

Dani slumped and uttered a little moan. "Oh, thank $#% I got that out of my system." She peeked up at Lucy and offered a sheepish smile. "Sorry. You can punch me now."

Lucy hesitantly raised a fist. "I wasn't planning on it, but if it'll make you feel better ..."

Dani flinched, but held her ground.

With a snort, Lucy dropped her hand and looked between them. "I feel like there's something we should talk about before we start working things out through bruises and beat-downs."

"Why, Lu," Ben said, "that sounds downright reasonable comin' from you."

Her fist came back up. "Though I'm willing to make exceptions if someone's really begging for it."

He winked at her. "Actually, probably best to lay it all out at once with Francis." He held his arm out, elbow crooked as if asking for a dance. "You're welcome to tag along."

Lucy swatted his arm down with her mop. "I never 'tag along' anywhere. I go or I don't."

"Ain't that the truth."

Dani bounced on her toes, boots thumping. "Let's get this over with." She headed off, leaving Ben and Lucy to share looks—hers bothered, his resigned.

When they caught up with Dani, she looked back over her shoulder. "Where's Jared, by the way?"

Lucy tilted her head in a vague direction. "Back in his room, playing in his sandbox."

"You built him a sandbox?"

"He *is* the sandbox."

At Dani's disapproving look, Lucy snorted and waved her off. "He's having a ton of fun, and I couldn't do my job while lugging him around all day. He's learned how to shift himself places, using the sand to move toy trucks and shovel himself here and there. When I left him, he was building a sand citadel."

"You mean sand castle?"

"Nope."

"Oh." Dani frowned, but then shrugged. "Well, so long as he's enjoying himself, guess there's no harm in it. Thanks for looking after him."

"Sure. I figure it's my good deed done for the year."

They reached a glassway, and Dani radioed in a request for transfer to the Chairman's office. Unlike with Destin, who'd forced any incoming employees to ride an elevator that doubled as a decontamination chamber, Francis had adopted a slightly more open-door policy, requiring just his authorization for his staff to directly access his office.

The glassway shimmered half a minute after Dani submitted the request, indicating it had been reoriented to admit them to the requested destination. Dani squared her shoulders, but glanced back at Ben. He gave her a thumbs-up, and she returned a tight smile before vanishing through the glassway.

Ben followed with Lucy on his heels. They popped out into the Chairman's office, a large chamber with white marbled flooring and walls, all accented with gold and silver. A crimson carpet provided a walkway from the entrance to the far end of the room, where there sat a glass-topped desk with a carved marble base. Francis sat behind it, scribbling away at one of his endless reports with a gold-plated fountain pen. The floor-to-ceiling window behind him showed Denver's nighttime skyline, with skyscrapers gleaming silver in the moonlight and strings of lights marking off streets, all with the mountains laid like a jagged swath of velvet in the background.

Francis rose and came around the front of the desk. Despite his severe features, the smile he graced them with actually came across with a hint of warmth and kindliness, despite their having interrupted his daily routine. Ben considered the subtle changes in the man since he'd taken on the role of Chairman. Where most people Ben had known in the position had grown detached and coldly efficient in how they ran HQ, Francis had made a concerted effort to remain connected to the lower-paid rabble, hearing their concerns and encouraging them one-on-one when he had the time.

He's gettin' better at the whole father-figure thing. And he must be practicin' that smile in the mirror every night before bed. 'Course, if he's lyin' to our faces about gettin' all murdery, ain't no friendly bedside manners gonna keep him on my good side.

Francis clasped hands in front of himself. "Janitors. I wasn't expecting you. Did you get word of the latest ...""

He trailed off as Dani stomped his way, clutching the Employee Handbook. Ben wanted to hold her back, but a big part of him was proud of her taking this sort of stance. Took him years to get up the gumption to even consider the Chairman might be wrong about something, much less confront one to their face.

Francis' golden aura brightened as Dani approached, but he looked more confused than concerned. "Janitor Dani? Is something wrong? Did your date end poorly?"

She planted herself a few steps away. Her arms trembled as she shook the Handbook at him, though Ben couldn't tell if the shaking came from her anger or from hauling around a binder that could double as a sledgehammer.

"Chairman," she said, "I want to know why you lied to us."

Ben watched Francis for any flicker of hesitation. For any twitch that might suggest the Chairman was attempting to hide the truth. Instead, Francis' confusion only deepened.

"Lied? About?"

"When you authorized me to take time off for the date tonight, you said you wouldn't interfere. That the Cleaners wouldn't take any action against Sydney."

Francis nodded. "I did."

"Then imagine my surprise when a Cleaner pops up in the middle of the whole thing, blasts Sydney's head off his shoulders, and says he was doing it on orders from you."

The Chairman's eyes narrowed. "Who is claiming this?"

"This Roofus guy—"

"Rafi," Ben said.

"Yeah, him." Dani swept a hand about. "He comes charging in like a maniac and guns it straight for Sydney, and lays the smackdown. Then when Ben and I confront him, he says he's acting on your orders before running off."

"The chimney sweep?" Francis looked past Dani to Ben. "Did this happen?"

Dani shifted to make Francis focus back on her. "Why are you asking him? I was there, front and center. Can't just take my word for it?"

"I didn't say I don't believe you saw what you say you did," Francis said. "I simply know there are ways of making people see things that aren't quite real."

"It was Rafi all right," Ben said. "Weren't no Scum tricksiness. He went at Sydney like a dog chasin' a fat squirrel covered in barbeque sauce, and then goes and says you sent him."

Dani drew herself up. "Well? What do you have to say about that?"

Francis frowned down at her for a full minute. Then he took off his fedora, revealing his close-cut black curls. The light of his aura swelled until even Ben squinted against the glare. Dani had an arm across her eyes to shade her face, but she didn't take so much as a step back, even as Francis looked ready to go supernova.

His figure turned white-hot and the room vibrated as waves of Pure energy swept through it. His voice rang out, clear and strong, "By the oath of my office and the power invested in me by the Board, I swear in the name of Purity and all that the Cleaners stand for that I did not order any attempt on Sydney's life, nor did I have any hand in or knowledge of operations that might've led to such."

The light winked out, leaving Ben blinking spots out of his vision. Dani cautiously lowered her arm as Francis held a hand out to her. His smile now held a shade of weariness.

"If there's any lie to what I just stated," he said, "then the Board is required to tender my immediate resignation and permanent removal from the Cleaners."

CHAPTER SIXTEEN

Dani knuckled away the last afterimages from Francis' display. She squinted up at him, trying to figure out what had just happened. Did he think getting all shiny and shouty proved he was being honest? If that was all it took, maybe she should yell more and carry a flashlight to beam in people's faces whenever they doubted her.

Adjusting the Handbook under one arm, she looked back at Ben and Lucy. "Um ... that was a good show, but how do we know he's telling the truth?"

Lucy clomped up and laid a hand on her shoulder. "Back off, girlie. He just opened himself up to an emergency Board evaluation. When he does that, they can access his thoughts and scour his emotions inside and out. They can tell if he's not being truthful, and they don't accept lies sworn in their name. If he was lying, he'd have just been stripped of his power and position."

"Oh." Dani grimaced at Francis. "Sorry?" Inwardly, she cautioned herself to not just swallow everything they fed her. She remained the fresh meat in the ranks, well aware of how much she had no clue about when it came operating on their side of reality. Plus, it still rankled when she remembered how Destin had tried to use his Chairman's power to compel her submission to his authority. How could she be absolutely certain Francis wasn't doing the same thing, just more subtly?

"No need to apologize." Francis donned his fedora once more and buttoned his jacket. "I believe you had good reason for making that accusation. It concerns me more that an employee is apparently running around, making claims to act with my authority. Why don't you give me a full report and we can try to determine the facts? And then we can discuss the attempt on Sydney's life."

"Wait," Dani said. "Attempt? How do you know it was just an attempt?"

Francis chuckled. "You're more angry than distraught, focused on the possibility that I might've tried to deceive you instead of mourning someone who would've wrongfully died. That suggests he somehow lives despite Rafi's attack." He looked between all of them. "Am I incorrect?"

Ben sighed as he joined the two women. "It's been an excitin' evenin', sure-for-shootin'."

He and Dani took turns filling in the Chairman on events from either perspective. Dani tried to hide her occasional half-smile as she described how enjoyable the evening had actually started out, how she and Sydney had been getting to know each other on a more personal level, without the nature of their work or opposing ideologies looming between them.

They detailed when the evening festivities became a fracas as the dust devils appeared. As Ben explained the Scum woman's appearance from within a porta-potty, Dani didn't bother concealing her scowl. Everything this woman did seemed designed to infuriate and cause widespread destruction. And for what? Not that Scum needed a particular logic, other than spreading the influence of the Corrupt Pantheon throughout the world; to Dani, though, it felt like this woman worked according to an unknown plan, or had a particular goal in mind that each event brought her closer to.

When they finished, Francis looked like he'd downed a few shots of raw sewage. He looked between them. "Where is Sydney now?"

Ben shrugged. "Oh, we gots him tucked away in a nice, tidy spot where ain't nobody and nothin' gonna sniff him out for a good long while. See, since it looks pretty much like we were bein' downright dirty dealers when it came to holdin' our word about not, y'know, gunnin' for his guts, we thought we owed him a hidey-hole until we could set things right."

"You owed him nothing," Francis said, lips thinning. "None of us were behind the attempt on his life."

Ben made a sucking sound through his teeth. "I ain't sayin' we was, but seems to me keepin' a clean image counts for more, 'round here. Bettin' the Board would get all huffy if their top man was accused of tellin' dirty, dirty lies."

Francis considered this for a few seconds. "Be that as it may, I need no one bothering to defend my reputation. As for Sydney, I would hazard to guess that he's currently sitting in one of your vans down in the main garage."

Dani made a peeping noise in the back of her throat, but Ben just chuckled. "Now that's soundin' like somethin' so stupid it'd circle right back 'round to make us a buncha clever ducks if we pulled it off."

Dani eyed the Chairman closely, but he made no move to summon other Cleaners to act on his deduction. Francis' gaze flicked her way. She averted hers at first, but then forced herself to lock eyes. Her earlier anger had dwindled to a simmering frustration, and this was no longer directed at him, but at their situation. Her initial focus on Francis' supposed betrayal had at least given her a concrete target, but now this had been taken away, leaving her flailing once more. Could she trust him after all, despite the evidence? In the same way, was she making a horrible mistake, trusting Sydney, even to a small degree?

Francis scanned them all and crossed his arms. "This woman. We're certain she's the same in both instances?"

Dani nodded firmly. "Unless two near-identical women are wearing the same getup while running around creating deserts, it has to be."

"And according to you," Francis nodded at the other man, "she manifested dust devils in a matter of moments? From nothing but the earth around her?"

"Yuppers." Ben made wavy motions, like a cheesy stage magician. "She was all *whoosh*. And the dust devils were all *zip*. And I was about to start writin' my last will and testament before Rafi went all save-the-daysies." He coughed. "Leastways, until Rafi went all murder-head-splatty with Sydney."

Dani shot him a look. "If this is how you speak to Jared, it's no wonder he's not talking out loud yet."

"You're gettin' my point, ain'tcha? Just 'cause I does my explainin' colorful-like don't make it wrong."

"If your explanations were any more colorful," Lucy said, "you'd need crayons and a color-by-the-numbers book."

He snorted. "Naw. Never could stay inside the lines."

"If we could focus, please?" Deeper lines sharpened Francis' thoughtful expression. "This does not bode well. The sort of rapid summoning this woman has demonstrated, especially accomplished without ceremony or prepared materials, suggests she possesses an enormous amount of raw power."

"Enough to create deserts?" Dani asked.

"It would seem so." Francis picked up his gold pen and spun it through the fingers of one hand, the closest thing to a nervous tic Dani had ever seen him exhibit. "So, this woman—"

"The Scummoner," Dani said.

Everyone paused and looked her way.

"Scummoner?" Lucy echoed.

"Sure." Dani held up either hand. "Scum who can summon. Scummoner. Makes sense to me."

"Hm." A hint of a smile ghosted across Francis' face. "Quite so. I'll be sure to add it to the company's official Scum categorization records."

She stared. "You're going to actually use something I came up with?"

"Of course," the Chairman said. "I appreciate positive employee contributions."

"Do I get a prize for positive contribution?" *Like a pay bonus or extra vacation time? Or a free pass on the next section of the Employee Handbook?*

"I'll write a memo so the entire company knows you're responsible for the new denotation."

"Swell."

"This Scummoner," Francis continued, "is, unfortunately, acting in our blind spot. She possesses power and motivation, but we have no real clue as to where the power is coming from or to what end she's using it."

"Actually ..." Dani cocked her head. "There was something she said that stuck with me. When I confronted her, she said she was 'practicing,' whatever that means."

Ben grunted as if a sudden thought flicked his ear. "That so? When she popped out of the TURDIS—"

"The what?" Dani cried.

He eyed her. "Ain'tcha never watched *Doctor Who*, princess?"

"Of course," Dani said, "but what does that have to do with this?"

Lucy muttered while glaring at Ben. "Just like they use sewer drains and mucky pipes to get around, some Scum can also use porta-potties that haven't been properly cleaned as ... well ... transportation. Like we use the glassways. We've used them, too, at times, if they're clean enough, but they're very unreliable. The only upside is their connections don't have to be maintained like windows or mirrors. It just depends on what state they're in when someone tries to get through. Going in through a clean one and coming out from one that hasn't been worked on in a few months is not a pleasant experience."

"It's a little germy-wormy, scummy-wummy," Ben said.

Groaning, Dani hung her head. "You have ruined that show for me, forever."

He grinned. "And there's another checkmark on my bucket list. Anyhoo, she started yappin' about puttin' on some sorta performance or show, actin' like I was part of the audience."

"So she's in this for the spectacle?" Lucy asked. "Just to show off how much damage she can cause?"

"It could be as simple as that," Francis said, tapping his pen on his palm. "Plenty of Scum fail to rise above their baser impulses of hunger or savagery. They destroy simply to destroy in the name of Corruption. They spread plagues just to enjoy the suffering they cause."

Dani frowned. "I think it's more than that."

"Why so?" Francis asked.

"Her attack on Cheesman Park might've been a test, sure, one to see how much her powers could do. But it feels like too much of a coincidence that she arrives to whip up another desert right where Sydney and I were. Plus, there's the whole picnic-turning-to-dust-devils thing." She explained more about how Sydney had planned to surprise her with a picnic, with the basket winding up full of dust that turned into the pair she'd put down.

Lucy harrumphed. "You still sure you want to be playing defense for this guy? They could've easily been working together. He lures you out. She plants the dust devils. They take you out, and he comes through looking innocent."

"He was just as surprised by the dust devils as I was," Dani said. "He even tried to destroy them first before—" She bit back

"Before what?" Francis asked.

She hesitated, keenly aware of Ben watching her again. "Before everything went to &$% with the desert and all. Besides, he'd promised not to use his powers during the date."

"Convenient excuse for letting the dust devils take you down," Lucy said.

"But when desert appeared, he stopped that from destroying us both."

The other woman shrugged. "Self-preservation."

Dani bit the inside of her cheek in frustration. "But if he and that woman were working together, why did she create a desert that threatened him as well? Those deserts eliminate all life in their path—they're total Nothingness. He would've died, too, if caught in it."

"To make him look good?" Lucy asked. "Because she knew he could handle himself?

"It just doesn't feel right," Dani said. "It feels like there's something bigger going on."

"I bet you'd like to think so. But excuse me if I point out the kind of trouble our *feelings* got us into not too long ago. You were hardly immune to that, and I'm just trying to keep us from making some of the same mistakes." Lucy eyebrows slammed down together. "Nothing Sydney's done and nothing you're saying, girlie, is proving he's any sort of hero."

They matched glares for a few seconds. Lucy looked as unmoving as a boulder, while Dani kept looking for cracks in the woman's logic she could keep chipping away at.

Francis broke the standoff by stepping forward, edging between them. "Whatever the truth about Sydney's intents and loyalties, those are questions to be answered later. Our primary concern must be identifying this Scummoner and stopping her before she creates even more lifeless zones."

Dani bit her lower lip. "Those two things might be more linked than you'd like. See, Sydney—"

The radio standing on Francis' desk crackled to life.

"Chairman, there's been an incident in the main garage. We believe we've cornered a Scum attempting to infiltrate HQ. Requesting heavy Ascendant presence."

"#$%^!" Dani's stiffened.

Francis looked to Ben. "Clever ducks, are you?"

He grimaced. "Mebbe more like clever platypuses?"

Dani whirled and raced for the mirrored office entry, hampered slightly by the bulk of the Employee Handbook. "We have to keep them from hurting him!"

"For Purity's sake," Lucy called after. "Why are you so determined to keep this @#$%&@* from getting what he deserves?"

Dani looked over her shoulder as she reached the mirror and pressed a palm against it. "He might know who the Scummoner is." She faced the glassway again. "Garage."

The surface shimmered and she plunged through. She stumbled as she emerged onto asphalt, the massive book throwing off her balance. Orienting, she charged along as best she could to where Ben had parked, passing dozens of uniform, white Cleaners vans along the way.

It didn't take long to spot the disturbance. A group of Cleaners clustered around Ben's van, which stuck out from the rest of the company fleet thanks to its dented bumpers, scratched paint, cracked windshield, and its white paint being several shades of dingy.

The Cleaners formed a semi-circle in front of the van, mops, brooms, feather dusters, plungers, and squeegees at the ready. One janitor had a water elemental spouting like a constant fountain in front of him, while a maid kept a miniature tornado poised over an upraised palm.

An Ascendant stood within their ring, three-piece suit a brilliant white against his golden glow. As Dani neared, she spotted Sydney hunched between the driver and passenger's seats, peering out at those assembled.

The Ascendant's voice echoed through the garage. "Surrender, Scum, and we will make your death painless."

Sydney's laugh rang out. "Oh, yes. That's exactly the sort of threat that motivates a man to give himself up without a fight."

Dani shoved through the surrounding Cleaners and caught herself just before bowling over the Ascendant. "Wait," she said, catching her breath. "Don't hurt him. He's under protection."

He eyed her with a mix of confusion and disdain. "Scum? Under protection? The only time that's true is when they're locked away in the Recycling Center."

"You want me?" Sydney leaned out the passenger window, which he must've rolled down at some point. He raised a fist, which pulsed with a purple aura. "Which of you will I turn to dust first before you lay me low?"

"You're not helping," Dani shouted.

"Apparently neither were you when you left me to huddle in this reeking rust heap," he replied. "I almost baked alive in here. You promised me safety, and yet you are gone no more than half an hour when I'm beset on all sides."

"Oh, for ..." Dani stood in front of Sydney, turning and holding the Employee Handbook up in front of her like a shield. "Back off, all of you."

The Ascendant stared at her in shock, as did the other Cleaners. "You're siding with the Scum?"

"I'm keeping a promise," she said.

The Ascendant sneered. "You swore your service to the Cleaners, not this monster. Protecting him makes you a traitor."

"No." Dani said, struggling to keep her arms from trembling at the book's weight. "I'm protecting him so we don't lose a valuable resource that could keep more of those deserts from appearing. You want the Chairman to find out you eliminated the one resource that might help us stop more death and destruction? Huh?"

The other Cleaners glanced at one another in confusion. As they did, Sydney crouched enough to put his head level with hers.

"What're you doing?" he whispered.

"Stalling," she said through clenched teeth. "Want to help a little?"

"My powers appear to be uncooperative once again."

"Then be dramatic. Put on a show. You're good at that."

He growled low. Then he shoved his torso further out the open window so he could raise both arms.

"I'll do it," he cried. "You know what my kind is capable of. I see the terror in your eyes. Cowards and weaklings, all of you. Come any closer and I'll bring this whole building down on your heads. Woe be upon any who dare the wrath of Entropy! Woe, I say!"

"Whoa, boy," Dani muttered. "I said dramatic, not drama queen."

Nevertheless, the Ascendant backed up a step, as did the other Cleaners. Then he recovered, features pinched with fury. He strode toward her, aura brightening with each step.

"I will not stand for this. You are in the center of Purity's power. The bastion against all manner of Corruption. We will not allow any Scum or anyone who sympathizes with them to so much as—"

"Oh, shut the $#%^ up, already." Dani spun and launched the Employee Handbook like a discus, the effort almost cracking her spine and dislocating her shoulders.

Still sneering, the Ascendant raised his arms to catch the book. It slammed into him with the force of a raging bull going for the red cape, and he made a noise like someone trying to projectile vomit all their inner organs at once. Lifted off his feet, he flew backward into a plumber, and the two of them collapsed to the ground, unmoving.

Dani boggled at the downed Cleaners for a few heartbeats. Then she raised her gaze just as the others standing about returned theirs to her. Their expressions became stormier, their grips firming on their various cleaning implements.

A weak laugh quavered out of her. "Uh … I didn't really think it'd work that well …"

The Cleaners began closing their semicircle, one going to stand over their downed teammates.

For Purity's sake, I'm going to have to fight my own coworkers again. It's like the Recycling Center all over again. Except this time, there's no possible escape, even into the Gutters.

Sydney cleared his throat. "Ben doesn't happen to leave the keys in the glove box, perchance?"

"Pernope." Dani took up a sparring stance and woke the smallest glimmer of her power.

"Hold!"

She turned as Francis, Ben, Lucy, and five more Ascendants raced up. With the Chairman and Ascendants all aglow, each in matching suits, it felt like a cavalry born from a men's fashion catalog rushing to the rescue.

"Cleaners," Francis called as he jogged up, "back away. Leave the Scum untouched." Seeing the plumber and Ascendant on the ground, he frowned over at Dani and Sydney. "For the moment."

Dani lifted her hands in surrender. "My bad."

Francis came forward, a shimmer of power showing in his eyes as well. "Sydney, your betrayal of the Cleaners and crimes against Purity are well known to me, as they likely are to everyone here. Why would you return?"

Sydney's attempt at looking indignant was spoiled by having half his body leaning out of a van window. "I was promised amnesty."

"By those without the authority to give it, I'm afraid." Francis clasped arms behind his back. "And amnesty is hardly a thing I give lightly, especially to someone so notorious."

"Oh!" Sydney clapped. "I made the notorious classification. Soon I'll reach nefarious. Perhaps someday I'll be filed under 'downright loathsome.'" He smirked at Francis. "I take it your subordinates have explained the circumstances and reason for my even deigning to consider gracing HQ with my illustrious presence?"

The Chairman nodded. "I'm aware. But that does not mean I agree with their actions."

"Of course you wouldn't," Sydney said. "Because that would mean the Chairman's untarnished image might be compromised. But considering my brother's actions while he held that title, I'd say there's plenty to mar the office's reputation already. So why don't we drop the façade of hard-nosed justice and get on with negotiation?"

"The Cleaners don't negotiate with Scum," an Ascendant shouted from behind Francis.

Francis rubbed his forehead and sighed. "While most of the company would certainly enjoy seeing your head hung on a wall, as Janitor Ben suggests, the Board does provide special dispensation for select enemies of Purity." He aimed a finger at Sydney. "Provided they have something of actual value that would help avert more damage than they might themselves cause. Well?"

Sydney hummed in thought, staring up at the ceiling. "Now that you mention it ..."

"Sydney," Dani whacked his ribs with the back of her hand, making him cough, "play nice, or I will back off and let them dog pile you while I take pictures and laugh."

"You wound me with such vile threats." Sydney made a show of hanging his head in defeat. "Nevertheless, you know me too well. The shame of such an ignominious defeat would overshadow my soul for eternity. Therefore, I must acquiesce to your demands." He grimaced at Francis. "If you swear to give me sanctuary, I will tell you all I know about the Scum creating desolation within the city."

Francis remained unwavering, unsmiling.

Finally, Sydney grumbled. "And I will aid you in stopping her, if it is within my power to do so."

The Chairman turned to the rest. "Stand down."

Several of the Ascendants who'd arrived with him gasped softly.

"But sir—"

Francis' aura flared and his voice took on a metallic timbre. "That is an order, Ascendant."

The sense of his presence and authority pushed against Dani, not in any physical manner, but against her very mind and soul. She resisted it on instinct, but it still muffled any thoughts of direct rebellion, making it difficult to even imagine disobeying his orders.

The other Cleaners hunched, none able to look at the Chairman directly. As one, their aggressive postures wilted, and they shuffled into a more orderly line to await further directives. Francis gestured to them all.

"Return to your current duties. I admire your initiative and dedication, but this situation is handled." He singled out a couple Ascendants and waved them to the prone Cleaners. "Get them to Maintenance, and then inform the handymen there that they'll also be receiving an unusual patient for analysis and possible treatment. Ensure the proper safeguards and quarantine measures are in place."

The Cleaners hustled to comply, picking up their unconscious coworkers by the arms and legs and carrying them off to the nearest glassway. The others scattered in all directions. A few glanced back doubtfully, while others shot Dani furious looks.

She pumped a mental fist. *Hurrah. More friends in the company. Can't wait to chum it up with them at the holiday party. I'll bet there'll be a line to try and drown me in the punch bowl. Better bring scuba gear.*

The van's side door rattled open and Sydney poked his head out. His unblinking, incredibly wary look made Dani imagine a gopher popping up from its den, checking for hawks and other predators.

"Are we done here?" he asked. "I've already had my head knocked off once today, and I'd prefer it remain where it is for a goodly while."

Francis spun about. "Welcome back to HQ. I hope your stay will be short and uneventful."

The entropy mage straightened and tugged at his tux jacket. He started to step down into the empty parking spot next over. As his foot hit the ground, his leg rippled and dusty patches bloomed all over his body. He collapsed. Where he struck hardest, sand sprayed from his form, leaving jagged clumps all over his form.

"Whoa." Lucy whistled. "Girlie wasn't kidding."

"Sydney!" Dani rushed to his side.

He shut his eyes in concentration; the scattered portions of himself recompiled and color bled back into place to make him look whole and human again.

"A little help?" Sydney stretched a hand out. His elbow drooped, and more sand drizzled from it as yellow streaks appeared along his arm. "I appear to not be quite myself."

CHAPTER SEVENTEEN

"This is most distressing," Sydney said from his seat on the patient bed.

Ben patted him on the back, just hard enough to send ripples across the entropy mage's dust-body.

"Hang in there, bucko. We'll getcha taken care of, sure-for-shootin'. And if not, we'll make sure you don't get stuck in a bucket the rest of your life. Mebbe we can make an hourglass outta you. That way you can keep on feelin' all useful-like."

Sydney scowled up at him. "You have no idea how much confidence that inspires. And I do think you're taking a little too much pleasure in my condition."

"Naw." Ben chuckled. "If I was doin' that, I'd have a vacuum cleaner in hand and be switchin' it from sucking to blowing every other second."

Sydney raised an eyebrow. "I suppose there are worse ways to amuse yourself."

Ben looked to the handyman tending Sydney—a soft-featured woman whose green Cleaners uniform was offset by the gold-and-black laced hijab that covered everything but her face. "Any diagnosis yet?"

The handyman eyed Ben sidewise, her disapproval shown in the slightest quirk of her lips. "Perhaps if I were not being interrupted."

Ben stepped back to give her more room to work. Her hands glowed green as she hovered them over Sydney's body, moving here and there, her eyes occasionally taking on a verdant shine as she peered and probed deeper.

The group stood around one of the patient beds in a Maintenance bay, where handymen hurried about, tending to Cleaners suffering from all manner of maladies. Across from Sydney's bed, a handyman lectured a maid on proper equipment upkeep while gingerly tugging razor-sharp feathers out of her bloody arm. The maid lay stiff, looking pale and sweaty, but uncomplaining as the healer removed the chanted feathers and sealed her skin over with gentle touches.

A hall led to a ward deeper within the bay, where more serious cases were taken. Occasional moans and soft screams emanated from there, and many of the handymen who emerged from that section looked a bit more harried and worn than their coworkers.

Standing on the other side of Sydney, Dani kept glancing at the doors leading into the emergency ward. Having retrieved her Employee Handbook after using it as an improvised cannonball— which Ben silently applauded her for—she now hugged it against her chest as if its weight reassured her. Lucy stood beside her, as stolid as ever, though the way her gaze remained fixed on Sydney told Ben she was making an effort to not be unnerved by the whole situation. The three of them certainly had reason to be a little unsettled after the harrowing experience of narrowly surviving a blackshard attack in another Maintenance bay.

Still, he found the place soothing, perhaps a side effect of so many healing auras being active in once place. The Cleaners never had enough handymen on staff, much less in the field, especially with HQ's round-the-clock need to tend to wounded employees. Whether mending bones, purging supernatural diseases, scouring infestations, or quarantining rotting beasts, handymen remained critical to the company's survival.

Ben made a mental salute to the memory of Lopez, who'd sacrificed himself during their fight to take down that corpse-controlling fleshmonger, Dr. Malawer. Not for the first time, he wished the handyman was present, not just because it would mean he'd still be alive, but because the guy had kept some of his moral compass intact even when everyone else had been ready to fling each other into the nearest wood chipper.

Always was one of the best of us, Lopez. Wish you was here, still fightin' the good fight—even if you was a bit of a stiff at times.

With a sigh, the handyman stepped back from Sydney and her aura winked out.

"Well?" Francis asked. He stood in the center of the room, surveying not only Sydney's inspection but also monitoring the whole bay's activity, as if preparing a mental report on how to improve operational efficiency.

The handyman went over to a sink and started washing her hands as if simply examining Sydney had befouled her.

"He is both here and not here," she said.

"What does that mean?" Dani asked. "We've got a Schrödinger's Sydney?"

The handyman returned to Sydney and pinched his shoulder, plucking away what looked like a fragment of his jacket. However, once the material tore free, it turned to dust, which she rubbed from her fingertips.

"His body," she said, "appears primarily to be made of silica and calcium carbonate, if I'm sensing correctly."

Ben raised his hand. "Smaller words, please?"

The handyman gave him a flat look. "Sand."

"Ah. Gotcha."

"So he's not real?" Dani asked.

Sydney drew himself up. "I am entirely—"

"Partially real," the handyman said.

The entropy mage hunched and sulked. "I am feeling far too judged, right now."

"Define partially," Francis said to the handyman.

She frowned. "His body is obviously either not present or has been transformed into this false composite, much like a dust devil's form. However, he shows a level of cohesion and identity a Corrupt construct would not possess."

"That's because I'm not a construct," Sydney said.

The handyman remained focused on Francis. "If I didn't know what he was made of and simply scanned his vitals, I would be inclined to think this a real person sitting here."

"I am a real person!"

"I'm a real boy," Ben whispered in a falsetto. Only Lucy caught this, and she scowled at his not taking the situation more seriously. He winked at her, but she just rolled her eyes.

"I detect mental activity," the handyman continued. "A heartbeat. Breathing. A suggestion of flesh and blood … but all of it oddly distant, like an echo." She shrugged. "I'm sorry. That's the best I can explain it. He's here, but not here."

"Is that why his powers ain't workin' proper?" Ben asked. "'Cause he's tryin' to broadcast 'em long distance or somethin'?"

Francis and Lucy looked at him in confusion, while Dani and Sydney appeared equally irritated.

"Oh, right." Ben tried to look chagrined. "We was keepin' that a secret, weren't we?"

Sydney bowed his head. "It's a wonder that employee gossip hasn't already proven the ruin of this company." Sighing, he looked up. "Very well. In the interest of transparency, yes, my powers are not exactly at their peak. And while I am ever-eager to display the breadth of my abilities, I must admit the sort of magic we've witnessed recently would be beyond me—or at least, not in my usual repertoire of talents granted by Entropy."

"Agreed," Francis said. "We've never known an entropy mage to display any gift for conjuration or construction. Simply eradication and destruction."

Sydney bristled. "Simply? Simply? You truly have no idea of the complexity behind the thermodynamic workings of reality. Entropy is an elegant thing. A fine-tuned equation that keeps existence in balance."

"You're not making any friends here," Lucy said.

Sydney smirked at her. "Pity. I was so looking for a third wheel for my next date with Dani. We did miss a certain level of belligerent awkwardness on this last outing."

"Next date, huh?" Dani asked.

Lucy curled her upper lip. "For someone made of sand, and totally clueless about how he got that way, you're acting pretty confident. Makes me think you're hiding something."

"We all hide things," he said. "My own brother hid his dalliance with Filth. Ben hid his infection by the Ravishing from Dani. And Dani obviously hides her affection for yours truly."

Dani snorted, though Ben felt an uncomfortable tingling in the stump of his right arm as he recalled Sydney exposing the Corruption that had almost claimed him. *Guess we're equal now. Though I's still thinkin' he got the softer landin'.*

"Francis here ..." Sydney scanned the Chairman up and down. "Well, no doubt he's hiding his crippling addiction to group hugs and cuddle sessions. And what about you?" He studied Lucy. "What darkness lurks deep within?"

"Enough," Francis said. "I didn't grant you sanctuary for you to try and sow dissent among my staff."

Sydney grinned slyly. "I've sown nothing, my dear chap. As you might say, I've simply pointed out what already exists. Everyone has secrets."

"Then why don't you tell us the one you promised?" Dani asked. "Who are we dealing with? Who is creating the deserts and summoning dust devils like they went on sale?"

"The problem is," Sydney said, "once I hand over any information I possess, what's to keep you from upholding your end of the bargain?"

"My integrity," Francis said.

Sydney looked as if the Chairman had suggested taking a high dive into the nearest septic tank without so much as a snorkel. "Trust is such a precious commodity these days," he said.

Dani leaned in to catch his eye. "I trust you, remember?"

Lucy scoffed. "Might as well trust a rabid bear to behave in a butcher shop."

The mage snorted. "While I'm hardly so impolite, dear lady, I have, over the years, heard certain people suggest you rather resemble—"

Ben made a growl that rather resembled a bear itself. "Watch it."

"Or what?" Sydney asked.

"Or I'll surprise you. I still got one fist left, don't I?" Ben certainly enjoyed making mundane threats, but he also flexed his internal senses like he used to when he was a true Cleaner. They stretched through the room ever-so-slightly, pinging off Sydney's Corrupt energies and putting a tiny bit of pressure on the Pure energies of his coworkers. He hid a grin behind his scowl, half wishing Sydney would call his supposed bluff.

Lucy looked at Ben curiously. "Thanks," she said, "but I can handle myself."

"Sure 'nuff. But that wouldn't be near as fun as poundin' a few manners into him myself."

She grinned. "Maybe we could tag team."

Sydney pouted at the floor for a minute before sighing heavily. "Very well. Since I'd quickly tire of Ben strutting around like a rooster in heat ..."

"Bears and roosters?" Dani asked. "You're really fixated on animal metaphors. Maybe you should've taken me to the zoo."

Sydney nodded to Francis. "If it is who I think it is, her name is Ella Zhang. Cross-reference that name with past Denver Art Museum exhibits. See if you can pull up a photo."

The Chairman went to a wall and tapped it, creating a glowing screen. Shutting his eyes, he kept his hand pressed against it as images flickered across screen, too fast for Ben to follow. After a few seconds, these slowed down until, like the spinning wheel of a lottery slot machine, a final image clicked into place.

A face peered out at them: an Asian woman, young and smooth-skinned, with dimpled cheeks. Her dark hair hung down to her shoulders. She wore the smallest of smiles, as if shy, but also inviting someone to lean in for a more private conversation.

"That's her," Dani cried. "That's the Scummoner."

"Scummoner?" Sydney asked.

"Scum who can summon," Ben said. "Was Dani's bright idea to call her that."

"Intriguing nomenclature, but I suppose it suffices in this instance."

"I didn't get the best look," Lucy said. "We're sure that's our target?"

Ben imagined the woman wearing a floppy hat and sundress. He nodded. "If it ain't her, then she's got a pretty spiffy twin runnin' around, whippin' up deserts like cake batter."

"I don't even know what that last part means," Lucy said.

Francis stepped back from the wall and spoke as if reading off an invisible file. "Ella Zhang. Twenty-nine years old. Born in Phoenix, Arizona. Moved to Denver to attend the Art Institute of Colorado. Graduated with a degree in industrial design. Worked several jobs before going freelance and establishing a small, but steady career producing sculptures for businesses and private clientele." He frowned at Sydney. "She disappears off public records seven years ago. Not long after your own defection."

Sydney slid off the bed to stand. "And as you might surmise, there's a correlation. That's when she became my student."

"Student?" Francis asked.

"Among other things. Pet project. Lover."

Dani's eyes became slits. "Pet? Lover?"

Sydney cleared his throat. "Just because, deep down, I believe life is inherently meaningless and all will end in oblivion doesn't mean I can't enjoy a little beautiful company," he grinned at Dani, "and brief moments of pleasure."

She groaned. "And I already don't like where this is going."

"After giving over to Corruption and my subsequent departure from the Cleaners," Sydney paced as he explained, "I went into a period of wandering. I traveled far, discovering the extent of my new entropic powers. I kept away from Denver, for the most part, knowing Destin would have a keen eye out for me. Yet I returned every so often to irk him. During one of my visits, I encountered Ella. I attended an exhibit at the art museum displaying a variety of local artists, where I intended to obliterate a few million dollars' worth of irreplaceable artwork."

"According to the latest estimate," Francis said, "you've destroyed several billion dollars' worth of property since you turned to Corruption."

Sydney's lips quirked. "I once might've been proud of that. But then again, if all comes to nothing in the end, what does material value really matter?"

Josh Vogt

"No existential theorizing right now," Dani said. "What happened at the art show?"

"I met Ella, of course. I first explored the exhibit, trying to determine exactly which pieces would be most delightful to eradicate. While studying a particularly gauche painting, she came up and asked me my thoughts on the piece. I won't bore you with the details of our conversation."

"Thank Purity," Lucy said.

"Suffice it to say, her wit and insight on a variety of topics snared my interest. She demonstrated a vibrancy. An irresistible spirit." Sydney glanced at Dani. "Much like yours. I found myself spending an inordinate amount of time with her, revealing far more about myself than I ever intended. We spent many a day debating philosophies of all manner. She kept trying to show me the beauty in the world, in creation, while I wore down her every argument until she finally accepted the inevitability of Entropy and the futility of fighting our fates."

"You …" Dani wore a growing look of disgust and horror. "You were trying to Corrupt her."

"Some guys go for the wooin' with roses and chocolates," Ben said. "Some go for food and a flick. And some try to turn your mind and heart blacker than sludge. Karen never woulda called me the romantic type …"

"Because you aren't," Lucy said.

"Hey. Play fair."

Sydney squared up with them, not appearing proud, but neither shying away from their accusing gazes. "I showed her another path. I showed her reality from my perspective." He clasped hands behind his back and bowed his head. "I didn't expect her to respond with the zeal she did. I just wanted someone to understand me. Instead, she wanted to become more—or at least to possess the same power I did—to explore and experiment, creating her own twisted version of the world." He swept a hand through his hair. "I expected her to be shocked, if not utterly dismayed at what I was. I expected her to flee in terror. Instead, she wound up clinging to me all the tighter, refusing to let me be until I gave her every secret I knew. Until I could promise her a portion of my power." He wiped

174

off a sleeve, scattering grains, as if feeling her hold on him. "That was impossible, of course."

"Whadja do then?" Ben asked.

Sydney turned his back and stared at the wall. His voice became distant, as if drifting across the years. "I broke her heart. And I then broke everything she ever created until all was ruin. Every piece in progress. Every sculpture on display throughout the city. And I left her weeping in the dust, certain that she would despair, retreat, and spurn me forever." He put a hand to the wall and leaned against it, as if burdened by a sudden weight. "I suppose, with her reappearance and seeming possession of the power she craved, that I underestimated her even more thoroughly than I thought."

"Bucko, you're one rank, unchin-snouted flap-dragon," Ben muttered. Francis drew a notepad from a jacket pocket. Before the Chairman could scribble down anything, Ben spun and thrust a finger at him. "Don't even be thinkin' about addin' that to the foul-filter. That's classic literature. You should be proud of me."

Dani's voice cut through the room, hard and edged like sharpened steel. "You destroyed a woman's life. And you did it for the fun of it, until it wasn't fun anymore."

Sydney faced her. "By the end, it was more out of desperation. I never thought I'd ever be on the receiving end of such unwanted and relentless attention. But I didn't kill her."

"You might as well have! You $#@%&*$!" Dani marched over and rammed a fist into his gut hard enough it popped out of where his spine would've been.

A cloud of dust sprayed out across the wall. Sydney's eyes bulged and he bent over, clutching her elbow.

"That is distinctly uncomfortable. If you would please remove your appendage from my innards."

She yanked free, flicking dust from her glove. "Be glad it wasn't your head again."

He lifted said head, jaw clenched. "I'm not the same man I was back then. I've been trying to prove that with my recent actions."

"Why?" Dani asked. "What changed? What makes you so different now?"

"'Side from bein' a sandman?" Ben shrugged as everyone looked at him. "What? Better than him bein' a snowman."

Dani focused back on Sydney. "So what caused this supposed change of heart?"

He frowned. "I can't exactly recall what inspired me to pursue a different sort of life. Perhaps I tired of being nothing but an agent of destruction. Perhaps you awokewoke something in me that I thought was long dead. All I know is I want to make a more positive difference, moving forward."

"That's not enough," she said. "I need something more than vague wishes and wants."

His frown deepened. "I truly can't recall. Things are a bit of a blur until recently."

She cocked her head. "What do you remember last? Before you sent your strip-o-gram guys?"

"Strip-o-gram?" Ben and Lucy said in tandem.

"Shut up," Dani said, without looking at them. "I'll give you the details later." She stiffened. "Actually, never mind. We're never talking about that again."

Sydney pressed a palm to his forehead. "Ever since realizing my current state, I've been plumbing the depths of my mind to determine the same thing—plus try to determine what might've triggered this transformation. Strangely, now that I focus on it, my memory is full of holes since the time we last were together. After our time in the Gutters, I get a sense of wandering, questioning, and then nothing but darkness until I came to myself here in Denver and sought you out." He made fists, and sand drizzled from his knuckles. "Perhaps Ella has something to do with this change, and it has affected my memory."

"Can you at least help us stop her?" Francis asked. "Before she causes further destruction? You obviously remember her from before. There must be something more you know we could use."

Sydney closed his eyes. "I remember some of the places that were important to her. Her apartment. Her studio. A couple galleries and a shop in a little strip mall that carried her work. If she's back, she may simply be hiding out in one of those until she's ready."

"Ready for what?" Dani asked.

"To create her next masterpiece, I'd wager." He reopened his eyes and thumped a fist against his thigh. Several fingers puffed into dust, and everyone stared as they reformed. Sydney wiggled them as if to reassure himself they still worked. "My condition appears to be worsening. I'm unsure how much longer I'll be able to maintain cohesion—and if I can't, then I doubt I'll be much assistance."

Ben looked over to where the handyman who'd inspected Sydney now worked on mending a plumber's broken leg. "Whaddya say? Think you can patch him up?"

She didn't bother to look up, eyes and hands aglow. "I already tried, testing to see how he would react. The energies sank into him and vanished without so much as a ripple. It's like his body is a bottomless pit. Nothing there to react to the healing. I doubt there's anything we could for him."

Dani glanced at Ben, and he saw the glint of an idea in her eyes. "Whatcha thinkin', princess?"

"I think I know someone who might be able to help." She jerked her head at Sydney. "Why don't we go introduce him to his nephew?"

CHAPTER EIGHTEEN

H old up, girlie." Lucy stuck her mop out to bar the exit from the Maintenance bay. "You want to expose Jared to a monster like this?

"Jared?" Sydney asked. "What a normal name for an impossible creature."

Dani scowled at him. "He's a boy, not a creature."

"The last thing we need to be doing is helping him," Lucy said, pointing her mop at Sydney. "We've already been way too lenient. Now you're talking about helping him get his powers back?"

Dani matched her scowl. Lucy could be crabby, yes, but the other woman seemed even more dead set than usual on seeing nothing but the evil the man was capable of. Had Sydney done awful things? Absolutely. Did he need to face the consequences of his actions? Dani wanted little more than to administer them all herself, leaving him weeping and begging for forgiveness.

Yet despite everything she'd just heard, deep in her gut, past all her anger and disgust, a flicker of hope remained that he might be truly trying to make amends or change his ways. She didn't know exactly why she clung to this, but there it was. Perhaps she hoped more for Jared's sake than Sydney's. If an entropy mage could be redeemed, or even begin working toward repairing some of the damage he'd done, then maybe Jared would have a better chance of staying on the path of Purity.

"I'm not saying we have Jared cure him," she said, "but what if what happened to him earlier is somehow linked to what's going on between Sydney and Ella? I mean, he did turn into sand just before the deserts appeared and Sydney started having problems."

Sydney jerked slightly. "He did?"

Francis tapped his pen on his chin. "It is true the boy has shown strange correlations with unique phenomena. The Board has been trying to determine ways to gauge the extent of his abilities. This could be an opportunity to test that. But it could also lead to disaster."

Dani waved at Sydney. "If what's happening to him started affecting Jared like this, then if it gets worse for Sydney, it might hurt Jared, too. What if it even kills him? And we need Sydney's help if we're going to stop this Scummoner from wiping out more of the city."

Ben placed his hand on Lucy's mop, but she stiffened and pushed him back a step.

"Lu," he said, "I know you're worried. I ain't gonna deny I'm not either. But it ain't just about Sydney here. Sure, he ain't exactly all puppy cuddles and rainbows, but somethin's wrong with the kiddo, and I'm thinkin' Dani might got a point. I'd knock my own teeth out with a brick if anythin' happened to Jared and we'd been able to stop it."

She swatted his hand aside. "Ben, you know what this guy is capable of. You know what he's done to us, to our friends and coworkers over the years. How can you even think of wasting another second on him?"

"I see you've fully bought into the propaganda Destin spread about me in my absence." Sydney splayed hands, palms up. "Did I destroy? Yes. Wantonly. Yet much of that was mere buildings and public structures. Mass murder? I'm not usually one to say it, but you think too highly of me in that regard. However, it appears Ms. Zhang is willing to go far further than I in that matter. I doubt it'll accomplish anything to claim it, but I truly wish to stop her before this situation gets any worse. Chairman," Sydney stepped Francis' way, "how many lives, Cleaners or otherwise, can you confirm me to be directly responsible for?"

Francis' features pinched. "Much of your brother's files on you were redacted or otherwise incomplete. He names you as the culprit for the loss of several scrub-teams sent out to stop you, though."

"And you trust his record keeping, now knowing who he fraternized with?"

The Chairman fiddled with his gleaming pen, making it twirl as if to match the swirl of his thoughts. "As much as I hate to admit it, it does throw his claims into doubt."

"Chairman, please don't tell me you're even considering this." Lucy thrust her mop at Sydney again. "What if this was all a ploy to get him back into HQ? To get him access to the kid he wanted to kill on first sight? Or let him be a Corrupting influence, like he just admitted to being with that poor woman? Or to get his powers back now that he's past our main defenses? We can't trust him."

"You're right," Ben said.

Dani snapped her gaze to the janitor. What was he up to? Ben smiled at Lucy, soft and sad.

"You trust me, don'tcha, Lu? And Dani. Trust us that we're tryin' to do the right thing, here. For Jared and for all of us."

"For Purity's sake." Lucy glowered at them all before slinging her mop over her shoulder. "Of course I trust you. You've earned it. But Sydney hasn't, and anyone can make a mistake in who they decide to trust, including you two. And I think you're making a huge one."

"If it wasn't for Sydney, the two of us wouldn't be alive," Dani said. "Neither would Jared. And Destin would still be in charge, as Corrupt as ever."

Lucy snorted. "Like I said before, self-preservation. That's all he's about."

"Who isn't?" Sydney asked. "I admire your desire to protect your friends; to protect the company you care so much about. My enmity was ever aimed at my brother, not the Cleaners as a whole. With him gone, I've rather lost my taste for direct opposition of your efforts." He went over to Francis and held his hand out for the notebook the Chairman held. "If I may?"

Francis' eyebrows rose, but he handed the pad and a pen over. Sydney scribbled on this for a minute and then handed it back.

"There," he said. "No need to torture it out of me. Those are the details I can recall of the various locales Ella might be employing in the area. Hopefully one of those will provide a lead. I also hope that I might survive long enough to accompany you when you do corner her."

"Why?" Lucy asked. "So you can betray us to her?"

He grimaced. "My hope would be to confront her and discover how she's gone about acquiring her powers. Perhaps I could give you enough insight to neutralize her, or even stop other Scum from following the same path. At the least, I could distract her long enough with an emotional appeal for you to ambush her and bring her in via quarantine."

Francis walked slowly to the center of the room so they all ringed him. He studied each of them in turn, lingering longest on Sydney before ending with Dani.

"You truly believe he can help us?" he asked her. "That he's willing to do so?"

Dani wanted to look at Sydney, but kept her focus on Francis. She reached her thoughts back into a darker chamber of her mind, where she imagined her elemental others residing.

"What do you think, ladies? Are we walking ourselves into a trap?"

Foreign thoughts bubbled and flickered up in reply, and Fire-Dani said, *"Maybe. It's hard to tell with you humans. But if all this is a trap, it's not one of his making."*

Dani barely masked her frown. *"Not his? What do you mean?*

"Well, we're talking a nice little family reunion coming up, aren't we? But aren't you forgetting Jared isn't Sydney's only living relative?" Fire-Dani continued.

"You think his brother is involved? Last we saw Destin, he was being hauled off by Filth to be her toy, or whatever she wanted from him."

"And maybe she's playing with that toy, using him to get to Sydney ... and us."

"If so, even more reason we need to stop whatever's going on."

She blinked at Francis, who waited for her answer. "I think we can trust him as far as Ella's concerned," she said. "I think he really wants to help us stop her."

Francis tapped the brim of his fedora. "Then I grant you admittance to the child. Of course, the Ascendants watching over him will keep all precautions in place." He fixed Sydney with his gaze. "In your weakened state, it would be little trouble for them to deal with you."

Sydney nodded, but kept quiet, which surprised Dani. *No quip? No comeback? I still can't tell if his keeping a serious attitude is a good sign or not.*

"I'm going with," Lucy said. "If I'm going to be on Jared's babysitter rotation, the least I can do is make sure he stays safe."

"I expected as much," Francis said. "I'll make preparations for your visit."

"I gotta talk to Francis for a sec," Ben said. "You all go on ahead. See what the kiddo can do. Then we can plan exactly how we're gonna stick that fly-bitten joithead of a Scummoner back in the porta-potty where she belongs."

Dani looked at him quizzically. "Not sure what that means, but I like the sound of it."

"Mebbe after all this, I'll teach you how to sling Shakespeare slurs right and proper. Y'know, make myself useful."

They shared a brief smile. Then Dani headed for the door to the Maintenance bay. "Come on. Time's wasting."

Sydney made a half-bow to Lucy. "Ladies first?"

"You try any tricks," Lucy said, "and I'll show you how little of a lady I can be."

He chuckled and caught up with Dani as she opened the door and led them out into HQ's maze of white-tiled halls. Lucy tromped along behind them, mop head hovering a jab's-length away from Sydney's back. They walked in silence for a few minutes, Dani concentrating on Jared's room, trusting the strange magic of the place to guide them there sooner rather than later. The halls were oddly quiet at this hour, and even their booted footsteps seemed muted. Only a couple of Cleaners appeared at random junctions, hurrying to and from jobs. They gave the trio wary looks, but passed by without question.

At last, Sydney broke the hush. "Why do you insist on calling this ... Jared ... my nephew?"

Josh Vogt

"He's Destin's kid," Dani said. "That technically makes him related to you."

"How can we be family if he isn't even human?" Sydney asked.

She frowned at him. "He's half-human. And you're going to be nice to him."

"Or you'll find out my beliefs on spanking," Lucy added.

Sydney smiled toothily. "I see you've both taken on the role of mama bear. That's rather darling."

"You said his head grows back, right?" Lucy asked.

Letting Lucy take charge of violent threats for the time being, Dani focused on navigating, not wanting this to take any longer than necessary. After several more turns, they passed through a glassway and came out in the small room that served as the antechamber to Jared's room. A pair of glowing Ascendants stood on either side of the double door entrance.

Dani approached the Ascendants. "We're here to—"

"We know," the one on the left said. "The Chairman informed us, and he's monitoring the room remotely, as are we. The room is prepped to go into full quarantine mode if anything goes wrong."

"Quarantine," Lucy muttered. "Great. We know how good that feels."

"If it makes you uncomfortable, you don't have to come in," Dani said.

Lucy's glower provided all the answer necessary.

With a nod at the Ascendants, Dani went through the doors. The other two followed her down a short hall, which admitted them to Jared's bedroom.

"Isn't this quaint." Sydney scanned the area, taking in the bed with superhero-patterned sheets and pillows, the shelves stacked with comic books and novels about swords and spaceships. A door to the side led into a small bathroom, revealing a Samurai Jack shower curtain. Jared never used the toilet, so far as Dani could tell, but he did love to brush his over-large teeth with his Captain America toothbrush.

A low plastic tub a couple feet square had been set in one corner, near the foot of the bed. Sand filled this, currently shaped in an impressive, towering castle. Dani went over to crouch by this.

"Jared?"

Sand flowed up to one large tower to form a dragon perched atop it.

"Dani? What do you think? I got the idea from one of the books Ben read to me."

She grinned. "It's amazing. I didn't know you were so talented at art."

"Thanks! This is way better than playing with Legos."

"I bet. But we've got to put playtime on hold for a little. You've got company. I want to introduce you to someone." She stepped aside and waved Sydney forward. "This is your Uncle Sydney."

The castle collapsed, and channels in the sand formed a giant stylized eye. It blinked.

"Uncle?" he repeated.

"Yes. You can call him Uncle Sid, for short, if you want."

Sydney made a face. "He most certainly cannot."

Lucy rumbled. "Be. Nice."

Sydney cleared his throat and stepped forward. "Hello. Jared, is it? I ... er ..." He looked to the ladies, seemingly at a loss. "I hear you're made of sand, too. How's that going for you?"

The eye became a fish that dove into the miniature sand dunes. A foot-tall figure rose from the center, roughly humanoid, looking more like a robot than a person. *"I remember you. You fought my daddy back on the gray world. You helped save me."*

"I did indeed." Sydney smirked. "Nice to know someone appreciates my efforts."

"My daddy was a bad man," Jared said. *"Are you?"*

Sydney's grin faded. "Some might consider me bad. I've certainly done bad things in the past, but I'm trying to make up for it now. Besides, I helped keep your father—my brother—from doing more bad things."

"Why? If you were bad, why try to be good now?"

"Despite what some think, people are capable of change." Sydney peered at the sandbox. "What about you, Jared? Which one are you?"

"Sydney ..." Dani said in warning.

The sand figure shifted, features sharpening to form a knight in armor, complete with sword and shield.

"I'm a good boy," Jared said. *"Dani and Ben tell me that all the time."*

"And that's one thing we don't want to change," Dani said. She moved beside Sydney and whispered. "What do you think you're doing?"

He held a hand out in a placating gesture. "Simply seeing what sort of son my brother has wrought. After all, as you insist, he is family."

"That's not what we're here for," Dani said. "You can have your family bonding time later."

"What is family bonding?" Jared asked.

Sydney smiled at the sand knight. "Oh, merely time taken to enjoy one another's company, trade stories and jokes, finding all manner of teachable moments, and sharing experiences that make for lifelong memories. At least, that's what I hear. Destin and I never really partook in such activities."

"Why does that not surprise me?" Dani asked.

"It sounds like what Dani and Ben have done with me. Does that make them part of our family?"

Sydney blinked. "I ... perhaps it does. Family need not be defined merely by blood, after all." It was Dani's turn to smile. He appeared a little bothered by the idea, but shook off the look a moment later. "Any other questions?"

"You said bonding means teaching things. Can you teach me what being sexy means?"

Lucy made a choking noise behind them.

Sydney's eyebrows shot up, and he chuckled. "My boy, nobody can possess every talent in the world, but there are at least a handful of things I might consider myself a maestro of. When it comes to the matter of allure and desire—"

Dani lightly smacked Sydney's shoulder. "We can talk more about that later. Or never." She shot him an incredulous look, which he returned with another grin. "Jared, your Uncle Sid is kind of falling apart. He's not supposed to be sand. He's supposed to be human. Is there anything you can do to help him?"

"I don't know. I haven't been able to stop being sand either. Why do you think I can help him?"

"You're different," Dani said. "You can do things nobody else can. Even turning to sand doesn't hurt you—but it might kill him if it gets worse. Would you just try? If nothing works, it's okay. I know you'll do your best."

She held her breath as long seconds ground by.

After a minute, Sydney sagged slightly. "It's entirely understandable. It's a pity, but we can't expect too much of the boy and, after all, just as with everyone, my death is inev—"

"I'll do it," Jared said. *"I'll try."* The knight swirled into a raised hand. *"We're family, right? Maybe if we bond a little now, it'll help."*

Dani and Sydney exchange a look. She tilted her head at the sandbox. "Well? What're you waiting for, Uncle Sid? Dare to bond a bit."

Sydney crouched and reached out to press his palm to Jared's. Dani struggled to see, but it looked like their flesh merged, becoming mingled sand particles that whorled about. Ripples passed over Sydney's body, his form splitting in places to reveal the dust beneath before closing up again. He gasped and looked ready to collapse for a second before firming up again.

Jared's hand closed over his, and both fists became a singular ball of sand that swirled with striations of brown and yellow and black. Sydney went still, head bent so they couldn't see his face. They remained locked together this way for five minutes, no sound in the room except Dani's nervous tapping of a boot toe, Lucy's heavy breathing, and the soft shushing of moving sand.

Dani's nerves teased her power awake, and she had to push it back down, fearful that it might disturb whatever Jared was trying to do. Finally, she couldn't stand it anymore. "Well?"

Jared's and Sydney's hands reformed and broke apart.

"She's spying on us."

Dani's rubber gloves squeaked as she clenched her hands. "#$%&. I mean, who's spying, Jared?"

"Not nice to spy. Sneaky lady. I'll show you where she's hiding."

Sand sprayed up from the box, making Sydney stumble back. He straightened, his expression one of total bewilderment.

"What is—" He cut off and went still as his face suddenly smoothed over into a blank, flesh-colored mask.

Lucy moved for him, mop poised to strike. "I knew he was up to something."

Dani flung an arm out. "Wait! I don't think he's doing anything."

The smooth portion of Sydney's face bulged and warped, forming eye sockets, a nose, and a mouth. Looking little more than a bland mask at first, the features sharpened by the moment, until Dani finally recognized who it was.

Ella Zhang opened her eyes and looked at them from Sydney's body. She smiled oh-so-prettily.

"Oh, hello," she said, with his voice. "It seems my little game of hide-and-seek is over. Whatever will I do?"

CHAPTER NINETEEN

I want in on this," Ben said. "And I don't wanna hear no back talk from you."

Francis crossed his arms, somehow not forming a crease in his suit jacket as he did so. "In on what, exactly? And you do realize that, as your superior, whatever I say to you can never really qualify as back talk."

"On this job." Ben went over to the Maintenance bay's sink and picked up a mug sitting in the cabinet above it. The mug had been shaped like an oversized prescription bottle, with COFFEE listed as the necessary medicine, with instructions to *Drink Until You Feel Human* on the ceramic-printed label.

Oughta get Lu one of these.

With deft use of his pinky, he turned the water on and filled the mug before shutting the faucet off again. He turned, sipping to slake his parched throat.

"And sure you can. You're the Chairman. You could sass the Board if you wanted to. 'Sides, what's the point of havin' that bein'-in-charge stuff if you ain't gonna back talk your employees every now and then?"

Francis studied him with a familiar expression—one that meant he was trying to figure out what Ben was up to.

"The point," he said slowly, "is respecting my superiors."

"Respect." Ben made a farting noise that made a couple handymen look his way before returning to their patients. "Please. Respect is for ... for ..." He scrunched his forehead in thought. "Ill-nurtured puttocks." Eyeing Francis over the rim of the mug, he grinned. "I think I remembered that one right."

Francis sighed. "Do you ever tire of wielding humor as a blunt weapon?"

"Naw. If my jokin' got too sharp, I might actually be dangerous. Could cut myself, if I weren't careful."

Francis took off his hat and inspected it. "You're claiming to use low humor in order to protect us from yourself?"

"Ain't I a saint?"

"The saint of bad puns, perhaps."

"Ooch." Ben grimaced, but chortled. "Good to see you still gots your sense of humor, too. That's always one of the first things to go when folks start slippin' away from bein' a proper person and becomin' just another of Purity's puppets."

"None of us are puppets so long as we work and serve of our own free will."

"I gotta agree with you there. And us agreein' on somethin' is scary enough." Ben swallowed another mouthful of water. "But back to what I was sayin' before you tried to get all distractifyin'. I want in on this job. I wanna help take down this Scummoner."

"And what would keep the first dust devil she summons from grinding you to paste?" Francis asked.

Ben flexed his arm, careful not to spill his drink. "My powers, Francis. They's comin' back."

The Chairman couldn't have looked more dubious if he'd had the word tattooed on his forehead.

"Hey." Ben jerked his chin at the other man. "You was the one who approved my idea. You even wished me luck on it."

"I did," Francis said. "But in all honesty, I didn't actually expect results."

"Y'know what? I didn't expect none either. My suggestion was one of my dumb jokes, and I thought you pranked me good right back. But the joke's on both of us 'cause somethin' in here"—he tapped his chest with the mug—"is comin' back to life."

"You're sure this isn't simply wishful thinking?" Francis asked.

"I ain't that ham-brained. It's been mostly spits and spurts so far, but it's happenin'. I'm gonna be a real Cleaner again, sure-for-shootin'."

The Chairman pinched the bridge of his nose. "You really think getting water unexpectedly splashed in your face has reactivated powers a godling took away from you?"

"Don't be callin' Jared that where he can hear it. We don't want him gettin' any deluges of grandeur. Mebbe it's the stress of me havin' to be all paranoid about gettin' ambushed. Mebbe it's one of them self-defense mechanistics kickin' in gear. Mebbe it was just a matter of time. I ain't sure. But I know one thing. Dawdlin' around HQ ain't gonna do me much good anymore. I need to get out and start flexin' this mojo if I want it back up to full strength anytime soon."

"And if you're slaughtered out there because you face a foe you simply can't handle anymore? Part of my duty as Chairman is to protect the Cleaners as much as the people and places you all protect in turn."

Ben started to reply, but his tongue suddenly felt overly large and dry. Coughing, he chugged the rest of the water, refilled the mug, and gulped that down too before he felt able to talk again.

"That's a risk I'm willin' to take. You don't gotta be responsible for what happens to every single body in this building, Francis. You can't be. It just ain't sensible. I'm askin' for this proper-like, but you know I'll try anyhoo even if you say no. And are you really gonna pull the 'lock 'em up for their own good' routine? Sounds like somethin' Destin woulda done. I know you better than that, and you know me better than that."

Francis replaced his hat, the brim hiding his eyes. "Very well. You can be on this job, alongside Janitor Dani and the others."

Ben gawped. "You mean it?"

"On one condition." Francis met his gaze. "Prove it."

"Eh?"

The Chairman raised his chin. "Prove it. If you can show me an inkling of the power you once held, I will accept that it, plus your rather extensive experience, will be sufficient to at least keep you alive out in the field."

"I've already been out on jobs without my powers," Ben said.

Francis' lip thinned. "Yes, and I recall you having to be rescued in certain instances. If you can't fulfill my one requirement, I have others who can be assigned to this alongside Dani and Lucy."

"But ain't none of 'em gonna work as well with 'em as I can."

"That might be true if you had any measure of your old abilities back. Otherwise, you might as well be flicking pebbles at any Scum you encounter. You'd be a distraction, at best. A liability, at worst."

"Ain'tcha heard of David and Goliath?" Ben swirled the water in his mug before draining half of it. "A pebble can do a lotta damage. Just gotta know right when and where to hit the target. And don't nobody know how to hit Scum in the soft bits like I does."

"True. So for now, until you can bring me proof, maybe you would be better suited giving training to your coworkers, showing them how to hit those soft bits as well."

Another gulp emptied his cup and he went for another refill. *Jeepers. Guess I got so distracted with work, I forgot to drink all day. Gotta be careful. Need to keep this body goin' strong if I want to be workin' again.*

"I got witnesses," Ben said, once he had another cup ready to wet his tonsils. "Like Rafi. He was right there in the cafeteria when I ... oh. Tarnation."

Francis' mouth twisted in distaste. "Yes. He does pose a disturbing puzzle. One I intend to solve. However, our priority is this Ella Zhang. So if you wish to participate in her downfall, show me the slightest proof that you have any power returned. Otherwise, you will remain here in HQ, performing your duties as a consultant. Though, if any other Cleaners go on dates, I suppose you could moonlight as a chaperone."

"You can't sense the energies in me?" Ben asked. "'Cause I got my magic radar back. Enough to sense you and everyone else. Even started gettin' the skeevies off Sydney when he was sittin' here."

Francis raised a hand toward Ben. Ben concentrated on projecting a sense of the power he knew he had. In the past, the power would've come to him without a thought, flowing through him, shaped by his will to interact with his tools and the watery elements he was most familiar with. Now, though, even with his whole mind bent toward the effort, he barely felt the energies welling up to pop few bubbles on the surface.

C'mon, Benny, you old scurvy-riddled badger. You can do this. Ain't as easy as it was, but you still got that oomph and pow and whammo and sockazam ...! And mebbe you've been readin' Jared a few too many Batman comics lately.

After a few moments, Francis lowered his hand and shook his head.

"I don't sense anything. I'm sorry."

Ben bared teeth. "Then you ain't tryin' hard enough. Or you just don't wanna sense it, 'cause it always kills you to admit that you's wrong."

"As I've shown in the past, I'm willing to change my mind when I find myself in error. But only when there's proof."

The two men locked gazes. Ben felt a heat rising in his, while Francis' eyes remained infuriatingly cool. Ben had stared down plenty of ravening Scum beasts, but the other man had the willpower of the whole Board backing him up, giving him as much a sense of authority as he needed to enforce on others. Ben wanted to see the Chairman flinch; to see him back down from an ironclad stance, just once. Francis was hardly the worst Chairman Ben had known, and a far sight better than Destin, he could thank Purity for that. Yes, Francis had even proven flexible in the right situations, willing to question an undermined authority and bend company procedure.

Yet once Francis dug his heels in on an issue, entirely self-assured in being right, Ben might as well have been trying to move a mountain by sneezing on it over and over again. It didn't matter how long they'd worked together. It didn't matter how much Ben had been vindicated, even when he went against official policy or asked for forgiveness instead of permission. Take away the man inside the suit, and Ben would always be going into the boxing ring with the Chairman and the Board.

It ain't never gonna be enough, is it? No matter what I give, no matter what I sacrifice, no matter how much I prove myself, it's all gonna be ashes swept into a trashcan in the end. To them, we're all just means to an end.

193

Janitors ain't any more important than their mops. Maids ain't any more important than their brooms.

Ben tightened his grip on the mug handle enough for a knuckle to pop.

And the problem is, ol' Benny here knows all that, and he still can't give up bein' here, workin' day in and out. They know they gots me hooked. That I ain't never gonna walk away. Not until I get a clue about what happened to Karen. But to do that, I gotta get my powers back, and that ain't gonna happen unless I can get out there and do some real work!

Carl's bubbling made him realize he'd been standing there more than a few seconds, glowering so deep his eyebrows were getting sore. But deep inside, that flicker of power had grown into a sizzle. His hand shook, and he almost felt like he could make the water in the mug boil with a thought. Instead, he channeled that energy into a ball at his core, like he'd done so many times over the years, keeping an unforgiving hold on it. He imagined himself being at a carnival, holding a softball while Francis sat just across the way, perched on the seat of a dunking booth.

The thought made him chuckle, and the power he contained swelled ever-so-slightly.

Benny, ol' boy, mebbe you can give him a good show after all. Just don't you be missin'.

Ben lowered the shoulder of his missing arm, like a pitcher winding up for a fastball.

"You want proof, Francis? That whatcha really want?"

Francis shrugged. "I've made it clear what I require."

Ben gripped the mug tight and stepped one foot forward. "Then you can take your proof and shove it up your suggestion box, you dull and muddy-mettled rascal!"

As he raised the mug, Francis' eyes widened.

"Ben, wait, I can feel—"

Ben slung the mug at the Chairman's feet. Francis' aura flared as the mug shattered. Ben kept his arm outstretched, wringing out every drop of power he could summon, forcing it to act according to the vision he'd locked into his mind's eye.

Several patients and handyman cried out at the sudden crash and the unexpected brightness as Francis' aura momentarily bleached color from the room. Ben winced against the glare, but refused to let it distract him. Slowly, Francis restrained his power, and the two of them stared at the sight at his feet.

The mug had exploded into a dozen pieces, sharp shards that could've gouged skin and jabbed eyeballs out—if they weren't all contained by the half-sphere of water Ben had formed around the impact point. The liquid the mug had contained moments before now contained the mug's remains, including several fragments that poked partially through the shield.

Ben went to one knee as the effort caught up with him. He let his arm fall, and the watery globe splashed down with it, mug pieces clinking and splashing into the puddle in front of Francis. He gulped air and waited until his pulse stopped playing percussion in his ears before looking up.

Francis inspected him with dazed fascination. "Your powers. They are coming back."

Ben managed half a grin and licked dry lips. "Toldja so."

The handyman who'd inspected Sydney rushed over, hijab slightly askew, revealing a few inches of jet-black hair.

"What do you think you're doing?" she hissed through her teeth. "There are wounded here."

Ben braced his hand on a knee to push himself standing. "Just provin' a point."

She adjusted her hijab, eyes and hands flashing with a green aura. Turning, she swept a hand through the puddle, scooping up mug shards. In a matter of seconds, the mug was whole again in her grasp. She gripped the handle and whipped around, aiming it at his forehead. Ben jerked back, and the mug stopped a few inches from scrambling his face into a Picasso forgery.

The handyman glared at him with eyes sharp enough to make a hawk look like a cross-eyed dunderhead.

"If you don't leave here immediately, I will shatter this against your thick head. Then I will heal you, repair it again, and repeat as necessary until I declare you cured of your stupidity." She twitched the mug an inch closer. "Have I made *my* point?"

Ben leaned over just enough to see Francis, who looked as flummoxed as Ben felt.

"Howsabout we continue this little chat outside?"

"I believe that would be wise," Francis said.

Backing up slowly, Ben reached backward until he felt the door, which slid open on contact. Once safely out in the hall, he leaned against a wall, laughing softly to himself. He patted the spray bottle.

"Didja see that, buddy?"

Carl fizzed. *Why'd you leave? Things were just getting entertaining.*

Ben glared down at his partner. "You got a death wish for me or somethin'?"

Bubbles and swirls: *Absolutely not. You were with talented healers. You would've survived.*

"Mebbe. But probably not without addin' a few lumps to this here handsome kisser."

Francis followed moments later, walking a little faster than usual. Ben eyed him.

"She kicked you out, too?"

The Chairman straightened his hat. "I thought it prudent to remove myself to avoid disturbing their patients further." He caught Ben's look and returned a wry one. "I may run the Cleaners, but the handymen run Maintenance."

"I hear yah. They're the best at what they do, so let 'em do what they do best."

"Concise, as always."

"So speakin' of what a guy does best," Ben hitched his thumb through a belt loop, "was that proof enough?"

Francis shook his head ruefully. "Always so dramatic, Benjamin."

"Whenever you say my name like that, it always makin' me feel like I'm gonna get bent over your knee for a spankin'."

The Chairman raised a finger, mouth open to reply, hesitated, then lowered his hand. "I'm not even about to respond to that. I always seem to forget how much I regret giving you a way to challenge your situation, rather than simply encouraging you to accept it."

"Yeah. That ain't gonna happen anytime soon."

"Perhaps that's why I continue to give you those opportunities. To discover how you will beat the odds next. You have never ceased to surprise me."

Ben clapped him on the shoulder. "But you hate surprises, don'tcha? Muddies up all those reports."

It was Francis' turn to laugh low. "Oh, hardly. I have an entire department dedicated to processing unexpected documentation. As I learned early on, the only thing one can count on in this reality is the unexpected."

"Well, then you can keep countin' on me."

"I intend to. As far as this job is concerned—"

Francis' eyes widened. His pupils dilated just before his head snapped to the side. Ben looked that way, nerves tingling, but saw nothing but the opposite wall.

"What is it?" he asked. "Whatcha seein'?"

Francis looked back at him, eyes returning to normal. His features gained a sharpened quality, like a knife just drawn from its sheath.

"It's Jared's quarters. Dani. Lucy. Sydney. Somehow they've triggered the quarantine."

CHAPTER TWENTY

ani's hand went to her belt, seeking any tool she might use as a weapon. However, in her haste to confront Francis and then deal with Sydney's predicament, she'd left everything in her van. Even the Employee Handbook had been stashed back in her quarters for when she had the time to finally return to her studies.

Rookie mistake. How many times have people reminded me to keep something close by, even a squeegee?

Ella's face on Sydney's body was disturbing enough, but that his voice emerged from her lovely lips ramped up the creep factor.

"I didn't mean to interrupt," Ella said, looking between Dani and Lucy. "Please keep going. Things were just starting to get interesting."

"What've you done to Sydney?" Dani asked. As she spoke, she woke her power, which twisted and snarled inside her like a ravenous tiger waiting to pounce and maul the instant its cage was opened. She ground her teeth, keeping the bulk of it in check while sending cords of energy into the surroundings—and connected with nothing.

Right. She'd forgotten. They kept Jared's containment quarters cut off from any natural elements, with things like light and water provided magically so they couldn't be as easily tapped into for aggressive spell work. Of course, that never stopped him from demonstrating his unique powers, but it certainly hampered hers.

Only the air offered itself as a possible weapon. Dani latched onto this, but tensed to keep everything still for the moment. Whipping up a gale in such tight confines would threaten Lucy and Jared just as much as Ella.

Ella beamed at her. "Me? Oh, nothing. I've just been keeping an eye on all his misguided wanderings for a while. After all, when you care about someone, you want to make sure they're doing all right, don't you? Like when your crusty old friend was spying on you earlier."

"There's a big difference," Dani said. "I asked Ben to come along. I don't think Sydney would appreciate knowing you're hitching a ride."

Ella fluttered a hand. "What's it matter? We both know this isn't the real Sydney. At least, not his real body."

Dani caught Lucy's eye. The other woman made a subtle nod and sidestepped, mop still poised as she eased around to Ella's blindside. Dani gestured widely to try and keep the Scummoner focused on her.

"So that really is Sydney we've been dealing with?"

The Scummoner's laugh was far too airy for Sydney's voice, and it made Dani want to stuff soapy sponges in her ears.

"Of course it is, silly. Do you think even the best copy of the man would be able to pass off as the real thing? It'd be like trying to sell macaroni art as a newly discovered work by Leonardo Da Vinci."

She has a point, Dani thought.

"Where's his real body then? What'd you do with it?"

"Me?" Ella placed a hand to her—or Sydney's—chest. "Why do you have to keep blaming me for all this? I'm just the artist. He provided plenty of raw material for me to work with. I'd hate to see it all go to waste. Just because he doesn't appreciate the beauty of my craft doesn't mean I'll stop the work. He'll come around in the end. One way or another."

Lucy had moved behind the Scummoner by then, one slow step at a time. Ella seemed to have forgotten all about the other janitor, but Dani still moved closer, hands spread to keep the insane artist fixed on her.

"One way or another?" she asked. "What does that mean? What's happening to him?"

"It doesn't concern you," Ella said. "Just leave him to me and I promise I'll take good care of him."

"Look, I know what he did to you," Dani said. "I know how he treated you. The pain he put you in. I'm kind of like you, that way. We have something in common."

The woman's expression and voice turned cold. "Don't pretend you know anything. We have nothing in common. You're just the latest in a string of playthings he toys with until he either breaks you or gets bored and moves on. Only I ever really meant anything to him. Only I ever really understood him, even when he didn't understand himself." Ella sighed, sounding sad for her. "That's the difference between us, Dani. You still pretend that what he's shown you isn't true. When I was with him, he helped me see the world for what it actually is. But right when I was ready to give everything over to what he stood for, he backed off, too scared of commitment. That was what hurt most, that I truly believed, only to realize he didn't. Now he's trying to lie to himself all over again." She lifted her arms and studied them as if they were alien limbs. "He doesn't deserve the kind of power he was given. That's why I came back. To help him."

Dani frowned. "Help him how?"

Ella cocked a hip, one arm bracing the other as she tapped her cheek. "By relieving him of the responsibility he no longer wants to have. He's a bit like a child, haven't you noticed? Wanting all the fun but none of the consequences. But it's time for him to grow up, and I'm here to—"

Ella stumbled and her chest bulged as a mop head punched through it. Lucy shouted from the other side. "Got her, girlie! Do your thing."

Dani started to conjure as potent, yet small, a whirlwind as she could, aiming to spiral it into a focused vortex. Maybe if she dispersed Sydney's body enough it'd break whatever possessing spell Ella obviously had on him—and still let him reform like he had after Rafi's attack.

But before Dani could summon more than a rough breeze, Ella snapped an arm back. It bent at the shoulder joint as if boneless, and everything from the elbow down turned into a column of sand. This broadened and shot out like a battering ram, hitting Lucy in the chest. The janitor flew backward and slammed into a toy shelf, while sand continued to pump out from Ella's arm, pinning her in place. Worse, the dust holding her increased, building up toward Lucy's head as the woman writhed and tried to break free. She'd be smothered in moments.

As she kept Lucy pinned, Ella stared down at the mop impaling her. Sand filled in the cavity it had created. Gripping the metal handle just below the head, she smiled at Dani.

"Excuse me for a moment."

Her hand turned into a yellow blur, like a buzz saw made of sand. A high-pitched whine lanced through Dani's ears, and she winced as sparks flew.

With the Scummoner distracted, Dani brought cupped hands together, holding them a few inches apart. She drew as much air as she could contain into her hands. Her breaths turned shallow and dizziness assaulted her balance as the air within the room turned noticeably thinner, but she fought past this and kept her grip on the growing mini-cyclone between her palms.

She poured more power into it until every air molecule seemed to vibrate in her grip, threatening to scour the skin off her bones the instant she lost control.

The Scummoner's hand returned to normal, and she plucked up the mop head, the shaft sheered through to leave a stump a few inches long. The rest of the handle clanged to the floor behind her.

With a cry, Dani thrust her hands out and launched the cyclone straight at Ella. The Scummoner raised her head and her eyes widened just as the concentrated air hit her like a cannonball.

The blast struck Sydney's body and exploded in a cloud of dust that billowed through the room with stinging force. Toys and books went flying to all corners. The spaceship lamp on the bedside table shattered into powder. Posters shredded and the lights flickered before stabilizing.

Dani sucked in a breath, but then choked as dust scratched and tickled her lungs. She bent over, hacking, but each attempt to recover just drew in more. She covered her mouth and tried to filter air between her fingers, wishing she'd had the foresight to bring a dust mask. Her throat and sinuses burned, and a smell of salt and decay clogged the air.

A cloud filled the room, creating a grainy haze that made Dani's eyes water. She couldn't make out anything more than an arm's length in front of her, though she thought she saw a vague figure still standing just out of reach.

Then, with a quiver, all the dust dropped to the floor at once. What stood in the center of the room looked more like a dust devil than anything human—though devoid of the constructs' usual horned features. Grit and sand swirled across the surface of the humanoid figure, which still clutched the mop head in one hand.

Its head tilted slightly, and Dani sensed it focusing on her. A second later, Ella's face popped back out on the front of the head, like a mask slipped into place. She breathed deep, as if having woken up from a delightful nap.

"How unique," she said. "And I do love unique experiences."

Lucy remained stuck to the wall, now with just her nose and eyes visible through the sand pile continuing to glom onto her. Her gaze fixed on Dani, shining with both fear and determination. Even though Lucy couldn't so much as budge, Dani could easily hear her saying: *Do what you have to, girlie.*

Dani hunched, hands cupped again as she began to create another mini-cyclone. *Let's see how many of these she can take.*

Ella frowned in disappointment. "Repeating yourself? Boring. Try to be a little more creative. See how I've got your friend out of the picture so easily? I could do the same to you, but I'd rather use my imagination a little."

She lashed out with the mop head. Her arm extended several feet further than should've been possible, curling around to strike Dani from the side. The mop whipped into her shoulder and sent her stumbling. She caught herself on a shelf and turned just as another strike came in—this time leading with the severed handle.

Dani screamed as the metal stump struck her straight in the sternum. The hit sent a shockwave down her spine and up into her skull; her cry cut off as she choked on the pain. She tried to pull away, but Ella kept the handle grinding into her, held in place by inhuman strength.

Dani clawed for purchase, sweeping action figures to the floor. She kicked and stomped, but her boots swept through nothing or thumped uselessly against the floor. Her power fled as her concentration broke.

"See?" Ella's voice had an underlying hiss to it now, like serpent scales gliding over hot sand. "Isn't this much more interesting? I wonder if I carve enough of you away, what beauty would I reveal?"

The pressure on Dani's chest increased until everything felt on the verge of popping like an over-inflated balloon.

Then Jared's cry echoed through her head. *"Leave them alone!"*

A jet of flame roared just in front of Dani, turning the mop to ash and leaving a jagged, glassy clump at the end of Ella's arm. The sudden release of pressure dropped Dani to her knees. Gasping for breath, clutching the giant bruise that was her chest, she turned her head to the flaming, smoking figure standing in the corner at the foot of the bed.

A pair of green-gold eyes peered out from the form, flickering like glowing gemstones. Jared raised fists with black-and-red skin glowing like magma. He punched toward Lucy, and another spear of fire shot out from his hand. It melted the column of sand and snapped it off. The pile that had formed over Lucy collapsed, and she flopped to the floor. From across the room, Dani couldn't tell if she moved or breathed.

"You should be nice to others', Jared said, stepping out of his sandbox. His bare feet left char marks on the floor. *"If you aren't nice, you get a timeout."*

"Jared." Dani tried to reach out to him but her shoulders and chest spasmed. *"Be careful."*

Ella turned Sydney's body to face Jared, but Dani could still see the smile broadening on her displaced face.

"There you are, you impossible little boy," she said. "Aren't you cute? But naughty, too."

"I'm not a bad boy. I'm a good boy."

"Hasn't anyone taught you that it's not polite to hit a lady?"

"But you are a bad lady! Let my uncle go!"

"Your uncle has been bad as well," Ella said.

"Maybe. But he's trying to be good now."

"It doesn't matter what he's trying to do," Ella said, with another light laugh. "He is what he is, and he must do what he must do. Just like you."

The boy hesitated. *"What do you mean?"*

"Aww." Ella held a hand out as if to cup Jared's cheek, though he remained well out of reach. "It's okay to be confused. You'll understand in time. And then you'll look back and realize I was right all along."

"I don't like you. I want you to go away."

Ella shook her head in disapproval. "She was right. You do need to be taught better manners."

Even with a head made out of fire, Jared's confusion still came through clear enough. *"She? She who?"*

"Jared." Dani coughed and spat to clear her throat at last. "Don't listen to her. She's just trying to confuse and trick you. She's Scum."

"Just like Sydney is Scum," Ella said. She waved at Jared. "Just like your father turned out to be. So, what does that make you, you impossible little boy?"

"I'm ..." Jared's fiery form dimmed, smoke occluding his features for a moment. *"I'm up past my bedtime, and I want you to go away so I can brush my teeth and Dani can read me a story!"*

The ember glow of his skin flared bright enough that Dani had to squint to not be dazzled. His form split down the middle, one half remaining fire while the other shifted into water. Steam rose where the halves met, but evaporated too quickly to cloud the room again.

He raised his hands and made a grabbing motion. Deep within both the water and the flames, Dani glimpsed cords of both white and dark purple energy twining about, a web of power that filled the boy's entire being. Threads of this Pure and Corrupt energy shot out and jabbed into Sydney's head, burrowing in.

Ella's dark eyes went wide, and her lips parted in a shocked scream—one that went on and on, until it rang in Dani's ears like sirens.

Dani staggered to her feet and yelled through the noise. "What're you doing, Jared?"

The boy's mental voice lowered an octave and his words plopped into her mind like ice cubes. *"Helping Uncle Sid. She's hurting him. I'm hurting her back."*

"No, Jared!" Dani waved her arms, unable to get closer to the searing power strung between Jared and Ella. "Stop it. You shouldn't be doing this!"

He looked at her, confusion gleaming even in his gem-like eyes. *"But she's been bad. Doesn't that mean she needs to be punished?"*

"Yes, but ..." Dani groped for a rationale, even as Ella's screams continued to claw at her mind. The woman sounded like she was being torn apart. Maybe it was fitting for the level of destruction she'd caused, but if Jared started lashing out at any perceived threat, using his powers to cause pain whenever he wanted, then where would he stop? How soon before even those closest to him were seen as deserving punishment for supposedly behaving badly?

"But it has to be by the people who are in charge, Jared!" she cried. "It has to be done right. The Cleaners will take care of her.

The heat in the room rose, and Dani had to shield her face from Jared's molten body. At the same time, the hissing from his watery side added a hellish soundtrack alongside Ella's tortured shrieks. Fresh steam plumed from the boy, and Dani dropped to her hands and knees to let the hot cloud gust overhead.

"I don't want her hurting Uncle Sid."

"Then just make her leave," Dani said. "You can do that, can't you? This is your room. She's not allowed to have playtime here. So make her leave, but keep Sydney here."

The bedroom had become the Devil's own sauna, with Jared barely visible now among the boiling clouds of steam. Only the flickering of his body through the mist let Dani know where he stood, while Ella's cries pinpointed her easily enough.

Then the crackling and hissing and screaming and bubbling all dropped away at once, leaving Dani's ears feeling hollowed out. A new noise filled the silence: that of a deep, indrawn breath, one that went on far longer than it should've before popping lungs.

The steam swirled and spun in on itself into a gray vortex that dwindled down into a tight funnel, like a horizontal tornado. Dani blinked droplets from her eyes to see Jared sucking the cloud straight into his mouth until the last wisps disappeared. His lips sealed, and his watery half bubbled, while his fiery side flared.

Across from him, Ella tottered where she stood, looking dazed. Jared went up to her and scowled.

"Go away, and never come back."

Her eyelids fluttered. She blinked and focused on him, her smile returning as if nothing at all had happened. "You are going to be so much fun."

He grabbed her face and yanked. Ella's grinning features elongated, nose stretching out like Pinocchio had sworn the earth was flat in a court of law. She managed a last few slurred words as

"Bad boy. Very bad boy …"

Her face tore away from Sydney's head like a mask. The instant it did, her expression went slack and lifeless. Jared turned and flung the scrap against the wall, where it shattered into pieces like clay shards. Dani imagined Ella's tinkling laugh even as the fragments clinked to the floor.

Sydney's body tumbled to the ground, limbs splayed.

"Uncle Sid!" Jared knelt by the entropy mage and shook him.

Dani ran to Lucy, but the woman groaned and sat up just as she reached her. Lucy fixed on Sydney right away.

"Is he …?"

"It was Ella," Dani said. "Not Sydney. Jared took care of her. We're safe now."

Lucy puffed a laugh. "Never going to be safe so long as he's around."

Dani frowned, unsure if she spoke of Sydney, Jared, or both. She braced and hauled the janitor to her feet. But right as Lucy regained her balance, a deep green glow suffused the walls and cast the whole place in an emerald hue.

"What's happening?" Dani asked.

"Quarantine." Lucy turned a circle, eyeing the ceiling and walls. "Whatever went down triggered the wards here. We're about to get put on ice for a bit until the Board can announce the all-clear."

"$%#&@$#," Dani said. "Can't they tell it's already over?"

"Company procedure. Better safe than sorry."

Dani grabbed the woman's shoulder. "Can't you override it or something?

"We're already inside it. Just hold your breath and we'll wake back up in Maintenance in a while." She eyed the walls. "Hopefully."

Dani cringed, anticipating the highly unpleasant sensation from her last experience with quarantine. The energy drew inward, forming a sphere that rapidly shrank to contain them.

As it did, Jared stood, fists at his side.

"But I was good. I don't want a timeout!"

"It's okay, Jared," Dani said. "It'll just be temporary and then they'll let us out once—"

"No! I was good! I won't!"

He grabbed at the air above his head. A thread of green energy broke away from the shrinking sphere and came into his grasp. He yanked.

The emerald energies condensed, the surrounding cloud congealing into streamers of power that writhed apart. With a sound like water swirling down a drain, the quarantine spell funneled down into Jared's waiting hand. They condensed there into a bright ball of raw power.

Jared studied this as if holding a new toy. Then he clenched his hand, and when he uncurled his fingers, the energy had vanished, and the room remained as normal—despite the mess of toys now scattered about.

"Oh, Purity save us," Lucy whispered.

"I take it that's not supposed to happen," Dani whispered back.

"Nope. He just defused a spell put in place by the Board. They're not going to be happy about that."

Jared faced them, a grave look making him seem far older than the teenage boy he seemed to be. A moment later, he smiled.

"Dani, I'm tired. Can I have a bedtime story?"

The bedroom door burst open, Francis and Ben charged in, followed by the Ascendants who'd been guarding the room. They all halted on seeing the three standing, with Sydney on the floor, missing a face.

"Glad you could make it," Dani said, wiping damp hair off her brow. "I was about to order room service."

"What happened?" Francis asked. "The quarantine activated but then appeared to disperse. But I don't believe the Board authorized its deactivation."

"Jared happened." Dani indicated the kid with her eyes, while also giving Francis and Ben a warning look to not press the issue right then and there. Not in front of the boy. "But who did what and why isn't important, right now. We need to get Sydney back to Maintenance and—"

A rasping gasp made her jump as Sydney's body arched. His face reformed, mouth gaping as he sucked in a deep breath. He lurched upright and planted hands on the floor to catch himself.

Lucy hopped back. "For Purity's sake! I thought he was dead."

The Ascendants had taken up posts inside the door, and they too tensed as the entropy mage reanimated, but Francis gestured for them to stand down.

"Yeah," Ben drawled. "He's provin' about as easy to kill as a mutant cockroach."

"Bad analogy," Dani muttered, though Lucy seemed accepting enough of the comparison.

Sydney looked at each of them in turn. "Did I miss something?"

Ben tapped the side of his own head. "You, uh, got somethin' on your face there."

Sydney cocked an eyebrow. "Should I assume it is something other than the normal array of prepackaged features?"

Dani peered closer and realized Ben was right. A dozen tiny splotches marked Sydney's skin, looking like flecks of glass. They glinted when he moved, but otherwise remained almost invisible unless pointed out.

That must be where Jared struck him. What was he doing to Ella?

She glanced at Jared. The boy stared at the floor, as if ashamed. She went over to him to get a closer look. He remained split between the two elements, with water on his right side. But the previously fiery portion had cooled and hardened into what now looked like gray stone. She touched his back lightly and, on finding it cool, put her arm around his shoulders.

"Must be a side effect of Ella taking control," she said.

"Ella?" Francis asked. "She was here?"

Dani nodded at Sydney. "She ... well ... I guess she projected herself through Sydney. His sand body was linked to her somehow, and she was using it to spy on us."

"Was?" The Chairman eyed Sydney with fresh suspicion.

"Yes, was." Dani squeezed Jared in encouragement. "Jared was trying to help Uncle Sid and sensed her presence. He exposed her, and she attacked, so he kicked her out. I think that's what activated quarantine."

"Uncle Sid?" Ben grinned. "Oh, I'm gonna get mileage outta this one."

"Focus, Ben," Lucy said.

"You're certain she's gone?" Francis asked.

"*She is.*" The Ascendants twitched as Jared's voice wove through the room. "*I made her leave here forever. She can't ever come back. But I don't know where she went. I'm sorry.*"

"Nothing to be sorry about," Dani said. "You were awesome. A real hero."

He smiled tentatively up at her and pressed closer.

Francis didn't appear appeased. "This complicates things. Depending on how long she was using Sydney's current state to observe us, she might've studied the situation from within HQ. If she's aware that we're aware of who she is and her activities, it might accelerate whatever timetable she has set. We need to determine where she is as soon as possible, before she can slip away ... if it's not already too late."

"I know where she is." They all turned as Sydney rose on wobbly legs. "She's at the strip mall," he said. "Lying low at her old gallery. It's closed down now, but she broke in easily enough. There's an abandoned construction site where they were remodeling part of the mall before most of it closed. Lots of raw earth for her to work with. She's been using an old and rather decrepit porta-potty left there to get around Denver, with a recall spell in place."

Ben started to make whirring engine noises until Lucy smacked him silent.

Dani waved at the half-wrecked room. "I'd hardly call this lying low. And how do you know all that?"

He scratched at the glassy spots on his temples. "Whatever connection she had with me must have gone both ways. When she took over this body ..." He pressed a palm to the glassy spots on his head. "I must've received a sense of her location in return, as well as picked up on some of her surface thoughts about the past couple days."

Francis checked something in his notebook and nodded. "I'll start assembling a team to accompany the rest of you to confront Ms. Zhang while I monitor the operation from here."

"Come on," Lucy said. "He just nearly got us killed and we're going to keep trusting he's not leading us right into another trap?"

"Lucy," Dani began, but Sydney held a hand her way.

"One moment, if you'd please, lovely one. Allow me."

She gave him the stink eye for the misplaced term of endearment, but backed up a step, clearing the way between her and Lucy.

Sydney moved to stand before the janitor. He looked down on her sadly, while she looked up at him with murder in her eyes.

"I know you hate me, janitor," he said, in a voice so soft Dani had to strain to hear. "I know you despise me. I know you and many of those here at HQ think I'm a monster. Maybe I am. I don't really seem to know myself anymore. But there is one thing I do know." He briefly scrubbed a hand over his forehead. "I am tired. Tired of feeling like nothing but a source of pain and destruction. Tired of being seen as nothing more than Entropy's lapdog. And tired of being hunted by those I would rather fight beside once more."

Lucy's face scrunched up in doubt, but Sydney didn't flinch.

"You want me gone? Very well. I will let you do what you wish to eliminate me. If you want to put me into a furnace and melt me down to embers, then I will let you."

"Sydney ..." Dani began, but his glance signaled for her to stay quiet a moment longer.

"I will let you do whatever you feel will bring any sort of justice for the wrongs I've committed." He tapped fingers to a temple, where the sand forming him had been fused to glass. "But only after I help you defeat Ella."

Lucy's deepening frown rumpled her cheeks. "Why insist on joining us for that? If you really wanted to prove you're trying to put aside all the old, bad blood, why not just stand in the corner and wait until this is all over? Let us handle Scum like we're supposed to and don't get in our way."

"I feel it's necessary for me to stay involved," Sydney said. "I am your one and only connection to her. Without me, you're fighting blind. With me, you have some sense of her, and perhaps a weapon you might use against her, if all else fails." He didn't quite smile at Jared, but his glance at the boy held a shade of consideration. "I believe my nephew when he says he removed her connection to me, however it was forged. But should she appear again in this form, I hope you'll take the advantage of attacking her directly through me. In fact, I highly recommend being prepared to do so."

"I'll be the first in line," Lucy said. "Fine. You want to try to make up for what you've done? Be my guest. But whatever happens with Ella, don't think anything is going to spare you from the consequences. I will see you pay."

He bowed and made as if to take her hand and kiss it, but she backed up, glowering.

However, when Sydney started to rise, his torso sagged as if a rubber band had suddenly replaced his spine. He dropped to hands and knees, a couple fingers turning to dust on impact.

"Uncle Sid!"

Jared broke free of Dani and ran to Sydney's side, trying to support his shoulders.

Is it bad, Dani wondered, *that I don't find it odd to be seeing a half-stone, half-water boy hugging a man made of sand? My "normal" threshold is so totally off base.*

Sydney coughed, and dust spewed from between his lips. "It seems you may not have to worry about what to do with me after all. I am having ..." He grimaced and shuddered. "Difficulty keeping myself together." Half his face blurred and started to slide off in a grainy slab. He pushed it back into place, but then his arm drooped as well, joints going soft and the colors across his flesh and clothes starting to run.

Francis had his radio out. "I need a handyman to the hybrid's containment unit, immediately. We have rapid decomposition on our hands and—"

"*It'll be too late,*" Jared said. "*We have to do something right now.*"

"Like what?" Dani asked.

The kid straightened, though he kept one hand on Sydney's back. "*I have an idea. Maybe it can save him, or at least stop this until we can figure out what's causing it. We need a mommy.*"

Dani and Ben shared a concerned look. Did the kid mean his mother, Filth? Sydney had summoned her once before, but she doubted the Corrupt Petty would respond to a call for help from within the Cleaner HQ itself. "Jared, I don't think your mother would really be available right now."

He shook his head. "*No, not mommy. Mommy!*"

Dani looked at Ben again, but he just made a single-shoulder shrug.

"Sorry, kiddo. Still not gettin' whatcha mean."

Jared ran into the bathroom, returning a moment later with a roll of toilet paper, which he handed to Ben.

"Uh ... thanks?" Ben held it up to look at Sydney through the tube. "But I'm thinkin' he's needin' a bit more than a bathroom break."

Jared knocked fists on his head, one side splashing, the other clacking stone against stone. Then he perked up and dashed over to where a selection of comic books had been scattered during his fight with Ella. He sifted through these until he came up with one in particular and displayed the cover. It was partially shredded, but enough of the art remained for Dani to get a clear idea of what it had shown.

"Oh." With the tiniest smile, she went and plucked the toilet paper from Ben's hand. "I think I get what you mean. He's going to hate this, you know."

CHAPTER
TWENTY-ONE

This is utterly humiliating," Sydney said, from his seat in the back of Dani's van.

"Shush," Dani said, keeping her focus on the road. "It worked, didn't it?"

He muttered a reply. She glanced in the rearview mirror, but he remained swathed in shadows, sitting alongside one of the Ascendants Francis had sent along for the job—a recently promoted young man named Wilton who kept glancing nervously at the entropy mage. The Ascendant's aura remained inactive, partly to preserve Dani's night vision as she drove and partly to avoid broadcasting their approach to Ella, should she be sensitive to such things.

Lucy sat in the passenger seat, taking so much care to avoid looking behind her that she might as well have been wearing horse blinders. She stared at the van ahead of them, its dented fender and rusted spots marking it as Ben's. Dani had been surprised when Francis included her friend and mentor on the team, alongside another Ascendant and a plumber, who rode with him.

Dani stifled a yawn and pushed her tiredness aside. How long since she'd last slept? Seemed like ages ago that she'd been preparing for her date ordeal with Sydney, and now here they were, riding in to try and save the city from a madwoman. Couldn't things ever be simple?

Probably not, where the Cleaners are concerned. But, hey, at least I'll never be bored. Better dead than bored out of my mind all the time. Dani paused, rethinking that inner declaration. *Hang on. Those are my two options? Bored or dead? I might need to find a little middle ground there.*

Francis' voice came over several radios at once.

"We're still searching for viable glassway anchors, both within the structure and nearby, in case we need to send in reinforcements. Unfortunately, because of its mostly empty state, much of the property hasn't received proper maintenance and cleaning in some time, so its windows are too dirty to allow us access."

"What about bathroom mirrors?" Lucy radioed back.

"Cracked or missing."

"All of them in the whole strip?" Dani asked. "That seems strange."

Lucy relayed this to the Chairman.

"Not strange," he said. *"Likely deliberate, either on Ms. Zhang's part when she reclaimed the space or by other Scum who wished to use the property as a safe haven."*

"You think we could run into other Scum besides her?" Dani asked.

"Unknown," Francis replied. *"If there are, they are likely of middling consequence compared to our Scummoner target."*

Dani grinned at his using the term she'd created. Maybe she just had to learn to take satisfaction in the small achievements when it came to this job.

Wilton tabbed his own radio on. "What about normal people, sir? Should we be expecting many bystanders?"

"Doubtful, Ascendant Wilton. There are only a few shops and offices that remain active, mostly under the property owner's purview. And at this hour, I wouldn't anticipate anything being open to draw customers in the first place."

Ben's voice filled the channel. *"Francis, I don't reckon you got a preference about whether we drag this chickadee back kickin' and screamin' or in a buncha little pieces?"*

"If she can be bagged-and-tagged and safely brought into the Recycling Center for detainment and questioning, that would be ideal," Francis said. *"However, she has shown no compunction against using lethal force, and our*

priority is to keep her from unleashing another one of these deserts. Do what you must."

"*Roger that.*" Static fizzled for a moment before he spoke up again. "*Whoopsies. Didn't mean to call you Roger, Francis. My bad.*"

Dani and Lucy shared an eye-roll.

"He's in a fine mood," Dani said.

"He thinks his powers are coming back," Lucy said.

Dani started. "What? Because of that whole water ambush thing he's been putting himself through? I didn't think that was serious."

Lucy slumped back in her seat. "Not sure, but he must've convinced the Chairman of something, otherwise I can't imagine why he'd be going with us for this."

"But that's ... that's incredible!" Dani thumped the steering wheel lightly.

"Don't get your hopes up." Lucy plunked an elbow down on her armrest. "Knowing Ben, he's just mistaking having a little gas as his old power."

"Then why would Francis agree to let him come with us? You know how protective he's tried to be."

Lucy eyed her. "Because it's Ben and he rarely gives up unless he gets his way? Francis might've just figured it wasn't worth the trouble."

"Well, I'll be hopeful for once. It'd be awesome to really work with him again."

Lucy laughed shortly. "You say that now ..."

"Marvelous," Sydney said. "Just as my powers and fortune wane, his appears to wax."

Lucy finally twisted around to scowl at him. "Quit bellyaching. You should feel lucky just to be alive."

Sydney sighed and shuffled in place. "I'm not sure exactly which category of luck this condition places me in. There are some who might beg to be put out of such misery."

"You just have to ask." Lucy patted a toilet scrubber hooked on her belt.

The entropy mage sniffed loudly. "Please. I'm not such a weak soul that I'd quail at mere pain. I intend to see this through, however agonizing it is for both my body and my dignity."

"Could be worse," Dani said.

"Enlighten me as to how that could be."

She caught a glint of his blue eyes in the mirror. "We could be carrying you in a bucket."

He looked aside. "I suppose you have a point."

Ben turned down a side street and Dani followed, the vans lumbering through Denver's suburban outskirts. The huge half-bowl of the Broncos football stadium loomed in the distance, swathed in shadows that made it look like a strange temple to the god of concussions and tailgating. The downtown Denver skyline formed its own miniature mountain range, twinkling like rimed peaks despite the gloom. The vans passed block after block of condos and row houses, most dark with the occasional illuminated window indicating an early riser. Lampposts splashed light across the streets, and Dani spotted a couple joggers panting their way along the sidewalk, breath frosting the air with every other step.

Weirdos, she thought. *Who in their right mind would get up at such an ungodly hour to punish their body like that? You've got beds, people. Use them while you can.*

She stifled a yawn and reached for her coffee thermos, which sat in the cup holder next to Lucy's. Dani's thermos already contained enough bitter brew to keep a whole army awake after a thousand-mile march, but it looked like a gecko standing next to Godzilla when compared to Lucy's enormous container. Dani glanced over at the janitor.

I don't understand how she slurps down so much coffee without having to sprint to the restroom every five seconds. I mean, unless she wears diapers or—

Dani hastily knocked her thoughts off that track and focused on driving. Just driving. Nothing else but the road and the job. Definitely not diapers.

The sky had lightened by the time the strip mall came in sight, with the first rays of sunlight slicing their way through thinning shadows. The vans turned into one of the lot entrances, passing raised concrete basins that might've once held bushes or flowers, but now contained little more than dirt mounds and a single withered aspen tree, bare of leaves.

The strip mall boasted the name Lowry's Landing. In its prime, which Dani guessed to be at least a decade or two prior, it must've housed a few dozen shops and restaurants. Concrete walkways ringed several central parking areas. This was further surrounded by the old shops themselves, two stories of dingy taupe-spackled fronts and faux brick façades crammed around large windows, their empty darkness broken up by sporadic Space for Lease or leftover Everything Must Go! placards tacked and taped to the glass.

As they drove in, Dani saw only a few shops which looked to be in business on either floor: a small clothing exchange and thrift store, and a candle store, of all things, that boasted its stock of Every Fragrance Imaginable!

I wonder if they have the raw sewage or blot-hound barf scents. Or the refreshing scent of bleach. Maybe I could start that as a side business. Cleaners Candles, bringing you the totally authentic smells of Purity and Corruption.

They parked the vans around the nearest corner, where a pair of small alleys cut one of the main mall buildings into quarters. Dumpsters, electrical boxes, and piles of trash lined these alleys, with employee back entrances spaced out evenly along the way. A few hundred yards from where they stopped, a large portion of a mall section had been demolished, leaving foundation and piping exposed amongst a tiny forest of steel and concrete pillars that would've once been hidden by drywall or other decorative elements. The foundation led off into a construction site that was surrounded by a low chain-link fence, marked by orange and yellow sheets of plastic. Mounds of earth and gravel filled the space within, with more exposed piping jutting out here and there.

Across the street, a few early commuters pulled cars up to the pumps of a gas station, while one patron steered toward the car wash off in a corner of the lot.

Shutting the van off, Dani reached back and grabbed a dustpan and hand broom, along with a large bottle of sani-gel, which she tucked into a zippered pants pocket. She and Lucy exchanged looks, and the other woman nodded. Technically, Francis had Lucy in charge of this job, with the Ascendants along to monitor and intervene if their power was needed.

"Scan the area," Lucy said.

Dani hopped out of the driver's seat and went into a crouch, pressing a palm to the asphalt. As she took a deep whiff of the chilly

219

morning air, she also let her power seep out into the elements, gauging the potential for any local disaster she could cause if the situation called for it.

Until then, she'd never realized abandonment had a smell. The strip mall reeked of it—a combination of stale air, a hint of sweet rot, a chemical tang she couldn't quite identify, and, of course, all of it heavy with the stink of dust.

Even the elements responded to the touch of her power lethargically. Cords of Pure energy wove out from her into the earth, but the ground seemed oddly sludgelike, not so easily shifted or cracked apart. Flickers of electricity sparked through a few sets of shop wiring, but much of it appeared to be cut off, as was much of the water in the piping.

Dani felt certain nobody had really cared for this place in a long, long while. It all felt so sad and worn out, like opening a closet to see a decades-old wedding dress hanging there, faded and moth-eaten, never to be worn again. She could almost hear the place moaning as the life ebbed out of it after years of neglect, and she fought a strange impulse to press herself to the ground in a full-body hug to comfort the area at large.

Dani blinked and rolled her shoulders back, pulling her hand away from the ground. As she did, the aching, longing sensation faded, leaving her with a hollow feeling in her stomach.

Great. I'm thinking about trying to give a strip mall a hug so it doesn't feel lonely. For Purity's sake, I must be more tired than I thought.

She expanded her energies, searching through the nearby shops, seeking any hint of Corrupt energies. There was definitely a nasty vibe to the area, but she couldn't tell if it came from any real Scum lying in wait, or just the mall's dilapidation and her paranoia. She pushed further, until the energies began to thin, reaching the limits of how far she could extend them. At last, she drew it all back in, leaving a ball of power pulsing within herself, eager to be unleashed the moment she set it free.

She brought her radio up and signaled the team.

"No immediate threat. Everybody out and ready for action."

The sliding doors on both vans opened. Dani's rolled smoothly on oiled tracks, but she winced as Ben's rattled and slammed back against the frame, the metallic echo sounding like a gunshot in the crisp air.

Lucy and Wilton emerged. The Ascendant wore the usual white three-piece suit, relying on the raw power of his aura as both an offensive and defensive measure. Lucy, on the other hand, had her toilet scrubber, sponges, a new mop, and steel wool gloves readily available in her jumpsuit's various pouches. A holstered spray bottle full of bleach sat on one hip, and a chanted squeegee hung from a cord on the other.

Ben unfolded from his seat and retrieved a mop of his own from the shelving in the back of his van. The metal tip had been outfitted with Taser nodes, and Carl burbled in his usual place. The other Ascendant—whose name Dani had missed—joined Wilton, while the plumber, a heavyset, bearded man called Laurence checked over his plunger and the drain snake looped over one shoulder.

Dani sized them up, and then realized they were missing someone. She rapped the side of her van with her knuckles. "I mean everybody."

Sydney's sigh resounded from inside. "Must I?"

"If you don't get out here right now," she said, "I'm sending the van through the car wash with the windows down."

A hand bound in coils of toilet paper gripped the side of the door. Sydney pulled himself into view. The toilet paper wrap continued down his arm, the tissue panels stamped with a hint of flowery embroidering. Several layers of toilet paper covered his entire body until only hints of his physical form could be glimpsed between the bands. After being secured, the wrappings had then been tended to by a handyman, who had enchanted the paper to be as strong as nylon while retaining its flexibility. Jared pitched in as well, though the handyman was at a loss to explain exactly what the kid's touch and outpouring of energy had infused the paper with. The theory was that while Sydney's sand form couldn't be cured at the moment, it could at least be reinforced, keeping him together long enough for them to complete the job.

It also made him look like a mummy. Specifically, a cheap, Halloween mummy decoration that had staggered off somebody's lawn, fleeing in shame from trick-or-treating children who'd laughed at its spindly frame.

Sydney stepped down from the van, trying to display his usual poise and slouch to avoid being too noticeable at the same time. The toilet paper hid most of his face, but his eyes still expressed plenty of longsuffering, and his lips appeared permanently twisted in a sour knot. His wrappings fluttered slightly in the pre-dawn breeze.

"Satisfied with the spectacle?" he asked.

Dani couldn't quite contain her giggle, but tried to turn it into clearing her throat. By his deadpan look, Sydney hardly bought the attempt.

"It's a good look for you," she said. "Can't go with tuxes and suits all the time. Maybe you'll start a new trend."

"Not exactly the sort of legacy I was hoping to leave this world." He swept a trailing end of toilet paper over his shoulder like a scarf. "Still, one makes do with the materials available."

"Which way to the gallery?" Lucy asked.

He pointed toward the far side of the building they'd parked alongside. "Upstairs and just around the corner. It used to be between a jewelry store and some little boutique that sold designer handbags." He frowned at Dani. "You're sure you didn't sense anything amiss?"

"There's something weird about this place, for sure," Dani said, "but I don't detect a specific threat."

Lucy scratched at her arm before getting her toilet scrubber ready and slipping her steel wool glove on her right hand. "All right. Sydney, you're in front with me and Dani. Ben, keep Laurence company and watch our sides. Wilton and Hovitt, you've got our backs. Let's keep this quick and quiet."

"You betcha," Ben said, just a little too loudly. He shook his broom over his head. "Let's get this Scummoner done and buried deep."

They moved into formation, keeping the pace slow enough to scan the area while not becoming sitting targets. The Ascendants let their auras wink on, ever so slightly, to shield themselves from attacks while no doubt also remaining sensitive to any lurking

Corrupt energies. Ben had Carl's bottle in hand, pointing it this way and that like a one-armed sheriff trying to smoke out some cattle rustlers.

Dani eyed the dark windows as they passed, keeping an eye on their reflections. Certain Scum had shown the ability to pass through darkened mirrors, a perverted form of the glassways the Cleaners used. Hopefully they wouldn't encounter any blackshards this time. She couldn't see well into any of the vacant stores, and their reflections coasted over the dusty glass like ghosts made of static.

Easing up the nearest set of stairs, the group reached the second floor and headed in the direction Sydney indicated. Dani noted how Lucy watched the entropy mage just as much as she did their surroundings.

She's got some major trust issues, Dani thought. *Though I suppose if you were being forced to work alongside someone you thought was basically a serial killer, you wouldn't exactly want to let your guard down.*

She kept her power shifting through the area, but if Ella was nearby, she kept her own energies well concealed.

They turned slowly around a corner and everyone stopped on catching the sight ahead.

Sydney waved at a particular shopfront. "Er ... well, there it—"

"We got eyes, bucko," Ben said. "I ain't thinkin' we gotta guess where we're headin'."

The front of a small store had a glittering banner strung across it, with WELCOME! in shining foil letters. Balloons had been tied to the door and nearby railings. And if that wasn't enough evidence, the central window had been heavily scratched, as if by some power tool. The graded scratchings formed the image of Ella's heart-shaped face smiling out at them.

Dani fed a cord of power into the glass, testing it for a trap, poised to shatter it with a minor quake if needed.

A voice suddenly echoed through the mall, and Dani realized it came from speakers set throughout the area—no doubt once used to pump music or announcements out for shoppers.

"So glad you all could make it!" Ella's voice was immediately recognizable. *"I've prepared a lovely display for your private viewing."*

"She knew we were coming," Wilton muttered.

"Of course she did," Sydney said, with a derisive huff. "Once she was repelled from HQ she'd have to expect us to come after her as soon as possible. She was always clever, whatever she set her mind to."

"Oh, Sydney," Ella continued, *"I've missed how you make compliments sound like insults. It was one of your charms."*

"What do you want here, Ella?" Sydney spread his arms in a dramatic pose—spoiled a bit by the toilet paper dangling from his hands. "If it is I, then I am here."

"No, Sydney. You aren't. You're with me right now, and we are having a really fun time together. Just like we used to."

Dani looked at Sydney in confusion, as did the others.

He chuckle-coughed. "Ah-eh. I think you are confused. Foremost, I am not sure that, in hindsight, you can call what occurred between us to be all that much fun. Secondly, I am standing right here. Those with me can attest to that fact."

"You're nothing but a projection, silly Sydney. A desperate cry for help, because you didn't realize I'm already helping you. Don't worry. It'll all be over soon."

"Can anyone pinpoint where she's broadcasting from?" Lucy asked.

"I would guess the management offices," Sydney said. "She might have hacked into the system remotely, but such technical expertise was never really her forte."

"Any idea where those are located?" Dani asked.

He glanced her way, and she could sense his raised eyebrows under the wrappings. "I would start by looking for a door marked Management, perhaps." He crossed his arms and looked to the nearest visible speaker. "Why bother even being here if you knew our arrival was imminent?"

A trill of laughter came over the speakers. *"Because before I'm done with you, I wanted to thank you. For everything you taught me, and everything I've received from you."*

"I have not given you anything. I only took things away." He held a hand out, as if requesting hers to clasp in sorrow. "And for that, I am truly sorry."

"Don't be sorry, silly. And I didn't say you gave me anything. You are the gift, direct from your patron."

Sydney jerked up straight. "Entropy? You cannot possibly mean ..."

With a loud click and hum, lights popped on in every shop in sight. A rumbling started off in the direction of the construction site.

The team spun outward, their backs to one another, weapons poised. The air crackled slightly as everyone drew on their Pure energies, preparing to cast a variety of spells. Ben had his broom up, Taser nodes sparking on the handle.

"Sounds like this missy has enough tech smarts to get a generator goin'," he said.

Dani didn't answer, transfixed by what the restored lighting revealed. At least a dozen shops held a figure standing just on the other side of the front windows or glass doors—all of them looking like extremely realistic sculptures of people. Sand sculptures. Every one set in a tortured or agonized pose. A few showed glassy portions, as if their bodies had been melted by a blaze. Others had missing limbs or heads, with stumps left where the pieces appeared bashed off.

Sydney staggered to the railing and gripped it hard enough sand drizzled out between some of his bandage linings. He rasped a whisper, "Ella, what have you wrought?"

"What?" Lucy asked, coming up behind him. "What's she done?"

Ben gazed around, looking as confused as Dani felt. He turned and went to the nearest window, where he inspected it for a long minute.

"You see it, don't you?" Ella sounded increasingly mirthful, as if she was barely containing hysterical laughter. *"I really love working with new materials when I get the chance."*

"Parks," Ben said, voice strangely dulled. "Both times, she's gone and turned parks into deserts. Look at their clothes, Dani."

Dani stared until the realization seemed to shoot straight into her eyes to jab deep into her brain.

"Oh $%&. No. No, this is $%&^#@$ sick."

"What?" Lucy said louder, spinning on them.

Dani pointed at one of the sculptures. "Running clothes." At another. "Bike helmet." And a third. "A bikini. Like she was tanning."

Lucy blanched.

Ben tapped the window with the mop handle. The head of the statue inside twitched slightly, making more of itself crumble to the floor.

Dani gagged against the impulse to retch. "These are ..." She swallowed. "These were people."

CHAPTER TWENTY-TWO

Ben's breath fogged the window, briefly obscuring the sand-person on the other side. It continued to twitch and shift, as if some last scrap of humanity was trying to break free of the dirt form it was trapped inside of. He imagined he could sense the thing's pain, its longing to just be wiped out completely so it didn't have to suffer like this anymore.

Poor folks. Oughta put 'em all outta their misery. But first, I reckon we gotta deal with the loopy little lady who did this to 'em, otherwise she's just gonna keep on at it.

Ella continued to chatter over the loudspeakers, now sounding like an art gallery curator giving a tour through an exhibit.

"You'll note how each piece is totally unique. There will never be another quite like any one of them in the world. See how their new material still reflects their old bodies? Perhaps it says something about humanity's ability to project itself into nature."

Lucy came up beside Ben. "Purity save us. Are they still alive?" She looked over her shoulder at Sydney, her expression now holding more desperation than anger. "Is there any way to save them? To undo this?"

Ben and everyone else watched Sydney in doubtful expectation. The entropy mage bowed his head over the railing.

"I despise myself for saying it, but I simply do not know. I never would've even conceived of something so abhorrent, much less attempted it."

Ella's *tsk* echoed through the mall. *"This is just as much your doing as mine, Sydney. You can't deny that."*

His head snapped back up. "I can and I shall. Yes, I transgressed in the past. I wounded you, and I wish I had a way to heal that, like I once did. But this, now, is your choice. Your actions. Don't attempt to claim that I'm responsible for the lives you've taken."

"You were a seed of inspiration. But you refused to accept that. Now, though, I've been given the chance to plant and nurture you. And very soon, you're going to blossom. And you will be so beautiful, millions will ache even as we destroy them together."

"What's she talking about?" Dani asked. "She's talking like you're working together."

"We're not," Sydney said, seething through gritted teeth. "I swear. I would never have associated with her on anything like this." He raised his voice. "Whatever you're planning, Ella, stop. You cannot do this."

"But I can. And I am. After all, as you used to love reminding me, you can't stop Entropy."

"She's saying Entropy with a capital E, isn't she?" Dani asked, wide eyes giving her a spooked expression. She kept turning slow circles, dustpan in one hand, broom in the other, looking for something to whack.

"I fear so," Sydney said. "My patron."

"Hang on a sec." Ben pointed his mop at Sydney. "Entropy's like your boss, ain't he? Like Purity and all them are ours. One of the Corrupt Pantheon bigwigs."

Sydney nodded. "Of course."

"And like any boss, he pays you a salary. That power you got with those fancy hands of yours. But with bosses and peons like us, it's always the same. We get paid so long as we's doin' our jobs. Bein' good worker bees, buzzin' around and humpin' flowers and throwin' up honey for the hive."

"$%&, Ben," Dani said. "You can make anything sound disgusting."

Another slow nod from the entropy mage. Comprehension oozed into Sydney's eyes, and Ben knew he was on the right track.

"Then you pop up back here, talkin' like you wanna change your stripes back to spots. Ain't wantin' to kill in the name of Corruption no more. That sure does sound like someone givin' the middle finger to the head honcho."

"What're you talking about?" Lucy asked.

Ben went to stand before Sydney, locking the other man's gaze with his. "You was thinkin' about resignin'. Mebbe tryin' to come back to play for the home team. Weren'tcha?"

Sydney splayed his hands. "I am still at a loss to the events immediately before my arrival here to secure my date with Dani, but I at least know that my mind and heart have been torn in twain ever since we first met. I felt that perhaps more time spent with her, trying to understand that spirit that kept her fighting for life and the good of others might help sway me one way or another. Help me make a final decision."

They both glanced at Dani, who flushed. "I really made you feel that way?"

The bandages swathing his face made Sydney's smile more of a grimace, but it held clear sincerity, to Ben's figuring. "You did. You are a rare one, and you made me realize there are some things too precious to destroy."

Lucy made a soft gagging noise, but the others ignored her.

"So," Ben said, "what's a big boss like Entropy gonna do when one of his peons ain't doin' his job proper?" He lightly swatted Sydney's shoulder with the mop handle. "He's gonna fire you and hire a replacement. And I think we know who was right rarin' to fill your dusty shoes."

"Ah." Ella sighed. *"I do enjoy the sight of dawning comprehension. It's like watching a sunrise."*

Sydney spun and shook a fist at the mall in general. "Then if you are taking my place, foolish woman, why bother harassing me at all? Why not simply let me leave and fill the void in my absence?"

"Because I care for you too much to let you off that easy," Ella said. *"And because Entropy wanted to make a display of his own out of you. To show that he is not one to be spurned."*

"I suppose you and he have that in common," Sydney muttered.

"Aside from that, there's also the matter of your power. I had to prove myself worthy of it. I couldn't take it all on at once. But with each act I've done in Entropy's name, I've gained a bit more. Soon, I'll have it all, and you will fade into the oblivion you always loved so much."

"So all this," Lucy swept her mop about to indicate the mall's morbid sand sculptures, "is just you showing off for Entropy? You are some twisted hag."

"Naw, she ain't a hag," Ben said. "I'd go with callin' her a goatish, milk-livered mumble-mews."

"It's more than just showing off." Ella sounded miffed, and Ben hoped his insult had shot straight to her Corrupt little heart. *"I need all of my sweet Sydney to complete the process. But his stubborn little mind wouldn't return to his body."*

Sydney went still for a second, and then looked down at himself. "This is not truly me, then, is it?" He turned to the others. "I am here … but in mind alone. This form is a shell that I am merely animating."

Dani lowered her dustpan and broom. "Then where's your real body?"

Sydney used his chin to point toward the decorated art gallery. "With her, I assume. Or in some place she's secured for this so-called process."

Rattling made them all look to the scratched window at the front of the art gallery. It shook in its frame, and cracks stitched through it. A moment later, it shattered outward.

The Ascendants went shoulder-to-shoulder, auras flaring to shield the group from any shards. But the glass tumbled in on itself, grinding the pieces into finer fragments until a glittering cloud hung in the air. All at once, it sucked in to form a humanoid figure made out of dirty glass. Colors bled into this, and Ella stood before them, floppy gardening hat and all.

Her smile gleamed despite the shadows over her face.

"Your mind, Sydney, is the final handful of clay to finish molding my masterpiece." She bobbed her head at the others. "And I appreciate you bringing it to me."

Sydney grabbed Ben's uniform. "You have to get me out of here. You cannot let her take me."

He nodded and bumped the man into motion with his shoulder stump. "Let's go, bucko. We're scootin' our britches back to HQ." Ben jerked his head at the rest. "Everyone hustle together. We ain't gonna let this foot-licker get her sandy hands on Uncle Sid here, now, are we?"

The group drew together. The Ascendants maintained their barrier between Ella and the Cleaners. Dani took up a fighting pose she'd practiced for hours in one of the Cleaner's sparring rooms— hand broom out in front, dustpan drawn back to strike. Lucy sidled in, taking up opposite Ben like Sydney's honor guard.

Tarnation, but even if we're tuckin' tail and runnin', it feels good to have people hoppin' when I holler.

As the group moved back the way they came, though, Ella lifted her arms. Her entire body pulsed with a brief, black aura, which expanded from her and washed across the mall. The Corrupt energies seethed across Ben's skin, feeling like someone had dropped a bucket of cold, slimy maggots over him. Then it crackled away, leaving him and all the others twitching and making sounds of disgust.

"Oh, this can't be good," he said.

"Look," Dani shouted. "The sculptures!"

The statues had all lost their human appearances, features blended away while horns sprouted from their heads. Their twitching forms suddenly hove into action, each reaching for the windowpanes they stood behind.

"Down!" Lucy cried.

The Cleaners hunched and knelt as further filthy windows exploded around them. Most of the glass ricocheted off the Ascendants' auras, but a few shards still stung Ben's cheeks and forehead. The others all sported minor cuts across any exposed flesh as well.

As shards tinkled to the ground all about, they rose as one. A dozen dust devils now stood across their section of the mall, each one oriented their way. A handful lumbered toward the nearest stairs, while others formed sandy whirlwinds with their lower bodies and started hovering.

"Laurence. Dani. Clear them out below." Lucy jabbed her mop around like a general marking positions on a battlefield. "Wilton and Sherman, you keep that woman back. Ben and I will get Sydney out. Regroup at the vans. If anyone gets separated, radio in and get to the nearest glassway."

The plumber charged to the railing and leaned over it, planting his plunger's sucker on the outside edge of the concrete lending. With a heave that made Ben think of a beached elephant walrus, Laurence hauled himself over the edge. He fell, but jerked to a stop as his plunger remained adhered to the concrete. The wooden handle grew, lowering the plumber until he dangled just a couple feet from the ground. Then the plunger popped free. Laurence landed with a thud and the plunger shrank back to normal size. The plumber then charged the nearest dust devil, swinging the plunger like a battle hammer.

Dani remained in place, but the earth shook and the wind picked up. The concrete under Ben's feet trembled.

"Careful, girlie," Lucy called over her shoulder. "Don't bring the place down on our heads."

"I know what I'm doing," Dani yelled.

She made a gesture, and a giant crack tore through the plaza on the ground level. This split and shot through a couple storefronts, shredding their brick and plaster like tissue paper. Walls crumbled, and a dust devil went down, buried under debris. Yet the cracks grew, with a central one spearing up to the second level and slicing that mall section practically in half.

The whole mall quaked. Ben lurched, and Sydney dropped to hands and knees, only to be jerked upright by Lucy a second later. A support column across the way cracked, and a portion of the walkway on that side tumbled into rubble.

Lucy bellowed over the noise. "What did I just tell you?"

"Well, stay away from the walls," Dani shouted back.

Ben scooted along beside Sydney, with Lucy keeping the entropy mage shielded on the open side of the upper walkway.

A dust devil flew into sight just on the other side of the railing.

"Lookout, Lu!"

Lucy turned and fixed on her target. With a Mama Bear growl, she thrust her mop at the construct. It swatted her attack aside, grainy hands tearing some of the cords away. With her steel wool-gloved hand, Lucy grabbed up her spray bottle and hosed the creature down with half of the bleach it contained. The liquid ate into the dust devil's form like acid, deep enough that the black core animating it became visible.

The dust devil wobbled. Lucy speared her mop out again, and connected with the core this time. A yank jerked the dust devil into her reach. Lucy snapped the bottle back on her belt and then reached out to grab the core with her steel glove.

"I've dealt with dust bunnies worse than you," she said.

The glove glowed white-hot for a moment, and she crushed the core into ashen powder. Keening, the dust devil dissolved into a yellow cloud, which drizzled to the ground.

Below, another storefront exploded in a fireball that engulfed a dust devil. When the flames died, a smoking glass statue stood there, with its dark core visible through the charred surface.

Laurence ran into view. He slammed his plunger to the ground and then yanked up with both hands, tearing up a hunk of concrete as wide as his bullish shoulders. Spinning, he launched the concrete free, and it flew over to shatter the crystallized dust devil and crush the core.

"Teamwork!" came Dani's cry.

Sydney stumbled as one of his legs went wobbly, like a scarecrow's. Lucy hooked a hand under his arm and pulled him along double-time.

"I fear I'm becoming a bit more trouble than I'm worth," Sydney said between huffs.

"Becoming?" Lucy asked.

When they reached the top of the stairs, Ben checked behind them. Ella had just started to walk their way, face serene. A faint black aura throbbed around her entire body like a foul heartbeat. The Ascendants had their Pure auras shining so bright they could've put angels to shame. But the Scummoner's darkness remained fixed at the center of it, growing nearer. Orange and purple sparks sprayed where the boundary of her aura met theirs.

Ella flung a hand out, and dust streamed from her palm, making serpentine churnings toward them. Much of it diverted around the Ascendants, but several streams hit hard and the Ascendants stumbled.

"Wilton! Sherman!" Lucy hollered to the Ascendants. "Slow retreat. She's not the priority."

Wilton started to back away immediately, but Sherman held his ground for a few seconds longer. He only seemed to hear Lucy and realize his partner had moved when another pulse of black energy dimmed his aura slightly, it no longer being reinforced by the other Ascendant's.

Sherman turned to catch up with Wilton, but Ella unleashed another dusty whirlwind that swept around and cut him off. He hunched against the assault, and his aura made it look like a dust tornado containing a heart of fire.

With a casual air, Ella raised a hand and made a fist. The sand's spinning sped up even as it imploded on the Ascendant.

Sherman's scream resounded through the mall as the sand scoured the suit straight off him—and then everything else.

A breath later, and the barest of white cloth scraps fluttered to the ground. The Cleaners all stared at where the Ascendant had been, while Ella looked on with a measure of pride.

Ben cleared his throat. "I hate to be a voice of pessimysticism, but I'm thinkin' she's a might bit stronger than we reckoned."

"Keep moving," Lucy said. "Don't stop."

The dust devils roared back into action as the trio hit the ground plaza. Laurence fought just a few yards off, keeping the path toward the vans clear.

The plumber had lost his plunger at some point, and now had his pipe snake out, wielding it like a bullwhip against two dust devils. The metal cord snapped about and lopped off one creature's arm—though this grew back a moment later, if smaller. A sidewise slice chopped the dust devil in half, and Laurence grabbed the augur with both hands to lash out and strike the exposed core. The dust devil tumbled apart for good.

The second dust devil, though, pounded into the plumber from the side. It slammed into him, pummeling him with its entire body.

Laurence went down and somersaulted hard into the base of a pillar. He lay there stunned. The remaining dust devil stomped up and raised a massive foot to grind down onto his exposed head.

Ben raced over and plunged the Taser-tipped mop handle into the construct's back, right where he figured the core would be. It made a noise like a wood chipper as it sank in. Ben sent a surge of Pure energy through it, strengthening the handle and amplifying the charge—nowhere near what he used to manage, but it was something.

The tip connected with a hard object, and Ben blew the whole Taser charge in one blast. An electrical bolt seared out of the dust devil's chest, taking the crumbling core with it. The rest of the creature's body cascaded down over Laurence, who spluttered and wiped sand from his face.

"Thanks," he said to Ben.

The mop handle now ended halfway up in a blackened jut. Ben tossed it aside and offered his hand to help Laurence up.

"You betcha."

As Laurence regained his balance, a trio of dust devils rushed them, leaving grainy footprints in their charge.

Yet as they neared, a ravine opened up beneath them. All three fell, but caught the edges and began to pull themselves up. Then the split earth slammed back together with jarring force, and the visible parts of the creatures crumbled.

Ben looked over to where Dani stood halfway down the stairs, brush and pan pressed together like cymbals.

"Just three, princess?" he asked.

"Just?" Her voice raised an octave.

Ben pointed to the pile that remained of the one he'd obliterated. "Hey, gimme a break. I'm fightin' with one hand tied behind my back." He shrugged his armless shoulder. "Megaphorically speakin'. Gave that one a heapin' helpin' of Purity, though. Don't think it liked the taste much."

Despite the chaos all around, her face lit up.

"Your powers *are* coming back!"

One of the flying dust devils soared down at her head. Ben reached out, too far away to do anything.

"Dani!"

235

She turned and sliced the chanted weapons at the construct. The brush tore away much of its vortex, but its upper body continued to plummet directly for her. Her dustpan chopped in like an axe. Still, the dust devil remained animated and drove her to the steps. Her cry rose as it began trying to smother her.

Wilton leapt the railing and impressed Ben by sticking the landing a few steps above Dani without shattering both legs. He blazed like a star as he carved his aura through the construct and seared its core to cinders. With it dissipated, he helped Dani to her feet. Each with an arm over the other's shoulder, they staggered down the remaining stairs.

Ella appeared at the top landing, several hovering dust devils swirling above her head. Those remaining on the ground level plodded the Cleaners' way. The sound of them filled the air with constant wailing and grinding.

A heavy hand gripped Ben's shoulder. Laurence's voice rumbled in his ear. "Go while you can. We'll keep them busy."

Lucy shouted over near the corner leading back to the parking area. "Ben, come on!"

Ben hesitated as Dani and Wilton reached the bottom. His every instinct craved to remain in the fight. To not abandon his team. With his powers coming back, maybe he could still be useful. He could help.

As if sensing his thoughts, Dani raised her head and locked eyes with him. She mouthed: *Go. We got this.*

He scowled, but an unwanted voice of reason whispered through the surrounding storm. *Admit it, Benny, old boy. You just ain't up to snuff still. You're gonna distract 'em, makin' 'em work to keep you alive instead of sweepin' up the dust like they oughta. Give 'em space.*

Ben nodded at all of them, and then ran to join Lucy and Sydney. Lucy threw her mop over to the plumber, who looked at it with distaste. Then he shrugged and thundered at the closest dust devil. Dani and Wilton disengaged from each other and poised for their own attacks.

"Follow," Lucy told Ben. In a fluid motion, she scooped Sydney up, threw him over a shoulder, and raced for the vans.

Sydney's words came out bumpy as he was jostled along. "And ... thus ... my ... mortification ... is complete."

236

They rounded the building, boots thumping from concrete to pavement as they finally reached the vans. Lucy dumped Sydney at Ben, who fought to keep the man from falling. Lucy yanked the side door of Ben's van open, and then grabbed one band of Sydney's wrappings and used it to fling him inside. After she slammed the door shut, she shoved Ben toward the driver's seat.

"Get going! We'll hold them off a bit and then follow in the other van."

Ben dug his heels in at the last second. "Blood and buckets, Lu. I ain't gonna abandon everyone. I can still help."

"Shut your yap. I don't care if your powers are coming back or not. You're still the weakest of us here, and I need someone I can trust to keep an eye on him." She thumped the van with a fist.

Sighing, Ben set his hand on her arm. "A'ight. You just get out safe, hear? Can't stand the thought of losin' you, too."

Lucy's expression softened briefly, and she looked about to say something. Then her mouth firmed and her eyes hardened. Whipping out her toilet brush and snagging a sponge from a deep pocket, she spun and ran back for the mall, where the sounds of battle continued.

Grumbling, Ben dragged himself into the driver's seat and fumbled at the keys he'd left in the ignition. Sydney crouched in the back, hanging on to one of the metal racks holding an array of cleaning gear.

"What about the others?" he asked. "Where's Dani?"

"They're all makin' sure we stay in one piece. Once we scoot clear, they're gonna be right on our tail."

Sydney looked doubtful, but Ben didn't give him time to argue. With the engine growling, he made the tires smoke as he peeled out for the main road. After turning out of the lot, he accelerated, narrowly missing a minivan heading into the gas station on the left. The driver, a young woman in a business suit, gave him a cheery, one-fingered wave.

He grimaced. "Sorry, miss. Just doin' my job."

The roar of an engine snapped his attention to the road ahead. Another van zoomed toward them, coming in at an angle across the dividing line. It looked like a Cleaner's vehicle, except for being all black, and with a logo and writing along one side.

Ben had just enough time to make out the image: a cartoonish chimney sweep tipping a top hat, a tall brush held in his other hand.

"Aw, canker blossoms."

The chimney sweep's van rammed into the passenger side. The whole world lurched and spun. Tires and metal screeched as the vehicles careened off the road.

CHAPTER TWENTY-THREE

oughing, Ben raised his head and tried to figure out who'd swapped out his eyeballs with stickle burs. They stung in their sockets, tears blurring his vision. His ears rang like a whole flock of shrieking seagulls had gotten stuck in them.

He groaned as he slumped back off the wheel. His head lolled and thumped against the doorframe. Glass tinkled, and his sight cleared enough to show the smeared blood he'd left on the metal.

Gurgling made him aware of Carl's bottle somehow still attached to his belt. The elemental swirled about in alarm and worry.

Alive? Aware?

Another cough. "Yeah, buddy. Shoulda worn my seatbelt, though."

Countless cracks obscured anything through the windshield. Ben gripped the armrest to support himself, every muscle and bone creaking in protest as he turned to look behind.

"Sydney? You still in one piece?"

The side door had bent and torn off its track. The back of the van was empty. The walls were crumpled, equipment scattered everywhere.

It took several shoves to force the driver's door open. Ben half-fell, half-stumbled out. He waved his arm for balance until the ground decided to stop mimicking a trampoline. Tripping this way and that, he turned in dizzy circles, searching for the entropy mage.

"Sydney? Hey, where you at? Gimme a holler!"

The vans had stopped just short of crashing into one of the gas pumps. The woman in the mini-van had pulled off in a far corner, and looked to be on her phone. Calling emergency services, no doubt.

Gotta get this site contained before the local help gets here. Somebody's gonna get hurt if that happens.

At last, Ben spotted a white-clad figure lying some thirty feet away. Sydney sprawled on the pavement, arms and legs bent at crazy angles. The toilet paper still contained most of him, though one foot appeared torn off, and a streak of yellow dust trailed out of the stump.

Ben headed for the man, still feeling numb and shaky. A *clunk* and door slam made him pause. A muscular figure appeared from around the other side of the black van, backlit by the first red glimmer of sunrise. Rafi held his brush in both hands as he stalked Sydney's way, limping slightly.

Ben grabbed Carl's bottle and triggered the elemental. Carl sprayed out and formed a long blade, flowing the lower portion of it around Ben's hand to keep from being knocked from his grip. He managed to jog over and place himself between Sydney and the murderous chimney sweep.

Rafi halted and glowered at him, eyes almost as black as his uniform. "Move, janitor. You are not my target."

"You don't wanna be doin' this," Ben said. "Somethin's wrong with you, Rafi. We's supposed to be fightin' on the same side."

The chimney sweep continued to glare. "By the power the Chairman has invested in me, I order you to move."

"Yeah, 'bout that. Francis said you ain't got any orders from him. You've done got yourself downright confused. So why don't we just settle down and go figure this out over a nice cuppa—"

With a cry, Rafi bolted at Ben. Ben dodged the brush as it came down—and the bristles sank an inch into the pavement. As Rafi worked to yank his weapon free, Ben cut at him from the side.

Even standing still, the chimney sweep moved as if boneless, body swaying to let Ben's attacks whiff by, arms and legs bending jointlessly. He twisted and brought the brush up at Ben's chin. Ben leaned back, just far enough so a single bristle flicked the tip of his nose.

Smelling blood, Ben tried jabbing at the sweep. Despite being bulkier and wielding the heftier piece of gear, Rafi danced around him, making Ben feel like he was attacking a wisp of smoke curling up from a fireplace.

Rafi let the watery blade shoot just past a shoulder. He twisted and snapped the brush handle into Ben's arm. Pain jolted through his bicep and his guard dropped as tingling numbness claimed the whole limb.

The brush slammed into Ben's stomach. The bristles didn't penetrate his suit, but still felt like a hundred needles jabbing into him at once. He dropped. Carl's bottle rolled away as Ben clutched himself, trying to keep his vital organs from evacuating via the nearest emergency exit.

Ben's mouth felt like it'd been stuffed with sawdust. Every breath came choked and his throat seemed to shrivel up.

Boy howdy, could I use a drink right about now. He shook his head, trying to clear his fuzzy thoughts. *This ain't no time to be worryin' about throwin' down a few cold ones, Benny.*

The earth bucked, knocking him flat. Faint screams rose as pavement slabs split and slanted, exposing gravel and earth all around.

Regaining a semblance of awareness, he looked up, confused. His gaze fixed on the car wash, which shook, walls cracking and ceiling collapsing slightly. Pipes and tubing burst both within and without, spewing countless gallons of water and rainbow-colored foam into the air and along the ground, making it look like a water park ride designed by an avant-garde five-year-old who'd been jamming way too many crayons up his nose.

Then again … mebbe it is time for a drink.

Ben lurched to his feet and stumbled for the ruined car wash.

▲   ▲   ▲

"Go, go," Lucy shouted. "We're out of here."

Dani sprinted for the van, arm-in-arm with Wilton again—though she now supported him. Half the Ascendant's face bled from deep gouges where a dust devil had pierced his aura with a claw. Dani's left shoulder kept clicking, and that wrist had swollen almost too much to move. One knee threatened to buckle. With all the pain ruining her concentration, her power fluxed. One moment it threatened to unleash its full fury, enough to wreck the whole mall, the next, she barely kept it active, unable to summon so much as a puff of air or shift a pebble.

Laurence and Lucy stumbled along just behind them, followed closely by Ella's laughter. Dani spurred herself on with thoughts of getting the woman pinned down in a chokehold.

She pulled up short as she reached her van. Across the street, Ben's van stood stalled in the gas station, buckled frame and shattered windows evidence of it having been in an accident. Another van stood a distance off, in just as bad a condition. The other, though, had been painted black, with writing and images on the side. Dani couldn't quite read the writing, but she made out the caricature of a chimney sweep easily enough.

A dozen yards or so from the vans, a figure lay on the ground, white tassels fluttering from his body in the morning breezes.

"Oh, no. Ben! Sydney!"

Leaning Wilton against the van, Dani drew on what little strength she had left and sprinted across the lot.

"Dani, wait," Lucy called after.

Heedless, Dani aimed for the gas station. She stumbled a couple times, coming close to do-it-yourself facial reconstructive surgery, but caught herself and raced onward.

Across the road, Ben had appeared, and now squared off with a man Dani recognized as Rafi, Sydney's would-be assassin. The chimney sweep proceeded to dodge the janitor's every attack while bashing him around in return. A final smack to the gut dropped Ben, and Rafi walked by him, aiming for the still-prone Sydney.

Dani made it to the street and ran straight across, not bothering to check for oncoming traffic. A bus horn blared as it chugged past, missing her heels by less than a yard.

On his hand and knees, Ben struggled to rise. Rafi poised the brush to once more separate Sydney's head from his body.

"No, don't!" Dani cried.

She reached out with both her hand and her power—which tore loose from her control. The energies soared ahead of her with reckless abandon. Chunks of asphalt crumbled as a minor quake tore through the earth. The gas station shook, and the car wash sagged as its aluminum ceiling and support beams warped.

Rafi stumbled away from Sydney, blocked by a jagged wall of pavement. Shaking his head, he headed for the nearest end to resume his attack.

Ben had somehow regained his feet. Yet his back was to Rafi as he stumbled toward the car wash.

Where's he going? Sydney's the other way! Maybe the crash disoriented him. Probably a concussion. Broken bones? Internal bleeding …

Dani raced around the wall herself to find Rafi, who'd finally reached Sydney. As she neared, he slashed his brush across Sydney's body. The magically reinforced toilet paper snapped like threads, and the entropy mage's dusty form began to spill out through the gashes.

Rafi spun through the strike and brought the brush over his head.

Dani screamed a final denial as she closed the distance—but not before the sweep's brush came down and crushed Sydney's head into powder.

She tumbled into Rafi, which felt like trying to tackle a stack of concrete mix. Still, both of them went down and his brush spun away.

The hit sent shockwaves through Dani, and she saw the world in triplicate for a few seconds. Pain played her spine like a xylophone, and pounded her skull like a bass drum.

It took her a minute to turn down the volume on this agonizing instrumental. By the time she recovered her wits, Rafi stood over her. His gaze went from her to the pile of dust strewn about with shredded toilet paper. Pieces of this drifted off as the morning winds picked up.

Rafi retrieved his brush and nodded in satisfaction.

"I've completed my mission," he said. "I'm free."

He plopped to the ground and laid his brush across his knees. His gaze went distant. Expressionless.

Teeth bared, Dani tried crawling to Sydney's side. Her body barely responded. The amount of energy she'd been throwing around had drained her almost completely. She reached out for her elemental cohorts, but a deep-set weariness emanated from them as well. Too much at once. And too little to show for it.

Maybe ... maybe if I pull myself along by my nose ...

A whir of air and a spit of grit made her look up. A pair of dust devils flew down, each holding one of Ella's arms. They dropped the Scummoner to the ground next to Sydney and alighted beside her.

Dani moaned and managed to at least push her upper body off the ground.

"Get away from him." The words came out muzzy, with just enough of a squeak to make her sound like a kindergartner shaking her fist at a pro basketball player.

Ella winked her way. "Oh, hun. Don't. You'll just strain something important." She turned her smile on Rafi. "Thank you for removing his bindings for me. That would've been annoying to deal with. Not that I couldn't have managed, but I'm not above accepting a little help."

The chimney sweep didn't respond. He just kept staring off at nothing, face slack.

Ella knelt near the burst sand pattern where Sydney's head had been. The dust shifted slightly, suggesting the entropy mage might be trying to gather himself back together. However, Ella planted her hand in the center of the strike zone and her dark aura writhed into being.

"No ... please ..." Dani reached out, both with her hand and her power. Both wavered, trembled, and then collapsed.

Ella's power stretched out and ate into Sydney's form like layers of charcoal through salt. Any resemblance of humanity vanished as the dust settled into miniature dunes. She withdrew her hand, which now cupped what looked like an ember that glowed hot purple. She pressed this against her chest, where it absorbed and disappeared.

"There." Ella patted that spot. "All back together. Rest now. It'll be over soon."

Dani shoved up to one knee. With a shaking hand, she reached into a pants pocket and drew out her bottle of sani-gel. As Ella continued to coo to Sydney—wherever he was and whatever she'd done to him—Dani managed to unscrew the top and squeezed so the gel glopped over the outside of the bottom.

Biting the inside of her cheek, using the pain to sharpen her focus, she straightened and lobbed the bottle straight into the side of Ella's head.

The Scummoner cried out and slumped to one side. The gel ate into her head like acid, smoke rising where it had splattered and where it dripped down onto her shoulder and arm. After a few heaving breaths, she rose and faced Dani—at least, she turned what was left of her face toward her.

Her head had become a crescent moon, with the right side looking normal, but everything the gel struck had been exposed as compacted grit. What remained of her mouth split in a smile, and she giggled.

"Oh, my. You're as silly as Sydney. Trying to hurt me like that?" Ella reached over and tore a chunk out of one of her own dust devils. She slapped the sand against her head, and it molded back into her full, normal face. "Did you really think this was my true body as well?"

Dani rose as well, but on shaking legs. "Would ... you ... please ..." She bent over, fighting the nausea writhing through her.

"Yes?" Ella asked.

"Stop ... #$%&@#$% ... smiling!"

Dani stumbled for the other woman, determined to scatter every last grain to the wind, even if she had to use her bare hands.

Ella blew a flurry of dust from her palm, which struck Dani in the eyes and blinded her. Dani halted as fire blossomed in each socket. She scrubbed at her eyes with her rubber gloves, gasping all the while. She couldn't even focus enough to view the area through the elements.

"Look," came Ella's voice. "Your friends didn't want to miss out on all the fun."

Dani knuckled away the stinging grains and tears in time to see Lucy, Wilton, and Laurence run up. They all panted and sweated, and each looked barely able to stand. Still, they spread out to try and hem Ella in.

The Scummoner made a pretty pout. "You all are so adorable. It's really a shame we couldn't be better friends, and I'd hate to leave you without something to remember me by."

She raised cupped hands. The earth exposed by Dani's quake shifted. Clay and gravel swirled through the air, grinding itself to fine powder as knots of foul energy coalesced all around Ella. These knots solidified into fresh Corrupt cores an instant before the dust flowed around them and snapped into rigid forms.

Ten more dust devils stood newly constructed, demonic visages all oriented on the ragged and battered Cleaners.

Ella spread her arms and curtsied. "It's been fun. Thank you again for providing so much inspiration." With that, her body collapsed into a pile of dirty glass shards and grit.

The Cleaners went back-to-back as the dust devils circled them and closed in with implacable steps. Clawed hands rose. Their bodies swirled around and in on themselves, the noise of them making Dani think of gnashing teeth or the growling of ravenous stomachs.

Dani continued to blink uncontrollably. The world swam, making it difficult to single out a target.

She managed a pained whisper. "What do we do? Each take two and then split the difference?"

On her left side, Lucy shifted closer and bumped her with a hip. "Dani?"

"Hm?"

"Where's Ben?"

The ground shook. A gushing noise filled the air, followed by a splashing, like ocean waves. The Cleaners turned, and even the dust devils paused.

The car wash swelled as foamy water spurted from cracks in its sides and through gaps in the entrance and exit doors. Metal groaned as it buckled. Snaps and creaks echoed as rivets popped and plastic casings crackled. Then the car wash burst open. The ceiling tumbled away as a firehose-like spout of water erupted skyward. The walls slammed to the earth as a wave of water flooded toward them.

And Ben rode atop the wave, surfing it with boots planted as if he stood on solid ground. He held what looked like an oversized metal spray nozzle, with a rubber tube trailing into the water beneath him.

"Whoop!" His delighted holler cut through the crisp air. "Duck and cover, folks! I'll get this cleaned up in a jiffy."

He aimed the nozzle at a dust devil. A watery streamer shot out and struck the creature. The construct's sand shell blew apart and its core shattered under the force of the hit.

The wave swell lowered and thinned as it neared, until Ben stepped off the end of a shallow river like someone hopping off a curb. He swirled the nozzle, forming a whip that he lashed into two other dust devils, bisecting each.

A trio of dust devils charged him. Ben spread his arm and laughed.

"C'mon, then! Gimme a hug, you dusty ol' buzzards."

At the last second, a film of water snapped up to cover his entire body, shimmering with subtle flares of Pure energy. The three dust devils slammed into him as one, and their forms turned to sludge which covered the janitor from head to toe.

Dozens of liquid spikes shot out through this mud covering, and three of them had skewered cores. The mud shivered and then ran off as the watery armor flowed off of Ben.

"Hoowee. Ain't never taken no mud bath, before, but they ain't so bad."

Another nozzle shot decimated another dust devil before anyone could move. Then Ben tossed the spray gun to Lucy.

"Hold this for me, wont'cha, darlin'?"

Lucy fumbled to catch the sprayer. Dani guessed the look of utter stupefaction on the other woman's face matched her own.

Ben turned to the remaining dust devils. "Any of you fellas reckon you want a fair fight?"

Dani knew that dust devils were constructs. They didn't have minds of their own. They followed no purpose other than their creator's will. They couldn't be reasoned with, bribed, or intimidated into abandoning the reason they'd been brought into existence.

Right then, though, the dust devils all looked at one another. As if hesitating.

Then they stepped toward Ben as one.

He grinned and made a fist. "Good. 'Cause I weren't gonna give you one, anyhoo."

Two dust devils shot into the air, propelled not by any sandy vortex, but by the geysers that spewed beneath them. Ben thrust his arm out. A thin shaft of water speared out to decapitate another construct. With several chopping motions, he left that one in muddy chunks.

Dust devils fell as fast as Dani could blink, laid low by liquid blades, bludgeons, and whips. He even created a water squeegee and minced a construct into powder with its edge.

At last, a single dust devil remained. Ben flicked fingers and knocked it back a few yards with a powerful spray. It recovered and charged back in. With a pushing motion, Ben conjured an inch-high current, which formed a line between his feet and the path of the oncoming monster.

With each step the dust devil took along this, the water ate away at its form from below. Its feet disappeared until it slogged forward on stumpy limbs. Its knees disappeared, and by the time it reached Ben, it had vanished up to its waist.

Ben bent over and waved. "Hiya."

He rammed his water-armored fist into the dust devil's stomach, yanked out its core, and crushed it.

Straightening, he checked around for other targets, tensed to attack. He clucked his tongue in disappointment.

"They just don't make giant piles of livin', murderifyin' dust like they used to."

The Cleaners boggled at the janitor, who surveyed the half-flooded gas station with an air of triumph. He almost appeared to have forgotten they were there.

Dani came up behind him, steps sloshing. "Ben?"

He turned and, for the first time, seemed to notice their bedraggled state, plus Sydney's absence. He blinked and frowned.

"Did I miss somethin'?"

CHAPTER TWENTY-FOUR

"How did this happen?" Francis asked.

Ben stood in the center of the white-walled briefing room, with Lucy and Dani sitting on benches on either side of him. Dani held a scrap of the toilet paper that had clad Sydney; she stared at this, working it through her fingers as if trying to find something hidden within it. Lucy held a mug of coffee that could've doubled as a bowling ball, but didn't so much as take a sip—a worrisome thing, to Ben's reckoning.

For his part, Ben drank deep from a gallon jug of water he'd snagged from the cafeteria to cool his parched throat. It also finally got rid of the cottonmouth he'd been smacking his lips against ever since they got back to HQ. Wiping his mouth, he toasted Francis with the jug.

"Can't rightly say. Might've been a one-two punch of all the hubbub goin' on around me and all that water kickin' my powers back into high gear. Always did work best with water, y'know. Mebbe somebody up in the Pantheon went and had pity on me after all. But when the first drop hit me, it was like stickin' my finger in an electrical socket. You all know what I mean, right?" He glanced at the women, neither of whom met his eyes. Their expressions dour.

"I'm the only one whose gone and done that for fun? You're kiddin'." Shrugging, he dismissed their unresponsiveness as lingering exhaustion, despite both having been rejuvenated by handymen. "Some people don't know what they're missin' out on. Anyhoo, I'm hangin' on to life by my eyelashes and get on in that car wash, fightin' a real mighty thirst. Like the water was callin' to me. Just felt right. Once inside, it was like listenin' to music. Every drip and drop and splash and splash ringin' through me, gettin' louder and louder, echoin' inside me and callin' my power back to the surface."

"Fascinating," Francis said. "However, my question was regarding the job I sent you to accomplish." He checked his notepad. "One Ascendant dead. Another in Maintenance, alongside a plumber. The rest of the team requiring emergency medical attention. Our primary asset taken."

"What about Rafi?" Lucy asked, looking up from her still-untouched coffee.

Francis ticked off another item on his list. "Since you brought him back, he's remained in what seems to be a catatonic state. He's been placed in quarantine until we can figure out the cause of his erratic behavior. But he's not our priority right now."

Setting the jug on the ground, Ben summoned a trickle up through the air and into his palm, where he formed two liquid globs. He began tossing and catching these in an endless loop, one-handed.

"Bet'cha didn't know I could juggle, huh?" he asked Dani.

She reached over and slapped a ball out of midair, drenching her glove. The other splashed to the floor between them.

He jerked back. "Hey, now. Don't gotta be jealous of my talents, princess."

"What is the matter with you?" Dani shot to her feet and glared up at him. "Would you be serious here? Something horrible is going to happen and you can't stop grinning like an idiot and playing around. Didn't you hear what Francis just said?"

"Sure 'nuff." Ben retrieved his jug and took a gulp. "But he missed the part about me gettin' my powers back, plus a whole bunch to boot, and savin' all your hides. Ain't nobody gonna even say thankya?"

"Thankya," Dani said, deadpan. "With your powers—which, yes, is awesome—we can figure out what's going on with them later. But the Chairman's right. We failed. And we have to find some way to fix this before it's too late."

Her calling Francis by his title sobered Ben more than anything else. Ever since Dani had joined the Cleaners, she'd challenged the traditional authority structure, though in different ways and for different reasons than he did. Her giving it a nod of respect meant she was taking this personally, and was willing to submit to that authority if it meant easing her conscience.

While it grated, Ben tried to tamp down on the euphoria that kept bubbling up inside him. *I know it ain't natural, feelin' so goofy good when the world might be crumblin' on our heads, but sure-for-shootin' if I haven't missed this.*

He forced what he hoped was a grave expression. "Sorry, princess. You're right. I guess I'm just overflowin' with all sortsa fresh energy, and it's makin' me buzz somethin' fierce."

"Then let's put that energy to good use," Francis said. "Namely, averting whatever fate Miss Zhang has in store for Sydney and, as she threatened, millions of other lives."

Lucy finally slurped from her mug and raised her head. "Is there any way to track Ella from all the energies she flung around the mall? All the cores she created, or whatever spell she used to project herself there?"

"I have a scrub-team on site," Francis said. "They're investigating, as well as helping to clean up the damage as best they can while diverting more sensitive official inquiries into exactly what happened this morning. Unfortunately, the mess your encounter left behind is making it difficult to sort

Dani crossed her arms and sulked. "I tried to be as careful as I could. There were just so many, it was hard to pinpoint a single target. Plus, we were kind of caught off-guard."

"I'm not blaming you, Janitor Dani, or anyone." One of Francis' eyes gleamed as he glanced Ben's way from under his fedora. "Though I would've preferred a little less structural damage to the area. That's always a bit harder to explain away compared to merely having to mop up a few piles of mysterious muck and alter witness memories."

Josh Vogt

Guilt tweaked Ben's nose, but he distracted himself with another swig. "I'll keep that in mind the next time I get my powers snitched and then have 'em come back in a tidal wave of glory."

"There's something I still don't get," Dani said. "Why are Ella's powers so different? From Sydney's, that is. I mean, she claimed Entropy was giving her Sydney's power. That she was taking his place. Why aren't we just dealing with another entropy mage?"

"Just?" Lucy echoed. "As if one wasn't enough."

Dani looked to Lucy and then back at Ben. "But the Cleaners have dealt with entropy mages before, right? We've got the procedures for handling them. The containment units. If she was like Sydney, we might not be dealing with this whole problem."

Ben frowned, realizing she had a point. "Takin' his place don't mean she gets the same bag of goodies."

"Why not?"

Francis hitched his shoulders back. "When it comes to Corrupt energies and their manifestations, chaos often reigns."

"Hoo boy." Ben shook his head. "You've gone and given the Chairman a chance to lecture. Don'tcha remember me warnin' you about that?"

Francis shot another keen look at Ben. "When it comes to our enemies, understanding their ways can be the key to victory in the field."

"Is that a quote from that old book about fightin'?" Ben asked. "What's it called? *The Arts and Crafts of War* by Sunnyside Zoo?"

"*The Art of War*, by Sun Tzu," Lucy said.

"There should be an *Art of Supernatural Sanitation*," Dani said. "I'd devour that in a day."

Ben chuckled. "That'd be the Employee Handbook, princess. How's that goin' for you, by the way? You shove it down the nearest incinerator yet?"

"I'm making progress. The manual's attitude makes it a bit harder to deal with than I expected."

His brows drew down. *The manual's whatsit? Just how deep is she readin' between the lines with that thing? Only attitude I ever got while workin' through it was downright boredom.*

254

Lucy popped her neck. "*The Art of War* is a good read, actually. You should try it, Ben. The words aren't too big, and it gives you a lot to think about."

"Now why would I want somethin' that'd make me go and do that?" Ben's wink drew a scowl from Lucy, but at least it was better than leaving her to brood over cooling coffee. "Guess there are worse books a Chairman could work from. Seems like Destin took a page from the one about makin' love instead of war."

"Yes, and see how well that turned out for him." Francis tucked his notepad away and focused on Dani. "Sydney was a handyman before he turned to Corruption. He had powers from a young age, which oriented his way of thinking and manipulating them for years. So when he betrayed the Cleaners, those powers were twisted in a way that darkly mirrored their original form."

"So because he could fix things and people, he could only break them after he went bad" asked Dani?

"Or at least believed this to be the case," Francis continued. "It may be he held potential skills even he wasn't aware of."

"Like summoning dust devils, manipulating particulate matter, and projecting his mind into sand constructs?"

Francis nodded. "Think of us—Scum and Cleaners alike—as filters. The power we wield comes from similar sources, though even that can vary, depending on how we come by it, and whether or not a particular Pantheon member specifically acts as a person's patron. Even those who serve directly under the same patron may be gifted uniquely, or learn to employ them in vastly different manners."

"Great." Dani dropped back to her bench. "So the only thing we can know for sure about dealing with Scum is that we can never know anything for sure about what they'll be capable of."

A third look from Francis. Ben was starting to feel a bit singled out.

"It seems the same may be true for us," the Chairman said.

Dani ticked points off on her fingers. "So we don't know everything Ella can do. We don't know where she's taken Sydney. We don't know exactly what's she's planning—except for that it can't be good. The only thing we have to go on is that it probably

Josh Vogt

has something to do with the deserts she created before, but this time it could threaten millions of lives."

"Nice roundup," Ben said. "I oughta have you write up my reports from now on."

She glared, but did stick the tip of her tongue out the corner of her mouth, so no one else would notice.

Francis tugged a wrinkle out of a sleeve. "As far as her powers are concerned, we learn and adapt, as we do in any situation. As for what she's planning, our goal is simply to stop her and make that a moot point."

"How can we stop her if we can't find her?" Lucy asked.

"I was getting to that. Our help should be arriving now."

He gestured to the back of the briefing room just as the door opened. Four Ascendants, auras glowing hot white, walked in with military formation. They formed a square around another person, and Ben had to squint to see who they shielded.

"Aw, kiddo. No."

Dani must've recognized Jared at the same moment, for she gasped and ran that way.

Jared stood among the Ascendants, and back to his normal body. Shoulders slumped, he looked as pitiful as a puppy that had tried to drink from a fire hose. His gaze darted everywhere, and his bare torso made his rapid breathing painfully evident. He wasn't bound by anything, but the Ascendants had him hemmed in tight.

"What is he doing here?" Dani demanded, stopping almost nose-to-nose with one of the Ascendants. "What are you doing to him? Let him go."

The Chairman coughed on his end of the room. "I thought you'd be happy to see him let outside of what you so often refer to as 'his cage.'"

Dani looked back at Francis and snapped a hand at the boy— making one Ascendant shift aside to avoid getting a slap across the throat. "Not like this. What are you trying to do, traumatize him? For #$%&, Francis, you're smarter than this."

Ben couldn't help a little smile at her dropping his title again. *Attagirl.*

Jared's voice vibrated the air. *"I'm sorry, Dani. I must've done something wrong. I'm trying to be good, like you said. I kept apologizing but*

256

they wouldn't tell me what I did so I could fix it."

If Dani's voice had any more steel in it, she could've supplied a smelting factory for a year. "You didn't do anything wrong, Jared. Absolutely nothing. Some people are just being stupid. Like they are way too often."

"I was hoping he could help us," Francis said. "However, I felt that what I'd ask of him would be hampered by the various quarantine measures we'd placed him under. So I submitted a request that he temporarily be allowed outside privileges. The Board agreed, in lieu of the circumstances, but required him to be under constant guard. Just in case."

"Just in case of what?" Jared asked.

"Just in case someone tried to attack you or steal you out from under our noses, kiddo." Ben shoved the explanation out before either Dani or Francis could open their mouth. "Francis here was just tryin' to keep you safe."

Jared looked at him doubtfully, but then a toothy grin split his face. *"Ben! You're strong again."*

Ben flexed his arm, pumping the gallon jug like a dumbbell. "Yuppers. Benny ol' boy is back in action. Just no more munchin' on me unless you absolutely gotta, 'kay?"

"I promise. No more munching."

Dani kept glaring at the Chairman. "Did you explain any of that to Jared, or did you just have your goons go grab him and march him here?" Her eyes narrowed as Francis glanced aside. "Yeah. Figures." She pointed at the Ascendants. "Tell them to back off. Or I'll make them."

The Ascendant closest to Dani tilted his fedora up and looked past her to Francis. "Sir?"

Francis sighed. "Stand down. Keep the door secure, however."

The Ascendants stood aside to let Jared out, and the kid rushed to hug Dani. She stroked his hair and spoke soothingly, softer than Ben could make out.

He eyed Francis. "Really? This is your idea of bein' all nurturin' and whatnot?"

"Why do you think I let you and Janitor Dani watch over him?" Francis asked. "Few in HQ have the time or temperament to deal with children."

Dani glared across the room. "Once this is over, check your Employee Suggestion box. I'll get some ideas written up for a few childcare and youth programs the company can implement."

"I'll take them into all due consideration," Francis said. "In the meantime, let's focus on determining whether Jared is able to give us a lead."

Jared stepped away from Dani, looking eager. *"I can help? How?"*

"Your Uncle Sid's in trouble," Ben said. "And we ain't got much time to figure out where he's been hustled off to before somethin' even worse comes a-knockin'."

Francis strode over to Jared, who cringed. Dani tensed, and Ben watched them both, knowing Dani might push things a little too far if she thought the kid might be threatened. Even Lucy stood to watch the interaction, mug held like a shield. However, Francis kept his aura dampened and didn't give any hint of trying to assert himself in any supernatural manner.

The Chairman placed his hands on Jared's shoulders in a gentler manner than Ben would've guessed the man capable of. "Jared, your Uncle Sydney has been trying to help us stop a very bad person. But that person stole Sydney away and could end up hurting him if we can't figure out where he's been taken."

Jared raised his gaze while keeping his face down. *"Is it the mean lady?"*

"Yes. The one you took care of so well earlier."

"I don't like her. But I like Uncle Sid."

Francis smiled. The easy manner of it caught Ben by surprise, and he briefly wondered what the Chairman might've been like if he'd wound up having a normal life with a regular job, a family, kids, and all those domestic frills. The guy could've made a decent drinking buddy, maybe.

"If you can help us find him," Francis said, "we would greatly appreciate it. It doesn't even need to be a specific spot. If you can even just point us in a general direction, narrow down an area we can start looking, then that would be excellent."

Jared stared at his tennis shoes for a long while. *"Can I come with you?"* he asked. *"To make sure Uncle Sid is safe?"*

Francis looked to Dani, but she just raised an eyebrow. Sighing, the Chairman let his hands drop and clasped them. "I'm sorry, but no. This is a job for grown-ups. If you went along, you would probably end up getting hurt."

Ben heard the unspoken loud enough: Or accidentally hurt someone else with those chaotic powers. Or get exposed to a Corrupting element that would tip the balances of Jared's behavior for the worse.

"But maybe I could help when I'm older," Jared said. *"When I'm a grown-up."*

This time, Francis caught Ben's eye. Ben shrugged. "Whaddya want from me? I've been workin' this gig since my voice woulda shattered glass."

Francis pinched the bridge of his nose. "We can … consider it. A lot can change by then, but helping us now would go a long way toward showing your potential."

Jared stared up at Francis, the gold flecks in his eyes glinting, and the serious cast of his face already making him look older than the youth people often mistook him for.

"Do you promise Uncle Sid will be safe?"

That snagged Ben's breath. He stepped closer. "Kiddo …"

Francis snapped a hand up to stop him. Ben pulled back, surprised, but willing to let the Chairman dig himself into whatever hole he wanted. Dani would call him out the instant he—

"No," Francis said. "I can't do that."

Jared cocked his head, but remained silent.

Francis clasped hands behind his back. "Jared, what we do as Cleaners is dangerous. I think you know that. We try to protect people, to protect the whole world from Scum like the woman who took your uncle. But people have already died trying to stop her, and more people may follow before this is over—including Sydney—despite everything we do. It's the sad reality of the world we live in." He bent over to be at Jared's eye level. "I can't promise you what you want. But I can promise we will try our best."

The kid met Francis' look straight on; Ben half-expected sparks to flash between them. Then Jared nodded and smiled. *"Good. I wouldn't have helped if you'd lied."*

Francis straightened, studying Jared at a new angle. Dani smirked off to the side, until Jared turned and pointed at her.

"You have a piece of him."

Dani looked puzzled. Ben set his jug down and went over to pluck out the toilet paper scrap she'd half-tucked into a pocket.

"That?" Dani asked. "It's just part of the wrappings that held him together."

Jared shook his head. *"No. I made it part of him. Just a little bit. At least, the part of him that was here."*

Ben handed the scrap over. Jared took it, rolled it into a ball, and popped it in his mouth.

Dani gasped. "Jared, gross!" She darted over and held a hand out. "Spit that out right … uh …" She looked at her own hand, and then pointed at the floor. "Right there."

"Hang on, princess," Ben said. "Let the kiddo do his thing."

"What thing?" She waved at the boy. "Eating trash?"

"Eh. Builds up the immune system."

Dani shuddered, but let Jared be.

After several hard chews, Jared swallowed, the lump big enough for Ben to track it down his throat. Everyone stood staring at the kid, who didn't look at any of them in particular.

Then Jared gasped and bent over double, one hand clutching his stomach, the other clutching his head. He went to his knees. Dani hovered around him, touching and then pulling away, as if fearing making whatever was happening worse. Ben kept back and watched, knowing he couldn't offer more than silent encouragement.

Hang in there, kiddo. You can do this. I've already seen plenty impossible about you. Keep it up.

Jared shook several times, each spasm coming harder than the last. Then his head snapped back so he stared at the ceiling.

Dani made a choking noise, and even Ben sucked deep through his nostrils at the sight.

Jared's eyes were solid gold, shimmering orbs with flecks of white and purple glinting and disappearing. When his voice shifted back into Ben's head, it sounded strained. No. Not strained. Stretched. Thin, as if the words were coming over a greater distance than normal.

"Uncle Sid. He's hurting. He's fading. It's dark all around." He groaned. *"It … hurts."*

Ben knelt by Jared's side and laid his hand on the boy's back. "Not your pain. It ain't you hurtin'. You just focus on pointin' us toward old Uncle Sid, and we'll take care of the rest."

Jared quivered and his skin baked under Ben's touch—though he couldn't remember if that was normal or not. Yet his breathing eased and he began blinking rapidly.

"He … he's being torn apart. Keeps trying to reach out. So far away."

"How far?" Ben tried to keep his voice calm. "Gimme an idea how far we're talkin'."

"That way." Jared pointed at a wall. Ben knew the kid had an uncanny sense of direction, and could walk around HQ blindfolded if he wanted, even in sectors he'd never visited before. But they couldn't just start walking in the direction he indicated and hope to reach Sydney in time.

"Need it to be a little more specific."

With a deep, sucking breath, Jared fell forward to his hands. When he raised his head, his eyes had returned to normal.

"I … I know. I know where he is."

"Where?" Ben, Dani, and Lucy asked together.

Jared frowned. *"I don't know the name. I can just see it. Far from here."*

"Can you describe it?" Francis asked.

"A dead place."

"That sounds promising," Lucy said.

"Dead. Dry. Windy. Hot. Cold." Jared stood, hugging himself and shivering. *"Can you make a map, Mr. Chairman?"*

Francis went and pressed a hand against the near wall. This glowed, and a gold-lined screen appeared at head height.

"What region should I focus on?" he asked.

Jared shuffled over. *"Where are we?"*

Francis gestured and a landscape map of Denver appeared, crisper and more detailed than any satellite could manage. A live image, too, Ben guessed.

The kid stepped in front of Francis and began moving his hands, shifting the image in all directions. The Chairman looked at the others, chagrined.

"He seems to have taken control with little difficulty."

"He's a quick learner," Dani said.

They watched for several minutes as Jared continued to manipulate the map. It scrolled wildly this way and that. Spun in place. Zoomed in on farmland, and then back out to encompass the whole Rocky Mountain range. It zipped along rivers and then shot back down on lakes until Ben thought he could see fish just under the surface. Jared scanned over towns, tracked roads until they dead-ended.

Just when Ben started to feel nauseas from the whirlwind visual tour, Jared leaned in and slapped the wall. The map froze. Everyone moved closer to stare over the kid's shoulders.

From this view, a jagged line of mountain peaks stitched their way along, outlined by forested slopes that made Ben think of gangrenous flesh. At the southern tip of this, the range hooked around a barren area, a splotchy half-crescent that, from this distance at least, didn't appear to have much, if anything living on it. The earth there had a rippled texture too, as if someone had punched a giant hole through the crust there, and then sealed it over with a few layers of crusty spackling.

"This could be problematic," Francis said.

"Why?" Dani asked. "What're we looking at?"

"A place of interest. One we've had on file for as long as I can remember. It has never been the site of known Scum activity, but we've certainly flagged it as a potential locus of Corrupt power. We've just never confirmed it until now." The Chairman reached out and tapped the dead zone. "She has Sydney at the Great Sand Dunes National Monument."

CHAPTER
TWENTY-FIVE

Dani gave Jared a last squeeze, but couldn't force herself to kiss the top of his head before he headed back to his room. She so needed to figure out some sort of sanitary lip covering. Constantly slathering sani-gel over her mouth might help, but would be hellish on her skin, and cracked skin made it easier for germs to get beneath the surface.

"If it's late when we get back," she said, "I'll come tell you a bedtime story."

He beamed up at her. *"Okay. Or maybe Uncle Sid can come tell me one."*

"Sure." Her smile felt chiseled in place. "I bet he'd love to."

He slipped out of her hug and went to stand with his Ascendant escort, who headed out without delay.

Sighing, Dani turned to the others. Francis had just gotten off his radio, having finished relaying orders to various employees. With the others gone, the minimalistic briefing—which had felt cozy before—now seemed a few sizes too big. "All righty. Time for a battle plan. We've got our target. What's next?"

"Getting to it in any sort of decent time," Francis said.

Ben and Lucy frowned at each other. All this time, worry had tightened in Dani's stomach like a steel spring being wound tighter and tighter. At that look, it cinched in another notch.

"What's the big deal?" she asked. "Getting there should be the easy part, shouldn't it?"

Francis plucked his pen and notepad out and began sketching graphs and formulae she couldn't begin to decipher.

"It's a four-hour drive from here, at best," he said, "and I'm guessing our time is already running short. I would wager we have an hour, perhaps two at the most before Sydney succumbs to Ella, and that's being generous. I'm dispatching several teams via van, but I fear they'll arrive too late. We need to find a way to get a strike team on-site as immediately as possible if we stand any chance."

"What about the glassways?" Dani asked.

Francis spun his pen between his fingers. "I have window-watchers scouring the area for viable options, but it's unlikely. There are several towns nearby, but we don't have any established glassways in the area, and no active Cleaners who could help from that end. In smaller cities and towns, we simply don't have the resources to maintain as active a workforce. That means we can't keep up enchantments on windows or mirrors that might give us anchor points from here. A group of window-watchers might be able to create a long-distance link by sheer force of will, but again, it'd require more time than we can afford."

"And the Gutters?" Dani hesitated to suggest that gray realm, full of dead worlds and lifeless landscapes composed of nothing more than ash and stone and bone. She'd rather take a high-dive plunge into a dumpster full of rotting fruit than trek through the Gutters again, but if it got them to Sydney in time, it might be worth it.

Lucy shook her head. "We'd waste more time just trying to find the right entrance and exit spots. And if we ran into any sort of Scum tromping their way through it as well, it'd just delay us more."

"Fine." Dani pointed at the door. "Then get Jared back in here. When we were dealing with Dr. Malawer, he transported me to a janitor's closet at the hospital. There've got to be some of those down in one of those towns. Maybe even one in the park's visitor center."

"Is that how you popped over there?" Ben asked. "I was always wonderin'. Thought it mighta been a Catalyst trick we didn't know about."

Dani kept her unease tucked down deep. With her manifestation of powers being so rare, the Cleaners knew little-to-nothing about the inner workings of what she did. She figured few, if any, guessed at her having bonded to a wide variety of elementals who did some of the heavy lifting from time to time. Here she was, having pushed Lucy to trust Sydney and asking the others to trust her judgment of him, and yet she still kept secrets from them all. Not to mention the secret Carl had entrusted her with, as far as his real reason for being Ben's partner.

What if Ben's restored powers have something to do with that? She glanced at Carl, who'd remained abnormally quiet in his bottle on Ben's hip. *I should find a way to talk to him again. See what he thinks about this sudden change.*

As for her own powers, maybe after they wrapped up this gig, she'd find a way to lay it all out without it being too much of a shock—or get her put in quarantine just like Jared or Rafi.

"Janitor closets are not normally part of our transportation network," Francis said. "They're used more as emergency supply caches and safe houses. Though I don't believe that particular display of Jared's power was ever reported." He made a note. "After this is all resolved, please provide me with a full write-up of that experience for my review."

Dani winced. One more thing to keep Jared under their microscope, and more homework for her. Yet rising anxiety shoved her annoyance aside.

"Vans are going to be too slow. No glassways. No janitor closets. Fan-$#%^&@#-tastic." Dani pushed her curls back over an ear. "Now that we know where Sydney is, all we can do is stand here and watch and wait until everything goes to #$%@."

"It ain't over yet until the skinny man squeals." Ben pushed her gently Lucy's way. "Howsabout you and Lu knock heads together for a minute. Lemme talk to Francis here, and see if either of us can come up with a way to go roarin' in to save the day."

Dani met Lucy's eyes. The other woman's face was already rumpled in concentration as she peered into her mug.

"Don't suppose there's any whiskey in that?" Dani asked, planting herself beside Lucy.

The janitor eyed her sidelong. "This early in the morning? Careful, girlie, or you're going to have a problem with that."

Dani shrugged. "I just figure with as little sleep as we've had, it's technically still yesterday."

"Maybe. But do you really want to be drinking something that dehydrates you right before possibly going into an actual desert to fight for your life?"

"Coffee is a diuretic."

Lucy's glower could've sent plenty of folks running for the restroom. *I really wish Sydney hadn't compared her to a mama bear. Now whenever she gets this look, I don't know whether to give her a cuddly hug or to start running.*

"So any ideas?"

Lucy focused back on her coffee, swirling the mug and taking a sip every third spin or so. "A few, but they're all pretty impossible. Summon a Pantheon member and beg for help, seeing that Entropy's involved in this one. Sometimes they take it personally when other Pantheon members have taken too much direct action."

Dani thought back to her brief encounter with the Corrupt Petty, Filth, and the inhuman power the being had wielded. She hadn't even done much. Her presence alone had given Dani a few nightmares of being buried in maggots and forced to wallow in fetid muck. The Pure Pantheon members might not be so abhorrent by nature, but she preferred to avoid tangling with entities she could barely comprehend if she could help it. "I'd rather not go that route."

"No one would. But it's one of the more sane options we have left. We can skip down to Colorado Springs and cut some of the drive short, but it still could be too long. From what we've seen, I think Francis' hour or two timetable is generous." She huffed and went back to stirring up grounds.

Dani frowned, now also watching the coffee go 'round. The brown swirl reminded her of foul water going down a drain. This then linked her thoughts to different types of drains and plumbing. And in that odd logic leap, a few extra neurons connected and flickered with inspiration.

"Uh-oh."

Lucy popped a brow up. "Uh-oh, what?"

"I think I just got an idea."

"And that's bad? Spill."

Dani bit her tongue for a second, almost not wanting to say anything, lest she commit them to this course of action. But if it worked and gave them the jumpstart they needed to stop Ella …

She leaned in close. "Tell me if this sounds too crazy. Or disgusting."

▲ ▲ ▲

Francis took his fedora off, a signal Ben had started to recognize as the Chairman bracing himself for a particularly arduous conversation.

"What is it you really wish to talk about?" he asked.

"Just that and nothin' more," Ben said. "You know me, though, so you know how much this is makin' me bellyache just to bring it up but … what about the Board? Them and all their high-and-mightiness gotta have a way to kick us over there quick as a whistle."

"No." The word dropped from Francis' lips so hard and heavy, Ben almost took a step back to avoid getting his toes smashed.

His brow crinkled in confusion. "Why not? Millions of lives, Francis. That's what she done said. I ain't their biggest fan, but I don't think even the Board's just gonna chalk that up to acceptable losses."

"I believe a better solution will present itself," Francis said. "Even if the Board was willing to intervene, the cost of it might be more than it or any us might be able to live with in the long run. Convincing the Board that this would be a worthwhile effort, much less bargaining the return on its investment could likely take just as much time as finding our own way."

Ben narrowed his eyes at the Chairman. "You don't wanna get the Board involved. Why?"

"This isn't their purpose," Francis said, voice lowering to a mutter. "This isn't their job. It's ours. The Board works best at a distance, and the moment we start petitioning them on a regular basis for any sort of extra resources is the moment they will begin enacting even tighter control and stricter policies to run things exactly as they see fit."

Josh Vogt

"Look, I ain't gonna give any of those pasty-faced Pantheon patsies a hug anytime soon, but what's the good of havin' folks in charge if they ain't ever doin' much to help?"

Francis grinned wryly. "Why do you think there's a Chairman? The Board has tried to operate the Cleaners without one before, and it always proved unwise. Almost destroyed the whole organization once. They're too detached from their humanity, as you're well aware. And you assume the work they do is the sort you would be able to notice in the first place."

"And if we don't get a movin' in a jiffy? What then?"

Francis looked over at a wall, and Ben guessed he was seeing far beyond its blank boundary. "If time escapes us further, I will use my last act as Chairman to transport the strike team there with all power available to me. I'll then return here and monitor the situation until it is resolved—at which point, I will then submit myself to be stripped of my title."

"What in brooms and blazes are you talkin' about, Francis? Last act as Chairman?" Ben indicated the room. "Monitor from here? If you can get us there, why ain't we already suckin' sand? Why ain't you joinin' us on this hoedown? I figured you'd be more than a little peckish for a bit of action after so much filin' and administratifying."

Ben could've sworn Francis' hand tightened around his pen, if slightly. "While I admit I would enjoy bringing myself to bear against this Scummoner, I'm forbidden to leave HQ for the time being. If I took you there, it would be a direct defiance of orders and would effectively be an act of resignation."

Ben frowned. "Forbidden? You? Who'd have the ball bearings to …" He went slack-jawed for a second. "You're kiddin'. The Board again? The Board has you grounded? Sittin' on the bench until they blow the whistle to let you in the game? A choke collar 'round your neck until they let you off the leash? A—"

Francis' lips pinched thin. "You've illustrated it quite well, thank you. But it's not any sort of punishment. The Board is quite pleased in my handling of the company so far."

"So what gives?"

"They simply don't want to lose another Chairman so soon."

"Uh, what?"

The Chairman sighed and pressed a fingertip into the spot between his eyes, which he closed for a moment. Ben noticed it was his middle finger, specifically.

"Destin was one of the more field-active Chairmen in recent history. He never let his title keep him from the grunge work." Francis reopened his eyes. "However, it is being theorized that this could be what ultimately led to his downfall; that being in the field exposed him to some unknown Corrupting element, or caused him to cross paths with Filth and plant the seeds of their, er, peculiar relationship."

"And what do you think?"

Francis lifted his chin and a glimmer of his aura flickered about. "I serve the Board as faithfully as I can. As ever, I look for evidence, and I can neither prove nor disprove this theory just yet." He sighed at Ben's skeptical look. "Yes, I would enjoy being out there with you, as much as any of us enjoy work that could end our lives in horrible and mind-shattering ways. Until the Board gives me leave, though, I must do my work from here and trust you all to provide as thorough reports possible."

Ben scrunched one eye up. "Hang on. Is that why you keep us jottin' down reports? So you can gobble 'em up like candy? They let you feel like you're still out there, doin' Purity's good work? Lettin' you get that thrill vicarously?"

"Close. Vicariously. And I refuse to answer that insulting question. It would be ridiculous and entirely unprofessional for me to do something of that sort."

"But if we're runnin' outta time?"

"Then I will do what must be done." He looked behind Ben. "But I don't believe it will come to that."

"Chairman?" Dani came up beside Ben, Lucy on his other side.

Francis donned his fedora. "Janitor Dani. You have something?"

Dani scrunched her face up as if she'd swigged a bucket of paint thinner and then chased it down with formaldehyde. "This sand dunes place. It's a national monument, right? A park? Where tourists go."

Francis nodded slowly. "Yes. And?"

Dani visibly firmed herself up before continuing. "So, not that I've been to many of those—what with all the dirt and filthy animals and moss and bugs and all—but don't parks like that have sanitation facilities?"

"Certainly. But as I said, even if they have restrooms with mirrors, or a visitor center with large enough windows, we don't have a connection there."

"But maybe they also have …" She took a deep breath. "Porta-potties? Ones set around the park trails or at least nearby?"

Lucy flicked her mug, making a soft *thunk*. "Should've thought of it, myself. That hag was using porta-potties to jump around town, whether she was projecting into a fake body or not. Likely thing is she had at least one back down near her home base and used it to scoot once done here."

Ben tried to contain it, but the grin stretched across his face until his cheeks ached. He hooted in delight.

"Now that's just genius, princess. We gotta get ourselves a TURDIS."

▲   ▲   ▲

Dani adjusted her dust mask and safety goggles, ensuring a snug fit. Once they felt as comfortable as they could be, she touched each and fed the slightest bit of Pure energy into them. The dust mask suctioned tight to the skin around her mouth, but every breath still came easy, as if she wore nothing at all. The goggles similarly adhered to her face, and after a few blinks, she could see clearly, without even any blurring in her peripheral vision.

She checked her gear. While she planned to use her powers more at a distance, she knew better than to assume she wouldn't get drawn into the action.

Aside from replenishing her sani-gel—and giving herself a brief wipe down, just to quiet her agitation for a little longer—she also picked up a metal-handled broom and extended dustpan that'd let her fight constructs from a distance. She had a couple squeegees hooked to her belt in case the fight got too down and dirty, and a few bars of soap in various pockets. She'd taken Lucy's cue and procured a bottle of concentrated bleach water to soften up targets before wading in.

So armed, armored, and energized, she prepared to face her greatest challenge yet.

Plunging into a porta-potty.

The strike team had gathered in a corner of a Supply sector, with rearing shelves vanishing off into the distance, piled high with crates and bins full of all manner of gear. This area looked dedicated to plumbing and sewage-related equipment—particularly the half-dozen porta-potties that stood along the nearest wall, stretched between two shelving units.

The blue-and-white receptacles ranged widely in size; a couple Ascendants tended to the largest one of the lot, which was so massive, Dani figured she could've almost driven her van inside and had room to spare. The toilet unit within had a gaping seat that reminded Dani of the opening to an amusement park water slide, inviting the unwary to hop on in and enjoy the ride.

Why even make something like that? Who or what would possibly need facilities that big? Giants? Do giants exist? I really hope the Employee Handbook has a Scum bestiary in the appendices, or something.

Around ten Cleaners filled the prep area, all of them strapping on gear, securing masks, gloves, and goggles, or refilling bottles with liquids running the gamut of colors, smells, and viscosity. The Cleaners themselves were an arrangement of every immediate employee Francis could summon, and he promised others were being brought in from fieldwork and would be sent after them as soon as possible.

For now, they had several Ascendants, janitors, maids, plumbers, and a couple handymen to bring up their rear. One guy stood off to the side, a huge vacuum canister with a large, handheld nozzle attached by a flexible tube strapped to his back. Ben had referred to him as a dustbuster, but mentioned little else.

A handyman had come by each of them in turn, her touch washing away any hint of fatigue as well as the most minor aches and pains. Dani thought about doing a few jumping jacks or pushups to warm-up, but preferred not getting herself sweaty for as long as possible.

As they finished readying, they formed a line before Francis, who stood stiffly in front of the porta-potties, like a war general in white. His face had gained its hard-edged quality, his gaze and voice brooking no questions. The wall behind him displayed both Ella's and Sydney's faces.

"The objective is simple enough," he said, once they all assembled. "Reach the sand dunes and neutralize this Scum." He pointed to Ella. "The full extent of her abilities are unknown, but she is most definitely under Entropy's own influence. Dust devil summoning, control of sand and related matter, and projection of her awareness into composite bodies have all been witnessed, but be prepared for anything. On the other hand, this man," he indicated Sydney, "should be recovered and brought back to HQ. Alive and in one piece, preferably."

The Cleaners murmured, enough of them obviously knew Sydney's reputation. Dani noticed how Francis hadn't labeled him as Scum, which made her smile.

"Janitors Lucy and Ben are heading up this operation," Francis continued. The pair stepped out of the lineup as he named them. "I'll convey any orders through them, so obey them accordingly."

Lucy had her usual array of sanitary weapons, but Ben just held a new mop. Aside from Carl's spray bottle, the only other thing he carried was a large, bulging black pack strapped to his back, with an extra band securing it around his waist as well. Dani eyed this curiously. He braced the mop against the crook of his shoulder, picked up a small tube that curled around from the pack, and drank from the tip of this for a few seconds before letting it fall again.

Water, she realized. *Of course. We're going into a desert and he wants to bring as much ammunition as possible without having to dowse for anything hidden under the dunes.*

Lucy spoke up as Francis drew back. "I'll take point and make sure we've got the right location. Once everyone's through, then we wipe this Scum out of existence and save some lives. Everyone ready?"

The team chorused the affirmative.

An Ascendant held the door open. Lucy crouched slightly, and then ran for the entrance. At the last second, she jumped through the threshold and went feet-first into the toilet receptacle. The extra-wide opening admitted her easily, and she fell out of sight.

Dani tensed, waited to hear a thud or for the porta-potty to rock on its base.

Nothing. Not so much as a splash, though this didn't alleviate her rising dread any. In fact, it made it worse.

Half a minute went by as everyone waited. Then their radios crackled.

"This is Janitor Lucy. Confirmed arrival at the Great Sand Dunes, unless there's another Purity-forsaken giant pile of sand in the region I don't know about. Site's secure, but I don't think that's going to last."

A couple Ascendants went through next. Then Ben waved Dani over.

"You're up, princess."

Unlike the others, who'd thrown themselves into the receptacle without hesitation, Dani ducked into the porta-potty and peered into the basin first.

"I wouldn't if I was you," Ben said.

She jumped back. "Oh, $%#. It's deeper on the inside."

He chuckled. "The first step's the hardest. Woulda been better if you'd just taken the leap. Remember to hold your breath."

Legs wobbling, she stepped up onto the rim and tried not to think about what she was going to do. She wavered there, wishing with everything that there might be another way.

"Need a push?" Ben asked.

Locking eyes with him, she mouthed something absolutely filthy and took the step.

She dropped down and struck a layer that bounced her slightly, as if she'd stepped onto a trampoline. Rising for a moment, she saw a boundary formed of what looked like blue, crystal-clear gelatin. Then she dropped again, and this time her feet pierced the barrier and she sank deep.

Dani yelped at the cold surrounding her. Her body felt encased in wet plastic, a slimy, slippery sensation, heightened by the feeling of shooting along at rapid speeds toward ends unknown. Her vision flickered from blue to black and back. She focused on holding onto her broom and pan, squeezing them so hard her hands hurt, and using the pain to try and distract herself from the terror of the ride.

Her body swerved without warning, being shunted from side to side, up and down, rocketing through pockets of intense heat and

cold at random. She glimpsed sporadic circles of light above her—
or whatever direction it was—and thought she might be seeing the
open portals of other porta-potties, all of them connected through
some sideways dimension.

The receptacle disgorged her with a harsh slurping noise that
sounded like a dog hocking up its dinner. Dani stumbled and caught
herself against the porta-potty's closed door, making it shake. She
stood there, panting and trembling from hair to toenail.

Someone knocked on the other side.

"Dani?" Lucy asked. "I'm guessing that's you from the
panicked wheezing."

Dani clamped down on her breathing to try and normalize it.
She took a moment longer to gather herself, not wanting anyone
else to hear her whimper or see her shake so badly. The gelatin
covered her entirely, and she was thankful for the lack of any
mirror, otherwise the sight of herself might've sent her catatonic.

Shivering, Dani crept into the sunlit outdoors, where Lucy
waited. The blue gel slopped off her in chunks, while thinner
coatings of it slowly evaporated.

"Told you it'd be messy," Lucy said.

Dani scraped gunk from her hair and flung it away. "I want to
go home."

"No can do, girlie." Lucy pointed behind Dani. "But what you
can do is keep this whole operation from getting shut down before
it even begins."

Dani turned, and it took her a moment to make sense of what
she saw.

The porta-potty they'd emerged from stood on a patch of
packed gravel beside a small parking lot, where several signs
indicated trailheads or displayed safety warnings and park
regulations. True to the park's name, desolate sand dunes rose all
around, forming a skyline that was, in turns, jagged and swooping—
all of it appearing utterly out of place compared to the green-clad
mountains behind them.

Yet in the direction Lucy indicated, it looked like a rearing wall
of yellow and brown stone had been set into place, blocking the
view.

As Dani blinked, the wall shifted and writhed all along its length. Her perspective snapped into true, and she realized the immensity of the sandstorm front barreling their way.

CHAPTER TWENTY-SIX

T he wind picked up, the breeze rising to a roar that made
Lucy have to shout for Dani to hear her. The janitor waved
at the wall of sand rumbling closer with each second. It
seemed to boil and erupt even as it approached, and Dani
imagined she could see faces within it, and hear screams in the gale.

"Can you keep that off us?" Lucy cried.

Dani wavered for a moment. *This ... this is too big. It's blotting out
half the sky!*

She reached down and snatched out her bottle of sani-gel.
Popping the top and slipping off her dust mask, she squirted a hefty
dollop into her mouth and swished. The fumes shot up into her
sinuses and her eyes teared up. Her mouth burned, but it was such
a good burn. A clean jolt that dissolved her doubts—most of them,
at least—along with whatever gunk might've slipped past her lips
on the ride out.

She spat the gel out, replaced her mask, and hollered back.
"Let's find out. Keep our people coming."

She ran around to the far side of the porta-potty, putting blessed
distance between her and the absolutely disgusting portal. The first
gust slapped her hard, adding a stinging spray to the insult. Dani
instinctively shut her eyes and averted her face, but the chanted

goggles and mask did their jobs. Seeing and breathing clearly, she planted her boots and stared down the storm.

Her power awoke with an extra rush that left her gasping, as if it had been waiting for this moment to spring. She wrapped her thoughts and willpower tight around it, barely keeping it in check. If she lost control, the energies could make the sandstorm even worse, tossing in an earthquake or tornado for good measure. Yet the riled-up elements tugged hard and she stumbled a step.

The wind buffeted her, and now she heard laughter in it; Ella's laughter, growing louder as the wall of skin-scouring sand loomed closer.

Dani made fists and briefly shut her eyes. The world shifted to her internal sight. Color vanished, while she traced dimensions along the landscape, feeling movement all around in the air currents and rumbling of the earth. Off in the distance, water seeped through a wide, shallow creek bed, little more than a muddy strip of land on the edge of the dunes.

She reached down through the twining cords of power and called for the elementals connected to the other end—those inhuman creatures now bound to her whether she wanted them or not.

"I need your help, ladies."

The voice she recognized as Fire-Dani, one of the self-proclaimed leaders of her minions, hissed in reply.

"What would you desire, oh mighty one? Shall we break out the pep squad? We've been practicing some new cheers, but Dani is kind of proving hard to rhyme."

Dani ground her teeth. *"What is it with you and always the attitude? We have to work together, or we could die together. We've been over this."*

Words crackled like logs in a blaze. *"Yes, and it's always just work for us. You at least get some recognition. Some appreciation. You get paid.".*

You ... want to get paid?" Dani asked. *"With what? Charcoal briquets? Does Stone-Dani want some fresh topsoil?"*

"You're a smart girl," Fire-Dani said. *"At least, that's what you keep trying to convince people. I'm sure we can work out a deal."*

"I can't believe we're about to become our own personal sand dune, and you want to argue salary."

Silence. Dani imagined her fiery doppelgänger watching, arms crossed, a smug look on her face.

Dani punched the ground. *"Fine. Fine! We'll talk this over. Figure out a deal. But could please stop bringing this stuff up when we're dealing with life or death?"*

"Why? It's so much more effective this way."

A sense of multiple presences crowded the space right behind her. Dani didn't bother looking back, knowing it wasn't the other Cleaners suddenly supporting her.

A burning hand settled on her shoulder, but didn't char her suit. *"You need to focus."*

"I am." Dani flung a hand out at storm, which now filled her whole vision. Fortunately, her internal conversations with her elemental others always seemed to take mere moments. "On stopping that."

"Oh, right. Try to stop an enormous wall of made up of countless particles being blown in every possible direction. That's focus. Look past that. To the source."

Dani kept her eyes shut, questing out with cords of power—thrusting them into the storm, seeking the core sustaining the spell.

Then she paused. No. That wasn't right. The Scummoner's will had created this sandstorm. Conjured it, like she did her dust devils. But unlike the constructs, it had no core to destroy. Instead, Ella channeled her power to maintain it. To direct it.

Dani reached her awareness through and past the storm. It muddled her clarity, making it difficult to sense anything on the other side.

Stone-Dani's voice of grinding gravel muttered in her ear. *"Focus."*

Dani growled back. "I'm. Trying."

"Try harder," Fire-Dani said. *"You wouldn't want your whole team to pay for your failure."*

Dani looked over her shoulder, past the elementals only she could see. A portion of the team stood assembled, with most of them crouched and hunched against the grit-filled blasts of wind. A couple Ascendants had their auras up to shield them, but sand had already piled around their shins, and kept rising.

A concentrated gust almost spun Dani down. She caught herself as a wave of wind whipped past and struck the porta-potty. It went tumbling end over end. A janitor flew out from the open door and slammed into the ground, covered in blue slop.

"No!" Shoving herself up, Dani faced the brunt of the sandstorm again. Now half-blinded, she felt the pressure build that would soon send her flying through the air or bury her where she stood.

That hit was more directed, she realized. *Like a shot fired.*

More strikes soared and spiraled past, hitting all around the Cleaners. Dani shut her eyes and traced where they were coming from, reaching through the storm again, cutting past until …

There. A dark pulse of Corrupt energies. A bit higher in elevation, as if Ella stood atop one of the dunes.

Dani grinned as she formed a mental image of the Scummoner perched on high, thinking herself all superior as she tried to bury the Cleaners.

She reached out and thrust her power into the dune beneath the other woman's feet. Locking on, she then tore the earth right out from underneath Ella's feet.

She hoped she didn't imagine the distant howl as Ella got caught up in the avalanche. At the same time, she didn't need to see her topple.

Almost immediately, the wall of dust slowed. Clods of sand pattered the ground, and Dani dodged a few before they smacked her skull.

The storm stilled.

And then it collapsed; dust rained down. Dani covered her head and hunched, trying to avoid it pouring down her uniform collar. Blue sky appeared. In the distance, a particular dune looked like it had been attacked by a fleet of bulldozers. She studied this but didn't see any movement, nor did she sense the concentration of power that'd just been there.

Now where did she get off to?

She jogged over to Lucy, who was helping dig out a maid who'd gotten buried up to the waist.

"How many made it through?" Dani asked.

"We've got …" Lucy did a quick headcount of the Cleaners rising and dusting themselves off. "Nine. Including you and me. I already let the others know to stop sending anyone along. It'll have to do."

"Ben?"

"Here." He stood and waved from behind the downed portapotty. Hocking and spitting, he came over. "Don't suppose that storm goin' away means our target's already down for the count?"

"No." Dani scowled at the dunes. "Don't think it's going to be that easy."

The absence of the unnatural storm revealed the Great Sand Dunes in all their glory. Despite already feeling grimy, Dani couldn't help but be impressed by the view.

From their position at the base, the dunes formed their own miniature horizon, sweeping to sharp peaks and falling to round heaps. Ripples and subtle textures pockmarked their slopes. Softer winds plucked sand from the ridges and drizzled it along, while a snow-sprinkled mountain range rose over twice as high further in the background.

Slurping drew her attention back to Ben. The hose from his water pack ran under the edge of his dust mask. He nodded at the vista. "Pretty, ain't it?"

Dani snorted. "That's one way to sum it up."

"Hey, it ain't the most elaboratorial description, but you gotta give me credit for bein' efficient."

The Cleaners gathered themselves and what equipment had made it through. They all looked to Ben and Lucy.

"It should be too early for many tourists to have arrived, but there may be campers." Lucy pointed to the Ascendants, one of whom Dani realized was a healed-up Wilton. "If we run into anyone, we need you two to make good with the managerial manhandling and get them out of the area. Or at least as far from danger as possible."

"What do we tell them?" Wilton asked.

"Use your imagination," Lucy said. "Tell them there's the threat of an earthquake."

"I can make that more convincing," Dani added.

"No unnecessary earthquakes." Lucy gestured to the dunes. "You want to bring these down on our heads?"

"Hey, if I cause an earthquake, it's always necessary."

Ben let the tube fall from his lips. "Mebbe tell 'em someone's been buryin' toxic waste 'round here. That's always a good scare."

"Or we just get the job done before we have to worry about witnesses," Lucy said. "Can anyone sense our target?"

"Someone was manipulating the wind," a maid said. She pointed with her feather duster toward the dune Dani had made partially collapse. "And the storm came from over that way."

Lucy thumbed at the sky. "Get some altitude while we slog it. See if you can spot anything."

The maid swirled her duster around, and a whirlwind lifted her to hover high overhead. Dani eyed her fine-tuned control with envy. Maybe someday she could manage that sort of spell, but her power still lent itself toward destructive ends.

Ben held his mop out like a war banner. "Fan out, folks. Keep those eyes bouncin' around, and holler if you sense anythin'."

"Nobody get out of sight, though," Lucy added.

They trudged up the first slopes, toward the ridge where Ella must've been standing. Dani kept her power close at hand, connected to the earth all around. Unlike the deserts Ella had created, this place felt oddly alive. She could feel the rocks and dust all around them, like someone had scooped countless stars out of the sky and poured them here to be sorted out. Ambient heat suffused the whole desert and she could still sense a level of moisture trapped deep below.

As she took all this in, the top of the dune split and waves of sand tumbled down at them. The dustbuster—Isaac, by the name stitched on his uniform—yelled, "Get behind me!"

The Cleaners clustered as he stepped forward and flicked a switch on the vacuum canister strapped to his back. He leveled the nozzle and fired.

Frosty air blasted out in a tight stream, which he wove over the oncoming sand waves. Where the air hit, the sand froze in place, turning to icy chunks or locked down by jagged icicles. Sand swept by on either side of the group, but nothing struck them directly.

Instead, the way ahead had become a frost-rimmed path.

"Nifty." Dani studied the vacuum, as he deactivated the nozzle. "When do I get to use one of those?"

Isaac glanced back at her. "Sorry, kid. Dustbusting isn't a gig you can sign up for. You have to be recruited. And be able to manipulate temperatures with total precision. From what I hear, your powers aren't exactly the best match."

Before she could argue—not that right then was the best time to defend her repertoire—the top of the dune shifted again. Instead of tossing more waves at them, though, the sand swirled and disgorged Ella. The Scummoner stood there in high heels, the tips of which refused to sink.

Dani called up. "Ella. Another fake body, I assume?"

The Scummoner patted her own hips. "Oh, this is me, I promise. If you sculpt the same thing over and over, after a while it stops being unique and just becomes a forgery."

"Just like you're stealing Sydney's powers?" Dani said. "Claiming they're unique to you?"

"But they are." Ella strode a few steps closer, remaining atop the sand as if she walked on concrete. "See, I've broken down the original source material into something raw, which I've reformed into my own take on the role. Like an artist who uses recycled materials to create beautiful things."

Ben blew a raspberry. "Or, y'know, they just make big ol' heaps of junk they claim are all artsy so they can sell trash for a million bucks. It's just a big scam, if you ask me."

"No one did," Ella said.

"Aw, shut it, you rotten piece of worm meat."

She frowned. "Rudeness is a tool of a weak mind."

Dani could sense the grin behind Ben's mask. "Yeah, well who asked you?"

Lucy rolled her eyes and shuffled forward. "For Purity's sake, you flirt like a middle-schooler."

"You call this flirtin'?" he asked. "I ain't even got to the mud-flingin' part."

Lucy planted fists on hips and stared up at Ella. "You know why we're here."

"In a misguided attempt to rescue Sydney, I assume." Ella shrugged. "You shouldn't have bothered. Just a few more minutes and there'll be nothing left of him worth saving. Though, I guess you will get a fun show for your efforts. Do you know what will happen when I absorb the last of him?"

"Let me guess," Dani said. "You'll try to take over the world."

"Now why would I want to do that? Don't be so small-minded." She crouched and raised a handful of sand. "You've seen just a fraction of the power I hold now. I've been channeling the rest into quite the special spell. These dunes ... this desert ..." Ella swept an arm at the expansive park, scattering the dust. "It will all act as a seed. A scale model of the true desert I'll sculpt as it spreads out and covers this entire state—taking all life within it and giving it up as an offering to Entropy."

Dani exchanged stunned looks with the others. "Can I call her insane, or does anyone else want to take that?"

Ben stepped up. "Lady, you gotta be one—"

"You're insane," Lucy shouted over him.

Ben sighed. "Aw. Now that's just spoilin' a man's fun."

"Can she really do what she's claiming?" Dani asked.

"With the amount of power Sydney had now in her hands?" Lucy shrugged. "Maybe. Do we really want to find out?"

"Nope," Ben and Dani said at the same time.

Ella crossed her arms. "As much as I enjoy a good exchange of wit, yours isn't exactly on my level. Here. Let me provide a little entertainment alternative." She raised a hand and twirled it.

"$%&#, I know that gesture," Dani said.

Dozens of dust devils rose from the dunes all around them, shedding excess sand as their forms and features became defined.

Ben barked a laugh. "Aw, c'mon. You call this a show? It's just a repeat of last we dosey-do'ed. I want a refund."

Ella frowned. "Hm. Actually, you're right. This is a bit uninspired, isn't it?"

The dune shifted beneath her and she sank up to her waist. She plunged her hands into the sand. Gullies formed, causing sudden depressions, while other sections bulged up.

The top of the dune shot upward into a massive column of dust. A head formed, followed by a giant body, easily fifteen feet tall. Features solidified, and Ella looked down on them while more sand continued to pour up to create boulder-sized hands.

"Y'know," Ben shaded his eyes with his mop, "I always wondered what a literal uphill battle would be like."

"Sometimes I hate you," Lucy grumbled.

He chuckled. "Naw. I'm too handsome to hate. A'ight, buddy. Pop on out." Carl shot out of his spray bottle on his own and flowed up to Ben's shoulder and down his arm. He sealed the mop to Ben's hand and coated the length of it. The tendrils at the end writhed as the water sprite animated them. "I call dibs on the left ankle."

"Her left or ours?" Dani started to whip up the air around herself, preparing a small sandstorm of her own.

"Princess, why you gotta try to confuse me all the time?"

The enormous Scummoner pounded toward them, each step shaking the whole dune.

CHAPTER TWENTY-SEVEN

R eady for this, buddy?" Ben flexed his arm and dug his heels in.

Carl rippled against his hand. *Careful. Don't tire too quickly. Powers are still newly back.*

"Then we'll let 'em rip and see just how much we can do!"

Churning up sand, he charged straight up for the giant Ella. Behind him, Lucy shouted orders.

"Isaac and Oliver, you've got our right side. Dani, help Ben. Wilton and Travis, keep your defensive auras hot." She raised her voice. "Delilah, take any shots you get. Make them count."

"Yes, ma'am." The maid soared past Ben, heading for a dust devil. At the last second, she flipped her legs out in front and flung the air vortex at the construct. The dust devil blew apart, drizzling across the dune.

With a fist pump Ben's way, the maid whisked her feather duster about and took to the air again. As she rose, she flicked a gust of air at Ella's sand golem, which tore the tip off its nose.

Ella tried to grab the maid, but Delilah sped up and out of reach. Ben paused to suck a mouthful of water from his pack. He then focused and spat it into the golem's torso, where it splattered and turned a hefty portion of sand into mud, which sloughed off.

It didn't seem to do much damage otherwise, but it drew Ella's attention back to him. She stared down and sneered as she moved his way. He ran for her as well, and snarled at the Scummoner's oversized face as he neared.

Jeepers. Don't matter how pretty anyone is. Blow 'em up big enough, and they get downright ugly.

Ella bent over and swept a hand at him. Instead of dodging, he turned and aimed the mop like a lance. Carl widened the end into a watery shield, and Ben funneled Pure power through the elemental, reinforcing it.

The hand smashed into the shield—and blew apart into a dusty cloud, fingers pinwheeling away as they dissolved. Ella reared. Her cry hit him harder than her actual attack.

Ben whooped and kicked a pile of sand into the air. "Hope that stung, sweetheart!"

"Ben, look out!"

A body hit him from behind and knocked him to the ground. Dani rolled off him just as a giant sand foot stomped into the earth with explosive force. Dust sprayed them, but his vision and breathing stayed clear with the face gear.

He planted the mop and shoved to his feet. Dani jumped to hers and glared at him. "Stop gloating and just get her."

She turned and raked a hand through the air. A portion of the dune under one of Ella's sand golem legs was swept away. The churning sand buried a couple dust devils—at least temporarily, since Ben didn't figure the stuff would hurt them much—but it also made Ella stagger and go to one hand and knee. Wherever she touched, the boundary between her form and the dune she'd summoned it from blended.

He poised the mop. *Now what's the fun of gettin' without the gloatin'?*

Nevertheless, his boots carved furrows in the dune as he closed the distance. She turned her head as he came in, and her blank, yellow eyes widened slightly.

Spinning, he brought the mop in across her elbow with all his strength. "Batter up!"

Empowered by both him and Carl, the mop blasted through and blew the arm in half. Dust erupted from the hit. The lower arm portion collapsed, leaving a dangling stump.

"Hey, sweetheart." Ben bumped his armless shoulder up and down, showing off the empty sleeve. "We're almost twins."

"$%&#@%&$%, Ben!"

The sand beneath Ella's other golem leg swirled and poured in on itself, forming a sinkhole that ate up the limb before she could pull free. A gasp ripped through the air as the Scummoner dropped almost flat ... just low enough for the head to come into range.

"Let's give 'er a swirlie, eh, buddy?"

Ben aimed the business end of the mop at the Scummoner's ear. The bundle of strings began whipping about so fast, they blurred.

He stabbed this into the side of the golem's head. The mop chewed into the sand head like a buzzsaw, and sand sprayed about like sawdust. Ben shoved the mop deeper, moving it this way and that so it chewed the head into a shapeless mass in seconds.

With a shudder, the giant form collapsed into a heap. Ben yanked his mop clear and spun it around to tuck it under his arm. He studied the dust pile, searching for the Scummoner's real body.

Dani panted as she scrambled up the steep slope to reach him. She had her hands up, looking ready to attack in an instant.

Ben nodded at remains. "Nice sinkhole there, princess. And you didn't take down a house this time, neither."

"Har." She wiped dusty smears from her goggles. "Let's help the others and then figure out where ..."

The dune quivered. Then a geyser of sand knocked them both back several steps. When Ben caught his balance and the dust cleared, another Ella golem loomed over them. She smiled, and her voice tickled his ear, though her mouth didn't move as she spoke.

"I admire the effort. You do try really hard. Even when it doesn't really do anything."

She raised a hand, fingers pointing at the pair. Ben braced to block another blow. Instead, each finger speared out, becoming a column of sand that slammed into the ground in front of them.

The hit staggered him. He continued to lurch about as multiple strikes made the earth shake, while yellow-brown clouds obscured his view. He barely dodged a couple finger-columns that blasted down mere steps away, each one hitting with the force of a wrecking ball.

Ben stumbled through the chaos. Instinct flicked in the back of his head, and he threw himself forward just before the spot he'd been standing disappeared under another column.

Holding the mop close, he rolled through and came up in a clearer area. Dani was on her hands and knees a few yards away, shaking her head as if trying to fight a dizzy spell. At this height, he had a good view of the fights going on lower down.

Lucy fended off a couple dust devils, alternating between ripping off their arms and legs with her steel wool-gloved hand and decapitating them with her toilet brush. Yet more sand filled in the gaps almost as quickly as she made them. Nearby, a janitor wielded dual spray bottles, firing off globs of bleach water. Every hit steamed against the dust devils' forms, making them dissolve into muddy heaps.

Then a dust devil appeared beneath the janitor, wrapped its arms around his legs, and dragged him down up to his waist. The man tried to wrench free, but could only futilely twist and turn in place.

On another slope, a cloud of dust concealed most of what was going on there. Ben made out devilish forms moving about, and a flickering glow suggested one of the Ascendants was trying to hold his own against them.

Overhead, Delilah flew down toward Ella, prepping for another attack. However, Ella turned surprisingly fast for her conjured size. Her hand connected with the flying maid and swatted her out of the air. Delilah plummeted into a distant dune and vanished beneath the dust cloud her impact raised.

Ben ran to Dani. She had a small cut on her temple, and blood ran down her cheek. Yet her eyes were hard, her expression determined as she straightened. Then those eyes went wide as she pointed behind him.

Ben turned to see Ella's form rising another few feet, swelling as the roiling dust drew into her, adding to her mass. She raised both hands, clasped them together, and then shoved them at Ben and Dani.

Shoving his shoulder into Dani, Ben drove them both aside and to the ground. A single, massive stream of sand pounded into the dune. It continued to pour in—and then started moving their way.

Ben got up on one knee and started to draw out all the water he'd been drinking, adding it to Carl's form. He visualized a half-sphere covering him and Dani—a larger version of the spell he'd used to capture the broken coffee mug.

But as he focused, pain punched him in the stomach and head simultaneously. He gasped, his tongue suddenly feeling ten times too big for his mouth. His throat tightened, and his eyes stung, now so dry he could barely blink.

A flash of light half-blinded him right before the sand struck. Ben braced, but the hit never came. He looked up to see Wilton, the Ascendant, interposing himself between them and the spray. His aura shone white-hot, diverting the incoming gouts of sand. His three-piece suit remained crisp and clean, despite the battle and their surroundings.

Swallowing hard, Ben laid the mop down long enough to peel his mask back and suck down more water from the pack's tube. This made the pain vanish in an instant; his vision cleared and he breathed easy again.

Dani groaned as she sat up beside him. She noted Wilton, who nodded back at them and yelled, "I can handle this. Get clear and regroup with the others."

The two staggered out of range of Ella's attack, leaving Wilton to cover their retreat. Ben chafed at even having to retreat, but knew the wisdom of taking an opportunity to reconsider their tactics and launch a better assault.

Once clear, Dani grabbed Ben's arm and pulled him close to shout in his ear, "We're not going to win this way. She's got an inexhaustible supply to work with here."

He nodded, hating to admit they might be overmatched, but unable to deny the evidence. "Whaddya thinkin' we oughta do?"

She scooped up a handful of sand and let it drizzle through her fingers, staring at it as if trying to divine their best options. "We have to find Sydney," she said. "We can fight her all day long, but it won't matter if she still finishes him off. It's his power she's using, remember?"

"Great." He looked around. "You seen him mopin' around here? 'Cause I sure haven't."

Frowning, she flung the dust aside. "No. I keep sensing him. Little flashes of him, like he's close, but being restrained." She squinted up at Ella, a dark shadow barely visible through the cloud billowing around Wilton's aura. "The power exchange must require both their bodies being in the same area. Or close to each other. She's here ... so he must be, too."

"Well, then she's doin' a tidy job of keepin' him hidden right under our noses."

"Under ..." Dani stared at their feet. "Ben, you're a genius!"

"You oughta tell Lu that after all this. Wanna tell me why I'm so smart? Not that I'm disagreein'."

She grabbed his arm again and pointed down. "Underground. Under the dunes. That must be where she's got him."

"You sure 'bout that?"

"It's our best chance. Otherwise we'll all be buried soon. She could be chasing us all over the dunes, but she's sticking right on top of this one. There has to be a reason."

Ben channeled power into Carl and the mop. The elemental coated the threads at the end, spreading them into the shape of a scoop. The water hardened, turning the mop head into a makeshift shovel. "Guess we oughta get to diggin'."

"Hang on." She stuck a hand in his face and looked aside. "Can you help me with this?"

"'Course," he said, speaking to her palm. "That's we're all here for, ain't it?"

"Look," she went on, as if not having heard. "I already promised you. It's not like I've had time to think it over since we got here. And if we die, you won't be getting anything anyways."

He frowned. "Ain't nobody gone die today. We're gonna beat this. I can feel it in my gizzard."

She huffed. "You all can be really selfish, you know that? Millions of lives are at stake here. Yes, human lives matter! All of them. And yes, elementals, too. Don't you remember the Nothingness from the other deserts?"

"Hokey-doke, you've lost me. Is this some sorta code talkin' I didn't get the memo about?"

Her head whipped around and she dropped her arm. "#$%&. Was I talking out loud?"

Ben looked to make sure no one else had snuck up that he hadn't noticed. "Sure-for-shootin', princess. Who else were you thinkin' you was talkin' to?"

Her cheeks flushed, noticeable even through the dust coating her face. "I ... never mind. Just thinking out loud."

Despite the dunes baking under the rising sun and him already sweating from the fight, Ben felt a chill tickle. More than one Catalyst had been known to go loopy without warning. Something about their powers being unstable, the Cleaners theorized. Dani had seemed just fine so far—her prior mental quirks and compulsions aside—but nobody knew, really knew, what triggered other cases.

Mebbe after this, I oughta have a chit-chat with Francis about Dani. See if he's got any ideas bumpin' 'round that noggin of his.

He lifted the mop-shovel. "You want me to get us started?"

She shook her head. "I'll get Sydney. You keep Ella busy."

She jogged a short distance off. Studying the ground, she pressed her hands together, and then snapped them apart. The dune quaked, and a crevasse tore wide before her. Dust poured into it along the sides. Ben couldn't see the bottom.

"Back soon," she called. "I hope."

He raced to reach her. "Dani, wait—"

She stepped into the gap and dropped out of sight. An instant later, the sand sealed up over her.

He stared at the spot. Minor trembles triggered sandslides all around, and he was forced move to keep his legs from getting buried.

He scanned the dunes. Delilah remained motionless in the crater Ella had knocked her into. The other Ascendant was frantically trying to dig the janitor out, who was now buried up to his neck. Isaac spun full circles, spraying his freezing blast at ten dust devils who all converged on him. For each one he shattered, another took its place.

Motion in the corner of his eye made him turn.

Lucy had a dust devil in a headlock a few strides away. She tore chunks out of it with her toilet brush, trying to get to its core. But its head sucked back into its body and reappeared as it pulled free. Its arms swung full circles to smash fists into Lucy's gut.

The janitor somersaulted backward. Her brush flew away.

"Lu!"

Ben loped as quick as he could to her side. She stirred and blinked as he knelt by her. Lucy's dust mask had been torn open from the hit. She spat bloody sand to the side as she lurched to her feet.

"Where's Dani?" she asked.

"Gone to get Sydney."

"She knows where he is?"

"Here's hopin'."

She met his gaze, uncertainty flickering in her eyes. Then she nodded and that doubt vanished. "All right. What do we do until she gets back?"

"We do what Dani said." He turned Ella's way. "We keep this here fat-kidneyed devil busy."

"Right. Oh, and you should know ..."

"Hm?"

"You ever try to slip one of those old-timey insults past me, I will make you eat a book containing the complete works of Shakespeare."

So saying, she drew another brush from her belt and started bulling her way toward the sand golem. Ben grinned at her back.

"That's my jovial, burly boned truepenny."

"I heard that!"

He grimaced and ran after. "It was supposed to be a compliment."

Passing Lucy, he aimed for Ella, who remained focused on launching attacks at Wilton. The Ascendant deflected and dodged them, but was visibly tiring.

Closing the gap, Ben plunged the mop into the sand golem's chest and swept it around, stirring up the muck he made.

"I know you're in there. Why don'tcha come out and dance in person?"

The mop jarred to a stop. Ben tugged, but it wouldn't come loose.

The sand pulled aside to reveal Ella's real face within the depths of the golem. Her hands grasped the mop handle.

"I've a better idea," she said. "Why don't you join me in here?"

She yanked with surprising strength. Ben tried to pull away, but found himself being dragged inexorably closer as the sand started to close around him.

CHAPTER TWENTY-EIGHT

Darkness engulfed Dani. She fell longer than expected, just enough for her heart to make an escape attempt via her throat. When she hit the bottom of the pit she'd created, the sand beneath her shifted, absorbing the impact but throwing her off-balance. Her legs collapsed, sending her sprawling. Breathless, she could only lay there for a few moments as sand poured down on her back, the weight of it making taking another breath more impossible by the moment.

She tried to push up and her arms sank to the elbows. A glance skyward showed light beaming through the crack she'd made—just before it sealed over. Spots flickered in her vision, her brain trying to compensate for the total blackness; she pulled one arm free to knuckle at her eyes, only to remember the goggles sealed over them.

Trying to stand, she found the sand already had her lower body pinned, and the mound grew across her upper back and shoulders. She gasped and sagged beneath the weight. Struggling just sapped her strength all the faster as she pulled and yanked desperately.

Shutting her eyes didn't help, for her inner, elemental vision easily showed the space she'd formed rapidly filling in, gaps closing all around her, robbing her of any last bits of movement. She filled her lungs as much as she could and held the air in, trying to form some extra space around her as the countless pounds of dust pressed around her head, clamping down until she feared it would crush her skull like an egg being squeezed in a fist.

Yet after another few seconds of wriggling, pulse throbbing in her ears, lungs straining, the pressure stopped increasing. Dani stilled. She felt held in a full-body hug, firm and unyielding, as if she wore ten times more layers of clothes than normal.

That's it. Don't think of it like being buried. The sand dune isn't holding me. I'm wearing the sand dune like … like trying to move while inside fifty sweaters at once. The sand dune is my fat suit.

She dared to breath out. The sand shifted slightly, but she still had enough room to move her chest a few inches. Her mask remained in place, and the enchantment on it let her draw air without obstruction. Each breath eased the rising panic that had threatened to swallow her as surely as the sand had.

I just buried myself in dirt! What was I thinking? I am literally surrounded by potential contaminants. What if my mask fails? What if my goggles crack? All this dirt in my mouth … my eyes … my hair …

"Calm."

The voice of Dani's main earth elemental plunked into the center of her mind like a rock clacking on pavement. Unlike Fire-Dani, Stone-Dani spoke with little inflection, steady and emotionless. This helped her, though, as it leveled out her own emotions a bit, reminding her that she wasn't stuck here alone.

"Hey there. Still going to help?" she asked.

"Yes," replied Stone-Dani, "you've given us your trust. I intend to repay."

Dani almost sighed heavily in relief, but kept her breathing steady to avoid moving too suddenly and disturbing the settling sand around her.

"Awesome. So what do I do now? You said you had an idea."

"You must focus. Think of the earth. It is not a static thing. It moves, though slowly, building pressure. Yet there are times when that buildup is unleashed in a span of moments rather than ages."

"More earthquakes?"

"Controlled ones. Like the tiny tornadoes the book has had you practice. Hold the quake within you. Do not fling it out at random. Remain in command."

Dani twitched. *"Tornadoes and earthquakes are a little different from each other. If I mess up with air, I can just let it disperse. Can't really do that with earthy stuff."*

"You are the hypocenter. You are a tectonic nexus. Be the focus. Be the fault line."

That made Dani think back to a college general sciences course. After a massive earthquake had hit an overseas country, causing thousands of deaths, the instructor had spent a week discussing the natural disasters. She recalled a video illustrating how earthquakes began at specific points where underground rock broke, releasing the energy that caused the seismic activity itself to ripple outward.

Dani the Fault Line. Not sure I'll be adding that to my job description.

As her earthen-alter-self had suggested, she focused on becoming the focus. Rather than snaking lines of power out through the earth as usual, she instead knotted it inside herself, twining the energies in and around themselves in a roiling ball of potential. She gripped this tighter, condensing the power, increasing the tension on it.

Then, after a brief pause, she envisioned that ball snapping in half. She loosed the power, which rippled out from her in a wave of Pure energy.

The sand pressing in all around her was shoved back all at once. She breathed deep, relishing the freedom. She pushed to her knees and found herself in a small pocket within the dune, the sand having been compacted outward in a rough sphere, firm enough to hold its shape for the moment.

"Well done," commented Stone-Dani.

Dani smiled weakly. *"Thanks. You, too. I'll make it up to all of you. I promise."*

"We know."

She sensed the earth elemental withdraw. After another mental nod of gratitude, Dani turned her mind to the reason she'd come. With her now beneath the dune's surface, the ambient Corrupt energies she'd been sensing all along sharpened into a pinpoint of power deeper down.

She stood and oriented herself to this. Moving to one edge of the chamber, she pressed her body against the sand and unleashed another mini-quake. The dust blew away ahead of her, and she stepped into the new space just as the old one collapsed behind her.

In this manner, she continued to unleash a series of mini-quakes, each one emanating from her, opening cavities just big enough for her to move forward in fits and spurts.

She delved into the dune's base, the Corrupt energies nearing with each shift she made. Then, without warning, she quaked open the sand ahead of her and almost fell into a far larger chamber than she'd anticipated.

Catching herself, Dani opened her eyes in surprise. She shut them again just as quickly to restore her elemental sight—but then realized there'd been an odd light to the area she'd just entered.

She reopened her eyes to what looked like a natural cave, with rocky walls interspersed with patches of sand, about the size of a two-car garage with an uneven floor

And all of it was lit by a dim purple glow emanating from Sydney, who lay in the center of the floor. Rather than the white tuxedo he'd sported on their date, he wore a tattered black shirt, slacks, and scuffed shoes. The glow of his aura against his pale skin and the deep hollows of his cheeks and eye sockets lent him a cadaverous look.

Dani rushed to him. "Sydney!"

Her cry was a muted echo, and a few drizzles of dust fell from the ceiling. Sydney remained unresponsive even as she knelt beside him. She realized his aura wasn't steady. Rather, it pulsed slightly every few breaths. Even as she watched, it seemed to fade a bit, deepening the shadows in the place.

She stripped off her goggles and mask, keeping both dangling by their straps around her forearms.

"Sydney. Sydney?" She checked him over quickly, looking for any obvious signs of injury. He breathed, if lightly, and he had a pulse, if weak.

"Come on. Wake up. Please. We need your help."

She patted his cheeks. Then slapped them. She thumped a fist on his chest, raising her voice until she shouted his name, ordering him to wake up. All to no response.

300

At a loss, she sat back heavily, shoulders slumped. "I'm too late, aren't I? You're already too far gone. We lost."

In the fading light of his aura, he almost looked expectant. Waiting for something.

A crazy thought winged through her mind. Dani scrunched her eyes shut and shook her head hard, trying to cast out the unwanted idea. "No. No way. Uh-uh. It's stupid. Wouldn't even work. It's from a #$%&^@# fairytale, for Purity's sake."

She groaned as the idea refused to be dismissed.

"$%&#@$$%&#, Sydney, I am not going to kiss you like you're some #$%&^#@& Sleeping Beauty."

The softest whisper teased her ear.

"Why ... not?"

She looked up to see his lips puckered, ever so slightly. She stared until one of his eyes cracked open a sliver.

"I hate you," she said.

"There is ... reason to doubt." Sydney's gaze flicked about the cave and he grimaced. "Ah. This place. I thought it ... a nightmare."

"It kind of is." Dani pointed to the ceiling. "Ella's up there, right now, kicking our #$@%$ and getting ready to use all the power she's siphoned from you to unleash some sort of mega-desert, killing everyone in Colorado. Or so she claims."

Sydney groaned and tried to rise, but fell back. Dani helped him sit up. His blond hair fell loose over his brow, and his aura continued its weak flickering.

"I fear she might be quite capable of that," he said.

"How is she so strong?" Dani asked. "You turned things to dust or erased them completely. But all these other abilities? On this scale?"

He chuckled softly. "A simple enough answer. She is not holding back."

"And you were?"

Sydney's cheek twitched. "Always."

Dani hesitated, and then laid a gloved hand on his cheek. "Then I need ... *we* need you to not hold back any more. To help us stop her."

He looked her full in the face, his expression unreadable. After a long moment, he turned away. "No. I cannot."

"What?" She gripped his shoulder. "Sydney, you have to."

"It is not for a lack of wanting. It is for a lack of ability." He studied his hands, the trembling in his fingers traveling up his arm until his entire upper body shook. "You were … right. It's too late. I am undone."

"No. No, no, that's not true." She took one of his hands and squeezed it to stop the shaking. "There's still time. There's still hope."

He closed his eyes. "In time, in the face of the oblivion of eternity, even hope must die. Everything ends, Dani. You cannot deny it."

She grabbed his chin and forced him to look at her. "You know what? You're right."

He blinked. "Pardon?"

"You're right. We live in a reality where things decay. Where they die. It's a law of the universe. It's a plain fact, however much we try to ignore it." She dropped her hand. "No matter what I do to delay it, no matter how careful I am, one day, I'm going to grow old and die. So will everybody I know. My parents. The few friends I have. My coworkers. Lucy. Laurel and Hardy. Ben. Although," she sniffed a laugh, "maybe he'll have an easier time dealing with it his second go-round as a grumpy old grampa."

He smirked, but said nothing.

"But that's not happening right here and now," she said. "Now's a point where we can still act. Where we can still make a difference and save lives. Where we can give Entropy a big, fat middle finger right in its stupid face and laugh. We can't do it alone, though. We need you."

Sydney stared into the distance for several long breaths. Then he slowly lowered himself to lie back on the floor, eyes closed.

"I am sorry. You should flee while you still can."

Dani sat watching as she tried to figure out what she could do. Screaming and punching him wouldn't help anything. She didn't think getting all weepy and begging would change his mind, either. There was no deal she could strike. No date she could offer, no matter how pretty a dress she promised to wear.

Over the years of living out her germophobic obsessions, she knew how impossible it was to force someone to act when they simply didn't want to or didn't believe they could. How many times had family and friends tried to shove her out into the germ-ridden world, claiming they were doing it for her own good? Trying to make her face and overcome her fears? They never understood that, to her, the world had looked like a hopeless battle. An enemy she could never defeat, so why bother trying? Better to tuck herself away, put up as many boundaries and safeguards as possible, and handle the few tiny threats of exposure and contamination she could deal with.

In time, yes, she'd slowly learned how to cope in healthier ways, and her unexpected recruitment into the Cleaners had given her further strength—plus a few magical confidence-boosters. But Ella's threat didn't give them the luxury of time. It needed to be dealt with immediately, or the world might be broken in a way that could never be repaired.

Dani's skin tingled with the rush of an idea. She stood and looked down on Sydney, who appeared less substantial by the moment.

"Sydney, I want you to listen to me." If he did, he gave no sign, but she forged on nonetheless. "Remember the squirrel? The mostly dead one you told me about on our date? The one you found and cared for, even though deep down, you thought it might be hopeless to save it? But it wasn't, because you tried. Despite everything everyone believed, you fought with all you had." She made a fist, glove squeaking. "Remember how much you wanted to make a difference? To help people? That's what this is now. A squirrel situation. You can fight. Just for a little longer. And if you gave up without that last bit of effort, I think that squirrel would be very, very disappointed in you."

Sydney remained motionless. His aura dimmed until she could barely see it, and darkness almost claimed the cave.

Then the purple glow swelled. He stirred and peeked up at her. An eyebrow quirked.

"Did you truly just try to give me a motivational speech based on a squirrel?"

Dani offered him a hand. "Did it work?"

His skeptical expression turned to amusement.

"I dare say it might have."

He grabbed her hand and she hauled him to his feet, shocked by how little he weighed. She put one of his arms over her shoulders and helped him walk to one of the cave walls.

"I'm going to get us back up there," she said, "and then we'll just do the best we can and see what happens."

"I suppose we shall." He coughed and glanced at her sidelong. "For the squirrel, m'dear?"

Dani grinned. "For the squirrel." *Those horrid little, disease-ridden rodents that I'd burn with flamethrowers if they ever got within fifty feet of me.*

With one arm around his waist, she pressed her other hand to a rocky portion of the wall.

"Hold on. This might be a bit of a rough ride."

CHAPTER TWENTY-NINE

Ben kicked and squirmed as Ella tugged him further into the sand golem. The portion he'd torn open continued to rapidly close up.

"Word of warnin' for you," he said through gritted teeth. "Never threaten a fella's partner. Get 'er, buddy."

Her pinched look of confusion flipped to shock as a portion of the water coating the mop slapped up over her whole face.

She released the mop, and Ben turned and flung it free, sending it and the rest of Carl flying back out into the open. The elemental's burble of dismay cut off as the sand flowed in and cut off Ben's view.

His arm became pinned to his side, and his legs might as well have been stuck in dried concrete. His head remained clear, though, poking into the small space Ella gave herself within the golem's form.

Black energy swirled about the Scummoner, and the water sizzled away. She wiped a few remaining drops off her mouth and flicked them aside.

"You Cleaners are an amusing diversion. But that's all you are." She made a fist, and the sand containing Ben compressed slightly, forcing a gasp out of him. "I appreciate effort, so I'll let you decide how I kill you. Would you prefer all your bones being broken? Your skin peeled off a layer at a time? Or should I just fill your lungs with dust and let you choke?"

"Real good thing you was never a game show host," he said. "I ain't thinkin' your ratin's would've been all that hefty."

"If you don't choose one," she said, "I'll just try them all. I mean, why limit yourself?"

The sand shifted around him, grinding against his suit, while a portion funneled up toward his mouth. Ben groaned at the pressure.

"Y'know, with you messin' around with all this dust and dirt, don't it leave you feelin', I dunno, a little dirty?"

"Are you about to get crude on me?" she asked.

"Naw. You ain't my type. I was more gonna suggest you takin' a bath. Howsabout it?"

He drew on all the Pure power he could, ripping it out of himself and reaching for the nearest, biggest source of water—his drinking pack. He poured the energies into this, channeling them with ferocious desperation, not bothering with any finicky visualizations. Just raw, supercharged liquid, so chock full of power it couldn't be contained.

Water exploded from the pack, tearing through the lining and bursting through the sand containing him. It whipped about everywhere. Ben's arm and legs pulled free, and he dove for the Scummoner, thinking if he could just knock her unconscious, it might be enough.

Ella shrieked and reeled as she water plastered her pretty dress to her slim body. She flung her arms out, and twin spikes of sand shot out from behind her to ram into his chest.

Ben gasped as they flung him backward, flipping him through the new hole he'd made in the golem and out into the bright light. He hit the dune slope and rolled. Tumbling uncontrollably, he tried to grab for purchase, but couldn't snag anything firm enough with his one hand.

Bumping and flopping, he finally slid to a stop near the bottom of the dune. He lay on his back, heaving breaths. His chest ached like he'd tried to hug a charging bull. His face stung all over, no doubt a mess of scrapes and scratches.

At some point, his mask and goggles had been torn away. His chuffs and huffs blew grit into the air. Licking his lips made him swallow even more sand, which scratched his raspy throat. An incredible thirst gripped him and underscored every movement with trembling weakness.

With massive effort, he turned his head to look back up the dune. He glimpsed Ella's scowl just before her golem re-sealed. It moved toward him, each ponderous step reminding him of how squishy he really was inside the suit.

He tried to rise but his arm and legs made a vote of no confidence and refused to accede to his demands. He thought he heard Lucy hollering his name somewhere in the distance, but couldn't get the strength up for so much as a feeble wave.

As the golem reached the slope's halfway point, it halted. Ben didn't know if the earth was shaking or if it was just him, or if it really mattered at that point.

That question resolved itself when a giant crack appeared just off to the side of where the sand golem stood. Ella stepped away from this, but the fissure kept widening. One of the golem's legs collapsed as the earth vanished beneath it. The golem fell once more, graceless, and its form broke apart as it was pulled into the still-growing crack.

The ravine shot up to the top of the dune, splitting it in half. Sand flooded down the slopes as the dune shifted violently, shuddering and spilling until a V-shaped crevice broke the dune apart.

At the base of this, not thirty feet from where Ben lay, a jagged spear of rock had appeared. Dani stood on the tip of this. Beside her was a familiar pale, black-clad figure. Sydney looked near skeletal and likely would've face-planted without Dani holding him up.

They spotted Ben and managed to make it down off the rock and over his way in a surprisingly short time, given Sydney's limp and Dani supporting him the whole time.

"Hiya," Ben managed to croak as their shadows fell over him. "Ain't supposin' either of you'd have a drop or two of water to spare an old geezer?"

"Hello, Benjamin." Sydney stood back as Dani helped Ben get to his feet. "I see your powers have returned. When did that occur?"

Ben swallowed a few times until he could talk again. He figured he didn't sound so much like a chain smoker as someone who'd just shoved an actual carton of cigarettes down their throat. "Oh, right. You wasn't there. Lemme tell you all about it after we finish moppin' up this mess, huh?"

A spray of dust made them look up as Ella descended from the sky, held aloft by a pair of dust devils with whirling lower bodies. They set her down a few paces away, where she scowled at the group.

"You think this accomplishes anything?" She stabbed a finger at Sydney. "I'm still bound to him. I'm wringing the last drops of power out of him even as we speak. All you get to do now is actually watch him die, just before it's your turn."

Dani moved as if to intercept, but Sydney held an arm out. "Let me handle this. Take care of Benjamin."

As Sydney limped toward Ella, Ben whispered to Dani. "All righty. Good plan. While he's distractifyin' her, we can circle 'round behind and—"

"No, Ben." She gave his arm a warning squeeze. "We let him handle it, like he said. That's what he came back to do."

He frowned, but his weakened state wouldn't let him do much else but stand and watch. Sydney stopped within an arm's length of Ella. His purple aura pulsed in time with her black one, mingling where they met. With each beat, his became harder to see, while hers grew impossibly darker.

"Ella." He bowed. "You have rather abused me."

She sneered. "You deserved every bit of it for what you did to me."

"I will not argue that. But this is between you and me. All those innocents should not suffer for my actions. My mistakes."

Ella waved that off. "You showed me that in the scope of eternity, concepts like innocence and beauty and all those other human constructs don't really mean anything."

"And there is where I erred. Perhaps with immortals or those such as the Pantheon, some concepts do not apply. But you and I," he gestured back to Ben and Dani, "all of us live in the present, where those things still most certainly matter."

She grinned impishly. "Then you all should be glad you won't be living for much longer. My last little gift to you will be the oblivious peace you've preached about all these years."

Sydney's shoulders drooped. "I cannot let you do this."

"No?" She gave a look of mock surprise. "Dear Sydney, how exactly do you plan to stop me when you can barely stand?"

He stepped in so they were inches apart. Her playful expression dropped away, replaced by wariness. She held her hands up, black energy crackling around her fists as if about to deck him.

"We are bound, as you said." Sydney smiled softly. "And all bindings are two-way."

He raised his own open hands and curled his fingers over hers. He drew one of her hands up to kiss the knuckles.

Then he pulled on the other to bring her into a kiss.

Beside Ben, Dani drew a sharp breath. Her fingers clutched tighter.

As their lips locked, Sydney's and Ella's auras merged, purple writhing on black. The energies sped up and thickened until they obscured the couple from view.

The dust devils that had brought Ella down collapsed, and the Corrupt cores that had been within them were sucked into the unified aura. All around the wrecked dune, any remaining dust devils shared the same fate, and each core added to the frenetic power.

The sand around the Corrupt sphere containing the two rose into the air to form an outer shell. It all spun so fast, the currents of energy becoming so chaotic, that Ben had to constantly blink away rushes of dizziness.

The wind slapped waves of sand over them. Ben started to shuffle back, but Dani stood rooted, and held him with a steely grip, keeping him from going anywhere as she stared into the maelstrom.

Roaring, screeching, and howling, the chaos continued to swell until Ben braced for the inevitable surge of uncontrolled energy. Just as it reached a peak, though, all the dust sucked inward, like iron filings to a super magnet.

The wind died. A final pattering of sand coated the area. The ground stopped shaking.

And where Sydney and Ella had been, stood a lone figure—a featureless statue of sand.

"What—" Dani shook her head, sending dust cascading from her fire-red curls. "What just happened?"

"Dunno," Ben said. "Mebbe we won? Mebbe we lost? Guess it depends on who that is over there." He pointed his chin at the figure.

As if in response, the sandy form twitched just so. Ben tensed, wondering if they were about to go back to square one. Dani muttered to herself.

"Come on …"

An arm moved, and the sand proved to be a shell as it cracked and fell off. A pale hand flexed. The rest of the sand quickly dropped away as Sydney shook free. Dust streaked his whole body; he tried to wipe a few spots clean but only succeed in spreading it around.

Dani finally released Ben. He teetered but caught his balance before exfoliating his face with the layer of sand on the ground.

"You did it!" Dani cried as she ran for Sydney.

He backed up and raised his hands, making her draw up short. "As much as I would enjoy your affections, I need a moment to gather myself, please."

"Oh." She clasped her hands in front of herself. "Right. Sorry."

A shout made them all turn to see Lucy slogging down one of the smaller dunes left over from Dani's destruction of the larger one. She panted and wiped sweat from her brow as she ran up.

"What happened? Where's the Scummoner?"

"It's gonna be just fine, Lu." Ben went up to her and put his hand on her shoulder, hoping she wouldn't notice how heavily he leaned on her. "It's over."

Sydney gave them all a lopsided smile. "Indeed, it is." He swept a bow and flared an arm out in a flamboyant gesture. "Though more for me than you. Fortunately, all of you will get to endure, while I must bid you farewell."

"What?" Dani looked to Ben and back to the entropy mage. "Farewell?"

Ben squinted at the other man. Something did seem off about Sydney, but he couldn't quite pinpoint it. Sydney still emanated Corrupt energies and appeared to be in control of himself, so what ...

Movement rippled up his leg and made him jump. He looked down to see Carl flowing up his uniform. Ben smiled. "There you are, buddy. Hope you ain't sore about me tossin' you into the dust. Couldn't see no other way to keep you from gettin' evaporated."

Carl fizzed and spat a blob onto Ben's cheek. *Throw me away again and I will block your bladder for a week.*

Ben had lost the spray bottle in the battle, so he simply reached down and let Carl absorb into his skin. The inrush of moisture eased the thirst that'd been throttling him, and he raised his gaze to Sydney with new clarity.

"You ain't got any water in you," he said.

Sydney looked at him oddly. "You can sense that now, can you?"

Ben's grin widened. "I think there's a few new tricks up my sleeves. Er ..." A glance at where his right arm had been. "Sleeve." He frowned back at Sydney. "You ain't really alive, are you?"

"Ben, what're you talking about?" Dani edged closer to Sydney. "He's standing right here."

"Naw, he ain't, princess. That there's another one of them dust bodies, like he had before."

Sydney inspected his fingernails. "Mm. Well, my mind seems to have stuck around a bit longer than I expected. Perhaps a sliver of my soul as well, if you believe in such a thing." He winked at Lucy. "Or if you could believe someone like me to be in possession of one."

Lucy eyed him suspiciously, as if thinking this to be another trick.

Sydney faced Dani, who looked stricken.

"No," she said. "You can't. Not now. You just did something amazing. Something good."

"Then perhaps it will end up meaning something." He held a palm up to her. "At least I go knowing the world is in far better hands than mine."

A tremble shook Dani, and she hugged herself, but didn't turn away.

Sydney lifted his head and gave Ben a jaunty nod. "Congratulations on the return of your powers, Benjamin. If anyone deserves to remain in this fight, it is you." He grimaced. "But a word of caution. Never forget that, beneath it all, you are still just a janitor."

Ben chuckled. "Oh, you can betcha I ain't never gonna have trouble rememberin' that."

"Hm." Sydney glanced at Lucy. "Janitor Lucy—"

"Goodbye," Lucy said. She hesitated and sighed, eyes squeezed shut as she forced out the words. "And … thank you."

He tilted his head in acknowledgement and turned to Dani once more. "I do hope that squirrel would be satisfied with my performance."

Her laugh had a quaver to it that threatened to tumble into a sob.

Sydney smiled. As the seconds trickled by, Ben realized the man had stopped moving altogether. No breath. No twitch of the eyes or lips.

"Sydney?" Dani reached out and brushed his cheek with gloved fingertips. His features crumbled into dust, and she gasped, jerking back.

His dissolution continued, shoulders and torso crumbling and wafting away on the wind. They stood in silence as his lower body eroded inch by inch, until the last grain was carried off and scattered across the dunes.

CHAPTER THIRTY

L ucy radioed in their coordinates, but it took another hour before the first Cleaner teams arrived by van from Colorado Springs. By then, several curious families had driven in and stopped to gawk at the scene, while a couple park rangers hustled onto the scene and began demanding answers from the team. Wilton spent a long while with them, trying to convince them of one scenario or another, but his battered state and white suit didn't appear to distract them much from the fact that a whole dune had been torn in half.

The rest of the team clustered around the now-righted porta-potty, trying to make it look like they'd all come out to deal with it. A little overkill, Ben figured, but it was their only real option until the scrub-team made it.

He studied the others, tallying up the damage. Dani sat in the porta-potties shadow, knees hugged to her chest, silent ever since Sydney's death. Lucy kept radioing in reports, even though Francis kept telling her to wait until they got back to HQ so she could get all the details properly reported.

Isaac, the dustbuster, tinkered with his vacuum, which had apparently overheated and clogged a bit. The other Ascendant stood behind Wilton, attempting to lend a silent air of authority, though he looked more dazed than determined.

One janitor had vanished beneath the sands, and Ben hated to think he might never be recovered. Maybe the scrub-team would have better luck finding the remains to get them back to HQ and into Storage. Delilah had limped in twenty minutes after everything blew over, clutching a feather duster that no longer had any feathers. She now sat beside Dani, staring at it as if waiting for it to sprout new plumage.

As for himself, Ben tried to sort through all the conflicting emotions that jumbled around inside him like mismatched socks in a dryer. On the one hand, having his powers back kept giving him a giddy rush that made him want to run around, hooting and hollering, despite his weariness—and that annoying thirst filling his mouth with cotton. They'd made the big bad go boom, and saved who-knew-how-many lives.

On the other hand, losing Sydney wrenched at him in a way he hadn't expected. Ben knew plenty who would cheer the entropy mage's death, and guessed there'd be plenty who wouldn't even believe his sacrifice in the first place.

Mebbe it don't matter how many know. Mebbe it's more who knows. He looked at Dani, who pointedly didn't return anyone's gaze. *Aw, princess. Ain't the time or place for me to butt in, but I know just a teensy bit how you're feelin'. Can't promise it gets any easier, but I can say it ain't gonna have that chokehold on your head and heart and lungs like I know it's got with you right now. Just keep breathin', and you'll work it through. And we're gonna be right here to help the whole way.*

He and Sydney had been fighting for different teams long enough that Ben wasn't quite sure what to make of him in the end. The man had been a downright dirty dog plenty of times, but maybe not the rabid monster Destin and others had framed him as. And Ben had seen how the man had affected Dani, and the hope she'd given Sydney in return. Sure, he'd had his smarm and had needed a few lessons on personal space, as well as how to take no for an answer. Yet Ben knew from experience how having the right person in one's life—no matter how mismatched they might first seem to be—could make all the difference. How it could make someone see life from a better perspective. How it could help a person stay human.

His sigh scraped over his tongue, which felt like a strap of brittle leather. Over by one of the families that had stopped in curiosity, a girl stood sucking on the straw of a juice box. Ben swallowed hard and fought the impulse to run over and snatch the drink from her.

Fortunately, two vans finally pulled in. One held a full scrub-team, with a pair of plumbers—ones no doubt who specialized in snaking out unwanted memories of the various witnesses who'd gathered. The other van held a couple janitors and a handyman, who set about dealing with the team's more serious injuries. Then the team was crammed into one of the vans, which headed out for the nearest glassway, leaving the others to deal with cleaning up the scene.

The whole drive was subdued, with little noise but the van's engine and occasional radio chatter. They reached the Springs and drove to a random shop with a sign that read: CLEANERS. After being ushered into the back of the shop, they trudged through a glassway hidden in a side closet and emerged into HQ's pristine halls. The transfer removed the last of any dust and grime clinging to them, but Ben still had to resist the urge to scratch at himself in unmentionable spots. Who knew a bit of sand could itch so bad?

Most of the team headed to Maintenance to finish getting patched up, but, in unspoken agreement, Ben, Lucy, and Dani split off to get the reporting bit over with. Yet after a couple turns, Dani also peeled away and headed for a hall in another direction.

"Where you goin', princess?" Ben called after.

She looked over her shoulder. "I need to tell him about Sydney."

Ben nodded in the direction he and Lucy had taken. "That's what we're headin'."

Lucy hip-bumped him. "She's not talking about Francis."

Ben drew his brow down, confused. Then realization blew an air horn inside his head. "Oh." He coughed. "Sure you don't wanna wait? I can give you a little company

Her tiny smile was overshadowed by the pain in her eye. "No. I think the fewer people, the better. Just for now, at least."

"Gotcha."

Once she left, Ben and Lucy made a quick detour through the cafeteria. He grabbed a gallon jug of water while Lucy swiped a mug and whole carafe of coffee. They reached the Chairman's office

Josh Vogt

swiftly enough after this. Francis waited for them, his desk cleared for once, and gestured for them to begin without any preamble. In between sips and glugs of their respective beverages, the two took turns conveying their experiences.

Once they finished, Francis sat in silence for several minutes. Then he took his fedora off and set it to the side. "I believe I have all the details necessary. I'll write the report up myself to process."

"Really?" Ben bobbed his eyebrows in surprise. "That's downright kind of you. What's the catch?"

"No catch," Francis said. "You've worked hard and deserve a rest, if a short one. Though I would ask both of you—and Ms. Hashelheim—to review my draft for accuracy before I file it."

Lucy stepped up. "Sir, one thing you should try to get right is Sydney's role in this. I was wrong about him. He really was trying to do the right thing. To make amends. I think that needs to be highlighted."

"Was he?" Francis held his hands up. "Or had he found himself overwhelmed and so used us in an attempt to get his powers back? Perhaps he intended to betray us in the end and just miscalculated what his rescue would cost."

"Aw, c'mon, Francis." Ben shook the jug, making it slosh. "You can't be believin' that after all this."

The Chairman leaned back in his chair. "I don't. But the Board may choose to interpret these events differently, in order to maintain their usual black-and-white view of events. It is increasingly difficult for them to accept that anyone touched by Corruption could ever be redeemed or fully trusted."

He looked directly at Ben as he said this. Ben felt a phantom ache where his missing arm had been, a limb that had been infested by Corruption. He thought of Jared, who balanced Pure and Corrupt powers of unknown potential within himself.

Ben glowered. "Yeah, well, if that's what they're gonna think, then put it in the report that I think the Board's a buncha lumpish, spur-galled whey-faces."

"You do realize," Francis said, "that Board members have shed most emotions, including the capacity to feel insulted—even if those insults are of the highest literary caliber."

316

"That's what they want us to think." Ben eyed the ceiling, imagining the Board looking down on them from on high. "But I'll figure out some way to get under the skin. I can be stubborn like that."

Lucy grunted, whether in agreement, disapproval, or both, Ben couldn't tell.

"There's another matter you both should be aware of." Francis leaned forward, fingers steepled. "The chimney sweep."

"Rafi? What about him? He talkin' yet?"

"The opposite, actually. He's escaped."

"You're kiddin'." When Francis' hard look indicated anything but, Ben spluttered. "How?"

Francis sighed. "I don't know. That, in itself, is perhaps more disturbing than his escape. Aside from slipping out of quarantine, there is no trace of him throughout the entire facility, nor any record of him leaving via glassway."

Lucy frowned. "If he was Corrupted, our wards should've picked up on that and blocked him from getting out. Or getting far at all before setting off plenty of alarms."

"Exactly," Francis said. "Which means that whatever is influencing him doesn't register as Corrupt elements." He pointed at Ben. "When he attempted to assassinate Sydney, he claimed to be doing so under the Chairman's orders, correct?"

"Sure sounded like it," Ben said. "There's this thing called lyin', though …"

Francis raised a hand. "However, he did not specify which Chairman gave him those orders."

It took Ben a few seconds to follow the mental crumbs Francis was laying down. "You's thinkin' he's followin' orders from one of the international divisions? He did just come back from Europe, right?"

"Yes," Francis said. "But no, that's not what I believe to be the case. The target of Rafi's violence makes me suspect another individual at work here."

"Individual?" Lucy drained her current mug and refilled it. "And target. So someone who would want Sydney, specifically, dead. Someone who would—and could—compel a Cleaner to act

317

erratically, even break out of quarantine. And someone who claims to be a Chairman."

The jug crackled as Ben gripped the handle hard. "Destin."

Francis nodded, expression grim. "As Chairman, Destin freely wielded his ability to assert his will on others, subduing them, encouraging their obeisance. It may be that, at some point, he laid a more permanent compulsion upon Rafi, making him something of a personal weapon to eliminate Sydney whenever his younger brother made another appearance."

Ben grumbled. "Why you gotta make so much sense sometimes? Wishin' we'd seen the last of Destin after Filth dragged him off, kickin' and squealin'."

"If it's true, is it a passive thing?" Lucy asked. "Something he left in Rafi's head before being ousted? Or is it active, meaning he's somehow still got some power and is out there using and abusing them?"

"All questions we must now attempt to find answers for." Francis studied Ben again. "Not to mention the how's and wherefore's of the return of your powers. I know it's still a fresh development, but have you observed anything about your abilities we should know about?"

Ben flexed his arm. The water in the jug slopped about. He felt this physically, of course, but he also sensed the liquid and all the ways he could make it dance and dribble around, if he wanted it to. Could he always do that? It felt similar to the way he detected nearby Pure and Corrupt energies, so maybe he had in the past, but had just confused the two, seeing how he mingled his power and water so much over the years.

He shrugged. "Nope. Feelin' just dandy fine. I'm just rarin' to see just what I can do with all this spiffiness."

"But should something occur or be revealed, you will let me know immediately, correct?"

"Sure-for-shootin'."

Francis nodded. "Then you're dismissed. I've a report to write, and you should get some rest. I'll get you back on the work rotation in the next day or two."

Ben didn't bother hiding his grin at that. *Back to work!* Back to the job that had defined his life for so long. Back to sending Scum scampering and whipping wanna-be baddies into shape. This was going to be grand.

As they headed out, he spoke low to Lucy.

"I've been thinkin'."

"Dangerous," she said.

"Hush it." Ben nudged her. "Now that I gots me a little fuel back in the tank, I ain't gotta squat on the sidelines no more. 'Sides from gettin' back to work, there's somethin' else that's been tuggin' at my noggin'. Some answers of our own we've been huntin' awhile."

Lucy went quiet for a few moments. Once they emerged from the glassway leading from the Chairman's office and back into HQ, she stopped and looked up at him.

"You mean Karen. All the things we still don't know about what happened to you two down in the Sewer."

"Yuppers. I figured you and I could kinda team up again. Get to the bottom of that barrel of mad monkeys. Wanna go talk about some sorta plan of action? Hopefully one that involves lots and lotsa Scum weepin' and beggin' us for mercy."

She eyed the jug he held and the carafe in her hand. She raised her mug. "How about over drinks?"

He bumped her glass with the jug. "Cheers to that."

CHAPTER
THIRTY-ONE

J ared?"

Dani peeked into the quarantine bedroom. It had been picked up since Jared's confrontation with Ella; the shelves had been set back in place, toys, books, and comics were all back where they should be. The bed was made, and she doubted the whole room had a speck of dust left on any surface.

Except for the sandbox still at the foot of the bed. The sand within didn't move as she entered, and she crept up, not wanting to startle Jared if he'd returned to this form.

"Jared?" she whispered.

The sand still didn't stir as she crouched beside it. Was he sleeping? Could sand sleep?

"Jared, it's Dani. I have something I need to tell you."

Sniffling caught her ear. It came from behind the closed bathroom door, which she'd ignored at first since Jared never used the bathroom. Yet noises were definitely coming from there now.

She rose and opened the door. Wads of toilet paper scooted aside as she swung it wide, revealing Jared sitting cross-legged among piles and streamers of toilet paper. He stared down at a full toilet paper roll he held in his lap, but otherwise it looked like he'd shredded, crumpled, and unraveled every other roll that had been stored in the bathroom.

"Jared, what in the world ..."

He raised his head, face miserable, gold-flecked eyes shimmering with unshed tears. His skinny chest bumped with hard breaths.

"I tried to protect him, but it didn't work." He held up the full roll. *"It wasn't enough. I was dumb to think it would help."*

"Oh, Jared." She went over, took the roll from him, and then sat to wrap her arms around him. "I'm sorry."

He shook against her for a few minutes, silently weeping. She tried to keep her own breathing steady for his sake. There'd be time to process things on her end later. For now, she needed to be strong.

Once he settled, she grabbed up a few paper balls and helped dab his face clean. He kept sniffling, so she placed a few tissues in his hand, which he blew into from time to time. She put a hand on one knee, just as a reminder that she was there. Then she realized he looked like ... himself. No elemental outbursts or other odd changes.

"You're back to normal," she said softly.

He blinked at her. *"I am?"*

She tried for a smile. "Well, normal for you."

"Is normal good?"

"That's," Dani quirked a corner of her mouth, "a tricky question. But I'm curious. How did you know about your uncle?"

He made a one-shoulder shrug. *"I felt him fade."*

"Yes, he ..." It took a couple seconds for the choked sensation to fade. "Sydney died doing something very brave."

"When will Uncle Sid be back?"

"Back?"

He stood, taking her hand and leading her out into the bedroom. *"In those,"* he pointed to the stacks of comics, *"people keep coming back when they die. Especially if they've done brave things."*

"Oh." She took his hand in both of hers. "I'm sorry, Jared. Those are just stories. That doesn't happen in real life. I wish it did."

He withdrew his hand and made a fist, which he stared at. *"What if I could bring him back? Make him come back?"*

Dani froze. She felt like she'd been walking along a somewhat familiar path, moving toward a known destination, and then turned a corner and found herself strolling across an alien landscape, utterly lost, without compass or map—a sensation she'd had numerous times ever since she first crossed paths with Ben, and one she really wished would stop blindsiding her.

She chose her words carefully. "I'm not sure. I don't know if it'd actually be a good idea to do that."

"Why not?" He tilted his head, birdlike. *"If you could do something that would stop it from hurting so much, wouldn't you?"*

"Can you?" Dani took his shoulders and squared him to her. "Could you bring someone back?"

"I've been reading things about the Cleaners. Whatever they'll give me from the library or Records department. It's not much, but I've read about something called recycling."

She sighed. "That's just something normal people do. Lots of people recycle. It's a way to try and conserve resources. To reuse old materials."

"No," he said. *"This is different. I can tell. What I read almost made it sound like people, and other things, could be recycled, too."*

She frowned. News to her. Then again, she still was just getting to Chapter Two of the Employee Handbook. Maybe this recycling thing got talked about later on.

"I'll look into it," she said. "Until we learn more about it, though, no trying to bring him back, okay? Or anyone."

He ducked his head. *"Okay. Are we going to have to ask for permission? Because I don't think they'd let us, anyway."*

Dani didn't have to guess at the "they" he spoke of. "I don't know. I'm not sure how that works. But why do you think they wouldn't let us?"

He went and hopped onto the bed, sitting with his back against the wall. *"They didn't like him. They wanted him gone."*

She joined him on the bed, careful not to muss the sheets too much. "Your Uncle Sydney was a good man."

"But Uncle Sid also did bad things, too, didn't he?"

She winced. "Kinda. Whether he meant to or not."

Jared's face creased in thought. *"So, he was part-good and part-bad. Is everyone like that?"*

"Probably. Whether they like to admit it or not."

"Even me?"

Dani sighed. She didn't have the mental reserves to launch into a philosophical debate about the nature of good and evil, or whatever moralistic structure she could squeeze Purity and Corruption inside. If Jared did have anything in common with his uncle, it was his constant probing and questioning of reality, trying to peel back the surface and poke at the workings behind the scenes until they made sense. Right now, all Dani wanted to do was peel back a blanket and burrow under it for a few days.

"Let's talk about that later," she said. "How about I tell you a story, instead?"

He pushed his lower lip out. *"But it's not bedtime yet."*

"Bonus story. About your Uncle Sid."

That both brightened his eyes while bringing back a shadow of his previous grief. *"Okay. But I have another question first."*

"Sure. What?"

"What's 'being sexy' mean?"

Dani groaned, and pressed a palm to her forehead. "Oh, #$%@$#%&, Ben."

▲   ▲   ▲

A couple hours later, Dani finally made it back to her quarters and flopped onto her bed. She buried her face in the pillow, thanking Purity for a self-sterilizing room and furnishings that didn't require her to decontaminate them every time she wanted to sleep.

Try as she might to block out the world, though, her mind continued to buzz on residual energy. From the moment Sydney popped back into her life to the moment he left, it felt like she'd gone into overdrive, and was just now able to start cutting back on the adrenaline. Her body might've been exhausted, but her brain still bubbled and boiled over with unresolved conflicts and questions—some of which would never be answered with Sydney's departure.

Huffing, she flopped onto her back and surveyed the room. Maybe if she found something to distract herself long enough, her brain and body would finally beat each other into submission, and take her into unconsciousness with them.

She rose, stripped, and took a luxurious shower, leaving the door open so once she emerged, her quarters had been invaded by a cloud of vapor. By the time she'd given herself a full-body coat of sani-gel, the steam had mostly evaporated, and she shivered as she retrieved her uniform. Her outfit had cleaned and repaired itself in the meantime, with nary a stitch or scratch out of place, and her black boots gleamed.

She turned to check herself in the mirror, and realized she'd left the sliding closet door halfway open. The dress she'd worn on the date hung there. Unlike her uniforms, it retained the damage done during that night, with water, dirt, and grass stains all over it, plus a few tears and ragged threads.

Dani's eyes locked on the outfit, feeling like it might escape the instant she stopped looking. She continued to watch it as she went to the closet and eased the door shut. Only when she stared into the eyes of her reflection did something unknot in her belly and let her breathe again.

Snapping her gloves on, she got a tub of mealworms out of the mini-fridge next to the dresser and gave Tetris something to chase. She watched the bearded dragon scurry after the helpless grubs for a few minutes, enjoying how a creature so prickly in appearance could be so cute.

At last, she went to her desk, where the Employee Handbook waited. Hauling it off, she let it thump to the floor and then sat on the edge of the bed, where she could still read its cover and pages.

"Recycling," she said. "Know anything about it?"

The title letters blurred and rearranged.

Recycling. A conservation and waste reduction process that turns old materials into new products.

She flung a pillow at it, which bounced off and skidded across the floor.

Nice one, Dani. Real effective. Next time maybe you should toss the whole mattress. That'll teach it.

"I'm not talking normal recycling. I mean the recycling that can affect people. That can bring people back from the dead and ... uh ..." She braced herself on her arms, head back, rolling her eyes at the ceiling. Even as she said it, she knew how insane it sounded. She started to fumble for another way to frame it until she looked down again and saw the new text.

You are not ready.

Dani counted off twenty blinks before she trusted herself to talk.

"Ready? You mean it's real?"

The words snapped into a new formation faster than they normally did.

Where did you encounter this information?

Dani hesitated. That was awfully probing for a book, even a magic one. Why did it need to know that? "Just heard someone mention it while out, you know, doing my thing." She shrugged. "Doesn't matter. But if you're not going to tell me about it, how about we have a study session. Maybe that'll help me sleep."

You find me boring?

"No." She threw her hands up. "I find you fascinating. I want to sit down and read you cover-to-cover a hundred times over until everything in you," she jabbed a finger at the book and then at her head, "is in here forever. What I find insufferable is the countless little tests you give me to prove that I'm ready to move on to the next page, much less the next chapter."

The book went blank. Dani stiffened. It had never done that before. Had she insulted it? Was it sulking?

With a slap—and a rather petulant one at that—the book swiveled its front cover open and flipped its pages to the one that read *Chapter Two: On Matters of Bathing.*

Extra text appeared above this. All of chapter two is now open to you. Once you have finished, your next task will be assigned.

"The whole chapter?" Dani asked, rising to her feet. "And just one thing to complete before getting to Chapter Three?"

Yes.

"Okay. See? This is progress." She knelt before the book and eagerly started turning the pages, skimming the new content. Her reading slowed as she took in the diagrams, the major section headings, and image captions. "Wait, what is this? The Bleach Bow? The Hygienic Handstand? The Plunger Plank? The Spray Bottle

Salute?" She struck the book, bruising her hand in the process. "This doesn't have anything to do with baths."

The text faded on one page, replaced by:

Do you not already know how to bathe yourself?

"Sure, but ..."

The pages ruffled under her hand, and she released them so they flipped back to the chapter beginning. There, text read:

A Cleaner must bathe both body and mind in Pure focus, Pure balance, and Pure calm in order to fully unleash and most effectively wield the powers contained within. This series of poses is designed to help Cleaners submerge more fully in their energies and achieve the mental and physical clarity necessary to reach the next level of service.

She stared in rising horror. "You've got to be kidding."

There are twenty-eight meditative postures. I suggest you begin practicing, as all are tested in the final assignment.

Whimpering, Dani sat back hard against the bed.

It's not enough that I have to practice Cleaner kung-fu. She put her head in her hands. *Now I have to deal with Cleaner yoga, too!*

ABOUT THE AUTHOR

Author and editor Josh Vogt has been published in dozens of genre markets with work ranging across fantasy, science fiction, horror, humor, pulp, and more. He also writes for a wide variety of RPG developers. His debut fantasy novel, *Forge of Ashes*, is a tie-in to the Pathfinder roleplaying game. WordFire Press launched his urban fantasy series, The Cleaners, with *Enter the Janitor* and *The Maids of Wrath*. He's an editor at Paizo, a member of SFWA, and the International Association of Media Tie-In Writers, and is also a Scribe Award and Compton Crook Award finalist.

Find him at JRVogt.com or on Twitter @JRVogt.

He is made out of meat.

IF YOU LIKED ...

If you liked *The Dustpan Cometh*, you might also enjoy:

Crecheling by D.J. Butler

Into the Fire: Samantha Kane Book I
by Patrick Hester

Taylor's Ark by Jody Lynn Nye

OTHER WORDFIRE PRESS TITLES BY JOSH VOGT

The Cleaners Series

Enter the Janitor

Maids of Wrath

Solar Singularity
with Peter J. Wacks and Guy Anthony De Marco

CPSIA information can be obtained
at www.ICGtesting.com
Printed in the USA
LVOW12s2103160218

566878LV00004B/522/P